Jeremy Brooks was born in Southampton in 1926. He was educated at John Bright School in Llandudno, after being evacuated to North Wales in 1940. He enlisted in the Navy and spent time at Magdalen College, Oxford before seeing active service in the Mediterranean. After the war he studied Stage Design at the Camberwell School of Art. He moved back to North Wales in 1953 with his wife, the painter Eleanor Brooks, where they rented a cottage on the estate of Clough Williams Ellis at Llanfrothen. They would have four children. To support himself while writing fiction he occasionally worked as a wine waiter in the restaurant at the Portmeirion Hotel and was later to write a novel, *The Water Carnival* (1957), satirising the Italianate village. *Jampot Smith* was published in 1960, *Henry's War* in 1962 and *Smith as Hero* in 1964.

He later embarked on a theatrical career, which included a period as the literary manager of the Royal Shakespeare Company with Peter Hall from 1962 to 1969. He was responsible, with Kitty Hunter-Blair, for a number of groundbreaking adaptations of plays by Russian dramatists including Maxim Gorky and Nikolai Gogol. An adaptation of *The Government Inspector,* in which Paul Scofield starred, was particularly well received. He worked extensively for theatre, television and radio producing many original works and adaptations including (with Adrian Mitchell), a version of Dylan Thomas's *A Child's Christmas in Wales*. He also wrote poetry, children's books and worked extensively with Theatr Clywd at Mold, producing a notable adaptation of *Medea*. He was renowned for helping the careers and development of younger writers and was a founder member of the Theatre Writers' Union.

His last published work was a collection of short stories, entitled *Doing the Voices* (1986). He died in 1994.

JAMPOT SMITH

JEREMY BROOKS

PARTHIAN

LIBRARY OF WALES

Parthian
The Old Surgery
Napier Street
Cardigan
SA43 1ED
www.parthianbooks.co.uk

The Library of Wales is a Welsh Assembly Government initiative
which highlights and celebrates Wales' literary heritage in the
English language

The publisher acknowledges the financial support of the Welsh
Books Council

The Library of Wales publishing project is based at
Trinity College, Carmarthen, SA31 3EP
www.libraryofwales.org

Series Editor: Dai Smith

First published in 1960
© The Estate of Jeremy Brooks
Library of Wales edition published 2008
Foreword © Merfyn Jones 2008
All Rights Reserved

ISBN 978-1-905762-50-7

Cover design by Lucy Llewellyn
Printed and bound by Gwasg Gomer, Llandysul, Wales
Typeset by logodædaly

British Library Cataloguing in Publication Data

A cataloguing record for this book is available from the British
Library.

FOREWORD

This novel is about growing up. It is a meticulous, delicate exploration of the joys, disappointments and adventures of a diverse group of adolescents growing up together in a small town, and negotiating the emotional crosscurrents of one another's lives. In its portrayal of youthful love and conflict, with all its attendant anxieties and conspiracies, it succeeds in being what one critic called a 'small classic about the delight and pain of sexual awakening.'

The novel expresses the emotional stresses and hopes of its young cast through acutely observed exchanges and a vivid exactitude of description. The town's streets, the beaches, the bicycle rides, the rain – as well as the debates, the misadventures, the conflicts and explorations – are all finely observed in a prose which, in the manner of its characters and its hero, is deceptively casual. *The Times* called his style 'fastidious' and *The Irish Times* considered it to be, 'Exact, funny, sad and beautiful; it is, I think, a masterpiece.' One reviewer, in *The Observer*, referred to the novel's 'golden, Turgenevian light,' a prescient as well as perceptive comment, perhaps, as the author was later to be a prolific adapter of Russian writers and dramatists.

I first read *Jampot Smith* in the early 1960s, soon after it was published, and when I was myself much the same age as the characters portrayed here. Not unnaturally, it spoke directly to me of adolescence and of the raw emotional entanglements and frustrations, as well as the happiness, which youthful love, and the challenge of sex, could bring. The seeking out of ideas, the emerging convictions, the dilemmas of pacifism; these also spoke to me and I distinctly remember being intrigued by something the author had captured in the characters and philosophies of 'Epsom' Jones and Dewi Hughes. That was then. The welcome republishing of *Jampot Smith* almost fifty years after it first appeared will, I suspect, bring other features of the novel to the forefront. For this is a novel, yes, about growing up, but it is also a novel about a very specific place and time – it is about life in Llandudno during the Second World War. One of the author's obituarists expressed the view that *Jampot Smith* will 'outlast its period and provincial setting.' But this is a novel of its period and of its, and many other, 'provincial settings': the small, rounded, towns of Wales and Britain.

It is a novel about Wales during the Second World War but a Wales which is unfamiliar to many of us – small-town Wales, comfortable Wales, middle-class Wales and, in a fascinating way, a partly English Wales. Not unlike contemporary Wales, perhaps, but a Wales which it is difficult to find in our histories and our consciousness (although it should not be entirely unfamiliar to readers of Emyr Humphreys). Llandudno, 'where the bay swung smoothly round between the grey fists of the two headlands, the Great Orme and the Little Orme,' was planned and built for tourism as the railway came to the North Wales coast in the 1850s. It was a highly popular venture with elegant hotels, promenade and pier on the spectacular seafront. Unlike the rest of Wales, the 1930s was a time of growth and prosperity for the North Wales coastal resorts, attracting, as they did, visitors from the prospering south-east of England and a new generation of holidaymakers liberated by new holiday entitlements. And then, with the war, came the Inland Revenue.

Rural Wales was hit by a wave of urban immigration during the war; the story of the evacuees from the bombed-out cities of England is well known. Less well understood is the equally significant flight of professional people and middle-class families. Much of this migration was voluntary and individual, but much was also strategic and organised as key services and factories were moved into safer regions. The BBC's Light Entertainment section moved to Bangor; the Inland Revenue came to Llandudno and brought Jeremy Brooks's Scottish father and his family with it. (Along with future Prime Minister James Callaghan and his wife.)

This move took the author from school in Brighton at the outbreak of war, when he was thirteen, and marked the start of his long relationship with Wales, one which was to last until his death in 1994. This novel is autobiographical to a remarkable degree, a partial memoir as well as a novel and most of the characters, and the relationships, are based on real people he knew at school and in the town. Llandudno itself, its relative comfort, its beauty, its ordinariness is a constant, and changing presence and the seafront, but also the suburban streets and the nearby hills and mountains, are all portrayed with intimate detail. Street names are often mentioned in an off-hand manner, as if the reader was sure to know them. This is a characteristically skilful technique, emphasising, as it does, the impression that the town was indeed these young people's bounded world, was all they knew. And for the author, 'although a pack of lithe, savagely jeering Welsh boys had given me a bad time in my first term,' it was to be his home during his growing up. This was his safe haven, like the Music Club, the room upstairs, that they danced in. Unlike Brighton, this was a co-educational world with endless permutations of boy-girl/girl-boy and the associated admixture of emotional obsession and innocence. A world of holding hands on bicycle trips and walks, armed with sandwiches and lemonade and disarmed by anxiety and longing.

But for these young people any haven was temporary for they all knew that the war would not let them rest, that their time would come. In the early years, the boys prepare a hideout and arms to launch a resistance movement should the Germans invade; later they watch Liverpool, so close, burn over the waters of the still bay. They listen to the bombers overhead, uninterested in the town between the Ormes; later still they passionately debate the legitimacy and morality of war. This is a wartime novel but with its focus firmly on the strange ordinariness of life on the Home Front, despite wartime conditions and dislocations. *Jampot Smith* is about growing up in Llandudno during the Second World War – its period, and its 'provincialism', is of its essence.

Jeremy Brooks left Llandudno to go, briefly, to Oxford and then into the Navy and the war. He then attended the Camberwell School of Art and began a life-long relationship with the theatre. His parents remained in Llandudno for some years after the war and Jeremy would visit North Wales as, during his time at school there, he had been bitten by the mountaineering and rock-climbing bug. It was on a climbing trip to Snowdonia in the late 1940s, one day when it was too wet to climb, that, exhausted and drenched, he discovered the village that was to be his home, off and on, until he died. Llanfrothen is a curious place in its geography, more of a dispersed parish than a proper village although until relatively recently a church, post office, pub, shop, and garage clustered near the terrace of Garreg. But it was curiouser still in its cultural and social composition.

The village was largely owned by one of its inhabitants, Clough Williams Ellis of Plas Brondanw – the colourful and energetic creator of Portmeirion, which lay a couple of miles away on the Merionethshire coast. Not only did Clough attract many creative and talented people to the area but his wife, Amabel – herself a Strachey, and a one time left-wing literary editor of the *New Statesman* – had a wide circle of Bloomsbury and political acquaintances. Over the years, several of these friends had come to live or stay in cottages on the Brondanw estate. Bertrand Russell lived near Portmeirion for decades, as did the novelist Richard Hughes and Jeremy's first novel, *The Water Carnival*, drew heavily, and satirically, on this world.

Jeremy finally decided to come to live in the village in 1953, along with his artist wife, Eleanor. The cottage they moved into, and which remained so important in both their lives, was called Gelli. It lies some miles from the centre of the village, in a remote location by the river. It was, and remains, one of the most beautiful places on God's earth. The poet Adrian Mitchell described it as, 'The cottage of many caves, / The simple complicated trees / And the best grass in the world.' It was also, when they arrived, derelict, and one day a man from the council, not quite a government inspector, walked up the stony path along the riverside to inform them that they couldn't live there as it was unfit for human habitation. That man was my father, and they were to see a great deal more of him over the years for in 1949 my parents had become tenants of the Brondanw Arms, the village pub (my mother prefers to refer to it as an inn) which was the hub of this strange world. Jeremy was to dedicate his fourth novel, *Henry's War*, to 'the Landlord and Customers of the Brondanw Arms'. By the 1950s, these customers and neighbours included the historians, Edward and Dorothy Thompson; the communist farmer, John Jones; the physicist and Nobel Prize winner, Patrick Blackett; and the artist, Fred Uhlman. These intellectuals were soon to be joined by the outrageous surrealist, Philip O'Connor, who wrote a suitably baffling book about the place entitled *Living in Croesor*. The historian and communist, Eric Hobsbawm, later moved in along with many others drawn into the circle by Bertrand Russell's militant opposition to nuclear weapons.

The pub brought the literary, academic, and creative visitors and inhabitants together with local quarrymen, agricultural workers, farmers and others, including the adolescent me. It made for an interesting social and cultural mix which Jeremy much appreciated and admired and which not only nourished me but made me entirely ill-prepared to meet what was out there in suburban Britain. It was an argumentative culture and alcohol was a great disinhibitor, and the arguments would continue in Gelli, or elsewhere, long after the pub had closed. Nationalism, communism, war and peace, Welsh and English, these subjects would be gnawed on like tasty bones until the early hours. Jeremy was normally a reserved figure who loved the mountains and fishing but he also oversaw, and contributed to, this occasionally raucous discourse. He was not alone in seeing this disputation as creatively cutting across class and educational boundaries in a way which he believed impossible in London and which he privileged as being uniquely Welsh.

It was in Gelli, in this milieu, that Jeremy wrote first *The Water Carnival* and then *Jampot Smith*. *Jampot Smith* is, arguably, the best of his four novels and, according to Eleanor, to whom the book was dedicated, it was the novel he was himself most satisfied with. Living the literary life in a Welsh village and without external income was singularly difficult in the 1950s, before the advent of computers, mobile phones and faxes. Despite brave attempts to fund his writing by reviewing and reading for publishers and, rather unconvincingly, by rearing hens and pigs, Jeremy and Eleanor and the children eventually decided to return to London in 1959, when Jeremy became Literary Manager of the Royal Shakespeare Company. Despite living in Kentish Town, they remained regular visitors to Gelli, and to the Brondanw Arms, and I recall them as being a semi-permanent presence. They finally decided to abandon London for good in 1990 and return permanently to Gelli. Jeremy lived there, still working, often on adaptations for Theatr Clwyd – and he died there in 1994. Eleanor lives there still.

Jeremy's attachment to Wales lasted for almost sixty years, but it was the incomparable Gelli that was his Eden; not Llandudno. It was there that he lived the literary life, bohemian, but also immensely hard-working; it was there that he wrote and wrote; it was Gelli, and its surroundings, and its people, which he loved with real passion. His triumph in *Jampot Smith* was to re-create the very different Wales of Llandudno, and of his adolescence – its ordinariness and its innocence in the extraordinary times of war. It is a major contribution to Welsh writing not only because of the quality of the prose and the universality of the themes woven into its capture of adolescence, but also because of its portrayal of time and place through its unique angle of vision.

Merfyn Jones

JAMPOT SMITH

One

Throughout our youth in Llandudno, Gregory was ever the nasty prophet of our loves. Like a woman, he seemed to know in advance what shifts might be expected in the changing pattern of our relationships and never failed to heighten the embarrassment of any dying affair by recalling to all parties the accuracy of his earlier predictions. Yet he was himself so socially inept, so clumsy, gauche, obvious, that we regarded him as a sort of clown, placed among us as a warning of what might happen if we, too, took ourselves a little too seriously.

It was to Gregory that I owed one of the biggest setbacks in my growing interest in girls; and it was Gregory, I wryly recall, who first drew my attention to Kathy.

My usual approach to school, in those early, unsociable days when I had no friends apart from Gregory, was across the fields between the gasworks and the Links Hotel. There was a point at which I could just manage to jump the ditch which divided the fields belonging to the farmer from the school playing fields, and it was just as I was making this jump that this girl, Kathy, sprang up suddenly from behind the hedge on the other side of the ditch and bounded away towards the school. Surprised by this sudden apparition, I missed my footing on landing and slid back into the ditch, soaking one leg and staining my grey flannel trousers with the green juice of crushed grass. Cursing inexpertly, I scrambled up and chased after the girl – safe against catching her, I thought, for she had already reached the long wall by the tennis courts before I was halfway across the field.

This, I knew, was the girl referred to by Gregory, a few days earlier, when he had said 'There's a wench in 3B yearning after you, Bernard. Quite a looker, too!' I had myself seen her more often than might have been expected, but, until she sprang up from behind the hedge that day, had not enough conceit of myself to believe that she could have selected me, out of the scores of available boys, as the object of her attentions.

As she reached the tennis courts, that day, she disappeared behind the long wall which separated them from the playing-fields; and when I reached the corner of this wall myself I saw that she must have slowed down as soon as she was out of sight, perhaps even have dawdled, for I was now nearly on top of her. I did not know, myself, if I wanted to catch her or not, but there was now no avoiding it, and clearly no doubt in her mind. As she reached the school door she paused and stood as, since, I have often seen her stand: as if poised for flight: one foot on tiptoe, her body bent forward supported by a hand against the corner of the wall, her head turned over her shoulder to look at me. Very quietly, as if she hardly dare speak aloud, she said 'I hope you didn't get too wet – Bernard!'

Then she turned and flew towards the girls' cloakroom. She knew my name!

After that I began to see this girl about everywhere: in the school, on the beach, outside the Library, or simply cycling quietly along, alone, down the Conway Road on some unguessable errand. She always seemed, if she were not on her bicycle, to be running. Perhaps I would be walking up to Llanrhos to buy tomatoes from the market gardener there, when suddenly this girl would appear, running away across the fields behind Bryn Maelgwyn; running, it always seemed to me, with a sort of desperate intensity which had nevertheless about it a kind of purposelessness, as if she were running because she must run, but was not running to any place in particular. Or I would be scuffling my way moodily along the beach between the Ormes, kicking at the tide-wrack in the vague hope of uncovering a dead German, when I would suddenly hear a clattering of stones somewhere in front of me, and a few moments later this girl would come flying desperately along the Promenade above, her head down and her elbows swinging.

She seemed to have plenty of friends, though. One of them, called Dora Maguire, was in my class at school, and though I had never spoken to her we had once exchanged exasperated smiles over some swanky scholastic exploit of Gregory's. Often I saw Kathy, with Dora and two or three other friends, standing in a little knot on one of the wide pavements in the centre of the town on a Saturday morning. She always had her bicycle with her on these occasions, and would stand there, listening to the excited chatter of her friends, with her head lowered and on one

5

side, looking up at them sideways with a smile which seemed to keep her always a little removed from them; with one foot on a pedal and her hands clasped side by side in the centre of the handlebars, looking as if she were ready, at an instant's notice, to swing into the saddle and pedal furiously away.

This first sight of Kathy happened to coincide with, and was completely swamped by, another incident, which occupied most of my interest up to the time that I met Jones. Gregory had somehow made friends with a girl from another form, called Freda Humphreys, and for several weeks had been spending his time wheeling his bicycle up and down Mostyn Street out of school hours, with Freda, and her friend Pat Hughes. I twitted him often, but with no real interest, about this attachment. Freda had a face like a sad tortoise, with no chin to speak of and a long stringy neck; a spectacularly unattractive girl, which I suppose was the secret of Gregory's success with her, if it can be called success. So far they had done nothing more daring than to walk side by side through the town in an embarrassed silence, and I supposed that that was enough excitement for Gregory to be going on with. He admitted to me once that she was 'a bit dim' – a common form of assessment with Gregory – but continued to pursue the relationship with what seemed to me to be pointless diligence; eventually taking the very rash step of making a date with her for a Sunday afternoon.

This was where I came in. Pat Hughes was the fly in Gregory's ointment, and it was to get rid of her – or, rather, to cancel out her presence with mine – that my co-operation was required. Following a pattern often observable among schoolgirls, Pat was as attractive as Freda was plain: freckled, brown-eyed, rather plump, but definitely attractive; a fact which considerably strengthened my objections to Gregory's scheme, for attractive girls were more frightening than plain ones. I quite appreciated, though, that without my help the whole undertaking was impossible. Even so I might well have refused, and enjoyed the feeling of power which Gregory's chagrin would have provided, had I not one day come suddenly face to face with Pat Hughes in one of the school corridors. We met at a corner, both travelling fast, and nearly collided; and then for an instant stood still, looking at one another with surprised recognition – though what it was we were recognizing I could not say. After that I knew that I would join Gregory on his Sunday afternoon outing, even though I was terrified at the prospect of spending a whole afternoon in the company of two girls.

I decided to adopt, as safest and most suitable for the occasion, a detached, careless manner; a manner designed to say, to anyone who was interested 'I am faintly, but not disagreeably, surprised to find myself in such company as this; vaguely curious to know what we are to do with ourselves to while away the afternoon, but not sufficiently involved with the outing to make any suggestions; I am prepared to make myself agreeable, but not to put myself out to entertain anyone.'

I had arranged to meet Gregory outside the Library. Out of some unreasoned desire for an initial advantage I was myself a quarter of an hour late, yet I still had to wait five minutes before Gregory appeared. He was in his dullest, most lugubrious mood. One would never have thought that twenty-four hours before he had been extolling the exquisite joys in store for us both. He kept yawning hugely and I, not then recognizing the yawn as a symptom of extreme nervousness, took it for deliberate ennui and became suddenly furious with him: pretended that I had been at our meeting place at the appointed time and raved angrily at him about the ethics of punctuality. Gregory responded with a braying laugh, uncomfortably loud, and turned away from me to march briskly up to the doors of the Library and back, like a soldier on sentry-go. Then the girls appeared.

They walked towards us rapidly with their heads bent together, chattering absorbedly, laughing softly, as if oblivious of their date. They didn't look towards the Library until they were almost on top of us; and then Freda looked up, gave a quick nervous smile, and said: 'Oh, hello!' just as if we had met accidentally and she was not sure if she had time to stay and talk to us.

'Hello,' said Gregory. The four of us stood grinning weakly at each other, all wishing that we could just mutter some easy pleasantry and pass on. Freda said 'Well!' in an interested voice, and looked brightly all round her as if she were at a party summing up the evening's possibilities.

Gregory said hurriedly 'You both know Bernard Smith, don't you?'

'Oh yes!' said Freda brightly.

'No!' said Pat, in a surprised voice.

I said feebly 'I've seen you both... around, and waved

my hand vaguely to indicate the fashionable places in which we were all bound to have seen each other before.

'I saw you,' said Pat surprisingly, stressing the pronouns in a meaningful way, 'in the Science corridor last week. I thought you were going to say something!'

'I nearly did!' I lied. Suddenly I became conscious that both Freda and Gregory were staring at us in horrified amazement, and realised that we had each been committing the solecism of owning prior interest in – and even intention towards – the other. Hurriedly I said 'Well, what are we going to do, Greg?'

Gregory instantly became bored, almost inarticulate with ennui. 'I thought we might walk along the dunes towards Deganwy,' he hazarded faintly. We had already begun to walk aimlessly up Lloyd Street in the general direction required for a walk along the dunes, and so we silently acquiesced to the proposal.

In retrospect I should perhaps admit that it was heroic of Gregory to have got the suggestion out at all, for it was a damning thing to have to say: implying, as it did, not only that he had thought about the subject in advance, but also that he was willing, even eager, to spend the afternoon simply keeping company with the two girls, without any other entertaining object in view. It would have been so much easier had the cinemas been open, when he could have suggested going to see this or that film without admitting any more than that it would not be inconvenient to have the girls accompanying him.

This was the first intimation I had ever had that Gregory was capable of exercising initiative, and it came as a surprise. I was used to thinking of him as a wholly passive object. He was soon to make my mistake even plainer.

I had been expecting that we would walk in a bunch, with Freda and Gregory side by side and Pat and me on the outsides, me next to Gregory and Pat next to Freda, as I had often watched groups of four walking away from school in the evenings. Our conversation then would naturally have fallen into the usual classroom form of semi-serious banter, a kind of double-talk which, once one knows the rules, can be carried on indefinitely with very little mental effort and absolutely no danger. Subconsciously, this is what I had prepared my mind for, but Gregory, for all his indecision, had obviously never even considered the outing in that light. For within five minutes of the meeting outside the Library he had forced Freda on half a dozen steps in front of Pat and me, and was talking to her in low, urgent, confidential tones, about his collection of penknives. Pat and I were left, virtually, alone together.

This was something I could not possibly have foreseen, and I found myself floundering wildly, bereft of all possible attitudes. The attitude into which I had so carefully thought myself in preparation for the afternoon, was now quite out of the question. Pat, I thought at first, was equally at a loss: at any rate, she was silent. But her silence had, I think, a different core to mine: while I was busy frantically searching my scarcely formed personality for an aspect of myself which it would be proper to present to this girl, she seemed to be attempting to sum me up, to discover from my face the touchstone that would release us both.

By the time we had reached the tennis courts at the end

of Lloyd Street, and were passing into the narrow pathway which skirts the eastern edge of the town playing fields, Pat and I had exchanged perhaps half a dozen non-committal remarks:

'Do you like 3D?'

'It's not bad.'

'Have you known Gregory long?'

'Ages. Six months, at least, I should say.'

'Lucky it's such a nice afternoon.'

'Shouldn't wonder if it rains this evening.'

And so on. None of them very revealing, none leading to any sustained conversation: and yet there was a feeling between us that already the ice was beginning to break up. I had still failed to find an attitude, and it was Pat who was doing most of the hard work, finding questions to ask, and expressing real interest in my evasive replies. But I think that already Pat was beginning to show me that I could do without an attitude in her company.

It would be pointless to go over our conversation as we followed Gregory and Freda – who were getting further and further in front of us all the time – through the West Shore back streets that led to the dunes. We were still being carefully impersonal, exchanging the bare facts of our lives, the when and how of our physical existence.

As we walked, I had been slowly and methodically tearing to pieces an empty matchbox which I must have picked up in the house at lunchtime. First I tore off the top label and then the bottom one, scrap by scrap, meticulously, looking down intently at my busy hands as we walked. Then I began to strip off slivers of wood from each end of the outer box. I was just beginning to work on the little drawer itself, pulling the blue paper away from the white wood, when, after a long silence, Pat suddenly said 'What are you tearing that matchbox to pieces for? You've been doing it ever since we met!'

I looked at her, and then at the box in my hands. I threw the box away and stuck my hands deep in my trouser pockets. I was so shattered by this immediate personal probe that I found myself saying distinctly, without embarrassment 'I guess I was just nervous, that's all.'

Pat laughed, and immediately I knew that she too had been nervous, so that my own nervousness became acceptable – and unnecessary.

'Do you feel better now?'

'Much better.'

We grinned at each other, and I had a crazy impulse to take hold of the girl's hand and swing it. I got my hand halfway out of my pocket, but had not quite the confidence to do it.

After that we were silent for some time. We had been alarmingly near to each other for a moment, and suddenly we both had an instinct to catch up with Freda and Gregory; we started to run, skating gracelessly through the shifting sand of the dunes, over the pebbles, and down on to the firmer, wet sand of the shore, trying to overtake them. On our left I noticed, for the first time, the concrete pillbox that was being built among the sandhills; on our right, the wet, wave-rippled sands stretched for miles, with, it seemed, only a narrow strip of silvered water separating them from Puffin Island, off the coast of Anglesey. Our feet sank inches deep into the sand, leaving trails of shining puddles as large as an elephant's foot. Pat wasn't much of a hand at running, and was soon badly puffed.

When, only twenty yards or so behind Freda and Gregory, we finally slowed down again, I found that the afternoon had somehow changed its quality. I was no longer at a loss for an attitude, for Pat had by startling me into admitting the inadmissible truth, made attitudes impossible. The afternoon, settling quietly into its golden self, suddenly filled with throbbing possibilities; not, as when one is in love, possibilities of endless juxtapositions of oneself and one's beloved, but possibilities opening in every direction at the thought of all the people that were in the world, with each of whom, it now seemed, some sort of communication could be established if one so desired.

A stiff March breeze had begun now to whip in across the sands, and above the mountains across the estuary a livid bank of clouds was beginning to pile itself up, waiting, it seemed, only for the cover of darkness to roll down on to the town. The sun slanted in downwind, low and feeble, but able, by the very obtuseness of its angle, to lend a certain romantic mystery to the ordinarily dull little hills above Deganwy. It was none too warm, though Pat and I, after our sudden burst of speed, were glowing pleasantly. The pair in front of us had stopped, apparently arguing. Gregory was wearing a fatuous grin and Freda, flushed from the wind and looking almost attractive from a full-face view, was protesting vigorously and negatively on some subject. As soon as we were near enough, she appealed to me.

'Bernard! Tell Gregory it's much too cold to sit around doing nothing!'

13

'Much too cold!' I agreed vaguely. Conscious of Pat coming up behind me, I was scarcely attending to whatever silly squabble these other two were engaged in.

'He wants us to go and sit down on the dunes!' said Freda.

'I only wanted to look at the view,' said Gregory. 'It would be sheltered up there, anyway.

I said 'Well, you carry on looking, boy, and we'll carry on walking.'

'That's right!' said Freda. 'And we'll send someone along later to chip the ice off you!'

Suddenly Gregory turned on me, his face mean with anger, and said 'So you got here at last, then? You two took so long about it we wondered what you were up to... hiding yourselves away together back there!'

I was so amazed at this – it seemed to me – completely irrelevant, groundless attack, that I could not find a word to say. Pat had to speak for me. She said 'I think you're rather silly, Gregory!' Her voice was so distantly disdainful, and her use of the word 'rather' so shattering, that I was glad I had failed to think up a retort. I did not begin to understand Gregory's flash of maliciousness, for it was most unlike him to impinge on one's attention at all. Normally, his importuning for notice and affection was so doglike and acquiescent that it seldom rose above the level of a background irritant.

But as we walked away I felt perversely grateful to Gregory for his outburst; for Pat's eye had met mine as she turned away after quietly squashing him, and a flicker of agreement had passed between us, in which we dismissed

Gregory as beyond redemption, even by love. So new to me was this kind of instantaneous silent conversation, that I felt my throat constricting with the pleasure of it; and by the time I had gained her side again I had already forgotten Freda and Gregory and their senseless quarrel.

'Let's walk along the top,' said Pat. She glanced sideways at me, inviting my appreciation of her irony, as she added 'He can look at his view from up there!'

We climbed slowly up through the sandhills towards the little clay and sandstone cliff which separated them from the golf links above. Further along towards the Black Rocks the cliff dwindled to the height of a man, and a little gully gave access to the path running along the top. At the base of this gully we paused, to wait for the others.

Pat said 'I love this path up here. It's like flying!'

And so it was: in the same way that riding on a switchback is like flying, only more intimately so, since one used here one's own muscles to swing up and down the sudden dips and swells of the smooth turf. The ground sloped down, inland, towards the golf course, and fell sharply to the dunes on the seaward side, so that the edge one trod was airy, almost detached from the solid ground.

'I often come here,' I said. 'Oh... !' I waved my hands helplessly. 'Often!' It seemed to me that we were having an intense and absorbing conversation, that with every letter of every syllable of every word of the few sentences we exchanged, we were revealing ourselves with an almost sensuous abandonment.

'I like it when it's really rough!' said Pat.

'When the spray comes right up!'

15

'Like walking a tightrope!'

'When it's rough next time... !' I said, letting the unspoken suggestion hang without quite daring to bring it out.

But Pat said warmly 'Yes!' as if the invitation had been complete.

Freda and Gregory had still not appeared. We were just turning to climb the gully so as to look down on the dunes from above, when we heard, quite close to us, a muffled exclamation from Freda. Then she appeared, stumbling clumsily over a dune not twenty yards away. From its crest, still stumbling forward, she saw us, and began to shout something. Then her feet slipped as she misjudged the steep slope in front of her, and she went tumbling down through the marram grass and into the hollow below. At the same instant Gregory appeared on top of the dune from which she had fallen. He did not see us. He was panting and hawking with laughter; and, seeing Freda beginning to sit up in the hollow to which she had rolled, immediately jumped down beside her.

'Got you!' we heard him cry.

Freda cried out again, unintelligibly. From where we stood we could not see them any longer, for Gregory, arriving in the hollow, had grabbed Freda's shoulders and rolled her sideways so that they both disappeared behind an intervening dune.

All this happened so quickly that Pat and I were involuntary and, on my part, incomprehending witnesses, without having time either to ignore or influence the horse-play. I, feeling that Gregory was almost certainly being a fool but that it was no business of mine, turned back to the gully as soon as they were out of sight again, and started to climb. Then I saw that Pat, after a moment's hesitation, was not following me, but instead had started to run back towards them. Feeling even more bemused, I climbed down again and sauntered uncertainly after her.

From the commotion taking place in the hollow, when I reached it, I thought for a moment that Gregory had attempted to murder Freda. He had just the sort of silly, unapologetic grin he would be bound to wear after committing a murder. Pat, I was surprised to see, was kneeling by Freda with her arms around the other girl's shoulders. Freda was sobbing. Gregory, with his hands pushed down and outward in his trouser pockets, in a clown's stance, was rocking backwards and forwards on his heels. 'Oh! Good heavens me!' he kept saying impatiently. 'Oh! Good heavens me!'

Just as I arrived, Freda, sniffing heavily and utterly repulsive with her streaky tears, red eyes, and tangled stringy hair, looked up at me in furious amazement, and, in a trembling, accusing voice, said 'He kissed me!'

'Did he?' I said vacantly.

Gregory gave a sudden alarming hiccup, winked at me conspiratorially, and said again 'Oh! Good heavens me!'

Pat, who existed for me in a bubble of warmth which did not touch the others and which they, I thought, could not affect, glanced once towards me without meeting my eye, and then continued her ministrations to Freda. 'It's all right, dear, I'm here. Don't you take any notice of him. Look, use my hanky, that's right, there, you're all right now, I won't let him come near you....'

She was talking, I thought, as if Gregory had really intended to do Freda some actual physical harm. Quite coolly, looking down at them all from the crest of my sandhill, I thought it was all rather a lot of fuss about nothing. I knew girls made a fuss about being kissed, though I didn't quite understand why this should be so, since it seemed to me a harmless, even a dull, activity. Certainly not one which should be able to bring on such hysterical, horror-stricken display of fear and emotion as this. Even Pat was open to criticism in that, instead of belittling the incident, she appeared to be deliberately inflating it.

'You boys!' she said fiercely, taking both Gregory and myself in the icy sweep of her eyes, 'you're all the same. I thought you might be different, but you're not. Don't you ever think of anything else?'

'Oh! Good heavens me!' cried Gregory, 'do stop making such a fuss and let's get on!'

'Oh! Oh!' wailed Freda. 'How can you!'

'I thought you wanted to look at the view?' said Pat viciously. 'Well, sit down and look at it and I hope you enjoy it, because Freda and I are going!'

Freda, still sniffing and very much disorganised, was now on her feet. The girls had their arms round each other's waists – an exclusive attitude which pairs of girls often employed at school, effectively shutting off the boys from any communication with them.

'Come on,' said Pat, and they started down to the sands, heading back the way we had come. I said stupidly, still not believing that that bubble of warmth could have dissolved so quickly and completely 'Where are you going?'

'Home!' said Pat decisively, stopping and turning for a moment to look back at us.

'Oh! Good heavens me!' exclaimed Gregory, as if in a last paroxysm of impatience.

'Home?' I echoed.

Pat said 'We're going home and we're sorry we ever came out with you and we hope we never see you again, ever, so there!'

'Boys!' she said finally, scathingly. 'Boys! Honestly!'

Then the two girls, entwined, turned on us their dignified, outraged backs, and stomped off back along the shore.

'Well!' said Gregory, resignedly.

'You great goof!' I said.

Beyond the girls I could see the tracks in the sand we had made on the way out: Gregory's and Freda's close together, and, further seaward, yards apart from each other, Pat's and mine. I could see the trampled place where the four of us had met and where Gregory had proposed sitting down in the dunes to look at the view. The tracks of Pat and myself had a nostalgic fascination for me. I remembered wistfully, surprised and offended, how happy I had been while I was making them. I felt suddenly a passionate sense of longing for a magic only just found and so soon irrecoverably lost. I knew it was irrecoverably lost, not only because what had happened between Freda and Gregory must always henceforward stand threateningly between Pat and me, but because the words Pat had spoken could not be taken back, nor could it be pretended that they meant something else. While she had been speaking her eyes had dipped for a moment at mine, and I was sure that she had tried to pass with them some disclaimer of her words.

But this only máde my sense of loss worse, my grievance against Gregory more profound.

'Well!' said Gregory, shrugging his shoulders. 'What shall we do now?'

'I'm going home,' I said. I had already started back towards that little gully, intending to cross the golf course to Maes Du Bridge, and walk back via the gasworks.

'I've got to collect my bicycle. I left it at the Library.'

'Well, collect it then!' I said. Gregory was puffing along behind me, and when I reached the top of the cliff I didn't wait for him, but started off fullspeed straight across the golf course, from the ninth tee to the first.

'I don't know why you're so waxy!' Gregory shouted from behind me. 'Look here, man, they're only silly girls!'

I did not reply, but walked on as fast as I could. I could hear Gregory stumbling and panting behind me, half-running in an attempt to catch up.

'Anyway, it was my party. I don't know what you're so worried about. You'd never even met them before.'

A pause, more stumbling, and a gasp of exasperation. 'What's the hurry, man?'

I walked on. Gregory cried out, and I could not stop myself from glancing round. He was sitting on the edge of a bunker, nursing his ankle, and drooping melodramatically. 'Oh!' he called pitifully. 'Oh, Bernie, I think I've sprained my ankle!'

I hesitated for a moment; and then, realizing what an almighty racket he would have put up if he had really sprained his ankle, I walked on again, faster than ever. Sure enough, when I looked back for the last time, Gregory was walking perfectly normally, but very slowly, away towards the corner of the golf course nearest the town. His hands were in his pockets and he was whistling very loudly, as if he hadn't a care in the world. I don't suppose he had.

Behind us the livid clouds had already toppled down over Conway, and their blunt, threatening fingers were exploring the sky above my head. The afternoon, which at one moment had seemed to be blossoming so richly with golden promises, had now turned cold on me, so that what little spark of understanding had been set to smoulder in me had consumed itself, or been hidden by the dead ashes which followed.

'Girls!' I muttered to myself, as I strode grimly down the long straight road towards the gasworks. 'Girls! They're all the bloody same!'

Before I reached home it had begun to rain.

Two

In that first spring, when the essential parts of my new life had still not come together, I spent much of my free time alone on the pebbly beach of the North Shore, where the bay swung smoothly round between the grey fists of the two headlands, the Great Orme and the Little Orme. Even in fine weather there was seldom more than a scattered handful of wanderers dotted along the mile of shore, and most of these would be on the wider belt of sand up at the town end, where the encrusted snout of the pier strode on stiff legs into the sea. But there was always something happening on the beach, or on that segment of the Irish Sea enclosed by the shallow pincer of the bay. On the morning when I met Jones for the first time there was a mad woman alone out there on the sands. Of course I didn't know that she was mad when I first saw her.

I had been sitting for some time on the pebbles, just below a ridge of shingle which obscured from sight the town on the other side of the promenade, and I was playing the game I often played down there on the beach. I would pretend to myself that I had no knowledge of what lay out of sight beyond the rim of the beach; and when I had washed my mind clear of memory, when the engendered mood was strong enough, I would walk backwards down the shingle, waiting with real excitement for the first signs of the town to appear above the lip of the promenade. There seemed always to be the chance that by some alchemy the whole view might have changed: a wild jungle, of palms and creepers, suddenly have sprung up in place of the town, with tigers and wolves peering out from the darkness between the trees... and as I walked backwards, expecting some miracle of this kind to have occurred, and as the town, with its rows of drab hotels, with their curious minarets and towers, and domes, rose into view, I would see all this familiar scene as if for the first time, and be filled with wonder and curiosity at the thought of people building these buildings, and living in them, at the thought of all the mysterious things that must be happening in this town which I had suddenly discovered....

It was while I was walking backwards that this woman, whom I had noticed and dismissed from notice a few moments before, started to sing. It was then I realised that she was a madwoman. She sang in a high falsetto, four notes over again 'La-la-di-da, la-la-di-da...' Very high and pure and mad the sounds came to me from out there across the sands.

I turned, and sat down to watch her. She was in the act of taking off or putting on a shoe, and in a moment I saw that she had been taking it off, for now she was walking away, taking a mad, curving course out towards the breakwater, leaving the shoe behind her, tiny and forlorn, on that great expanse of sand. And I saw now that her other shoe had also been left, a hundred yards nearer to me, in solitary isolation not far from the edge of the shingle.

She hung her handbag by the strap from a post of the breakwater. Then she mounted the top plank of the break-water and moved unsteadily along its edge, swaying dangerously from side to side until she reached the next post nearer the sea. Before she reached it she nearly fell: I saw the arc of her swaying increase, and she completed the few yards to the next post at a run, off balance, reaching forward to clasp the post desperately for support. But after a moment's rest she moved off once more, more confidently this time, passing the next post with scarcely a pause, and continuing easily now, a few feet above the gently lapping waves, on her way out to sea. I turned my back on the sea once more, thinking half-heartedly to pick up the threads of my game, but almost at once I was arrested by a cry from the madwoman, a faint, far cry, as if she were at the last ebb of her strength.

'Hi, you! little boy!' she cried.

I turned and stared at her. She was sitting now on the square top of the final post of the breakwater, her hands in her lap and her feet folded demurely together on the edge of the top plank. It was apparent immediately that she had not been calling to me, for I saw that, on the far side of the breakwater, nearer to it and further out to sea than I was, had appeared a youth of about my own age. Like me, he had tied the laces of his boots together and hung them round his neck. He had rolled his trousers up to the calf, wore a corduroy lumber jacket open down the front, and had his hands in his pockets. He had turned to stare at the madwoman but moved no closer. Curious about the madness of this woman, I walked down slowly on to the sands, passing the first shoe on my way.

'I say, little boy!' the woman called. 'I've left my handbag on the end of the breakwater. Could you fetch it for me?' She had straw-coloured hair which sat like a bird's nest on her head, pulled down (as if it were a detachable cap) almost over her eyes. The youth looked towards the landward end of the breakwater, and then back at the woman, hesitating, and I felt the moment hardening, with the three of us in our triangle there, far out on the sands, under the sky.

The other boy moved landward, and I looked at the woman again, perched on her pole in the sea like an ungainly bird. Then she shouted again, this time at me. 'Hi!' she shouted. 'You other little boy. I left my shoes on the sand back there. Could you fetch them for me?' I hesitated, just as the other boy had done, and as he was doing now, thinking that the shouting must be for him. Then I too moved landward; and, not having so far to go, but having to collect one shoe and then the other, and complete my triangle, it happened that the two of us, on our different sides of the breakwater, converged on the woman together.

I held the shoes gingerly, keeping them away from me, using as few fingers as possible, partly to show my desire not to damage them and partly because they were very old, very soiled, and not pleasant to the touch. I noticed that the other boy held the handbag, which was of cheap, very dilapidated, imitation shagreen, in the same fashion. I looked at him, across the breakwater, and he looked at me, we neither of us looked at the woman. When we came close to her, holding out our offerings wordlessly, from as far away as possible, she started to look all round her – but there was only water there – and said in a confiding voice

'I ought to have worn my Wellingtons. Angela said I ought to wear my Wellingtons.'

We exchanged glances, the other boy and I. His eyebrows were suspended high in his forehead, and with his free hand he kept pulling his upper lip down over his teeth, which protruded, and over his lower lip. There for a moment it would stay, he looking sober and surprised at once, like a circus clown; and then it would slowly roll back, like a patent blind, and three huge front teeth would pop out, gleaming, at unexpected angles. The right-hand upper incisor was missing, so the three remaining ones seemed to pop out of his mouth sideways, altering the whole shape of his face whenever they appeared. He did it again and again while we stood there, and I watched him, not wanting to look at the woman.

The woman had taken the bag and hung it over her shoulder. Now she took one of the shoes which I was proff-ering and, balancing precariously with one foot on the edge of the top plank of the breakwater, pulled it on. Then she did the same with the other. She seemed to have some difficulty putting them on, and I noticed that she had put them on the wrong feet, left for right and right for left. But I didn't dare say anything. The sea had wet the rolls of trouser-leg round my calves, and I was standing on tiptoe in an attempt to avoid soaking them any further.

With her shoes on, and her handbag clasped firmly against her waist, the woman stepped down into the water beside us. She looked at us each in turn, in a very worried way, and then remarked 'I hope you boys have got a towel, to dry your feet on.' And she waded thoughtfully away

26

through the shallow surf, the belt of her coat, held only by the buckle caught in a loop at her waist, trailing behind her in the water as if it wished to hold her back in the sea. Over the sand she went, sloshing heavily in her wet shoes, up the shingle and on to the Promenade in a straight, undeviating, determined course.

We watched her go in silence, grave with our speculations. A gull flew in front of us, shrieking wildly. I heard the other boy draw in air sharply through his teeth. I looked at him. He was pulling his upper lip down over his teeth. When he caught my eye he grinned, the lip flew up like a blind, disappearing, apparently, into the underside of his nose, and his whole face crinkled up like corrugated paper.

'Dotty!' he said, screwing one finger into his temple.

'Must be,' I said, 'quite dotty!'

We started walking quietly in towards the sand. Suddenly the other boy jumped right out of the water and back, making a tremendous splash. 'Dotty, dotty, dotty!' he shouted, and went racing in through the shallows, leaping wildly.

'Dotty!' I sang, dancing, high on my toes, after him.

It was a strange morning out there on the sands, with the sea disappearing into the sky and the little waves so calmly rolling up and unrolling their dainty carpets of lace. Somehow the madwoman had given the day a special quality, so that I might still have remembered it even if it had not been the day on which I met Jones.

Up on the Promenade, we rolled down our trouser legs, pulled on our boots, and assumed again the precarious poses of adulthood. Although it was the end of April, and nearly as hot as midsummer, the Promenade, like the beach, was almost deserted. In another few weeks Whitsun would have concentrated the crowds as if it were a sign; but at present the town was ours. We walked sedately along the very edge of the Promenade, making a little detour every hundred yards where the glass-sided shelters stuck out their square promontories above the beach. Our hands were deep in our trouser pockets. Sometimes we kicked a pebble in the direction of an obese herring gull, making it hop nonchalantly aside.

As we walked we exchanged credentials. Jones had only recently arrived in the town to join his father, who, like mine, had been evacuated from London with his office early in 1940. He had already taken some sort of entrance examination to the school, which I had been attending for two terms.

'What's the school like, then?'

'Pretty bloody.'

'Couldn't be as bloody as my last one'.

'You wait, man! It's bloody all right!'

Actually I rather liked the school, although a pack of lithe, savagely jeering Welsh boys had given me a bad time in my first term, and I had made no friends save Gregory. After the initial horror, co-education had been an exciting new experience for me, and much of the original excitement remained, for the whole field of girls was still an almost totally unexplored country. As we turned into the town, at the Cenotaph end of the Promenade, we ran up against Gregory, who was waiting outside a bicycle shop while the mechanic fiddled with the brakes of his machine. I intro-

duced Jones, glad that he should see me as a man sufficiently established to have friends, but anxious not to allow
Gregory to spoil with his clinging, lugubrious ways the
beginnings of this new friendship.

'New bug, eh?' said Gregory, with his gluey smirk. 'Well,
they give new bugs a pretty rotten time here, generally, but
you'll be all right now that you know us, eh, Bernard?'

'Ah, dry up!' I said. I was furious with him, and as soon
as he went into the shop to pay for the repairs to his bicycle
I grabbed Jones by the arm, hissed 'Hop it, quick!' into his
ear, and we fled, roaring with laughter, pretending that the
police were after us, down alleyways, through crowds of
shoppers, until we were sure we had left Gregory far behind.

'That Hawkins,' said Jones, pulling at his lip judiciously.
'Ain't he a tweeny bit wet?'

I agreed that the hottest sun could never dry off
Gregory's wetness, and indicated that it was only through
compassion that I allowed him to think of me as a friend;
brushing aside without difficulty all thought of the two
terms throughout which Gregory had been, virtually, the
only person in the school ever to speak to me.

As we walked through the town and down Gloddaeth
Street I pointed out to Jones the local landmarks: Haulfre
Gardens, the cliffs of Pen-y-Dinas, supposed to be an ancient
British encampment, and of Pen-y-Bwlch, above the Happy
Valley.

'Pen-y-what?' asked Jones.

'Bwlch,' I said.

'Bless you. What did you say?'

'Bwlch.'

29

'There you go again! What's wrong? Eaten something that didn't agree with you, man?' said Jones, full of concern. 'Have a peppermint, that'll fix you up. Now, what was that name?'

'Pen-y-Bwlch, you clown!' I said, laughing.

'Bullock. Bullock! Is that right?' Jones pushed his lips out as he said the word, blowing it out just as if he were breaking wind.

'Bwlch!' I said. We were both struggling with face-splitting grins.

'How do you spell it?'

'B-W-L-C-H,' I said. 'Bwlch!'

'Don't be silly, man, you're having me on!'

'I'm not.'

'You are.'

'I'm not!'

'Oh well, I suppose it's no worse than ought.'

'Than what?'

'Ought. A-W-T Ought.'

'Ought!' I said.

'Silly word, ain't it? said Jones. 'You might as well spell awl O-U-G-H-L. Ought, indeed!'

'Ought!' we said together, derisively.

'Bwlch!' we chanted. 'Ought!' For some reason we started to run, swinging on our arms in and out of trees and lamp-posts, laughing and leaping and shouting our two words back and forth like prancing cannibals round a cooking missionary.

Jones would never let a joke go cold on one; he always contrived to leave it at the very height of its powers. On this occasion, though, he didn't need to invent a distraction, for a very complete one was provided for us by the sudden appearance of Gregory, cycling slowly up Gloddaeth Street with his head sunk morosely between his shoulders. Jones saw him first.

'Hawkins-ho!' he cried softly, drawing me quickly behind a tram shelter. 'Do you want to see him?'

'No, for God's sake, man!' I exclaimed in a panic.

Gregory passed us slowly, slouched forward over the handlebars, his eyes on the road approaching his front wheel. His mouth was pursed up in a soundless whistle, his eyebrows raised as if in fixed surprise at what his bulging eyes saw over the rim of the wheel.

'Haw-haw-haw-HAWkins!' sang Jones suddenly. 'Oh, you bloody fool!' I cried furiously. 'You absolute bloody, bloody fool, Jones!'

Gregory sat up straight on his saddle, braked, wavered, and fell sideways on to a supporting leg. He didn't know where the shout had come from. There were several pedestrians on his own side of the road, and he inspected these first before turning has attention to our side. I muttered imprecations at Jones as we peered through the dirty glass of the shelter's centre division.

'Why!' said Jones innocently. 'He doesn't seem to have seen us. I'd better call again, hadn't I?'

'You dare!' I hissed.

Jones put his head back like a wolf about to howl, but he had scarcely started to breathe the aspirate before I had swung an arm round over his mouth, pressing his head into my chest. Almost at once we were on the ground, fighting hard. I was on top, but had to take my arm away from his face in order to stay there.

'Haw-haw-haw-HAWkins!' Jones shouted, as soon as his mouth was clear. 'Oh, Hawkins, here we are!'

'Shut up, you swine, oh, damn, shut up!' I panted, as we wrestled violently on the floor of the tram shelter.

I got my hand over his mouth again, but he pulled it off, grinning like a maniac, and shouted 'Help! Hawkins! Help!'

With a sudden twist I got my legs round his body, locked the feet together, and started to squeeze. My head was now crushed against his ribs by both his arms, but mine was the more deadly grip and I knew that he could not last long. He gave one last strangled cry of 'Hawkins!' and I increased the pressure.

'Beaten?' I asked.

'Hawkins!' he cried despairingly.

I squeezed harder.

'Beaten?'

'Hawk... Oh Christ, yes, beaten, let go, for God's sake!' Jones gasped. I gave a final squeeze for good measure, un-locked my feet, pulled my left leg from under him, and scrambled up, brushing the dirt from my clothes. Jones lay gasping on the ground like a stranded shark.

'Ambulance!' he gasped. 'Police! Fire! Murder!'

I stood grinning down at him, delighted with my victory.

'You nearly murdered me, you swine!' Jones said, looking up from where he lay flat on his back, his hands pressed tightly to his sides, his chest heaving. 'I wouldn't have thought such a weedy little chap could – '

'Such a what? Want some more?' I said, threateningly.

'Damn, no, give over!' Jones pushed himself to a sitting position, and then gingerly stood up, feeling himself all over as if for broken bones.

When we emerged from the tram shelter, Hawkins, of course, had gone.

'Why, bless me soul,' said Jones, 'the bird has flown. Ain't you disappointed, man?'

'Heartbroken,' I said.

'Fine way to treat a friend, I must say.'

'What, you?'

'Pore ole Hawkins.'

'Want another fight?'

'Go blow your nose!'

Squabbling amiably thus we made our way to the end of Gloddaeth Street. The tide, which had been rising all morning, was now nearly high again, and a sudden breeze was making the water slap fretfully against the stone groynes. The great lazy herring gulls swung indolently in front of us, lifting, braking, sitting on the air, sliding away sideways towards the surface of the water; sometimes hovering there, just over the waves, with their wings flapping wildly and their yellow claws hanging down behind them like a ladder from a helicopter; or skidding gently on to the surface, making a sharp little bow wave, then shrugging and shifting their flanks as they settled their wings neatly in place, bobbing and dipping comfortably over the swelling water. 'Smashing to be a seagull,' said Jones thoughtfully.

'Smashing!' I said.

We scuffled along the edge of the surf, turning the line

of tide-wrack over for flotsam and jetsam, but finding none, and skimming flat stones from wave to wave with deft, practised flicks of the wrist, Jones was better at this than I was: in anything needing co-ordination of hand and eye he was always streets ahead of me. But when it came to leaping from rock to rock in a chase across the big boulders higher up the beach I soon outstripped him; I just could not put a foot wrong, it was as if I had eyes in the soles of my feet, so sure and delicate was my leaping progress.

The light was bright and hard on the mountains across the water. The little breeze had dropped as suddenly as it had arisen. The noise of the gulls and the gently rolling shingle was now just a kind of silence, in which our own footsteps crunched loudly, so that we left the stones as soon as we could for the fine pale shifting sand below the beginning of the dunes.

'Good place,' said Jones, indicating the steep bank of sand-dunes which ran down along the shore towards the little spit of piled boulders that was the Black Rocks.

'Rabbits,' I said. 'There's rabbits in the dunes. Hundreds of them. Thousands.'

'What's that?' Jones asked, pointing to where, a few hundred yards down the dunes, some blocks of stone, a wheelbarrow, and a small triangular derrick were clustered together in a fold of the sands. 'What are they doing there?'

'Building a pillbox,' I told him. 'Beach defence, you know. Shall we take a decko?'

The pillbox was nearly finished: and a box it was, a building some five feet high, and, inside, eight feet square, made of reinforced concrete blocks the same colour as the sand. It had a three-foot-high entrance hole at the back, and three gun slits at the front, facing the sea. The workmen had piled sand and tufts of marram grass on the roof, and the wind, an unwitting collaborator, had already started the sloping drifts which would eventually creep right up to the gun slits, obscuring them entirely if the sand was not kept at bay. Already the new building had become an almost indistinguishable part of the dunes. Jones and I crawled in through the entrance hole, and crouched side by side at the gun slits, looking out across the soft water to where Puffin Island, that bell of birds, was suspended in the midday haze.

'What would you do,' I said suddenly, startling myself as I uttered the thought, 'if suddenly hundreds of enormous U-boats surfaced off-shore and started to disgorge thousands of Jerry soldiers?'

Jones thought for a moment, pulling at his upper lip. 'Well,' he said at last, 'I'd send you back to give the alarm. And I'd stay here myself to make notes. You know, number of men, number of boats, and that.'

'Why should I go?' I protested. 'Anyway, you haven't got a pencil and paper.'

'You'd go because you're smaller and quicker than I am, you could get away without being seen. And I'd make my notes by scratching on the concrete with my penknife.'

'Fat lot of good that would be when the pillbox was captured by the first wave, and you with it!' I jeered.

Jones didn't answer. He just went on staring through the gun slit, still pulling at his lip, his brows drawn down in a straight black line across the bridge of his irregular nose.

'How old are you, Smith?' he asked at length.

35

'Fifteen in August. How old are you?'

'I'm fifteen this month. April the twenty-eighth.'

It seemed to me that Jones had managed to assimilate an awful lot of maturity in the three months' extra living he had experienced. I hoped that by the time I was his age I, too, would feel as poised and settled as he looked.

'How long do you think the war's going to last, man?' Jones asked.

'Ten years?' I hazarded hopefully; it was the equivalent of saying 'for ever'.

'If the Jerries land, I'm going to take to the mountains. My old man's got a shotgun.'

'My old man's got a .45 Colt,' I boasted. 'We could do some damage with that, man, eh?'

I didn't know whether it was a .45 Colt or not, but I'd often seen the massive revolver, a Great War relic, with half a dozen shells loose in the holster, lying in a corner among the shoes at the bottom of the wardrobe in my parents' bedroom. It was almost too heavy for me to hold with one hand.

'Two and a half years,' Jones said. I thought he was guessing the length of the war, but after a moment he added 'We've got to wait two and a half years before we can get in. The Navy'll take you at seventeen and a half.'

Seventeen and a half, I thought. I wondered if I would ever reach such an age, or die of fatigue first.

'Still,' Jones went on hopefully, 'they might invade. Then we'd all be in it, wouldn't we?'

'They won't invade,' I said. It seemed my role that afternoon to put the dreary view, Jones's to put the hopeful one. 'I expect we'll just starve them out, like last time. It can't take long.'

'I don't know,' said Jones. 'You can't tell. Anyway, if the Jerries did land we'd all look pretty silly if we were caught napping, I reckon we ought to have a Plan.'

'There's the Home Guard,' I said. 'We wouldn't be caught napping.'

'No, you ass, I mean us, you and me. We ought to get it all worked out. Just in case.'

'Well,' I said soberly, 'there's nothing like being ready for anything.'

'Quite!' said Jones, with an executive snap of his jaw. 'And you and I, Smith, are damn' well going to be ready if it's the last thing we do. If I was a Jerry, this is just the sort of place I'd choose to invade. And you couldn't expect the bloody Welsh to defend it properly. They'd probably go over to the Jerries, they're always yapping about self-government.'

'Are they?' I asked innocently.

'You know they are. Like the rotten Irish. And you know,' Jones said significantly, 'what happened in Ireland in 1916.'

'Oh, that!' I said, with a little laugh. I had no idea what happened in Ireland in 1916, but whatever it was, it sounded very subversive, mentioned in that tone of voice.

'Damn it!' said Jones violently, as if I'd been arguing with him, 'someone's got to defend this blasted place, haven't they?'

'Oh, sure!' I said vaguely.

'Well, then!' Jones looked sideways at me truculently, as if not trusting me to refrain from further argument. Then he turned back to his gun slit, working his jaw from side to side like a cowboy. Into the small field commanded by my own narrow aperture swam a seagull, head down, perfectly motionless, scanning the sands below for food. Beyond it, the sea shimmered indistinctly, without a surface, seeming to slope up gently towards the horizon, which was no great distance away, bounded on one side by the great hump of Penmaenmawr Mountain and on the other by the Two Sisters, twin vertical rocks standing up out of the sea two hundred yards from the westward point of the Great Orme. Somewhere out there, I said to myself, somewhere beneath that unbroken surface, the enemy are waiting, watching and waiting, ready to strike, ready to kill.

Somewhere over in the heart of Germany the bombers, their engines revving, were loading their tons of high explosive, the submarines chugging quietly downstream towards the sea. But I saw the enemy as a handful of close-cropped, moustachioed men in Kaiser Wilhelm helmets, rising suddenly out of the sea somewhere near Puffin Island and falling one by one to the deadly accuracy of Jones's shotgun and my Colt .45 revolver, while Llandudno slept peacefully through some such calm morning as this.

Three

Kathy entered my life quietly, like a ship, with its engines cut, sliding silently into its berth across a still mirror of water. After our first brief meeting on the threshold of the school, I continued to see her more and more frequently about the streets, the playing fields, the beaches, and the hills. It was Gregory, of course, who discovered and passed on her name; and by shadowing her, one day after school, hazardously through the streets from the Library down to Graig-y-don, I had found out where she lived. Gradually, she began to enter my waking dreams; became the audience, breathless with suspense, for whom I climbed the unclimbable mountains or broke the unbreakable stallions. So familiar did her presence become to me in these dreams, that it seemed only natural that in my active life our paths should cross so frequently.

In fact, our brief meetings became so regular as to be beyond the scope of coincidence; one broiling May afternoon – a Sunday – I stumbled across her, with two other girls, picnicking on the summit of Conway Mountain; the next evening, after school, when I was cycling by myself round to Rhos-on-Sea by way of Llangwstenin, she suddenly appeared on the road in front of me, walking slowly, but apparently puffed with running; and at Gogarth Abbey, two evenings later, where I was waiting for Jones, who had some errand to complete for his mother, I spotted Kathy walking lazily along the Marine Drive above me, seemingly intent on her own thoughts. Jones had still not arrived, and I was passing the time by throwing stones at the wheeling seagulls below me, when Kathy passed again on her way back. This time she saw me, and waved; and hesitated, so that for a moment I thought she was going to clamber over the wall and climb down the rocks to join me.

Now when our paths crossed we would exchange brief greetings, and often pause for a moment, looking at each other undecidedly, until one or the other of us made a sudden gesture of retreat. On one occasion, Dora Maguire held me talking, on some pretext, as she waited at the gate of the school long after the majority had left; and I, anxious to get away, had just impatiently cut short the conversation and turned to leave when I saw Kathy emerging from the girls' cloakroom, and realised that it was for her Dora had been waiting. But it was by then too late for me to stay, my excuses and goodbyes to Dora had been made, so there was nothing for me to do but cycle as quickly as possible away, knowing that by my obtuseness (for it had at last dawned on me that Dora had thought to effect a meeting between us thus) and impatience I had forfeited the chance of a perfectly simple, authentically accidental, introduction.

But, as it turned out, such an introduction became un-necessary. Shortly afterwards, as I was cycling down the Conway Road on my way home after walking through the town and back again with Jones – an after-school ritual which had the same social importance as riding down Rotten Row or along the Promenade at Longchamps – I came across Kathy, leaning over her bicycle and fiddling with the chain, which had slipped off the rear cog. Without any sense of surprise, and only the very faintest quickening of the heart, I pulled up beside her and asked if I could help. She looked up quickly as I spoke, and said quietly 'Oh, hello! No, I think I've fixed it now, thanks!' She gave a turn to the wheel, and I heard the chain click back into place. She seemed to have managed the whole operation without getting a trace of grease on her hands, but nevertheless went busily through the ritual of finding a clean white rag in her saddlebag, wiping her hands, folding the rag, and returning it neatly to its pocket. Then she straightened up, smiled shyly, and began to mount her bicycle. She had a frail gold chain round her left wrist.

It was a quietly miraculous event. Her tone, as she said 'Oh, hello!' had been familiar, unsurprised, as if she had only left my company a moment before; and so natural did it seem to me to be with her, that I was aware of nothing unusual in the ease with which we cycled off together towards the Links Hotel. When two eight-year-old urchins called from the pavement 'Sweethearts! Sweethearts!' as we cycled past, we exchanged smiles of compassion for them; and I was pleased to think that the thing was accomplished and obvious already, without my having had to expose myself to the dangers of taking action.

We rode in silence, for it seemed no embarrassment to have nothing to say. But when we reached the Links Hotel, where our paths necessarily diverged, we entered into a sudden furious burst of conversation – an exchange of information about ourselves – so that it was natural for us to pull up at the corner, supporting our bicycles with one leg on the ground, and put off for a few moments the parting which we both desired and desired to delay.

Kathy said 'That day you fell in the ditch... did you get wet?'

'Not much,' I said; and then 'Fancy you remembering that!'

'Oh!' said Kathy, beginning to laugh, but looking away from me, away across the fields towards Nant-y-Gamar. 'Oh, I couldn't forget that! That was the first time I spoke to you. And I can remember every time I've ever seen you!'

For some reason I wasn't surprised. 'So can I!' I said. 'I mean, remember every time I've seen you.'

Kathy said 'I bet you can't! I bet I can remember more times than you can!'

'I bet you can't!' I said, seeing the little incidents pass rapidly before my mind's eye like an endless moving tapestry.

'Go on then!' said Kathy, with teasing laughter in her voice. 'Tell me three... tell me five!'

'Well, there was the time near the Little Orme when you fell over, and the time on the road at Llangwstenin, and the time on Conway Mountain, and the time by the Library when you got your bike stuck in the tram-lines...'

I thought I was doing rather well, but Kathy said 'Oh, it doesn't count in the town, nor at school, nor if I was with other people, so that's only two!'

'That's not fair! Well, anyway, there was the time I saw

you up near Llanrhos, in the field, and the time by Pigeon's Cave, the time when – er – when...'

But I couldn't sort them out any longer; I saw only a jumble of images of Kathy in a hundred different poses, Kathy running, Kathy lying on the sand, Kathy poised for flight beside her bicycle as she was poised now, Kathy swinging round a corner of the school, her head cocked sideways like a bright sparrow, Kathy running like a fiend, Kathy walking, Kathy running...

'Three!' cried Kathy. 'That's only three! What about the time near Gogarth Abbey and the time near the gasworks, and the time I waved to you at Maes Du and you fell off your bicycle, and the time...'

She went on and on, breathless, faster and faster, talking against a strong current of her own laughter until we were both laughing and I had to say 'All right, all right, I give up! But I did remember all those times, only I couldn't think of them!'

'Ah!' said Kathy. 'But I could, couldn't I? And anyway, I've seen you hundreds of times when you didn't even know I was there!'

Kathy laughed still; and since there was no answer to such a charge, I laughed with her. And then, suddenly, she was moving, going, still laughing.

'Goodbye, Bernard!' she called.

'Goodbye, Kathy!'

The following Sunday, at midday, I was cycling slowly towards my home through the dingy back streets between the railway station and the gasworks when Kathy came

43

flying out of a narrow turning and nearly knocked me off my bicycle. She was pedalling furiously, with her head down and her hair streaming like a plume, and as she shot across the road in front of me we both swerved, so that for a moment we were travelling away from each other. I stopped and shouted; and Kathy, whose brakes were clearly not at all efficient, made a wide sweep in the middle of the road and freewheeled to a halt beside me.

'You're jolly dangerous,' I said. 'You nearly knocked me flying!'

'But I didn't, did I?' said Kathy triumphantly, as if she had achieved something positive. 'I missed you!'

'Only just. What's all the hurry, anyway?'

'Hurry?' Kathy opened her brown eyes innocently. 'I'm not in a hurry, Bernard.'

'You were going jolly fast. You looked as if you were in a hurry, anyway.'

For some reason she was now blushing, so I looked away. We had started to pedal along side by side towards the gasworks, and were at that moment passing the slaughter-house, so I said 'That's the slaughterhouse, there.'

'Oh no! Oh, Bernard!'

'What's the matter?'

'Is that what the – the smell is?'

'That's it,' I said. 'The smell of Death!'

'Oh don't, Bernard! How beastly! I shall never be able to eat meat again.'

'You will,' I said, laughing. But I could see that she was genuinely upset. I had spoiled the morning for her; she looked now as if she would never be happy again.

'Where were you off to, anyway?' I asked. 'Hurry or no hurry.'

Kathy brightened at once. 'I'm going to pick wild strawberries. I've got a theory there must be some wild strawberries at Dwygyfylchi.'

'Is it far?'

'Not very. Are you coming?'

It was so easy with Kathy: the hardest things were past and done almost before one had become apprehensive about them... frighteningly easy.

'I haven't had my lunch. Have you?'

Kathy laughed, 'I don't eat lunch,' she said. 'Not often, anyway.'

'I must go home for lunch. Mother would think I'd had an accident...'

'Go on then, I don't mind waiting.'

'Oh, I couldn't...'

Kathy went off into one of her mysterious wild swirls of laughter. 'Silly! Silly!' she mocked at me. 'Go on and have your lunch. I'll just... oh, I'll ride around, I'm quite happy, I'm always happy just riding around.'

I had to believe her, strange as it all seemed. So, while pedalled slowly out to the golf links and back, I tore into my house, gobbled my lunch, borrowed two shillings from my mother, and in fifteen minutes was out on the road again, a yellow waterproof cape strapped to my handlebars.

Kathy appeared almost at once, cycling quietly towards me as if she had known exactly how long I would take to eat my lunch.

45

'I bought some chocolate,' she said, 'in case it rains.

'Haven't you got a cape?'

'I didn't bring it – it would be sure to rain if I did!'

She was evasive, to begin with, about the exact location of this unpronounceable place, Dwygyfylchi. 'The other side of Conway,' was all she would say. But when Conway was already two miles behind, and we seemed to have been climbing steeply for a long time, she confessed that it was also the other side of the Sychnant Pass: in front of us was a long, slow climb before we could swoop down the valley towards the place of the wild strawberries.

'You're a cheat!' I said. 'Why didn't you tell me when we started?'

'You might not have come!' laughed Kathy.

I was at once thrilled and appalled by such confessions, which Kathy made as if nothing were being confessed. She gave herself away with every word she spoke, and I felt that I ought to reply in kind, but could not. My impulse towards honesty had already been corrupted by two terms of school warfare and by Gregory's sly, false knowingness.

Heavy grey clouds had gathered along the crests of the mountains between which we aimed to pass. As we climbed, pushing our bicycles, round the sharp curve of the road below the top of the Pass, the clouds on either side seemed to expand, stretching out to meet above our heads.

'It's going to rain,' I said, as we rested for a moment below the pinewood that closed round the final stretch of road before the top.

'I love rain,' said Kathy.

We had not talked much during our ride; and for me there

was enough excitement – almost too much – just in being alone with this extraordinary, laughing girl, who was at once so agonizingly shy and so innocently bold, without the added dangers and excitements of conversation. Once, peering sideways at her as I did from time to time just to make sure that she was really there, I caught her looking across at me in exactly the same wondering way. She blushed, and I stammered some inept platitude about the steepness of the hill; and then we both suddenly burst out laughing, it was wonderful the way we laughed together then.

The pine trees closed above our heads as we went on uphill, making a dark tunnel at the end of which we could see, in a semicircle of light, the highest point of the pass. As we approached the end of this tunnel we heard an irregular murmur from the dense mass of pine needles above, and knew that the rain had begun.

'Shall we stay here and shelter?' I asked. 'It may only be a shower.'

'No, let's go on, Bernard. I want to show you something.'

'You'll get wet.'

'I don't mind.'

Below us, as we stood at the head of the pass, the valley swept round wide and clear towards the coastal plain and the sea. The mountain flanks on each side still burned a reddish brown with last year's dead bracken, with here and there a flush of pale green where the new fronds were unfurling above the tangled corpses of their forbears. The dark clouds close above us had imprisoned the head of the valley, and we seemed to be looking out at everything through a pane of dark green glass, almost as if we, and the mountains and the valley at our feet, were fathoms deep below the sea. Yet along the coast, we could see, the sun was shining, pale solid light streaming in bars and curtains out of the sky.

'Follow me,' said Kathy. 'And not too fast!'

We freewheeled off downhill, our brakes rubbing and squealing. Kathy had cocked one leg forward round the front of her steering column, and with the foot was pressing the front of the mudguard hard down against the tyre: this was her only effective brake. I noticed for the first time how smooth and firm were her strong bare legs, red-gold in a green world.

After a few hundred yards Kathy jumped off her bicycle and ran it to a halt beside the wall on the right of the road. 'Here,' she said, 'leave your bike here. I want to show you something.'

'What is it?'

'I'll show you. Come on.'

On our left, facing across the valley, a short overhanging cliff curved up, saucer-shaped, to about twenty or thirty feet. Kathy walked across to its foot. 'Come here, Bernard,' she commanded.

'What is it?' I asked again.

'Listen.'

She cupped her hands round her mouth, lifted her head to the sky, and shouted 'Bernard!'

'... ernard... ernard... ernard... nard...nard,' sang the echo from across the valley. It was eerie and faintly disturbing; impossible not to feel that there was someone across there, mocking us; that the mountain knew.

48

'You try,' said Kathy.

'Kathy!' I shouted at the mountain.

'... athy... athy... athy... thy... thy,' the mountain sang softly back.

'Bernard!' shouted Kathy.

'... ernard... ernard... nard... nard,' sang the mountain.

'Isn't it horrid?' said Kathy. 'Some nasty little gnome across there, all rocky and mossy with bracken in his hair, and all he does all day is just shout back at people whatever they've shouted themselves. He never says anything new, it doesn't matter how rude you are.' She cocked up her head, staring challengingly at the mountain. 'Why don't you say something else?' she shouted.

'... ing else... ing else... else... else,' mocked the gnome maddeningly.

'Phooey!' said Kathy. 'Let's leave him alone, or we shan't have time to look for strawberries.'

While we had been playing with the echo the rain had thickened. We had been protected slightly by the overhang of the little cliff, but now suddenly the raindrops increased and, as if gathering momentum from their own increase, came sizzling down in ever-greater numbers, forming grey swaying curtains across the valley, humming as they came.

'Stay there,' I told Kathy. I'll get my cape.'

I ran across to my bicycle, slipped the straps from the cape, and scuttled back. Kathy, whose cotton dress was already clinging wetly to her knees, had crouched down with her back against the rock, her face raised to the rain. I squatted next to her and, spreading the cape as wide as it would go, we drew it up like a blanket to our chins.

'Bernard!' said Kathy, as if she had urgent news for me.

'What?'

'Isn't it lovely?'

'What is?

'Being here like this... I mean, us, and the rain, and all...'

'Yes,' I said.

It was lovely, there was magic in it somewhere, but I could not do more than agree, I could not add a comment of my own. There were deep waters here, I knew, and I was afraid of them. As long as we just crouched here, leaning against each other's shoulder, our heads inches apart and the spreading yellow oilskin making of us one squat form, and watched the curtains of falling water march swaying up the valley, seeing through them that other world of sunlight down there, three miles away, by the sea, then the magic was safe. But there were worlds beyond magic which words could open up, and I did not want to risk myself out there, however brightly the sun might shine. So I just said 'Yes,' and sensed the faint disappointment that would be clouding Kathy's eyes.

When the rain ceased we moved out reluctantly from under our uniting cape, became two people again, and laughed as we sped down towards Dwygyfylchi, with the wind drying our clothes and Kathy's thick brown hair swaying and lifting like a bird's wing behind her eager head. We found no wild strawberries by the banks of the little stream down there, though we did find a leaf that Kathy alleged belonged to a mean wild strawberry that hadn't bothered to flower; but nothing happened to us to equal that strange magic of the echo and the rain, and we rode home quietly, content with our great achievement.

Four

At the time I thought that these meetings were bound to flower, almost immediately, into some more solid relationship. It seemed impossible that they should not; after such shared experience we could hardly continue to meet, accidentally, as casual acquaintances; it would be too humiliating for both of us. And yet that, in fact, is exactly what happened.

It was clear to me, after our ride to Dwygyfylchi that the onus was now upon me to take some positive action; and indeed in my mind I pictured now with delight the scenes that must follow: we would take our bicycles, one sunny summer day, and ride down to Glan Conway to pick blue scabious in the water meadows; and as we walked we would hold hands, and there would grow up about us a precious, enveloping bubble of tenderness, and understanding, and we would lie side by side on the hillside and I would feast my eyes on her... it was very vague, what happened then, but there was great sweetness to be had at the end of it all.

Yet I did nothing, and came to know, finally, that I was incapable of doing anything to further this tentative, terrifying friendship. It was not, somehow, a relationship which could be fitted into the rougher, more earthy pattern of life that Jones and I were evolving for ourselves. I saw Kathy as often as before, and spoke to her on several occasions, but there was now a constraint in our manner; for we were both guiltily conscious of having failed each other in some vague but decisive way. Kathy's face would still light up when we met accidentally at a corner of one of the school corridors; but if we paused to speak there seemed nothing to say, and I would see a puzzled, almost incomprehending look come into Kathy's eyes, as if she recognized that something was wrong but could not understand why this should be.

Jones never mentioned Kathy, sensing perhaps how private and unsharable were my feelings about her; and I soon came to feel that there was something shameful in having such feelings at all, and began deliberately to avoid Kathy, going out of my way, sometimes, to reach one end of the town from the other, if I knew that she might be standing, with her bicycle, among a group of friends outside the Library or the Milk Bar. She cannot have known about these evasions, yet it seemed to me that she looked at me accusingly now, when we did meet, and I wished that there were something, soothing, but quite final, that I could find to say to her.

Dropping Gregory, as far as that was ever possible, Jones and I rapidly hollowed out for ourselves, that term, a secure little burrow in the rigidly stratified society of the school. Secure in each other's friendship, we were free agents, equals of anyone, at liberty, we felt, to draw our friends from the periphery of any clique – drawing them rather into our orbit than seeking, like others, to be drawn into theirs.

Thus by mid-term we had established friendly relations with Jimmy Raven, known as the 'Crow', whose father owned one of the large hotels now requisitioned by the Inland Revenue: a small, wiry boy with a mass of stiff yellow hair standing up straight from his forehead; and with 'Red' Glyn Jones, a rangy, independent youth so brilliant at sport that he had cut through all barriers without noticing them. There was a wildness, an intractability about Red which for me at least was romantic and slightly frightening; one felt always that at any moment he might do something quite terrifyingly reckless, yet in speaking to one his mild blue eyes gazed from his red face with almost vacant benevolence.

Usually, however, after school hours, we were alone together, and for the time being content to remain so. Indeed, if it had been in my choice, I would have prolonged this semi-isolation indefinitely, for I had far from exhausted the delights of Jones's company. But just as he was able, without embarrassment or loss of face, suddenly to capitulate in an argument once he saw that his position was untenable, so he could, from one day to the next, shift his viewpoint on some absolutely basic subject: as he did, in the middle of that term, over the subject of our attitude towards girls.

The first intimation I had of this important volte-face was an enquiry, one lunch-time, when we were lolling in the grass on the playing fields, as to whether I had taken any particular note of the two girls who had just passed us, their arms round each other's waists. They were circling the playing-fields, had already passed us once, and would certainly pass us at least once more, for we were now between them and the main gate to the school.

'When they come round again,' Jones said, 'take a dekko at the dark one!'

We were chewing the ends of long succulent grasses, searching for even more succulent ones as we chewed. We followed the two girls with our eyes, as, their heads bent together, both arms locked and entwined behind their waists, they marched purposefully, absorbedly, keeping step with each other, round the fenced perimeter of the field. They were dressed identically, in dark blue gym-slips, white blouses, green sashes, white ankle-socks, black shoes; but even at this distance, seen diagonally across the field, they bore no resemblance to each other. Blended now as their figures were, one could see that the taller, dark-haired girl was slim, trim, and neat, while her ginger-haired companion had about her the sort of dumpy disorder that goes with a warm nature and a ready laugh. As they approached us more closely, their conversation became animated, punctuated frequently with poorly suppressed giggles; and for a moment they fell out of step. They both changed step at the same moment, giggled, and then did the same thing again; this time their giggles were nearly shrieks; the dark one suppressed her hysteria first, frowned severely, and said something to her companion, who immediately changed step again.

Jones, searching intensively among the grasses, said quietly but clearly 'Left, left! Left, right, left!'

A burst of fresh giggling rewarded him. The dark girl said something to the ginger one, who pulled at her arm impatiently, leaning forward to hide her face and quickening her pace so that they once again fell out of step. This time they didn't bother to pick it up again, but hurried on towards the gate.

'Left... wheel!' shouted Jones, just as they reached it; and, as if at his command, the two girls wheeled left through the gate, almost running now, and disappeared on a gale of long-pent laughter at last released.

'Well?' said Jones.

'Well what?'

'What about her? The dark one? Bit of all right, eh, man?' Jones gripped his upper lip between thumb and forefinger and pulled it out into a grotesque beak, his enormous eyes bulging under surprised brows.

I said languidly 'If you care for girls, I suppose...' And rolled over on to my stomach, poking among the grass for another fat stem.

Jones was silent for a moment. He lay on his back, supported by his elbows, a long stem of grass sticking up past his nose and curving gently over above his head. His eyes were concentrated on the waving seed-pods, with which he was attempting to describe a circle by manipulating the stem with his teeth.

'You know, Smith,' he said at last, removing the grass and vaguely scanning the ground beside him for another. 'I've been thinking. I reckon we're missing a lot, you know, through sheer laziness. You and I, Smith,' (he produced his new word triumphantly), 'are too insular! We've shut ourselves up in a set of nice cosy little habits, and all the time Life is passing us by! We ought to go about in the world more, Smith, meet people, do things, get to know what's going on! It's all very well us being so self-sufficient and contented, but damn, man, we're missing a vital part of our education!'

'Such as what?' I asked. I had no idea what he was talking about, but it certainly didn't occur to me to question his assertion that in the six weeks since he had arrived at the school we had become, in one another's company, self-sufficient. I seemed to have known him all my life; already the unhappy two terms prior to his advent had dropped away into a past life, dismissed, if thought about at all, as a regrettable mistake on somebody's part; a period having only the vaguest of connections with the person I now felt myself to be.

'Complacent!' said Jones, vigorously whipping my backside with a thong of grass. 'Complacent, that's what we are, Smith! We're fast asleep on a soft bed of complacency. You are my smoking companion, Smith, and we're smoking opium. We're living a drowsy lullaby, and it's got to stop!'

'If you don't stop whipping my arse with that thing, I'll give you a good hiding for a start!' I said. 'That'd be one way out of your dilemma.'

'No, listen, man, I'm serious. This has gone far enough!' Jones waved his arm at the fields in front of us, at the row of council houses behind the gasworks and the Victorian facade of the distant Links Hotel. 'We've got to emerge from our comfortable little shell, Smith, and get out there, get out into the world, go out and meet people...'

'Yes, you said all that. So what?'

'So what what?'

'So what are you going to do about it? Throw a ball at Payne's and ask Councillor Probert?' (There was something obscurely, smuttily funny attached to Councillor Probert's name but I never discovered what.)

'No,' said Jones. 'I'll tell you what I'm going to do for a start. I am going,' he said, as if proposing an alternative far more daring than my flippant suggestion, 'to make the acquaintance of the dark young lady we have just been observing!'

'Good lord, man, is that all?' I exclaimed. 'Well, you're welcome, I hope you enjoy it. It should be easy enough. Personally, though, I think I'll stay a bachelor.'

I was disappointed, after all that build-up, that all he proposed doing was to go out with a girl. Though he was older than I, it would be Jones's first experiment in this direction, and I felt very experienced and cynical – an old roué, blasé with a thousand memories.

Nevertheless, Jones managed to involve me in his various schemes for getting to know Isabel Frith, which proved harder than either of us had imagined.

Gregory presented us with her name almost immediately, by saying to me one morning, soon after Jones had announced his interest in the girl: 'I hear Jones has fallen for Isabel Frith. Is he having any luck?'

I answered with an obscenity, but was pleased to have the information, for it was easier to fit a girl to a name without having to make dangerous enquiries than a name to a girl. The information proved correct, and Jones was delighted with the name, and was thenceforth constantly covering little scraps of paper with 'Isabel Jones' or 'Isabel Frith-Jones', in a dozen different styles of handwriting.

Various manoeuvres were tried in an effort to effect a casual but promising meeting between them, but each time something would go wrong with the plot, and weeks later Jones had still not succeeded even in speaking directly to the girl.

That she was aware of the attention being paid to her was obvious and inevitable – even, perhaps, desirable – and on several occasions when Jones and I, by design or accident, happened to be approaching her face to face, she crossed the road or the playground, or disappeared into a classroom, deliberately to avoid us. These unforeseen difficulties, of course, only served to make Jones keener than ever, and I was myself by this time beginning to feel personally involved in the contest of wits that was going on: for it had now become plain that Isabel was as interested in Jones as he in her, but that she was determined to keep him at arm's length for as long as she possibly could without risking a cooling of his ardour.

Jones's attitude was a mixture of deadly seriousness and high comedy, though he would have been most offended if I had suggested that the comedy was deliberate. Often, coming into the form-room in the morning, he would sink into his desk (which was near mine, though not as near as we would wish), heave a tremendous burlesqued sigh, sink his head into his arms, and hiss dramatically at me 'I've just seen Her. My God, Smith, my God! She looked at me! I can't bear it much longer!'

One lunchtime he came to me bearing a scrap of paper and wearing his gloomiest, most intense expression. 'Look here, Smith,' he said, 'this thing is destroying me! I've got a twitch!' He twitched his face grotesquely. 'And I've started writing poetry! Poetry! Me! I ask you, Smith!'

This is what he had written:

Isabel Frith,
Is the girl I would most like to go out with.
She already has a smashing figure
And it will doubtless be even better when she's bigger.
Oh I would run and fetch a burning coal from hell
For Isabel!

Jones pulled nervously at his upper lip as I read his verse, and when I handed it back his body was suddenly convulsed by an explosive shudder, and he growled 'Aaa-ah-ah!' like a wild animal, rolling his eyes, and clutching at the slip of paper with twitching fingers.

'It's a rotten poem,' I said. 'It doesn't scan. Anyone knows a poem's got to scan!'

'Ah well,' said Jones bitterly, if obscurely, 'it's the passion that's got into me, you see!'

Jones's particular interest in Isabel brought out in both of us an intense interest in girls in general which for a few weeks was so obsessive as to exclude practically every other mental or physical activity. Jones did not feel precluded, by his professed devotion to one girl, from expressing admiration for others, and for about a fortnight we kept a sort of fatstock book, in which each girl we knew or who came to our notice

59

was given a separate page, with a detailed physical description, an assessment of her probable character, her address, and a summing-up of her worth. Kathy did not appear in this book.

Although it was easy enough to get to know some of the girls, Isabel Frith and her friend Moira Evans continued to elude us, and to tease us, seeming to take a delight in slipping out of our carefully prepared traps, almost as if the game were being played out in the open, with all rules declared. We redoubled our efforts, until the campaign reached fever pitch. We thought of nothing else, talked of nothing else, spent all our leisure and much of our school hours in planning and pursuing. By this time I was as passionately concerned for the success of our campaign as Jones was. I scarcely thought of Kathy, and, if I did, it was as of a creature belonging to another world; not a duller world, but a world with which I was not at present in tune. I continued to see her, at school and about the town, and to exchange greetings; but I happened always, when I met her, to be in a tearing hurry; so that, just as in the days before I met her she seemed always to be running desperately off to keep some life-and-death appointment, so I, during this period, must have seemed to her to be passionately engaged in some urgent affair of state that left me no time to indulge the affections of my private life.

The object of our campaign was at last attained, as so often happens, purely by chance, on a Saturday afternoon. Ironically enough, we had spent the first part of the afternoon lurking around the neighbourhood of Isabel's house in Church Walks, up on the lower slopes of the Great Orme.

Again, it was Gregory who had gratuitously presented us with Isabel's address, but Jones had found out Moira's by the simple expedient of ringing up all the Evanses in Llandudno one after the other and asking 'Is Moira in, please?' It cost him 3s. 8d. in tuppences before he got the answer he wanted, and then it turned out that Moira's house was next door to Isabel's, a discovery that brought forth from Jones a stream of pseudo-Shakespearean obscenity: Shakespearean speech was his latest fad.

At about half past three that afternoon we gave up our vigil in Church Walks, and strolled up behind the Grand Hotel towards Happy Valley. On fine summer afternoons a concert party performed on the open air stage in the natural amphitheatre there, and one could lounge comfortably on the grass all afternoon, watching the show over and over again, only occasionally having to get up and stroll away for a moment or two when the men came round with the collecting boxes.

Jones, that afternoon, was in a ribald mood, hissing when he should have clapped, cheering the villain instead of the hero, and inventing, between-whiles, grotesque names for every member of the tired, struggling little company. 'Here's Mister Comely Bottomley again,' he said, as a florid, large-bottomed singer with a hoarse bass voice tripped up to the microphone. 'He's going to sing a duet with Lady Incipient Cough. What do you bet it'll be 'Drink to Me Only'?'

As Mr. Comely Bottomley began to rasp deeply through the slow rhythms of 'Drink to Me Only', Jones, who was sitting slightly behind me, took my head between his hands and moved it firmly round, away from the stage, so that I was looking sideways across the amphitheatre towards the scattered audience on the opposite slope.

'Employ your eyes, Smith!' said Jones. 'Observe closely yonder bank, with sage and myrtle cushioned. Observe even closer yon dirty big rock, and the grass below it. Is the area under examination?'

'It is,' I said. 'So what?'

'"So what", he says, little knowing what fate holds in store for him. Smith, I palpitate, I sweat like numerous horses! Smith, in short, I swoon. It is her, I do swear!'

'Her. Who?' I said obtusely. And then, becoming conscious, I realised what he meant 'What! You mean Isabel, the belle of the ball? Where?'

'There! goon of goons, where I told you. Oh, Smith, use your eyes, man! Look, slightly to the right of the old geyser with the newspaper over his face, and below the three disappointed virgins in black. Oh, Smith, tell me not I am mistaken!'

Then I spotted the two girls, lying side by side and face to face not far below three prim old ladies in black, seated on folding stools. The dark-haired girl's back was towards us, but her companion was certainly Moira. I had missed seeing them for so long because I was looking for the dark-blue of gym-slips, and they were now wearing light-coloured cotton frocks, which at this distance looked almost white.

'I've got them now,' I said. 'Yes, that's them. At least, it's Moira.'

'Okay, let's go. Unobtrusive exit, backwards.'

Bit by bit we began to move backwards. We didn't want to get up and walk off, as, among so many sitting figures, two standing ones would be conspicuous. So, still facing the concert party, we moved ourselves backwards on heels and hands until we were hidden from the two girls by the fringe of trees on the edge of the amphitheatre.

'What are we going to do?' I asked, whispering unnecessarily, as we stood up and began to walk round behind the curtain of trees.

'Walk up and pass the time of day,' said Jones confidently. Personally, I felt none of his confidence, and if there had been the faintest hint of an excuse would have postponed – for ever, if necessary – the approaching embarrassment. But I knew that I could now neither leave Jones to his own devices nor persuade him to abandon his intention; so, with a slightly sick feeling in my throat, I followed him with elaborate caution as he slipped round the outer edge of the amphitheatre until we were above the two girls.

'Reconnaissance first!' said Jones. We crawled out on to the grassy hump that concealed the top of the big rock which Jones had first pointed out. Lying on our stomachs and looking over the edge, we could look straight down on to the two unsuspecting girls thirty feet below us. They still lay face to face, not watching the clamorous goings-on on the stage, and were talking animatedly. They were poring over a little book which I took to be a diary, and Isabel kept pointing out things in the book which sent them both off into cataclysms of giggling.

'It's them all right!' said Jones grimly, as if he had tracked a gang of smugglers to their lair. 'Now, here's the plan. You go down the left-hand side of the rock, and I'll go down the right. When you get down, sit down on your haunches, and work your way forwards, keeping level with me. That way we'll come up on either side of them at the same moment. But make sure you take it slowly and quietly in the final stretch. Any sudden movement and the game will be up. Okay?'

'Okay,' I said. I wasn't at all happy about the idea of splitting up, but I saw immediately that it was by far the best plan. We moved off at once. The rock, set into the slope so that the ground drew a diagonal line across each side, was easy to descend on my side, and when I reached its lowest extremity I crouched down on my haunches and waited for Jones to appear. As soon as he was level with me, I started to inch my way forward down the slope. I noticed that the three old ladies had packed up and left, leaving the paper shard of a packet of biscuits to mark their resting-place. The man with the newspaper over his face was snoring erratically.

I let Jones get slightly in front of me. The two girls could not, from their positions, have seen back up the slope; but there was just a chance, for me, that a sudden movement might be reflected in the corner of Isabel's eye; and, of course, the same danger for Jones with Moira. But we were not seen. The nearer we approached the greater I allowed Jones's lead to become, until finally he stopped and beckoned me forward, making threatening faces and frowning horribly. He refused to move again until I was level with him.

The last few feet we covered with almost imperceptible movements. But again, at the last moment, I let Jones draw on ahead of me, and this time he was too close to gesture at me safely.

I was still about three feet behind Moira when Jones, sliding into position beside Isabel, said cheerfully 'Well, well, fancy meeting you here!'

Isabel gave a little yelp and rolled over to face him. Moira sat up straight, adjusting her skirt. Very slowly I moved down beside her. They were both looking at Jones, who was grinning unselfconsciously from one to the other.

'Well!' was all that Isabel could say.

'Surely we've met somewhere before?' Jones said politely. 'On Brighton beach, wasn't it!'

'I've never been to Brighton,' said Isabel stiffly, 'and I'm quite sure we have never been introduced!'

Moira started to giggle. Jones leaned forward and looked across Moira's shoulder at me. He said 'Isn't that odd, Smith? We were quite certain we'd met them before, weren't we?'

'Quite certain!' I said. My voice sounded odd to me – a bit husky.

Moira fell back, turning so that she could see me. 'Oh!' she said. 'Oh! Oh, good heavens, you frightened the life out of me!'

'Well!' said Isabel.

'I'm sorry,' I said contritely. 'I didn't mean to frighten you.'

'I should think not!' said Isabel severely. 'Look at the poor girl – she's knocked all of a heap!'

As the ambiguity of this phrase struck them the two girls could maintain their severity no longer. They collapsed in giggles, which became only stronger when Jones, with concern in his voice, said 'Ladies, ladies, control yourselves, we don't want you to be ill, you know!'

'They're all right,' I said, 'they're just knocked all of a heap.'

The hysteria increased.

And so our campaign ended in success. My embarrassment gave way quickly to excitement, as we walked together down the colonnade and I watched, out of the corner of my eye, the soft changing folds of the girls' summer dresses floating and swishing about their knees, saw the way their hair flowed like a medium in the sunlight, and admired, as I slouched along with my own hands deep in my trouser pockets, the prim, practised way in which they folded their hands together under their scarcely formed breasts. Whatever it was we all found to say is of no consequence. The sea air was about us and a mysterious excitement was within us. The pavements we trod might have been littered with gold dust, we'd not have stopped to brush it up. It could not have been more valuable than this mysterious, intoxicating cup of excitement on which we had at last laid our hands.

Five

Several weeks later, on a Saturday afternoon, the four of us – Jones and Isabel, Moira and I – were sitting in a row at the edge of the Pen-y-Bwlch cliffs above Happy Valley, looking out across the town towards the glitter of water in the Conway estuary, and the dark shapes of the mountains beyond. At our feet purple aubrietia, self-sown from the gardens below, grew in bushes between the cracked, weathered blocks of limestone. The air was so still and clear that there was a constant strong temptation to spread one's arms and swoop down like a seagull low over the roofs of the quiet town.

The end of the term was approaching, and with it my fifteenth birthday. We had been discussing, in a desultory way, the composition of my birthday party, which was due to take place in a fortnight's time. We had already counted off the boys: Jones, Gregory, and myself, with the Crow and Red Glyn Jones, formed a good nucleus, and we had decided to invite Kenny Owen, and Dewi Hughes. Kenny had come to notice because he was very friendly with Dora Maguire, Kathy's friend, for whom we both felt a distant, protective warmth. He was a blond, bony, Nordic-looking boy, who rather intimidated me, whenever we talked together, by the dazzling display of obscure technical terms which he seemed to have ever to hand. Dewi was a small, tidy-featured boy who had suffered badly from an attack of infantile paralysis when he was ten, and had only recently become strong enough to attend school again. For this reason he had been put in 3D, along with the other unknown quantities, arriving there a fortnight after Jones: and had made on both of us an immediate impact, with his quiet self-sufficiency and offhand acceptance of his handicaps. After years in bed, he was still learning to walk again; and having missed the grounding we had all shared in the common school subjects, his natural brightness was concealed by lack of knowledge; so that when he confided to me his two ambitions – to become an expert mountaineer, and to win a scholarship to a university – I was unable to take either of them seriously. But for all his handicaps no one ever dared condescend to Dewi.

'Seven men,' said Jones, when we had ticked them off on our fingers, 'if you call Gregory a man. Now we've got to think of seven women.'

'Won't we do?' asked Isabel ravenously. 'Seven boys just between the two of us – yum-yum!'

'You pipe down, young woman!' Jones commanded. 'Jones will look after you, and I don't want any trouble or I shall beat you with my best snake-buckle belt!'

'Ho, indeed! And what makes you think you've got any right over me, Mister Jones, I'd like to know?'

'Superior force of arms!' growled Jones, jumping at the girl and pinning her arms out flat against the grass, while she screamed and kicked without conviction. I looked on enviously, wishing that I could achieve such an easy, bantering relationship with Moira, and knowing that it was impossible. Because I could not, poor Moira had a dull time of it when the four of us were out together, for I felt safe in paying attentions to Isabel, and enjoyed teasing Jones in that way, but did not dare make any advances to Moira for fear she should take them seriously. I would walk beside her, of course, when Jones loped off with Isabel to fight for a kiss behind some hedge or in a dark shop doorway; but we had little to say to each other, and too often, as we walked, I thought of Kathy's laughter and the way her hair streamed over her shoulders when she pedalled her bicycle hard into the wind.

'Well, where have we got to?' said Jones, resuming the discussion of my party. 'Two women – '

'If you can call them women...' I said.

'If you can call them women,' Jones agreed, ignoring the rain of little punches that Isabel was delivering on his rounded shoulders. 'And then there's our little friend Dora and her pal....'

'What, Dora Maguire?' asked Isabel quickly. 'I didn't know she was a friend of yours.'

'Ah yes, a very close friend, ain't she, Smith?'

'Very close,' I agreed.

'You might almost say,' said Jones dreamily, holding up one hand with two fingers intertwined, 'that we were as close as that!'

'I see,' said Isabel icily. 'And I suppose Bernard and this 'pal' of Dora's are as close as that too?'

'Oh, closer,' I said, 'much closer.' I wasn't thinking of

Kathy when I said this, although it was she we were talking about. I was playing Jones's game according to his rules, and from this game, and the whole atmosphere surrounding it, Kathy was excluded.

'Well, Moira, dear,' said Isabel, getting to her feet and yawning ostentatiously, 'I don't know why we're sitting here talking to these two. They obviously have a very full programme, I don't think we'd better take up any more of their valuable time. Come on.'

Smoothing their skirts and linking their arms, with their noses in the air and their lips drawn down in a caricature of disdain, the two girls flounced off along the top of the cliff towards the point where a gentle slope fell smoothly down towards the path below.

'Wait 'til they reach the slope,' whispered Jones, as we lay there affecting to ignore their going, 'then we'll get 'em.'

As the girls turned downhill where the end of the little cliff dwindled away, they were unable to resist a last glance back towards us; but Jones and I were carefully not looking in their direction: we remained sprawling languidly in the attitudes in which they had left us. But as soon as the swell of the ground had hidden them from sight we crept swiftly back over the brow of the hill, and raced along, doubled up, to a point immediately above them. Peering over the lip of the hill, we could see them picking their way slowly and carefully down the steep slope, through patches of bracken and little boulders, towards one of the gates leading into the Happy Valley gardens.

'Right – now!' said Jones, giving me a push forward as he leapt to his feet; and the next moment we were bounding down the slope towards the girls, shrieking at the tops of our voices, taking great leaping strides which carried us forward yards at a time, weaving in and out between the boulders and bracken clumps, with the wind of our progress whipping tears from our eyes and the ground rushing up at us with pitfalls and snares, miraculously dodged, at every step.

As soon as they heard our yelling pursuit the girls too started to run, giggling, screaming, and stumbling, holding their skirts down and bumping into each other; but our speed by now was so great that the problem was not how to overtake them but how to slow down sufficiently so as not to overshoot them altogether. I started braking twenty yards behind them, digging my heel in and feeling the shock of each step jarring right up my backbone into my skull; I was still travelling too fast when I overtook Moira, and, thinking to slow myself, I grabbed at her shoulders, so that the two of us went teetering off down the remainder of the slope, clutching wildly at each other, until we fell together in an untidy heap right up against the fence at the bottom of the slope. For several moments we were so winded that neither of us could move, I had fallen half across Moira, with one arm under her head and the other, stretched across her, supporting the weight of my body as I pushed myself away to look down at her. She had fallen with her hair spread out around her head like a symbolic sun. She was breathing heavily, her plump new bosom rising and falling perceptibly against my chest, her mouth slightly open, and her grey eyes gazing at me with a mixture of fear and expectancy. Without thinking I bent down and kissed her lips – quite accurately – and felt them

71

soften and saw her eyes close and I seemed to sink into her, I was drawn down, deeper and deeper, as her lips became softer and softer....

Almost instantly I sprang away from her; the kiss cannot have lasted more than five seconds. Jones was coming towards me, swaggering slightly and still puffing, and behind him I could see Isabel pushing rather petulantly at her hair, patting the creases out of her clothes. Moira lay for a moment as I had left her, looking crumpled and dazed, her skirt twisted up to show a plump thigh pinched by the elastic of the blue school knickers. But almost at once she sat up, straightening her skirt and plumping out her hair with exactly the gestures Isabel had used.

Jones reached us in time to grab her hand and command 'On the feet, one, two, three – up!' in the tones of our gym instructor at school, as he pulled her to her feet.

'Thought you'd escaped from the Terrible Twins, did you, me fine ladies?' he said grandly. 'You'll have to run faster and further than that to get away from Jumping Jones and Striding Smith, y'know!'

'Oh yes, we all know you're just wonderful!' said Isabel tartly. She was obviously a little put out by the rough handling which she, as much as Moira, had just experienced; but at the same time pleased that we had not (as we might, if the whim had taken us) let them go their way alone. Moira was silent, subdued, as we all were, by the sudden violent action of a moment before; but as we walked quietly down through the gardens she suddenly took my arm and squeezed it, and looked up, smiling confidently, into my face. I forced a smile, but I was filled now with an overpowering panic as I thought of that terrifying kiss, and the way I had sunk into it, and the way Moira's half-parted lips had become softer and softer, as if she wanted to take something tangible away from me.

We took our girls to their tram-stop – both of them lived in Penrhyn Bay – at the corner of Gloddaeth Street, and then walked aimlessly back through the town.

'When we chased the girls,' said Jones, after a long silence, 'did you kiss yours, when you caught her?'

'Yes,' I said, wishing that I could deny it.

'On the lips?'

'Yes.'

'So did I.' He pulled his lip down over his teeth, and then sighed hugely and spread his arms wide as he said 'Ah, Smith, Smith, life is a wonderful thing, man, a wonderful thing. Up on yon beetling headland, for one terrible eternity, Time stood still for Jones! Doesn't it make you think about God?'

'No.'

'No, it wouldn't, you god-forsaken pimple, you. Doesn't it make you glow all over, though?'

'No.'

'Oh, Mother of Christ, the man's inhuman! Didn't you even like it?'

'Well,' I said doubtfully, 'I supposed I liked it all right...'

'For pity's sake what's wrong with you, then, man? You sound as if you'd been chewing aloes or something. Are you ill, boy?'

'It was the wrong girl,' I said.

Jones looked at me blankly for a moment, his jaw

dropping into an imbecile gape. Then he started to heave and splutter with laughter, slapping his sides with his arms, coughing and spitting and choking, shouting 'Oh! Oh, I can't bear it! The wrong girl! Oh no! No! I ask him what's wrong and he just says... he just says... it's the wrong – the wrong girl! Oh! Oh, Smith, you'll kill me, you really will!'

Exhausted with laughter, Jones had now reached a lamp-post and draped himself about it, still coughing and spluttering with his waning laughter, an object of smiling interest to passers-by. I stood watching him with my hands deep in my trouser pockets, smiling a little because of his laughter but not involved in it; serious, a little detached, and interested, now, in my own feelings.

'The point is,' I said, 'it was my first kiss.' I would not have said this to anyone but Jones, but I wanted to make the point quite clear, because it seemed important. I knew I could rely on Jones to see this, and he did.

'Your first? Honest to God, your very first?'

'First proper one.'

'Oh dear. Oh, that's bad. It should have been Kathy, you mean?'

'Oh, not that exactly,' I said hurriedly, although it was exactly that. 'It's just that there's no going back on a kiss like that.'

'Oh, I see what you mean.' Jones pulled thoughtfully at his lip for a moment, and then said brightly 'Still, you can make jolly sure that there's no going forward, can't you? You'll just have to cut the girl right out of your life...' He made a sweeping gesture with his arm. 'Cut her right out, like... like a wart off your thumb.'

'Not easy.'

'The path of righteousness, said Jones sententiously, 'is never easy. Means can be devised. For a start, for instance, let us both practise abstinence from the woman-habit for a few weeks. Give the wenches a rest. If we both do it, they may take offence, but no one will get hurt. And think how fascinating it will make Jones appear in the eyes of the fair lady Isabel!'

'You mean you really wouldn't mind?'

'Why should I mind, boy? The finest wine loses its flavour to the drunkard. We will sit back, scarred with the wounds of many battles, and savour old tales of heroism and stirring deeds!'

I think if there were anyone I truly loved at this period of my life it was Jones. I don't mean that there was between us any of that 'romantic love' of which I have since read in books about public schools; I simply mean that there was both comfort and excitement in his company, and I found with him, for the first time, that security of affection and understanding which my parents, poor dears, had been unable to provide.

Jones and I parted in Vaughan Street. As I turned back from my last words with him, I found myself face to face with Pat Hughes. I had not seen her – nor, until that afternoon, thought of her – for several weeks, and the conjunction of this sudden unavoidable meeting with the unreasonable fact that a memory of her had lain just below the surface of my mind ever since I had kissed Moira, made me speak immediately and naturally to her, as if the Gregory-Freda incident had never occurred,

'Hello, Pat!' I said. 'I haven't seen you for ages!'

'No,' she said. 'I've been in hospital. I missed the last few weeks of school.'

'Good lord! I didn't know. I'd have liked to have visited you, if I'd known.'

'That would have been nice,' Pat said simply. We stood looking at each other; I was actually wondering whether it would have looked silly if we had shaken hands, for that had been my first impulse; and then Pat said 'You look very well.'

'It's the wind. We've just been up on the Orme.'

'How lovely! I'm not allowed out much yet. I'm supposed to be convalescent still. Was that other boy with you? Who is he?'

'That's my best friend,' I said, hoping that Pat would grasp the extent to which Gregory had now been repudiated. 'His name is Jones.'

Rather grudgingly, after a pause, I allowed him a Christian name 'Raymond Jones.'

'He looks nice,' said Pat. 'Now I must go. Goodbye, Bernard!' Her wide, kind face crinkled in a smile and, after a tiny pause, she veered off sideways across the street.

'Goodbye.'

I wanted to say that I hoped we'd meet again, soon; and I wanted to invite her to my party. But neither course seemed possible. It was as if some transparent glutinous matter, composed of memories of Gregory and Freda and the things Pat had said on the sand dunes, hung like a curtain between us; a curtain which would stick to us and destroy us in some way if we tried to tear it aside.

Now, instead of walking straight home, as I had intended,

I continued on down Vaughan Street towards the Promenade. Once more Pat had stabbed through, with a simple, clean rapier, a body which I had always found solid and let the light gleam through the hole her blade had left. 'He looks nice,' she had said of Jones. I could not possibly, speaking to Dora Maguire of Moira, for instance, have said simply 'She looks nice.' Immediately I would have felt myself surrounded by emotional commitments, trapped in a maze of implications. And yet I wanted to be able to say such things to somebody – to some girl, I mean. But they were so difficult, these girls, their minds leapt in all directions to seize and distort one's slightest word. The only safety, in their company, was in flippancy – or silence.

It was an afternoon of meetings for me. As I turned to the right along the Promenade I nearly walked into Kathy. I was staring out to sea and I heard her say 'Hello, Bernard,' very quietly from close behind me, and I came back abruptly from my sea voyage and there she was, clean and lovely in her pale yellow summer frock, her bare arms brown and the quiff of hair that fell across her forehead bleached by the sun. She was playing ball with her Scotch terrier, a yappy little dog that had taken an aversion to me on sight and was even now backing away so as to get a good run up for the assault.

'Hello,' I said. 'All set for the party?'

'Oh don't!' Kathy implored. 'I can't find a thing to wear, Daddy's so mean about dresses, he just doesn't understand!'

'You look very nice as you are.'

Kathy coloured deeply, and turned away to throw the dog's tennis ball far down the Promenade. Then she looked up sideways at me and said 'Why did you ask Dora to invite me to your party, Bernard? Why didn't you ask me yourself?'

'I thought I might not see you,' I said untruthfully. 'I see Dora every day and... anyway,' I suddenly blurted, 'it was Jones who did the asking, not me, so there!'

Kathy said nothing for a moment, watching her ridiculous little dog somersaulting over itself as it tried to grab the still-moving ball. Then she said, very quietly 'I wish you'd asked me yourself, that's all.'

'I wish I had, too,' I said awkwardly; and Kathy coloured again and turned towards me, beaming. 'Ask me now!'

'All right. Kathy, would you please very kindly come to my birthday party on the second of August at six o'clock, please?'

'Oh, I'd love to, Bernard!' Kathy cried delightedly, exec-uting a sudden skipping turn in the middle of the Promenade. 'Thank you so much!' Then she started laughing, not at me or at anything we had said, but just because she was suddenly happy and loved laughter. 'Look, Wiggy, fetch it, fetch it! Good boy!' She slung the old tennis ball off down the Promenade again, and the dog went charging off, tripping over its own legs as it tried to come to a stop from high speed.

'I feel such a fool calling out Wiggy, Wiggy, all the time, but he won't answer to any other name.'

'What's his real name?'

'Winston Churchill. Isn't it silly? Daddy says Wiggy is spelt with an aitch, but he's got it without one on his collar. Daddy's like that. He only enjoys jokes that no one else can understand!' We walked on down the Promenade, leaning landwards slightly against the wind which had now sprung out of the west. Kathy's hair was blown out from her neck, baring the ear nearest to me, and her wide yellow skirt flared and swung to one side. Once again as we walked she looked sideways at me and caught me watching her, and laughed again – that laughter that she could find as easily as if pockets of it waited around her in the moving air, ready at a moment's notice to be pulled down and used as she used it now: not against anything, not to cover anything, never for advantage or in despair, but just as a quality to revel in, like the summer sun.

She had thrown the ball down the Promenade again, and this time the silly little dog, yapping away, overran it to such an extent that it rolled almost to a stop behind him while he was still looking for it in front. Finding that the ball had disappeared, he turned and came bounding back to us, wagging his rump, and leaving the ball far away in front of us, still rolling slowly, but now, impelled by the wind, curving round towards the edge of the Promenade.

'Fetch it! Wiggy! Fetch it!' cried Kathy. But Wiggy just jumped up and down, bouncing absurdly upon its stumpy little back legs, and yap-yap-yapping away as if it were utterly demented.

'Oh, you silly!' cried Kathy, starting to run towards the ball. I, too, ran, trying to overtake and pass her, but, to my chagrin, finding that she could run faster than I. Even so, she was too late, for long before she reached it the ball had toppled gently over the edge of the Promenade, bounced down the dozen or so steps to the beach and been grasped by the sucking tongues of the waves.

'Oh bother!' said Kathy, She turned on the dog, stamping her foot at it. 'You're a silly, silly dog, Wiggy. You don't deserve to have a nice ball to play with!'

We stood on the top step, looking down at the water. The ball was no longer to be seen, and I was filled with self-disgust that in this tiny crisis I should have proved so im-potent. What was the use of breaking unbreakable stallions for Kathy in my dreams if in actuality I couldn't rescue a tennis ball from the sea!

'I've got plenty of old tennis balls at home,' I said weakly. 'You can have them all.'

'So have I,' Kathy said. 'It doesn't matter at all....' But even as she spoke, she left my side, leaping down the steps four at a time to snatch the ball, which had been thrown right up nearly as far as the bottom step, from the jaws of another poised wave.

'Well done, Kathy!' I cried, as she ran triumphantly up the steps towards me clutching the ball.

'There you are, you old silly!' she said, throwing the ball towards the flower-beds on the other side of the Promenade. 'And don't be so stupid again! You might not be so lucky another time!'

I might not be so lucky another time as to see Kathy so fresh and untroubled, so full of joy and so undemanding. I might never feel so happy again. I might never meet her on terms that could not be betrayed, or speak to her in a voice which had nothing to hide at all. I might not be so lucky another time. But, walking back to my house behind the gasworks that day, I knew that there was a thing I had to do, a wrong that had to be put right. Somehow or other I had to steel myself to a gesture, a declaration that would be both public and private, that would say both to her and to the watching, ravenous eyes of our friends 'This is my girl; I need no other.' I looked forward to my birthday party with apprehension and joy.

Six

The first guest to arrive for my party was Gregory, I heard him at the door when I was still upstairs in the bathroom, trying, with water and nailbrush, to plaster my hair down flat across my scalp. By the time I came downstairs Gregory was already established in the kitchen as a culinary aide to my mother, who, for unguessable reasons, thought him a 'nice boy'. He followed me through into the living-room – the room at the back of the house which we used daily, the front room being the 'parlour' – carrying a tray of individual fruit salads.

'Hello, Bernie,' he said eagerly. 'Happy birthday! I say, there's a smashing spread in there. Have you seen?'

'Yes,' I said. 'I've seen.'

'Cider, too!'

'I know.'

'Makes me hungry just to look at it!'

'Well, you'll have to wait.'

Gregory fussed busily over the sideboard, trying to arrange the fourteen fruit salads in a square.

'It won't go,' he said.

'What won't go?'

'You can't make a square with a number like fourteen.'

'Can't you?'

'Of course not. Now if it was sixteen...' Gregory said longingly.

'What do you want me to do? Run out and invite a couple of strangers in so you could have enough dishes to make a square?'

I snorted and strode out of the room, only to find myself a moment later pacing restlessly up and down the parlour with nothing to do. The truth is that I was as nervous as a bride giving her first dinner party; and on top of this ordinary nervousness was the tension of knowing that this party had for me a special significance. It was essential that it should go well, but it was even more essential that it should turn into a particular sort of party, and this was something less easy to control.

Gregory had followed me into the parlour.

'I hear Beryl Johnson is coming.'

'Yes.'

'That's going to be... interesting!' Gregory rubbed his smooth yellow hands together as if in anticipation of a feast.

'Very interesting,' I agreed drily.

It was in fact all a monstrous mistake, and a considerable element in my present nervousness. Beryl Johnson, a spectacular blonde from 3C, happened to be known to Jones through some parental accident: I think his father and hers were in the same platoon of the Home Guard. Her home was a small cafe in Craig-y-don, and Beryl was sometimes to be found there serving behind the small confectionery counter at the entrance to the shop. Beryl was unlike the other girls we knew in every conceivable way: in her physical development, her use of make-up, her attitude towards boys ('men', she called them), and, I'm afraid, her intelligence: was in fact an archetypal 'dumb blonde'.

After the Crow had introduced us to, and invited to the party for me, two girls from the local Catholic convent, one of them his cousin, we were still faced with a shortage of one girl in the balance of the sexes. I toyed with the idea of inviting Pat Hughes, but was still not able to overcome the legacy of Gregory's behaviour on the sand-dunes and never got beyond mentioning the possibility to Jones. After that several names were suggested and discarded. It was ridiculously difficult. Somehow the terms of our contact with the girls at school precluded, at this time, any extension into the 'outside' world. And so the days drifted by, the party became ever more imminent, and still that essential balance had not been achieved. Until one day Jones came to me and gloomily admitted that, in a flash of what at the time he had mistaken for inspiration, he had invited Beryl Johnson to the party on my behalf. He made no attempt to defend himself. It was a disaster, and he knew it, but it could not now be undone. And whether Gregory guessed at my apprehension or not, I was certainly not going to discuss the matter with him.

I thought little of it at the time, but later realised that my mother must have made superhuman efforts on my behalf for this party, which had been her own suggestion. It was war-time, and at the height of the food shortages; and yet somehow she had mustered all the traditional ingredients of party fare: jellies, trifles, fruit salads, cream cakes, cheese straws, chipolata sausages – all those luxuries most difficult to obtain in those austere early years of the war. Retrospectively I would guess that my mother, recognizing how thin a foundation her own failing marriage was providing for me, estimated that the best she could do at this critical age was to give me an opportunity for showing my new friends, all at once, a cheerful, generous, and solid-seeming domestic background, which, even if they never came to the house again, they would remember as the basis of their thoughts about me. I think now that she was right, and that she was entirely successful in what she set out to do. Most new acquaintances exist for us in a vacuum, their characters only half-real, until we have associated them in our minds with some environment to which they obviously belong. This is even more true of the young, whose characters are still half-formed, than of the mature. That party on my fifteenth birthday served my friends as a reference point in their thinking about me during the next two years; and, because it turned out to be the first formal gathering of a group that was to survive, in varying forms, throughout our remaining school life, it also gave me a social importance to which I would never otherwise have attained. My mother was thirty-six at this time, and already deeply involved with the man she was to marry as soon as my own departure from the house brought her first marriage to a belated end. Perhaps she was still not too old to remember the vital importance, for the fifteen-year-old, of never being caught at a social disadvantage by his contemporaries.

Although I was in many ways dreading the start of the party, by the time the next guest arrived I was so tired of trying to keep up some sort of conversation with Gregory that I was heartily relieved to hear the bell ringing; and even more relieved when, opening the door, I saw Jones's face grinning at me from between a self-conscious Moira and a subdued Isabel.

The two girls were still giggling away in my mother's bed-room, while Jones, Gregory, and I stood stiffly in line before the fire in the parlour, when the doorbell went again, and the Crow arrived, bringing with him the two convent girls, Ann and Nancy. Hearing their voices below (I suppose) Isabel and Moira then made their stately descent, passing the convent girls on the stairs. The descending and ascending pairs exchanged frigid smiles as they passed, inspecting each other warily like strange dogs at street corners. One could almost hear them sniff. And both pairs, as soon as they were out of hearing of the other, put their heads together and had a hasty whispered exchange of observations.

In the sitting-room, as soon as Ann and Nancy re-appeared, both Jones and the Crow started a muted duet.

'Murders?' said Jones suggestively.

'Murders!' agreed the Crow in his deepest voice.

'Oh golly!' said Isabel. 'He's started already!'

'We – want – Murders!' both the Crow and Jones intoned. 'We – want – Murders!'

'Well, you can't have them,' said Mother, coming in with a wad of obsolete income-tax forms in her hand. 'Not until after supper. I've got a nice quiet game to keep you all busy until everyone's arrived. Now, listen.'

'Murders!' breathed Jones regretfully. 'Be quiet and listen, you!' said Isabel.

Mother's 'nice quiet game' was the one where everyone is given a Famous Name and you all have to find out what these names are by asking questions which can only be answered by Yes or No. It has the advantage of making people move around and talk to each other; but the disadvantage that the lazy or timid or unco-operative simply sit in corners and hope to be, or try to avoid being, approached by bolder questioners. It was apparent at once that Nancy was one of the timid sort; and the Crow one of the unco-operative. Mother, spotting the first, nudged me and nodded in Nancy's direction; so I spent the next ten minutes being unnecessarily obtuse, as a questioner, and deliberately misleading, when being questioned in return. But I was not sorry for this excuse to hide in Nancy's corner; she was not difficult to please, or dangerous, or a source of embarrassment; there was something slightly dog-like about her, and, as with Gregory, I accepted the position of head-patter to a tail-wagger with a certain lazy relief.

The Crow went through to the dining room and started to strum inexpertly on the piano, until chased back to his duty by Mother. He then went round asking 'Are you in Sport...? If you're not, I've never heard of you!' until he found someone – Ann – who said she was. But even then he couldn't guess her identity, and when he at last discovered, by direct question, that she was Amy Johnson, he started an argument, in which everyone joined, as to whether flying was a sport or not. He was very entertaining, but I hated him. By this time I hated them all, even Jones, hated the thought of Kathy, hated Ann and Nancy and Isabel and Moira and Gregory and the Crow. What right had they to invade our privacy like this, stare at our ornaments, loll on our armchairs, laugh and argue and shout as if this were just an ordinary public place? They were all strangers to me, I didn't know them or want to know them, they said nothing that was not absurd and certainly thought nothing that was not cutting and offensive to my pride. I hated them.

Red Glyn Jones, Dewi Hughes, and Beryl Johnson arrived in a group; whether by accident or design I never discovered. They were closely followed by Kenny Owen and Dora Maguire. Kenny, I thought, was not in a particularly good mood, to judge by the brusqueness with which, once inside the door, he abandoned Dora. Poor Dora, coming downstairs with Beryl Johnson, looked rather lost, and was obviously dismayed to find that her friend Kathy had not yet arrived. Dora wore large steel-rimmed glasses, which effectively hid the very real handsomeness of her thin, sallow Jewish face. She knew that neither in looks nor in the immediate impact of personality, could she rival any of the other girls, and, in the middle of my own apprehension, I had time to think that it was cruel of Kenny to abandon her so cavalierly. His reason soon became obvious: it was not bad temper, it was Beryl Johnson; round whom, as we had predicted, Kenny, the Crow, and Red clustered like flies round a jampot.

Jones had obviously remarked the same thing; for he now trapped me in a corner from which I could not escape and, gripping the lapel of my jacket in a conspiratorial way, said 'That jampot's deadly! We'll have to stop it, Smith. Can't leave all the other wenches panting for a man!'

'I can't do anything about it,' I said stiffly. 'You invited the woman, it's your responsibility, not mine.'

'Come, come, Smith! Don't be like that. You don't want to ruin a good party for a ha'porth o' tact, do you?'

'I suppose something could be done,' I said gloomily, 'if the party was worth it. But it all seems pretty dim to me, anyway, I don't see that it's worth bothering.'

'Nonsense!' said Jones vigorously. 'It's a smashing party! Cheer up, man, I expect Kathy'll be here soon.'

With the arrival of this second group of guests, the party which, apart from my own bad temper, had for everyone else started well, began to degenerate. My mother's plans had slightly miscarried, for she had not anticipated such a long interval between the arrivals of the first and the second group; and now, considering that the game she had planned to hold next was not suitable for those who had only just arrived, she started these on the Famous Names game although the first group had long lost interest in it. And so the party entered on one of those dragging pilgrimages through the doldrums which even the most skilful hostess is often unable to prevent. Despite the guessing game, employed to avoid just such a danger, three self-defensive groups came into being. In the bay of the window, her back to the sill, stood Beryl, holding court, with a sense of conscious triumph which dominated the atmosphere of the room, to Red, Kenny, and the Crow; around the fire the five girls, Isabel, Moira, Dora, Ann, and Nancy, huddled together, whispering and giggling and throwing occasional sideways glances spitefully towards the group by the window, or hopefully towards the door, where Jones and I, Gregory and

Dewi, hovered undecidedly. My mother, busy in the kitchen and imagining, I suppose, that we were still occupied with her guessing game, had not appeared for ten minutes.

Jones stood beside me quietly talking to Dewi about some new Glenn Miller records that had just appeared in the music shop on the corner of Vaughan Street. It was obvious that circumstances had proved too strong for him, so that he, like everyone else, was waiting patiently for some outside force to set the room moving again. To me, it seemed as if they were all waiting for Kathy, as if, until she arrived, the party could not properly come into existence. When, very faintly, the door-bell tinkled in the distance, as if whoever had touched the button had lost courage at the last moment and run away, Jones turned to me with a smile which seemed to echo the whole room's relief. 'There's Kathy now,' he said.

A fine mist of rain must have drifted in over the town some time in the last hour; for Kathy, coming into the hall, was covered with a soft fur of moisture, which, throwing back the light of the hall, outlined her in a tracery of pale fire; every strand of her hair was strung with brilliant, minute jewels, and the faint down between temples and ears, normally invisible, carried now a sheath of moisture whose glow seemed part of the radiance of her skin. I stood staring at her, forgetting to answer her greeting, forgetting to help her with her coat; seeing, not a shy fifteen-year-old girl valiantly struggling with social terror, but a visitor, almost, from another world.

'Hello,' said Mother, coming up silently – or possibly noisily, I'd not have heard – behind me. 'Who's this?'

I introduced them, rebelliously conscious of Mother's too-obvious immediate liking for Kathy; I could better have borne frank disapproval. To hear the warmth of her welcome, the solicitous, proprietary tones as she showed Kathy upstairs, waving away her excuses for being late, was like hearing someone else close behind one the door of a desirable room which one had not made up one's mind to enter.

I hovered in the hall. Mother ran lightly down the stairs again, half-sliding, with most of her weight on the banister.

'Time we had a new game,' she said brightly. 'Then it'll be time for supper. We'd better have the drawing game, I think. Come on, you'll probably have to do some explaining.'

'I'm waiting for Kathy,' I said stubbornly. I suppose I hoped Mother would insist on my following her into the sitting room.

But she said 'Oh yes, all right, she won't be long.'

As she left she said over her shoulder 'She's nice, Kathy.'

So then I couldn't wait for Kathy, but instead pushed into the sitting room ahead of Mother, avoiding her raised eyebrows and circling the room until I was as far away from the door as possible, standing next to Moira, who smiled expectantly at me.

Beryl now stood alone by the window; somehow, while I had been out of the room, a breach had been effected in the defences of the two groups of boys and girls, so that now the whole structure of the pattern had changed, Gregory, I noticed, at once, had at last managed to leech on to Nancy, from whose side he scarcely moved through the rest of the evening. On the other side of Moira, Jones and the Crow had imprisoned Isabel, each firmly occupying an arm of the deep armchair in which she was sunk. Kenny leaned non-chalantly against the wall opposite Beryl, with Dora standing forlornly at his side. Red, his habitual look of polite surprise grotesquely over-emphasized, was listening to Ann. The room presented a picture of neatly arranged well-bred sociability, as if, for a moment, everyone had agreed to mimic what they imagined would be the behaviour of adults at a cocktail party.

'Hello, Bernard,' said Moira, as soon as I turned to look at her. 'It's a lovely party!'

'Oh, do you think so?' I said coldly.

'Oh, I do!'

I had scarcely spoken to Moira since our accidental kiss above Happy Valley a fortnight before; Jones and I had carefully avoided the two girls – had indeed made as much a game out of avoiding them as a few weeks previously we had out of our pursuit of them – but to our chagrin they seemed either not to have noticed or to be attaching no significance to our disappearance. Moira looked up at me now with, absurd, touching confidence, perfectly sure that, of all the girls at this party, she was the only one to have any special claim upon me. I could not look into her face without remembering that meeting of lips; and, rather than remember that, I was prepared to avert my eyes from her all evening. But it was not all that easy. She was whispering something to me now, and I had to bend my head almost until our foreheads were touching to hear what she said.

'I didn't know Beryl Johnson was a friend of yours!'

'Oh, a very old friend,' I whispered. 'A childhood sweet-heart, in fact.' And as I spoke I saw, across the room,

Kathy's head appearing round the edge of the door, shyly smiling at the unknown terrors within the room. For a moment she looked straight into my eyes, where I was bent down with my head next to Moira's, and then turned irresolutely towards the hall behind her, and then turned back again to face the room, twisting quickly like a trapped animal. She would have rushed out blindly then, I think, before I had time to reach her, if my mother had not suddenly appeared at her side with a tray of glasses which she thrust, with a smile and a whisper, into Kathy's hands. Behind Mother came Dewi, beaming mildly and walking with elaborate care, bearing two large jugs of cider. He too smiled at Kathy, and nudged her forward with his elbow, and I felt a sudden spasm of jealousy that he should have touched her.

I crossed the room quickly to take the tray from her, and was rewarded with a smile that mixed gratitude with uncertainty. We walked round the room together, Kathy handing out glasses from the tray which I held while Dewi and the Crow followed us with the two cider jugs. It was not a long walk, for the room was small, but one of those fortuitous, difficult-to-break silences had fallen, and I could see Kathy colouring as she felt her actions becoming the centre of the silent room. I too felt myself to be in a dangerously exposed position, but for once my customary self-centredness was diverted by Kathy's obvious agony, and I searched feverishly for some witty and apposite remark with which to break the silence.

None came, of course. But suddenly Jones lurched forward from the arm of Isabel's chair, waving his empty glass erratically in the air. 'Shider!' he belched drunkenly. 'Jonesh wansh sh'more shider!' He wavered grotesquely in front of Dewi, his eyes crossed, steadying one arm with the other as he brought his glass into position below the poised jug. 'Jonesh-hup!' he hiccupped. 'Jonesh ish going play – hic! – play Murrers. Mush have sh'more shider to play Murrers.'

The Crow took him up softly, chanting 'Murders! Murders! We – want – Murders!' – and was soon joined by Kenny and – rather too commandingly – by Gregory. Isabel and Moira, giggling, falsely and loudly protested that no power on earth would induce them to play 'Murders' with such a gang of obvious ruffians, while Ann, Dora, and Nancy grimaced questioningly at one another, obviously unaware of the nature and implications of the game. Kathy, as soon as Jones had released her from her torture, had fled again to the doorway, where the possibility of quick escape from the room gave her some reassurance. She was joined at once by Dewi, who took his stand beside her with a diffident but unmistakable proprietary air.

With increased difficulty, this time, Mother persuaded the chanting boys that there would be no game of 'Murders' until after supper. The 'drawing game' was explained, sides were chosen, and the two teams separated, one gathering in the living-room, the other in the parlour. The captains detailed the order in which we were to take our turns, and with Mother stationed in the hall with her list of subjects, and the doors of both rooms closed, the game commenced.

Jones, our captain, had made a thorough mess of choosing his team. Dewi and Kathy were together in the other room; Kenny was separated from Dora; Moira was with us, Isabel with the others. I mimed fury and despair at him and he pretended to pull handfuls of hair out of his head, well knowing to what minor tragedies he had just played midwife. When I went out to the hall for Mother to whisper the new subject in my ear I had a quick glimpse into the parlour as the door opened and closed, and it was agony to see Kathy's head and Dewi's so close together over the drawings on the table: I heard Kathy's laugh, and by the time I had returned to my own team in the living room found that I had momentarily forgotten the subject I was supposed to draw. As we gathered in a circle round the coffee table, and I bent to do my drawing, I felt Moira pushing in beside me; as soon as there came an excuse for craning forward more closely she rested her plump forearm across my shoulders to support herself.

'Why, Bernard!' she whispered, not two inches from my ear. 'I didn't know you could draw so well!'

As soon as I saw that the game was nearly over I slipped away upstairs and locked myself in the lavatory. The situation was becoming intolerably complicated, and I needed to compose myself for the battle ahead. It was now clearer than it had ever been that some quite unequivocal public gesture on my part was essential. Dewi and Moira must quickly be disabused of their errors. I could see vividly, now, how their assumptions might all too easily become too rooted to discard without pain. I had no conceit of myself so far as Moira was concerned, for I knew that only a series of accidents had led her to look on me as her unchallenged property. With Kathy, it never crossed my mind to question her own desires; it was inconceivable that she should not feel as I felt.

When I came out of the lavatory I found Jones waiting for me on the landing, his black hair slicked back and gleaming with newly applied water. He looked at me owlishly, pulling at his upper lip.

'How's it going, matey?' he asked.

'Oh, beautifully,' I said sourly. 'I'm just brimming over with happiness, didn't you notice?'

'Yeah, I can see. I was wondering,' he added, looking thoughtfully down the stairs, 'if friend Dewi was getting in your way? You know you've only got to say the word, man.'

'How d'you mean, say the word?'

'He could easily be, dot, dot, dot, eliminated,' said Jones ghoulishly. 'But perhaps you know what you're doing, eh?'

'I think I do now,' I said doubtfully. Jones compressed his lips, shaking his head as if in despair.

'Ah, Smeeth, Smeeth,' he keened in a stage-Scots accent. 'Ah ken weel it's an awfu' long way twixt yer hairt an yer heid, an' there's nae a telyphone between, but ye'd mak yer auld friend unco' happy if ye'd nae worry sae much!' With this, a quick grin, and a sharp punch on the shoulder, Jones suddenly took off from my side, leaping like a maniac down the stairs, shouting 'Food! Food! Jones wants food!' I followed more slowly, grinning quite happily to myself.

The supper was a tremendous success. I suddenly realised, as I edged into the living-room, that my party was not only a good party, it was a momentous party. Before it there had been only a few scattered groups and individuals, unrelated to each other, without significance, lost in the social jungle of the school. Now, through my agency (I thought, forgetting that Jones and my mother had taken all the necessary actions) they were one: I knew that none of our lives (except perhaps Beryl's life) would ever be quite the same again.

I edged unobtrusively round the walls of the room until I had reached Kathy's side. Beyond her, Dewi was leaning in one of those awkward poses which I always thought must be so tiring to maintain – legs wide astride, hunched shoulders against the wall – but he and Kathy were not talking together. We exchanged blank, uncommitting smiles as I arrived, but I was no longer affected by his presence. I had decided to ignore his attentions to Kathy, and felt now only a faint twinge of compassion for his approaching disillusionment.

'Oh, Bernard,' said Kathy, as I reached her side, 'it's a wonderful party!' Her face was glowing with enjoyment as she turned it to me, and for an instant I saw the room through her eyes: alive, noisy, throbbing with interest. I saw her brows contract as her gaze swung to rest on Dora, the only person in the room who was not smiling. Kenny and Beryl, facing each other in the darkest corner of the room, had the engrossed air of scientists at the laboratory bench. At least, Kenny did; Beryl's eyes wandering from time to time towards Red Glyn Jones, the only obviously unattached male in the room. It suddenly struck me that Kathy – and indeed all the others – must think me responsible for having invited Beryl, and I longed to be able to explain, but all I could get out was 'I'm afraid poor Dora...'

'Oh, don't!' said Kathy, widening her eyes at me in horror; and at that moment Jones and the Crow started their chant again.

'Murders! Murders! We – want – Murders!' And at once everyone began moving through into the next room. Supper was over and forgotten, the party approaching its ritual peak.

Mother caught me as I followed Kathy out of the room.

'Are you having a nice time, darling?'

'Yes, thank you. It was a marvellous supper.'

'Good boy. Now listen, if you're all going to play that dreadful game, tell them they can't use the living room until it's been cleared, and no rough-housing, do you understand?'

'Oh, of course. Good heavens!'

I turned to leave her, but she touched my arm, saying softly 'Oh, and Bernard, I don't at all care for that Beryl girl. She's a dreadful little minx. Whatever possessed you to invite her?'

'It was a mistake,' I said shortly.

'You're telling me it was a mistake!' said Mother. But she looked relieved and let me go.

In the parlour, Jones, impatient to start, had already organised the first game of 'Murders'. As I entered, one of my father's hats, with three pieces of folded paper in it, was thrust under my nose, and I was told to take one. Isabel and Moira, who had been upstairs, entered behind me and took the other two pieces. My paper was blank.

'Now don't forget,' said Jones at large, 'as soon as you hear a scream, stay exactly where you are until the detective tells you you can move. And whoever gets murdered, give a good loud scream and fall down and stay down. And no false alarms, please!'

'I shall scream if anyone touches me, I'm sure I will!' said Isabel.

'Jones will look after you,' said Jones.

Dewi had drawn the ticket with a 'D' on it: he was detective, and had to wait in the parlour until he heard a scream. As we all jostled out into the dark hall I took note of Kathy's position and movement: she was with the fair-haired convent girl, Ann, and they were already mounting the stairs. I squirmed through the groups behind them and followed silently on their heels. Curtains had been pulled all over the house to shut out the lingering summer daylight, but there was no curtain on the small circular window above the half-landing, where the stairs changed direction, and the roundel of dark stained glass allowed a deep purple and green glow to suffuse the first few steps of the short flight of stairs facing it. The pupils of my eyes, having come straight from a brightly lighted room, were still too tightly contracted to make much of this gloom, but from halfway up the stairs I could see the shadow of two figures standing close together in the corner below the window. As I crept past, unheard and unseen, I recognized Kenny and Beryl and hurried on, feeling like an eaves-dropper who has heard the planning of a crime.

By the newel post of the main landing I stopped, wondering whether to move or stay still. I had lost Kathy and Ann, though I knew they could not be far away. I held my breath, trying to identify the little sounds, the whispers and creaks and giggles, that were now coming from all over the house. At first I could make nothing of it all; then there came, from my bedroom, Isabel's giggle, and a soft remark from the Crow which started the giggle again, louder but quickly suppressed. Then suddenly there was a crash from the box room upstairs, and I knew that my father's golf-clubs had been knocked to the ground. Soon the scream would come. I wished it would come, for the silence which followed the crash of the golf clubs was complete and oppressive. The darkness, too, had a tangible quality, as if one could put out one's hand and grasp a fistful of this lack of light. I wanted suddenly to be not alone, among all these hidden people who were not alone. Now that I had lost Kathy this game was for me wasting precious time; the moment for which I had been bracing myself was not yet upon me. I longed for the scream to come, for the lights to blaze on, for noise and movement.

I became aware of movement behind me. Turning, I saw against that darkly glowing window the unmistakable aureole of Moira's ginger hair. Panic seized me. It was unthinkable that here on this dark landing, I should find myself in proximity to that voluptuous comfort. Silently, keeping to the middle, I moved away down the landing towards the door of the dressing room at the far end. So surely did my memory guide me that I put out my hand and found the handle of the dressing room door without having touched either walls or door to check my position. Slowly, I turned the knob and eased the door open.

Inside the room – lying, presumably, on the bed – someone was sobbing. Dora. Her sobs were quiet, the exhausted sobs of one who has cried long and passionately and is now eased, but sobs on for lack of reason to cease, I began to close the door. It creaked once, and instantly the sobs ceased; then, as if the reflex could not by will alone be stopped, a last single shattering sob heaved itself up from the depths of the girl's body, a sob that trembled away on an expiration of breath like a soul leaving its body, so that it was impossible to imagine how, after a sob like that, she could walk upright again among the sanguine living.

Leaning back, a fierce guard, against the closed door of the dressing room, I imagined to myself the crumpled, pale-faced girl in there, her spectacles wet with tears, her whole compact little body racked with this grief. It seemed incredible that that oafish untidy lout, Kenny, could be the cause; yet it was so, and if he could be the instigation of such pain, were any of us safe from the danger of committing a similar cruelty?

'Hello, Bernard,' said Kathy softly beside me. I jumped so violently that my right arm hit her elbow.

'I'm sorry. Did I startle you?'

'How... Good heavens, Kathy, how did you know I was there?'

'You were humming, Bernard,' said Kathy contritely, as if it were her fault; 'or not humming, exactly, but a sort of hm-hmming, as if you were telling yourself off....'

'Yes?'

'Oh, nothing.' I was wondering if Dora had heard my hm-hmming, and identified me. I would not tell Kathy what I had heard in the room behind us.

We were standing very close together now, our shoulders touching, I could smell her hair. Now was the moment. If I were to turn and kiss her... if the lights were to come on and we were to be discovered there, our bodies so lightly touching, that would be enough. Dewi would see, before it was too late. Moira would see. If I moved my hand a fraction now, it would touch hers. That would be enough. There was no need to frighten her with a kiss.

Swift, surreptitious movement had suddenly infused the air on the landing; whispers, a giggle, a muffled swearword, footsteps feeling their way across the carpet.

'Oh, Bernard!' whispered Kathy, as if she could not bear the tension, the darkness, a moment longer.

When Jones screamed I was already moving blindly away across the landing. I bumped into someone and walked quickly on, stubbing my foot on the base of the newel post, filled suddenly with an unreasoning terror. There was movement everywhere. Then the lights came on, and we froze, an amazed, blinded tableau, hurriedly fixing into position the bright, enquiring smiles that visibility demanded.

I hardly noticed who else was on the landing, what dispositions had been achieved. Across the length of the landing I could see Kathy's bewildered face, and saw with her eyes the inexplicable madness of my sudden flight. I did not myself know what had happened. I understood nothing now, nothing at all.

Dewi, pulling with both hands on the banisters, lumbered up the stairs. 'Stay where you are, everyone,' he cried excitedly. 'Good heavens, it took you long enough, didn't it? I thought you'd all gone to sleep. Where's the body?' His quick-glancing eyes took in our positions. He gave me a friendly smile.

Red emerged, wearing his most vacant look, from the spare room on the landing above. Dewi went into my bedroom and emerged a moment later followed by the grinning 'corpse'. As we all trooped downstairs, the girls giggling among themselves and the boys swapping suggestive banter, I could still feel the tremendous ache inside me where lay the thing I had not done.

Back in the parlour I looked round curiously for Dora. She came in last, composed and smiling brightly. Kathy moved over to her at once and linked arms with her without speaking, and my compassion for her increased as I saw her hidden handsomeness fade beside Kathy's beauty.

Dewi's cross-examination was brief, alert, and sensitive. He wasted no time with the boys, except to check the alibis of those of the girls whom he suspected; he knew, as we all did, that no boy would waste so heaven-sent an opportunity by laying his hands on another boy. Within a few minutes of our gathering in the room he was saying 'Isabel Marion Frith, I charge you with the murder of Raymond Epsley Jones. Do you plead guilty or not guilty?'

'Guilty,' giggled Isabel.

Jones, grinning complacently, said 'I know worse ways of being murdered. Corpses to order, motive no object.'

'Epsley!' said the Crow mincingly. 'Oh, Epsley! More like Epsom! You look as if you could do with a dose of salts!'

'I think it's a very nice name!' said Isabel primly.

'Epsom!' scoffed the Crow. Jones started to strangle him, baring his great teeth like a maniac.

'Oh, do be careful!' cried Moira. 'You'll hurt him!'

'Epsom! gurgled the Crow, as he slid to a crumpled heap on the floor.

My slip of paper was again blank for the next game; and Kathy was detective. I wandered aimlessly through the sibilant darkness of the house, avoiding Moira, looking for company. At one moment I was next to Nancy, feeling the guilt of a poor host face to face with a neglected guest; but soon Gregory eased me aside and I left her thankfully, meaning to mount the short flight of stairs to the upper landing, thinking that I had heard Jones just ahead of me and needing the balm of his unshakable sanity. On the first step, with no warning at all, I walked into someone: a girl. There was a gasp, and for a moment the girl staggered, clutching at my arm.

'Oh!' said Ann's voice. 'Oh, dear, you did frighten me. Is it Bernard?'

'Yes.'

'Are you the murderer, by any chance?'

'No.'

'Well, thank goodness for that! This darkness... I get so nervous!' She didn't sound in the least nervous. 'I don't mind if I'm with someone, but I lost everyone this time. It's horrible being alone!'

She still gripped my arm, as if letting go would upset her balance again. I made a small, involuntary movement away from her, and she gripped tighter. 'Don't go, Bernard, please, I hate it by myself.'

'I wasn't going.'

'Only, you moved away, sort of.'

'Did I?'

She was very small. When she moved her head, strands of her hair brushed my shoulder, clinging to the nap of the new flannel. Through my arm, pressed against her side, I could feel the contours of her body, the firm swelling of her breast. I was within the faint cloud of her perfume – probably her mother's, stolen or borrowed for the occasion. Her left foot, calf, and knee, were touching my right foot, calf, and knee. The excitement of the contact mesmerized me, so that, consciously desperate to escape, I was unable to move.

The house had entered a complete silence. My breathing and Ann's pulsed quietly around us; yet, conscious of others so near, unseen, unheard, we were filled with the tension of the action that somewhere, with silent deliberation, must surely now be approaching its end.

My right knee was trembling.

'I wish they'd get on with it,' I said.

'Yes, it's awful, this waiting,' agreed Ann; but not as if she desired the waiting to end. Her knee pressed more firmly against mine. I closed my eyes, and felt the sweat prickling on the lids. My scalp itched with heat and I longed to scratch it, but my whole body was immobilized by tension and excitement; I lived in my right leg, my right arm, through them knowing, it seemed, the whole scope of Ann's small body. I tried to remember what sort of dress she was wearing, and, so private was our world of darkness, so completely unreal, so unrelated to daily behaviour, habits of mind, without thinking I brought my left hand across to feel the material.

I misjudged her height. My hand touched her right breast, which for a moment my fingers, expecting a shoulder, failed to recognize, so that they lingered there exploring. 'Bernard,' said Ann, expressionlessly.

I snatched my hand away, as if it were burned. My whole body had started trembling uncontrollably; Ann's was rigid. I tried to pull away from her, but the pressure on my arm increased. I moved my right leg away. Ann, turning slightly, moved hers behind it, pressing her knee into the back of my calf her thigh against mine. I took a deep breath, and held it. The trembling ceased. Somewhere in the darkness above us, a girl screamed. Moira. My breath came out in a long uncontrollable shudder. Lights went on all over the house. Kathy came running lightly up the stairs; behind her, leaping in ungainly strides with both hands on the banister, came Dewi, At the head of the stairs, looking guilty, stood Red. 'Where is it?' asked Kathy of him. 'Where is it?'

'Where's what?' asked Red, his bewildered expression replacing the guilty one.

'The body!' said Dewi, for Kathy, 'Oh, that. Up there, I think.'

Kathy walked past us as if we were not there. I realised that Ann was still hugging my arm, our legs were still interwoven. She smiled demurely at me as I detached myself from her.

'I was beginning to get quite frightened,' she said. She didn't say of what.

I moved up two steps so that I could see what was happening on the landing. Jones and the Crow emerged from the spare room, with Moira, struggling, slung between them like a sack. Isabel followed them, giggling.

'Put me down! Put me down!' cried Moira.

'She's dead,' said Isabel, 'but she won't lie down.'

'Corpses don't walk!' said Jones, firmly. They began to carry Moira, screaming mutedly, downstairs.

Beryl and Kenny came out of the bathroom, blinking. Kathy turned her back on them and came down towards me. I was directly in her path. Before she reached me she turned and said softly to Dewi 'I think the Crow did it, don't you?'

'Or Raymond,' said Dewi.

I turned and ran downstairs, passing Ann on the main landing; unable, for the moment, to think who 'Raymond' was.

Jones and the Crow had laid Moira on the settee; she lay back comfortably, smiling with self-satisfaction; this was her apotheosis, the moment for which she had been quietly waiting all evening. Without having had to do anything or say anything, without effort, without embarrassment, for a few moments she had become the precise centre of all attention. The party, for Moira, was a success.

I joined Jones near the fireplace.

'Where do you keep drifting off to?' he asked.

'Oh, I was up there... somewhere.'

'God, man, you should have been with us. Drama. Action. Excitement. The works!'

'I wish I had been!' I said sincerely.

Jones looked intensely into the distance, pulling at his upper lip.

'Watch 'em, man,' he advised quietly. 'Watch 'em! Women! Gorblimey! Deadly!'

I assured him I was watching 'em.

Kathy, diffident but determined, began her questioning. One by one she eliminated them. Dewi had been downstairs – he didn't say where – and was vouched for by Dora. Dora was vouched for by Dewi. Gregory and Nancy also had mutual alibis. Red was uncertain where he had been. 'Somewhere upstairs,' he said,

'But where, upstairs?'

'I don't know. One of the rooms.'

'Which room?'

'I don't know.'

Kathy gave him up. Without asking Ann where she had been, Kathy wanted to know if anyone had passed up or down the upper flight of stairs directly before or directly after 'it' had happened. (Kathy would not say 'murder' or 'body'.) She spoke of 'it' deprecatingly, as if it were something one would rather not think about, but about which it was her duty to discover the details. She prefaced all her questions with 'Do you mind' or 'Can you tell me' or 'Perhaps you could remember'; diffident, apologetic, yet determined to see her unpleasant task through to a successful conclusion. She didn't question me at all.

'Do you mind telling me, Raymond, what you were doing at the time of the murder?' Isabel giggled.

'Yes, I do mind,' said Jones. 'Strongly!'

'You were in the spare room?'

'Yes.'

'Doing what?'

'I was entangled with...'

Jones paused, waiting for Isabel's fresh burst of giggling to subside.

'With some golf clubs. Golf clubs. All over the floor. Highly dangerous to life and limb.'

'Was anyone with you?'

'I had the impression,' said Jones, looking vaguely round the room, 'that a young lady was in the vicinity, yes.'

'Which young lady?'

'At a wild guess, I should say – Isabel. But of course,' he added hastily, 'all cats are the same in the dark!'

'Why, Raymond Jones!' exclaimed Isabel indignantly. 'I never did!'

'Epsom!' growled the Crow. 'Raymond Epsom Jones, by damn!'

It didn't take long for Kathy to pin the murder on the Crow, though Jones and Isabel were deliberately ambiguous in their evidence, prodigal with red herrings, and the Crow lied wildly and protested his innocence convincingly to the last. Kenny and Beryl, standing side by side and watching the proceedings with a superior air, were ignored by everyone. The hat was passed round again. And again I drew a blank.

'Oh me gawd!' said Jones. 'I'm the rotten detective. All right you lot, vamoose! Aroint! Scram! Out lights, please, and let's have a nice brisk murder this time.'

Jones shepherded us impatiently out of the room, switched off the wall light and, with a last injunction to make it snappy, returned and closed the door.

Kathy was immediately in front of me; alone. Dewi was behind me, whispering to Dora. Silently I followed Kathy up the stairs; hesitated when she hesitated near the circular window, through which only the faintest hint of the dusk could now be seen; and followed again as, lightly and surely, she mounted the remaining stairs, crossed the main landing, and ran swiftly up the seven steps to the top.

I was close behind her, and we were alone. I had followed her without knowing why, purposelessly, because I had to. On the penultimate step of the top flight I stopped, suddenly terrified that she should discover my presence before I knew what I was going to do – if I was going to do anything – before I had an attitude prepared. Breathing shallowly, silently, quite still, I stood there, with one foot poised on the top step, straining my eyes and ears towards Kathy, somewhere there, almost within touching distance, in front of me.

Someone was coming up the stairs behind me. A firm, slow tread, searching and determined. I had to move. Kathy was leaning against the bathroom door. Opposite her was the door of the spare room. I felt for the jamb of the door, which was open, and silently slid round into the room. Inside I tripped over a golf club, and fell heavily against the wall.

Outside, in the enlivened silence, I heard an exclamation, low murmurs, and someone retreating again down the seven stairs. Then the rattle of the door handle, and someone else was in the room. The tension of not knowing who it was became unbearable. I would have to speak.

'Bernard?'

It was Ann's voice. It was not so much an enquiry of my identity as of my position.

'Yes. Mind out, there's golf clubs all over the floor.'

'Where are you?'

Ann's voice was purposeful.

'Here. On the left of the door. How did you know I was here?'

Ann laughed quietly, pleased with herself.

'I'd looked everywhere else. And then I heard you hum-humming to yourself. No one else does that.'

'Was I? Oh damn!'

Kathy would have heard me, too; would have known that I was standing within two feet of her all that time – how long had it been? – before Ann ever arrived. The muttering I had heard had been Ann bumping into Kathy; and the steps downstairs had been Kathy's.

'I'm going to murder you,' said Ann.

'What? Here? He'll know it's you at once.'

'No, he won't,' said Ann confidently. 'You'll see.'

'What... what are you... ?' I stammered nervously. 'I mean, how are you going to murder me?'

I suddenly remembered my hand touching her breast, and was thankful for the kind darkness. I put the hand which had touched her behind my back, and the other up to my throat, which had already contracted with fear at the thought of her cool capable fingers closing firmly around it. All my old fear of the dark came back. I felt cobwebs sticking to my face, small animals climbing my legs. The girl was approaching, her breath was warming my face from below. I pressed back into the wall, flattening my body desperately.

'I'll show you,' she said. 'It's really quite easy.'

Her hands found my shoulders. She was laughing. When she leaned forward I felt her breasts pushing into the soft hollow below my ribs. I closed my eyes; should I scream now, now? One hand crept round behind my neck, tilting my head forwards.

111

'Like this,' she said; and precisely, unhurriedly, she found my lips with hers, pressed herself into me, pressed her face against mine, her mouth parting until I could feel her tongue touching my firmly closed lips. If her weight had not supported me I believe I would have slid to the floor.

Suddenly she pushed herself away from me, laughing breathlessly. 'Now you can scream,' she said. 'Goodbye.'

Leaning weakly against the wall, feeling as if I were about to be violently sick, my mind went literally and completely blank, all images, all thoughts, sensations withdrawn. 'Now you can scream...' The words were still in my ears. I screamed.

I could hear my own scream still in my ears, and wondered who had screamed. I went to the door as the lights came on, and found the Crow and Moira staring curiously at me from the open door of the bathroom opposite. Down on the main landing, Kathy and Ann were leaning against the balcony rail, talking quietly.

Jones came bounding up the stairs, three at a time. 'Now then!' he howled. 'Stay where you are, everyone. One false move and you're a goner. No need to panic, Jones of the Yard is on the trail. You, there, Miss Sheldon, don't move. Now then, where's the body?'

The scream came from up there,' said Ann innocently. I moved back into the room as Jones, in two steps, bounded up towards me.

'Where? Here?' he asked the Crow. He put his head inside the door, winked at me, looked round, and bobbed out again. 'No body in there. You lot trying to fool me, eh?'

As he turned threateningly on the Crow, I jerked back to consciousness.

'Hey!' I called. 'I'm the body.'

Jones stormed back into the room. 'Well, you great goon, lie down and look like one! 'Sblood! Are you trying to make a fool of Detective Inspector Jones? You'll pay for it if you are, corpse or no corpse.'

'He's dead but he won't lie down!' said Isabel's voice from the doorway.

Jones rounded ferociously on her. 'And what do you think you're doing, may I ask? I thought I told you to stay where you were? Get back to your place at once. Suspect number one, that's what you are!'

'Oh, I didn't do it!' said Isabel scornfully. 'I wouldn't murder him!'

Feeling extremely foolish, and still trying to sort out the tangle of emotions aroused by that saboteur's kiss, I lay myself down reluctantly on the floor, my head pillowed on my arms among the scattered golf clubs. Jones looked down at me scornfully.

'Well, you're a rotten corpse, you are,' he said. 'If you ask me, this is the work of a woman... you wouldn't have been standing up and looking stupid if I'd had a hand in it. Come on, then, let's check over these witnesses.'

As he stood aside to let me precede him downstairs, Jones hissed at me 'Wipe your mouth, you clot!'

Surreptitiously, as we all trooped downstairs in a bunch, I screwed my handkerchief into a ball, wet it with spit, and wiped my lips. A faint pink smear on the white cotton rewarded me, and I realised that the unfamiliar waxy taste in my mouth had been lipstick. Ann had used the cosmetic with such discretion that, without this evidence, I would never have noticed she had it on at all. I had thought Beryl was the only girl at the party who was wearing it, but looking round now I realised with astonishment that several of them had tinted their lips, palely but unmistakably.

In the sitting room, his hands tucked importantly into his belt Jones took the floor. Normally, this cross-examination was considered the dullest part of the game, a necessary evil to be kept as perfunctory as possible. But Jones, entering fully into his part, blustering, bullying, snapping off questions almost before he had the answers to the previous Jones, brought the thing up to a pitch of breathless entertainment which it had never approached before, so that even I, troubled and apprehensive, was able to enjoy his virtuoso performance.

Looking round the room, Jones suddenly noticed, as I did, that Kenny and Beryl were not present. His face went dark with real anger, he strode out into the hall.

'Kenny!' he shouted. 'Kenny! Come on out, you slug!'

He waited in the hall until Kenny and Beryl, flushed and dishevelled, emerged from the triangular cupboard under the stairs. Beryl's thick lipstick was smudged grotesquely, for she had left most of it on Kenny's face, but only I, waiting in the doorway, and Jones could see this.

'I'm going upstairs,' she said coolly, and went, leaving Kenny to wipe his face furiously in the hall.

'What do you think this place is – a knocking-shop!' Jones hissed furiously at him. 'If you can't bloody behave, you can bloody go home. Now, get in there, and make yourself small!'

As Kenny slipped shamefacedly into the room, I took time off from my private troubles to admire and wonder at this new, startling, admirable version of Jones; Jones roused, Jones rampant with fury. But before I'd had time to do more than register the impression, Jones convivial was firmly back in place and the cross-examination had begun.

Though obviously suspecting Kathy, Jones went to work first on Isabel.

'Where were you at the time of the murder?'

'In the big bedroom, I – '

'Was anyone with you?'

'Well, I think – '

'Yes or no!'

'No. But – '

'But nothing. Did anyone enter or leave the room when you were there.'

'No, but – '

'I don't want your opinions or qualifications. Yes or no?'

'No!'

Jones was in fact leading himself astray by this bluster, for it later transpired, to his wrath, that Dewi had been in the same room as Isabel all the time, though they had only just discovered each other's presence when I screamed; but the bullying performance, pointless as it was, succeeded in reducing Moira, as well as Isabel, to giggling confusion, so that when he suddenly turned his attack on to Moira she was unprepared.

'What were you doing in the bathroom? Washing your hair?'

'Silly!'

'Contempt of Court! Any more of that and I'll have you in the dock. Watch it, madam, watch it! Who was with you?'

'Jimmy,' said Moira complacently.

'Who?' roared Jones. 'Jimmy! Never 'eard of 'im! Jimmy who, for Pete's sake?'

'Why, Jimmy Raven, of course, silly.'

'Silly! Don't you call me silly, young woman. The Crow, you mean, the Crow! Use the proper nomenclatter, can't you? Jimmy!'

'Epsom!' taunted the Crow softly.

'I'll Epsom you, lad, if you don't watch it. Now then, was Dora in the bathroom all the time?'

'Yes.'

'How do you know?'

'How do you think? I wasn't washing my hair.'

'Cheeky! That's enough of that.'

And now Jones was nearing home. I think he knew all along that either Ann or Kathy would be his final quarry, but the task of eliminating the others had provided an excuse for a fine display of repartee.

He turned gently on Kathy, asking his questions quietly but firmly. 'Now then, Miss Sheldon, you were standing at the stairhead throughout the period in question?'

Kathy nodded. She put her hands together in the small of her back, interlocking the fingers – a familiar gesture of hers when slightly embarrassed; and, as Jones questioned her, I watched her clasped hands being pushed further and further up her back until I thought her elbows must surely crack with the strain.

'Did anyone brush past you shortly before the murder?'

'Yes.' Kathy looked up at Jones ingenuously, smiling.

'Could you say who it was?'

116

'Yes.' Again that sweet, innocent smile.

'Well,' said Jones impatiently. 'Who was it?'

'It was Ber – the murdered man.'

There was a burst of laughter, and Jones smiled round at the room contemptuously, holding up his hand. Then he said, portentously 'But, Miss Sheldon, it was quite dark!'

Kathy, her hands now right up between her shoulder-blades, but still with that wide-eyed smile on her face, said 'Yes, it was dark, wasn't it? But, you see, he was humming, he's been humming all evening. So of course I knew who it was.'

Across the room, Kathy's eyes met mine, and slid away again, unsmiling.

The Crow yelled 'Hurrah for Kathy! Down with rotten old Epsom!'

Jones spun round on him. 'Quiet there! I'll have the lot of you in clink, stap me if I won't! Now then, Miss Sheldon, have you a reliable witness who can vouch for your position at the time of the murder?'

Kathy said 'Well, yes. Ann was with me, of course.'

'Is that true, Miss Skeeping?'

'Why, yes. We were just talking when – '

'Answer yes or no. Miss Sheldon, you were talking to Miss Skeeping when you heard the scream?

'Certainly I was.'

'How long had you been talking?'

Kathy smiled. 'Really, you know,' she said demurely, 'I couldn't say. As you pointed out, it was dark, and I couldn't see my watch. I don't usually time my conversations, you know!'

Jones began to splutter incoherently, raising his fists and face towards the ceiling as if in supplication.

'Back on the beat, you'll be, old Epsom, if you can't solve a simple murder better than this,' said the Crow.

Kathy was looking at me again. I knew now that she had known all along that it had been Ann who had searched me out, that the revelation I had feared as the inevitable end of Jones's questioning would have no further significance for her, beyond the knowledge that Ann had set her cap at me, whether I liked it or not. She must know, I was sure she knew, that the conjunctions she had stumbled upon were none of my choosing. And yet I still felt a sense of guilt, as if I had taken something from her which I must at all costs repay.

Jones, his questions exhausted at last, took a shot in the dark.

'Kathleen Penelope Sheldon, I charge you with the murder of Bernard Evan Smith. Are you guilty or not guilty?'

Kathy and Ann dissolved in helpless laughter.

'It was Ann!' cried the Crow delightedly. 'It was little Ann after all. Well done the fat lady in blush pink! Down with Epsom!'

'Not guilty!' gurgled Kathy. The room filled and glowed with her laughter, and I felt sick with love. The laughter caught, running round the small room like a flame through dry bracken, breaking in waves against Jones's rueful grin and Kenny's sulky hostility, making even Gregory's lugubrious grin burst for a moment into a wet, spluttering sound that faintly resembled laughter.

Mother put her head round the door, smiling pleasantly at our mirth. 'Last game,' she announced. 'It's after ten.'

Somebody found the hat, and, with the laughter still alive, it was passed quickly from hand to hand. It reached me last, and there were two slips of paper in it.

'Beryl!' I said. 'Where's Beryl?'

Mother, hearing my cry, came back to the door. 'She's gone,' she said. 'She came to say goodbye to me, but said she didn't want to interrupt the game.'

Kenny looked relieved.

I took one of the two remaining slips. It had a large M scrawled on it in pencil. 'Look at the other one,' said Jones, it might have something on it.' I looked, but the other paper was blank.

Gregory was detective. I grinned to myself, glad of an opportunity to pit my wits against his. But, as the lights were put out and I busily noted everyone's position and apparent intention, the grin left me, and I went cold with apprehension.

I knew now what I had to do. It had all been made desperately simple for me. The three previous games had laid down a pattern which I could not ignore. Isabel had murdered Jones. The Crow had murdered Moira. Ann had murdered me. The act of murder, here, had become a declaration. It was all quite easy. I had only to murder Kathy, and all mistakes would dissolve away.

It was not difficult to follow her, for Dewi accompanied her up the stairs and his lumbering, clumsy tread was unmistakable. And I would be glad of his presence, it would be a safeguard against... against something.

Kathy, too, seemed to favour the very top of the house. On she went across the landing, up the seven steps, and

119

now, without hesitating, turned confidently in the door of the spare room, picking her way (I supposed, for there was no clatter of golf-clubs) delicately among the bric-a-brac there. After her went Dewi; and after Dewi, myself.

'I wonder,' I heard Dewi say, as I reached the door, 'who's the murderer this time?'

'I wonder,' said Kathy. She really sounded as if she was wondering, and I nearly said 'I am,' both to commit myself, and to relieve their suspense. But I didn't. I would have to wait. As yet, I was sure, they were not aware that I was with them. I should have to make myself known gently, for the thought of frightening Kathy appalled me. But then, I realised, if I didn't make myself known, I might involuntarily eavesdrop upon things I didn't want to hear; things that would make me privy to thoughts that were not my own. It would have to be soon, soon. Feeling my way gently with each toe, I worked my way silently across the room.

My foot touched a golf club, making a tiny, almost unnoticeable, scraping noise.

'Who's that!' whispered Kathy, 'Oh, please! Who's that?' I froze. Not yet, not yet. There must be as little speaking as possible. There was nothing to be said that could not be said in action,

Kathy, I judged, was not little more than four or five feet away from me.

'Is anyone there?' asked Kathy doubtfully. It was just the floorboards creaking, I think,' said Dewi.

Kathy laughed nervously. 'I know it's silly,' she said, 'but I can't help it. This game terrifies me.'

'I don't think it's silly,' said Dewi seriously. 'It's terribly creepy, all this dark. And everyone except me can move so silently.'

'I know,' said Kathy, with compassion for Dewi's misfortune making her voice soft. I clenched my teeth hard in an unseen snarl. Kathy. Kathy. I must murder Kathy without frightening her, before it was too late.

'Hello' I said, as if I had just come in. 'Anyone in here?'

'Bernard!' said Kathy.

'I'm here, too,' said Dewi. It was said softly, but it was a warning. I took a step closer.

'Where are you?'

I knew exactly where they were, both of them. Only two feet separated them. I could, now, have put out a hand and touched either of them.

'Here,' said Kathy.

Now, now.

'Are you the murderer, Bernard?' asked Kathy.

'Yes.'

'Who are you going to murder?'

'Well,' I said.

I suddenly realised that I couldn't do it. The pit was too deep for me, I might never see the surface again. Her voice reminded me of the first time we had properly met, on the Conway Road; and of Kathy saying, with that laughter in her voice 'Anyway, I've seen you hundreds of times when you didn't even know I was there!'

Those were her terms. There could be no pretence with Kathy, no half-commitments. One loved and was loved, in the open, with all barriers down. Or not at all. The symbols and conventions of adolescent society were not enough. I couldn't go down there with Kathy. She was too vulnerable;

I was too vulnerable; someone was too vulnerable; I didn't know. I had to remain on the surface where the cuts and bruises were slight and soon forgotten. With Kathy, I felt, a failure in love would be a kind of murder.

I turned and murdered Dewi. I was violent; so violent that though still managing to laugh, he had to call out to me to stop.

Abruptly, I took my hands from his neck, turned, and loped off down the stairs. By the time he screamed I was leaning, breathing heavily, in the corner of the stairs under the circular window, talking to Nancy. When Gregory lumbered up the stairs he nodded severely at me, in overemphatic warning against trying my luck with Nancy.

Gregory failed to discover who had murdered Dewi. He accused Kathy, of course, and then, in turn, Jones, the Crow, Red and Isabel, until everyone was shrieking with derision, including Dewi himself. When the revelation finally came, there were howls of disgusted laughter, and several puzzled, slightly contemptuous glances at me.

Dewi said enigmatically 'I should have thought it was pretty obvious from the start.'

Then everyone started going home. Kathy came to me and thanked me for the party. 'It was a lovely party, Bernard, it was terribly kind of you to ask me. Goodbye.'

She said goodbye as if she would never see me again. Dewi was taking her home.

Jones, who was to walk with Isabel, Moira, and the Crow, up to Church Walks, said 'Humdinger of a party, man! We all had a smashing time.'

He pulled briefly at his upper lip. 'I hope you enjoyed it,' he said doubtfully. Ann left with Nancy, Gregory, and, surprisingly, Red. I remembered that in the final game it had been revealed that he and Ann had spent the time of darkness in the dressing room together.

Kenny, looking contrite, left with Dora, triumphant. Mother and I saw them all off from the front gate. Jones and Isabel, arm in arm, turned and waved from the end of the road. So did the Crow and Moira, also arm in arm.

'Well' said Mother, drooping slightly, 'that's that. We'll be on short rations for a month, I should think. Golly how those boys can eat! Still, I think it was really a great success, don't you?'

'Oh yes,' I agreed, surveying the chaos of the living-room from the hall, 'I suppose it was, really.'

Seven

Heavy with the weight of the unbroken summer weather, the bay lay still and quiet, as if marooned in the unending haze. Down on the sands, between two seaweed-covered breakwaters, a small boy was playing by himself not far from the edge of the advancing tide. Up towards the town a scattering of wartime holidaymakers had staked their claims at the edge of the shingle, but here, where the bay began to curve away from the coast road towards the rocks of the Little Orme, the beach was clear save for that one small boy, and ourselves.

Drugged by the sun, we lay in a long straggling line at the foot of a steep ridge of shingle. Epsom – Jones had been called 'Epsom' ever since my party – Epsom and I were moodily throwing pebbles at a little tower of larger rocks, surmounted by a flat, anonymous piece of cork which Gregory had found among the tide-wrack and claimed to be part of a naval lifebelt. For some time now neither of us had been able to hit this target, although at first our aim had been so good that we had to keep jumping up to remake it. Epsom was throwing bigger and bigger rocks each time, and had reached the point where, if he chose any larger missile, he would not be able to reach the target with it at all. It seemed to me that our whole lives had been spent thus, lounging by the indolent sea.

Isabel and Moira, sitting between us, were pulling on their dresses over their still slightly damp bathing costumes. They had decided to go home for tea, and Epsom and I didn't attempt to discourage them. We were none of us in a very sociable mood; it was mid-September, and the last day of the holidays.

It was always a relief to me when Moira got into her clothes again, for in the last six weeks she had become excessively plump, and her pink, unstable flesh bulged out of her old bathing costume, reminding me unpleasantly of the way that a partially deflated toy balloon bulges between one's fingers when squeezed tightly in the fist. Clothed, there was something rather magnificent about the swell of her bosom and backside and the solid strength of her calves, but even a state of partial undress had, with Moira, a suggestion of gross nudity about it.

Isabel, on the contrary, had during the same period fined down, lost whatever puppy-fat she had had, and developed – our main point of interest at this time – a bust that must have been the envy of practically every other girl we knew.

Five yards away from us along the beach, Ann and the Crow lay side by side, their heads pillowed on rolled-up towels, staring into each other's eyes. It was only during the last few days that they had discovered their mutual passion for each other, and now, with the end of the holidays upon them, they were about to be torn from each other by the fact of having to attend different schools. There had, that afternoon, been endless discussion about the possibility of persuading Ann's parents to take her from

125

the Convent and send her to the County School, and Epsom had come up with an ingenious plan for getting her expelled, without shame. But we all knew that such speculation was in the end worthless, and Ann and the Crow had settled now to a long, tender, silent farewell.

They would, of course, be meeting two evenings hence, at a session of the Music Club; and there was nothing to stop them meeting on any other evening, if they chose to; but these, it was felt, satisfactory though they might in themselves be, did not compensate for the loss of that almost hour-by-hour contact that was possible at the County School, and which made it possible for so many romances to run their impassioned courses, from start to finish, within a few days.

Beyond Ann, sitting upright on the shingle and staring out to sea in her self-contained way, was Nancy, with Gregory stretched out in a lumpy, ungainly position beside her. Nancy, I am sure, can have found little that was attractive or entertaining in her consort, yet throughout the summer holidays she had borne patiently the slack weight of his presence, even suffering herself at least on one occasion, to which I was an involuntary witness, to be kissed by him. Epsom explained the mystery of their relationship by saying 'Nancy is determined to qualify for a sense of sin even if she has to die of boredom in the attempt!'

This was too deep for me, and I subscribed to Isabel's less cryptic remark 'Well, at least he's male, isn't he? It's better than nothing!'

I was interested, in an abstracted sort of way, in the mysterious activities of the small boy down on the sands.

He was in fact quite a large boy, of about ten, I suppose. But he wore short trousers and a striped cotton T-shirt, which put him very much in the child class, so that I thought of him as 'the small boy'. He had built, with considerable labour, a long dyke, stretching from one breakwater to another, parallel to the advance of the incoming tide. Through this dyke, in three places, he had bored holes at sea-level, a practice which seemed to defeat the aim of the dyke, which was presumably to keep the water at bay on his particular stretch of beach. And now he was engaged in some further feverish digging near one of these holes, to an end which had not yet become clear. A faint desire stirred in me to go on down there and examine the scope and purpose of these defences; but it was so quickly suppressed that it never even reached my consciousness, which was still occupied with our vain attempts to knock over the tower of stones.

I was interested, too, in another part of my mind, in three figures on the other side of Epsom, part of our line but separated from us by a gap of several yards. They were Peredur Williams, one of the Crow's friends, who had become attached to our group within the past few weeks; Dewi, whom I had seen but rarely during the holidays and whose presence among us was usually the result of some action on Epsom's part; and a large, big-boned girl called Gwyneth Thomas, a friend of Peredur's. All three were members of the recently formed 'Music Club'.

The Music Club was, in a way, a direct result of my fifteenth birthday party, for its unacknowledged purpose was to keep together, during the coming term, the group which had so arbitrarily been mustered for the occasion of that party, and which, without conscious volition on anyone's part, had throughout the following six weeks re-formed itself so often that it had by now been consolidated into a compact unit of more-or-less familiar friends.

Dewi, surprisingly, had been one of the active founders of the Club, for although the idea of a club – any club – had been Epsom's, it was Dewi who, with his passion for music, had provided the excuse. Kenny, too, had been in it from the beginning, though when he finally dropped Dora altogether we began to see less of him; and his brief friendship with Dewi, which had been little more than a convenient echo of the friendship between Kathy and Dora, came abruptly to an end.

All who had been at my party, with the exception of Beryl, whose name never even cropped up in our discussions, were by common consent automatically made members of the Club; and to these original thirteen were added, during that summer, Peredur and Gwyneth, a convent friend of Ann's called Helen, and a tall, dreamy boy from 4B, Peter Hatchett, whom Epsom had picked up somewhere.

The leadership of the Club, in so far as any existed, had at first seemed to rest uneasily in my own hands, by virtue of my having been host at the party from which it evolved; but it was Epsom who discovered the attic at the top of the hotel where the Crow and his family lived, and who persuaded Mr. Raven to let us use it as our headquarters. This was really a stroke of genius, and in some way it lent Jones an air of authority which milked off what little leadership I still retained. Since we were only allowed to use the attic in the evenings, when the hotel, now in use by

128

the Inland Revenue as offices, was completely empty but for the Crow's family, our privacy was complete. There were other advantages. Much unwanted furniture and kitchen equipment was stored up there, and we found not only a workable upright piano, but such useful things as electric kettles, gas-rings, saucepans, discarded china, and endless curtains. The curtains we hung from the rafters so as to cut off the eaves of the roof, and in this space all the unwanted junk was piled. The Crow ran a power cable and light flexes up from the floor below, from somewhere a vast array of cushions was assembled (the furniture contained one settee and a three-legged stool, but no other chairs), and we supplemented the incomplete store, of china with cups and plates begged from our mothers.

It was finding a gramophone that caused us most trouble. It isn't conceivable that a Music Club should exist without a gramophone, even if a handful of the members can pick out tunes on a piano; in fact, it was with the express object, on the face of it, of listening to gramophone records, that the Club was founded. At first we were so busy making the attic – known as 'the Room' – habitable, that this particular lack didn't bother us. But soon the time came when there was no more work to do in the Room, and we found ourselves sitting around on the cushions admiring our self-sufficiency and listening to Dewi endlessly beating out 'In the Mood' on the piano, and gradually becoming aware that the Room, with all its admirable properties, still lacked its *raison d'être*.

Pressure was brought to bear, first upon Kenny, and then upon Dewi, both of whom owned gramophones. But, though both were willing to lend their records, neither would part with his machine; an attitude which was, as Epsom pointed out to a group of us one evening, though irritating to us, a very understandable one.

Further efforts were made. A Gramophone Fund was started, but after reaching its peak of twenty-three and ninepence with encouraging speed, stuck there, leaving us completely penniless; and, since man must eat and smoke, and five times this sum would be needed to purchase a decent gramophone, the Fund was gradually whittled away to provide buns and tea and cigarettes, even though the Treasurer, Gregory, resisted our depredations on it fiercely to the last.

The gramophone finally fell into our hands, unexpectedly, from the last imaginable source. We were all sitting round in the Room one evening at the beginning of September when Red, a rare visitor to our cell, entered with a large cardboard box under each arm. Smiling silently, and refusing to answer the barrage of questions fired at him from all sides, Red slowly unpacked his boxes, revealing to our incredulous eyes first a very expensive radio, and then a turntable and pick-up to go with it.

'I've got a dozen or so records, too,' said Red deprecatingly, as if he'd picked them out of the gutter. 'They're downstairs.'

While Gregory and Dewi dashed down the ladder, and down the five flights of stairs to the hotel entrance to collect the records, we tried to find out how Red had managed to bring off this coup. But he would tell us nothing. Over and over again we asked 'But where did you get them, Red?'... and always received the same enigmatic answer 'From a shop.' So in the end we gave up questioning him, and thanked him instead, accepting this gift of the gods as the due reward for our effort and initiative in bringing the Club, and the Room, into existence.

After a few meetings the character of our proceedings up in the Room changed slightly. At first an almost religious attitude invested the 'jam sessions', as they were called. An air of self-conscious idolatry pervaded the room, as if, in listening to our very ordinary and limited repertory of records, we were performing some solemn and uplifting rite. Dewi and Kenny smiled condescendingly at our enthusiasm, and began to bring along selections of their own records – wild, incomprehensible jazz if they were Kenny's; interminable, meaningless concertos, symphonies, and preludes if they were Dewi's. It did not take long to sort us out. Those few who genuinely enjoyed the 'classical' records could be relied upon to listen attentively to jazz, but the reverse did not apply, and for many of us, though we would not have admitted it, music was only tolerable, in the form of popular songs or dance tunes, as the background filling to more exciting pursuits. Thus, without discussion, the 'Music Nights' came to be limited to two each week, and Dewi, Kenny and Peredur, Nancy and Gwyneth, were left to sort out the balance of their programmes as they wished. For the rest of us the Room was simply a valuable meeting ground, a place for gossip and flirtation, a place to construct a world.

For all of us, I suppose, the Club fulfilled some special, in each case different, need. For me it provided a platform on which I could act out, in public, those emotional dramas

131

which I dared not privately pursue. For, while I was as anxious as any to increase my knowledge and 'experiences' of girls, I was unable now to allow myself ever to be alone with one: alone, that is, in any real sense, in any situation which would expose me to the dangers of other than physical contact. What intimacies did occur that summer had been snatched hurriedly in situations contrived deliberately by me to limit the time that I and the girl would be alone; or, if at all prolonged, had been conducted as it were publicly with Isabel and Epsom crammed into the opposite corner of our chosen shop doorway, so that, while the kisses might last an hour, nothing might be said that could not be said to the other two as well.

For I had a horror now of verbal commitment of any kind, a fear of saying anything, or having anything said to me, that might in any way be taken as constituting a private contact between my mind and the mind of whatever girl I was with. And the girls, it seemed to me, the girls were all after just that: contact, commitment, some particle of self-revelation which they could take away and cherish on their very own. In exchange for kisses, they wanted confidences. I took the kisses where I could: from Moira, mostly; for a brief period from Ann; once from Dora, meeting and being scared away by a staggeringly passionate response; and once, in Epsom's absence, from Isabel; but of confidences, I gave none. No doubt I was the cause of some dissatisfaction among the girls that summer; and no doubt, too, this very dissatisfaction was the cause of the unwarranted, and certainly unexpected, success which I found myself having with them.

Epsom was fascinated by this success; and, now that we no longer saw Beryl, he borrowed her nickname to apply to me.

'How the devil do you do it, Jampot?' he would ask, in an exasperated voice. 'What do you do to them, man? To my certain knowledge, Ann's the sixth wench you've dallied with in the past four weeks, and I wouldn't be surprised if you had a few up your sleeve that I don't know about. What's the secret, man? Do you slip 'em a pill?'

Six was a gross exaggeration, but he certainly knew enough about my courting activities to have occasion for surprise. I was surprised myself. I was diffident, fearful of rebuffs, clumsy and silent. But, spurred on at first by the conviction that my own experience and courage lagged far behind that of my fellows, and later by the desire to repeat and improve upon an experience which I had found pleasurable, dangerous, and balm to my self-esteem, I had forced myself to pursue Moira with reserved diligence, and, meeting there with instantaneous success, gone on to experiment even further, and even more dangerously, with Dora, Ann, and Isabel; so that, before I was even aware of any change having taken place within myself, I found myself suddenly appearing in and enjoying the role of successful philanderer.

By the end of the holidays I had gone back to Moira again, an arrangement which suited me well on account both of Epsom's continuing relationship with Isabel and Moira's comfortable, undemanding personality. Even with her, of course, I had to be on the alert for her sly, more and more half-hearted attempts to penetrate my defences, but I felt safer, more relaxed in her company than, for instance,

133

in Ann's. I was, as it were resting. The long summer stretched behind us like a decade of war.

Isabel and Moira were ready to leave. Ann, a few moments
before, had suddenly leapt to her feet, bent to kiss the Crow,
and dashed precipitately off to catch her bus to Colwyn Bay,
leaving the Crow sitting moodily alone, throwing stones
diagonally across the beach towards our still inviolate target.
   Gregory had also left to take Nancy somewhere, possibly
to his own house for tea. And as Isabel and Moira stood
over us to say their goodbyes – goodbyes that, though we
would all see each other at school the following day, had
none the less in them a particle of acknowledgement that
the summer holidays, which had been so rich in discovery,
had ended and were already worthy of nostalgia – Dewi,
Peredur, and Gwyneth also rose, collected their towels and
wet costumes, waved a greeting to us and left.
   After Moira had smiled her last smile at me and crunched
off up the beach, Isabel lingered a moment looking down at
Epsom, who had been a disappointment to her that afternoon. He was withdrawn, monosyllabic; and without being
rude had quite plainly given the impression that he would
be glad when the girls left us alone. Perhaps she was still
hoping that at the last minute he would come out with
some suggestion for that evening, but, though he smiled up
at her warmly enough, the mild enquiry in his expression
must have told Isabel that her lingering was to no purpose,
and at last she turned away, only very slightly downcast,
and followed Moira up on to the Promenade.
   The Crow crawled laboriously, on hands and knees, over
the shingle to settle at my side.

'Well... ' said Epsom. He sighed weightily. Down on the sands the small boy was running frantically backwards and forwards along his dyke, which the first unrolling tentacles of the advancing tide were now nearly touching, the dyke he had built a vast network of channels and connecting pools, all leading, eventually, to one enormous central circular pool about ten yards back from the dyke. At present, only a little surface water had seeped into this drainage system; and it was apparent that he had blocked, with large stones, perhaps, the three equidistant holes which I had earlier noticed him boring through the bottom of the dyke; for when the first lacy foam ran up to touch the outer wall of the dyke, no water, so far as I could see, penetrated to the other side.

'Have you noticed the smoke?' asked Epsom.

The Crow and I followed his eyes to where, beyond the snout of the Little Orme, a thin line of smoke, which might have been taken for cloud had it not been so isolated in the utterly cloudless sky, hung over the horizon.

Although we could not see the distant shore, we knew that below that pall of smoke the port of Liverpool spread out along the Mersey shore – burning.

'I was up on the Orme last night,' said Epsom. 'You could see the fires burning. Sometimes it was just a dull red glow, and then there'd be a sudden sort of explosion of fire, and sometimes a lot of explosions all together....'

'You might have told us you were going up,' I said.

'I didn't know. I just heard them come over and, well... I thought I'd take a look.'

The three of us were silent for several minutes, looking across the sea towards burning Liverpool. The little boy on

135

the beach had opened up one of the holes in his dyke, flooding the left-hand series of pools and channels; but a dam prevented the water from flowing into the central system, to which the big pool was connected.

The Crow said 'They're starting an Air Training Corps at school next term.'

'That's just it,' said Epsom.

'Are we going to join?' I asked.

'Well,' said Epsom, 'that's the point. I think we ought to make up our minds.'

'Well,' said the Crow after a pause, in a tone which suggested that he was puzzled by Epsom's implied suggestion that there might be two courses open to us. 'Well, anyway, I'm going to join. It's obvious. You must join something.'

'Is it? Must I?' said Epsom. He was not trying to be provoking: he was reacting seriously to the Crow's assertion that we obviously had to join either the A.T.C. or some other military training force. 'I don't know,' he said, after another pause. 'I've been thinking... '

When Epsom said 'I've been thinking...' I knew that we were in for a lecture. It was a phrase he used seldom; and only when he meant exactly that; not, as is commonly meant, that he had had a thought, but literally that for some hours, days, even weeks, he had been turning a subject over in his mind, and had now reached a stage of constructive thought that required expression in words. Thus he had prefaced his little lecture to me on the occasion of his *volte-face* over the matter of our attitude to girls, and when he had first propounded his idea for a Club that would keep together the group founded by my party.

136

'Has it occurred to you, Jampot,' he said, turning, not to the Crow, but to me, 'that the state of the war is in a pretty parlous condition?'

'It doesn't look too hot,' I agreed.

'On the contrary,' said Epsom, looking north-eastward with real gloom on his face, 'it's altogether too hot to my way of thinking. Much too hot.'

He took hold of his upper lip and twisted it violently. I had a premonition, then, of what was coming, remembering the brief conversation we had had on this subject on the very day that we met.

'What do you want us to do, then?' said the Crow derisively. 'Assassinate Hitler?'

Epsom, ignoring the Crow, suddenly became animated. 'Damn, man!' he said, knocking together the two large pebbles that were cupped in the palms of his hands. 'Look at the facts! We've been driven helter-skelter from Europe, run for our lives from Greece and Crete, holding on to Malta by the skin of our teeth! London's being pulverized, Coventry, Manchester, Birmingham... all being knocked to bits night after night with nothing but a handful of fighters to protect them! The Jerries can do what they like, now. Old Goering's only got to say 'Wipe out Llandudno' over his tea this evening, and you and I and the rest of us'd find ourselves failing to wake up tomorrow morning! In Africa we've been driven back into Egypt, and they're streaming across Russia as fast as their Panzers can drive. Before we know where we are, Moscow will have fallen and they'll be nipping down into Persia and Syria. The U-boats have got control of the sea from Norway to the Med, there aren't

137

enough aircraft for convoys, and the losses of merchant shipping go up almost daily. Those are the facts, man, not my opinions but the facts! And you,' he concluded, turning to the Crow 'want to join the A.T.C.!'

'Well, damn it all!' said the Crow defensively. 'It's not my fault I was born five years too late! Anyway, it's only another eighteen months, and I'll be able to get into the R.A.F.'

Another eighteen months: that meant the Crow was already sixteen, while I had only just had my fifteenth birthday. I, too, cursed the fact that I had been born 'too late', Epsom's exposition of the war situation was a revelation to me. I had to assume that it was all true, for little of all this had penetrated my enclosed world. Rumours would reach me, of the fall of Libya, of Greece, of the Italian entry into the war, of bombing, of disasters in far places which, though I could possibly find them on the map, had no real existence for me. But all these were isolated incidents; we were at war, and such incidents, I supposed, were bound to occur in war. They neither added to nor subtracted from my picture of the war, for no such picture existed except in relation to myself. I felt vaguely, conventionally, that I would like the war to last long enough for me to participate in it, to have the chance of being a hero, and any incident adversely affecting the allies was secretly welcomed by me as adding to my slender chances. That we would win, I never doubted; my only fear was that we might win too soon.

The picture which Epsom presented to my startled mind was believable only because it had come from him; and was grave only because he thought it grave. Had the Crow expounded the same set of facts, my mind would have refused them entry. But now I began to perceive a new possibility: that we might be beaten; or, if not beaten, for that was inconceivable, at least suffer invasion of our land. And that was something I could really visualize, for, like the bombing, it might affect me, and thus obtain reality.

'Eighteen months!' snorted Epsom. 'Eighteen months! Damn, man, the way things are going it's very unlikely that you'll live another eighteen months! Don't you understand, the Jerries are on our doorstep, the house is surrounded, they've set fire to the roof? And you want to wait eighteen months before you're old enough to get up and put the latch on the window or set a booby-trap over the door! You want to go up to the nursery and play with your toy cap-pistol while the rafters are burning to pieces over your head. Eighteen months, indeed!'

The Crow exploded into a commonly used, graphically obscene Welsh sentence.

'But damn it, man, what the hell do you want me to do?'

Very soberly, Epsom said 'I want you not to waste time playing with your cap-pistol, but to get busy rigging up that booby-trap over the door.'

'Meaning what?'

'Meaning this...' Epsom hunched forward, becoming urgent, practical, and confidential. As he talked, I watched the small boy on the beach opening up the right-hand hole in his dyke, to flood the other wing of his canal-system. The waves were lapping threateningly against the walls of the dyke now, and the small boy ran backwards and forwards along it, strengthening the weak places and paying particular attention to the site of the left-hand hole, which the passage of water had enlarged to such an extent that for a moment it had seemed that the boy had lost control, and that the dyke would be breached.

'You remember,' Epsom said, turning to me, 'telling me about the revolver of your father's, and the ammunition? And me telling you about the shotgun we've got?'

I nodded, remembering vividly the scene in the unfinished pillbox on West Shore.

'Well, I've got more than a shotgun now. I've picked up, second-hand, a deadly little .22 rook rifle that you could kill a man with easily if you were a good shot. I've got half a dozen Civil Defence steel helmets that Red got for me, some knives, blackjacks, and other odds and ends. Also I've been on to Pete Hatchett, who's a bit of a scientist, you know, and he reckons he can produce any number of bottle-bombs if we provide the bottles and can get hold of some 12-bore cartridges to provide the detonators. And there's various other possibilities I've thought up, which we might have a chat about if you're agreeable.'

Epsom looked at me enquiringly, but it was the Crow, still heaving pebbles at the tower of stones below us, who spoke. 'You reckon you're going to stop a German invasion with a .22 rifle and a few dud bombs?'

'I'm not talking about stopping an invasion. If an invasion happens it won't be our job to get in everyone's way, and get ourselves killed. We'd be more use alive. But look at it this way: if Britain's invaded, the Yanks couldn't go on holding their noses for ever, they'd have to come in; and the war would go on not in the field, but internally, you see, directed from America. All the troops and equipment would be evacuated to America, and what couldn't be evacuated would be destroyed. And then what would be left? Old men, young boys, the women, and us. We'd be the army then, the core of the Resistance Movement. It would be to us that the Americans would drop equipment, to help us that they'd land experienced saboteurs and leaders. Don't you see, man, we'd be all that was left here to carry on the fight! And think how much stronger we'd be if we were prepared first, if we'd laid our plans in advance, found our hiding-places, got stores of food and arms and ammunition! What we want is just a small band of men, sworn to secrecy, who would provide the core of a properly prepared Resistance Group. For security reasons we wouldn't want too many, the more who know the details the more chance of them leaking out. The whole strength of the thing would be in its secrecy. Half a dozen to a dozen at most would be quite enough to do the donkey work. And you two,' Epsom ended, with a grin that excused but did not lessen his seriousness, 'having heard my plan, are hereby sworn to secrecy about it even if you don't agree to join me.'

Even if Epsom's argument had failed, as it certainly had not, to convince me, I would have found his plan irresistible simply for the sake of this dramatic secrecy which it involved. But the Crow, I could see, though shaken, was not convinced.

'You'd look pretty silly,' he said, 'if you made all these preparations and then there was no invasion.'

'Oh me gawd!' moaned Epsom impatiently. 'What the hell do I care about looking silly? I'd look a bloody sight sillier if I'd thought the plan out and not put it into practice

141

for fear of looking silly, and then there was an invasion, wouldn't I? It – looks – to – me,' he said slowly, emphatically, as if speaking to a child, 'as if there's every possibility of there being an invasion, and that being so I think it's my duty to make whatever preparations for it that I can. Okay?'

'Okay,' said the Crow reluctantly. 'But look here: I'm still going to join the A.T.C., though I'll come in with you as well and do what I can to help. After all, you may be wrong; the war may go on for ten years for all we know. And I want to get as much of my training over as I can before I'm old enough to join.'

'Whacko!' said Epsom boisterously, full of joyful impatience for action now that he had won his point. 'You can be our contact in the A.T.C... might be very useful. What about you, Jampot?'

'I'm with you,' I said soberly, 'though I'll have to consider the A.T.C. business too. Even in an invasion, you know, they might be useful in stemming the advance.'

'Cannon-fodder,' said Epsom.

I had become more and more restless during these final exchanges. Down on the beach things had been happening fast. The advancing tide was now lapping the top of the dyke of sand; the centre hole had been opened and the water rushed through to fill the interlocking pools; but now I saw that the great pool was not, as I had thought, connected to this centre system; but that all three systems had outlets to this pool, and the outlets were still blocked. The small boy was now so busy building up and repairing the dyke, over which the sea now threatened to pour in several places, that

142

I could not see how he could possibly make the dyke strong enough to hold back the sea for sufficient time for him to go back and enjoy the supreme moment for which all this had been a complicated, subtle preparation: the opening of the inlets to the great pool.

Epsom said 'They might use the A.T.C. as cannon-fodder, I suppose.'

But I could bear it no longer. I leaped to my feet and tore down the shingle and across the sands to join the boy behind his battered dyke. There was a spade stuck into the sand inland of the great pool, and I grabbed this as I dashed past. Coming up behind the boy I called to him 'I'll look after the dyke, you go back and work the pool!'

The boy glanced at me without surprise. 'Och, reet-oh!' he said, in the broadest Scots voice I'd ever heard. 'If ye can hauld her for a wee minute we can mak' her goo!'

I attacked the dyke furiously, shovelling huge spadefuls of crisp wet sand on to the lowest places, whamming it down with the back of the spade, and strengthening the precarious bridges over the three original holes. Behind me I heard an exclamation of glee, quickly followed by another, and again another, as one after another the big rocks were removed from the inlets to the pool and the three streams of water rushed in, with all the force of their pent-up reservoirs behind them.

'Wheee!' sang the small boy, dancing with delight on the sands behind me. Still I was feverishly fighting my losing battle with the little waves, and then the boy called 'Reet-oh, lad, let it all come!' and I ran back to stand beside him, out of range of the water that would at any moment sweep forward towards our feet.

143

It was amazing how quickly it was all over, once the defences were breached. First there was just a slop of water over the dyke, washing some of the sand away; then the next wave swept over more easily, widening the gap, and, almost instantaneously, it seemed, more gaps appeared, all the way along the dyke, until the water poured over in a continuing wave, over the minor walls of the channels and pools, smoothing and softening the contours of the sand everywhere, reaching, finally, to the very lip of the great pool, on whose opposite rim we stood.

The boy, surveying the wreckage of his afternoon's work, which ninety seconds of the sea's insolent power had effaced almost entirely, heaved a contented sigh. 'Wheel,' he said, matter-of-factly, 'that was grand. Thanks for your bit of help!'

I handed him his second spade and turned to leave. Epsom, I found, was standing only a few yards behind us, his hands deep in his pockets and a wide grin on his face. For a moment I felt a twinge of shame for my manhood.

'You were only just in time, Jampot,' he said solemnly.

I turned to look back at the faint traces of our effort, unsure, for that moment, of a proper attitude.

'Well,' I said, 'I stemmed the tide for a bit.'

'You did,' said Epsom, 'you did. And may you die happy.'

Up on the shingle the Crow had at last succeeded in knocking over our tower of stones. But he was, I noticed, now several feet nearer to it than Epsom or I had ever been.

'And what was that peculiar performance in aid of?' he wanted to know.

Eight

Sentiment had no place in Epsom's choice of officers for the Resistance Group. No doubt I at first confidently expected to be appointed second-in-command, but if I did any resentment I may have felt at my failure to achieve this position was soon obscured by my admiration for Epsom's actual choice, Peter Hatchett. Peter belonged to that small, mysterious band of familiars known to us as the 'Dreamy Scientists'. Drifting mildly from library to laboratory, these harmless fanatics had for us an air of impenetrable otherness, as if we had been born and raised on different planets. Peter, the only one ever to seem remotely human to us, joined our group shortly after he had become famous throughout the school for an exploit known as 'Hatchett's Wield', in which a perfectly innocent-looking tumbler of clear liquid, left during the morning break on the piano in the main hall, had, after quietly seething to itself for twenty minutes, suddenly started to give off clouds of dense, acrid-smelling white smoke, which quickly filled the hall and the lower classrooms, and caused the Biology mistress to turn on a foam fire extinguisher which she was then unable to turn off. To be author of such a wield, for some, would have been fame enough. But Peter, whose long, unsmiling face seemed only to grow sadder as reports of his success came flooding in, had ambitions in the field of ballistics which might well have brought him further fame had Epsom not diverted them along more secretive paths. As it was, the armoury of the Resistance Group was constantly being enriched by new Hatchett inventions: landmines, sticky bombs, incendiary bottles, tar bombs, shrapnel bombs... largely at the expense of the Caernarvonshire Education Committee our plan for the coming conflict was gradually equipped with teeth and claws.

The Group had a strength of nine to begin with, though Kenny was soon discarded as being unfit for the great responsibilities ahead. 'You must regard yourselves,' Epsom once told us, 'as potential officers. This is not a unit, it is only the cadre of a unit. You are the men who will lead the troops we shall enroll when the time comes.'

'If the time comes,' amended the Crow.

This was on one of the rare occasions when the whole Group was gathered together in the same place. Epsom preferred usually to work in small gangs of three or four; that way he could control and direct us without danger of our getting out of hand. We were lolling on the uneven, sharp-cropped turf on the shoulders of Nant-y-Gamar, looking out over Llandudno into a long November sunset. We had just completed a 'carry' of food, arms, and equipment from the Room, where we first hid our stores, up to the newly discovered 'bothy' – a deserted, half-ruined, creeper-covered cottage buried deep in the Gloddaeth woods behind us. Gregory, who had joyfully taken over the duties of Quartermaster, was still back in the bothy, checking his lists by the light of a hurricane lamp – for it was always dark in there.

'If the time comes, if you like,' said Epsom, 'but that isn't the point. The way the war's going now anything might happen, I agree, the tide might turn at any moment. You've all got to accept the fact that these efforts of ours may be a complete waste of time. If they are, then I can only say it would ill become us to be sorry.' Epsom tended to become pontifical and literary in his speech when addressing us in his capacity as Commanding Officer; at times his rhetorical excursions achieved a certain lofty splendour. 'When the house is on fire it is folly to cease beating at the flames on the off-chance that someone has rung for the fire brigade.'

'I would have thought,' said the Crow, who, though he could not bring himself to leave the Group, never ceased to question the foundations on which it was built, 'that it is equal folly to train yourself to fight fires when the house is far more likely to be flooded.'

'False analogy, as usual!' cried Epsom.

Gregory appeared behind us, his Establishment Book under his arm, and as we all lumbered off down the hill towards Craig-y-don Epsom and the Crow bickered on happily over their analogies, a game which they were both willing to pursue to the point of absurdity.

'Flour,' said Gregory beside me, worrying to himself about the stores, 'we must get some more flour. Torch batteries, too. We haven't got nearly enough.'

'You'd better talk to Red,' I said.

Stocking the bothy would, of course, have been an

147

expensive business – if we had had any money to spend. As we hadn't, other means than buying had to be devised for providing the Group with the necessary stores of food, clothing, and equipment. Initially a certain amount of this had been found, by secretly ransacking our own homes of discarded paraffin lamps, primus stoves, cooking utensils, cutlery, blankets, and clothing. But it soon became clear that the gap between the essential minimum and the achievable maximum was never going to be closed by legitimate methods. Thus it came about that Red organised a series of elaborate 'Hocking Expeditions'.

'Requisitioning of essential war materials,' Epsom called it; another name might be 'organised petty thievery'. Each expedition was planned well in advance like a military operation. Epsom would enumerate our most pressing needs. Red was nominally in charge of the action, for it was he who would play the greatest part in actually laying hands on the goods required; but Dewi, assigned to him as Intelligence Officer, and Peter Hatchett would between them do the detailed planning that was essential for success.

If possible, the goods would be obtained from a chain store – Woolworth's was our favourite – for much larger hauls could be made from a crowded store than from a half-empty shop. On these occasions diversions – usually a scuffle or loud quarrel in the gangway opposite the one where the hocking was going on – would be planned in detail but not put into effect unless Red and his assistant came under obvious suspicion. My function at such times was that of co-ordinator; from some vantage point I would keep an eye on the hocking pair, and if necessary give the signal for the diversion to take place at the psychological moment. Sometimes, if the object to be hocked was large or in a difficult position, a double diversion would be laid on, with shouting and fighting going on in two different parts of the store at the same time. These were exciting, but dangerous: there was always the risk that too much disturbance would infuriate one of the supervisors into the pursuit of a possible scapegoat.

Raids on private shops were a more delicate business; here the diversion had to take place before the hocking, and continue long enough for the raider to get away with his loot. I was always very nervous about these 'shop hocks'; and apprehensive lest my mother should ask me to call at the same shop before the shopkeeper had had time to forget the faces of the young hooligans who had been rough-housing around his counters a day or two before.

Red, however, seemed to be utterly without nerves. There was never anything furtive about his manner. That bland, vacant expression would be on his face as he stood at the shop counter, slipping unpaid-for articles into the deep pockets of his raincoat. He behaved just as if he were either unconscious of what his hands were doing, or had a right to do it anyway, so that the question of discovery was irrelevant. I shall never forget how he stood one day in the music shop in Vaughan Street, with a pile of records under his arm, talking to the manager about how difficult it was to get one's orders through in wartime, talking, talking, incessantly, almost inanely, until a glazed look of bored impatience gradually took control of the manager's face, and he finally slipped backwards, smiling glassily, into his office, leaving Red to walk out of the door with the unpaid-for records under his arm.

The records, of course, were not for the Resistance Group, for by this time the origin of the hocking expeditions had been forgotten, though I believe they still went on in a less organised form. But Epsom and I – and probably Dewi and Peter – had ceased, by February of 1942, to have anything to do with them. The bothy on Nant-y-Gamar was sufficiently stocked, Epsom declared, for our immediate purposes, though we still had not nearly enough small arms and ammunition. Sabotage, however, had been declared our major function, and for that, thanks to Peter Hatchett, we were, we thought, as well equipped as any *maquis* band.

The records Red had been stealing were for the Room, where, during the dark winter evenings, we had been painfully learning the first steps of ballroom dancing. To begin with only Ann, who had had lessons, and Gwyneth, who had learned the previous winter, were at all proficient. As with most of our activities the dancing classes started casually, and were only later organised into regular twice-weekly events. As soon as they were established, however, their fame spread rapidly through the school and attracted more prospective members than we could possibly have admitted. An attempt was made to set up a committee to deal with all these applications, but it was soon found to be unworkable; there were too many of them, and the committee disagreed too violently, and we had to fall back on the old formless method of admission by unanimous consent.

Several new members were admitted by the committee, however, during its brief life. One of these was Pat Hughes. I avoided her for some time after she joined, feeling guilty towards her because I had, in an unguarded moment, voted against her admission. No one knew this except myself, for the final ballot had been secret; but I felt that I had wronged her, and had been ashamed of, and puzzled by, my action as soon as the votes had been counted and the result announced.

I still felt Pat's attraction, as a person, strongly. Physically, she was going through a stage of excessive plumpness which was not, like Moira's, comfortably voluptuous, but which made her seem always to be wearing too many ill-fitting clothes. Her brown, deep eyes were as reassuring as ever, but there was so little to excite me in her physical appearance that I found myself able to contemplate, for the first time, the idea of being friends with a girl without feeling impelled to flirt with her.

I found more difficulty than I had expected, however, in approaching her. The memory of Gregory's outrageous behaviour on the sand dunes was now so faint and distant that it could no longer, I was sure, come between us: but, while that obstacle had been fading, another had risen up in its place: my own burgeoning reputation as a rake.

It was a reputation of which I was proud; to which I had been at some pains to give substance, and, once it was established, to foster in every conceivable manner. I had in fact, at the time Pat joined the Club, been 'going steady' with Moira for an unthinkably long time – for six months, at least. But I was careful, at Club functions, at the dancing classes, and wherever else I felt I might be under observation, to flirt ostentatiously with those of the other girls with whom I felt it safe to do so, and this, since it served to support what everyone was already prepared to think, kept my philanderer's name alive, at the same time as it kept my relationship with Moira on a pleasantly tenuous footing.

Until Pat crossed my path again, I had revelled in my rakehood. Wrapped in the skin of this alter ego, I could skate lightly, safely, over the thin ice of personal relationships, touching others never so deeply as to affect them to more than a passing love or hate, attracting admiration not with the fallible reality, which must at the last disappoint with its inadequacy, but with the infallible created image, which, since it bore no relation to myself, could be made to do anything, satisfy all requirements, be complete. Gleefully I observed the growth of my notoriety; watched for the knowing glances that would be exchanged if I danced too many times, followed with my eyes too obviously, some temporarily unattached girl. Her reputation, I would think, won't be worth a fig in the morning; for it was commonly believed among those girls to whom I had not yet paid my attentions, and whom, for some obscure reason, those that knew better chose not to disabuse of the idea, that an evening out with Bernard Smith could end only in a fate worse than death.

How much of all this Pat believed, I had no idea. But, whatever her attitude, my own consciousness of my reputation made it impossible to face her without an uncomfortable feeling of ambiguity: a sense of which, perhaps, was at the bottom of my voting against her. For weeks I watched her, at the Club, at the dancing classes, in school, exchanging only the brief familiar smiles of those who know each other well enough not to want to know more. For a time it seemed, so strong was this sense between us of knowing quite enough about each other, that this passing acknowledgement must remain our sole means of contact, that we were debarred, through some quirk of fate, ever from coming together. But so insistent now was my curiosity to know what judgement those brown eyes held, that in the end, one evening at the dancing class towards the end of March, I forced myself to move naturally across the floor and ask her to be my partner in the next dance.

'Why, Bernard,' she said, in a tone which I uncomfortably failed to interpret, 'this is an unexpected pleasure!'

Pat for all her plumpness, danced well, avoiding that infuriating habit, common among the other girls, of fighting for the leadership of the dance. Also uncommon was her patent enjoyment of the dance itself; an enjoyment most obviously manifested in her almost unique dancing position: leaning back against my supporting arm, keeping a space for movement between our bodies, and dancing, not just from the knees downwards, but from the waist. I found it a pleasant change from having to support the slumped weight of a girl's torso against my chest, with hair in my mouth whichever way I might turn my head and never room enough to move my feet more than eighteen inches at a time. Pat's position had only one disadvantage, and, since it was Pat I was dancing with, it was an important one; she could, and for most of the time did, look straight into my face.

For the first two circumambulations of the floor we said

nothing, intent on finding a comfortable physical adjust-ment before attempting the more hazardous mental one. Then, as we approached the gramophone end of the room for the second time, Pat said 'I was beginning to wonder if I'd done something wrong!'

'My dear Pat,' I said, in a patronizing, 'grown-up' voice which I had found remarkably successful in intimidating other girls. 'My dear Pat, what are you talking about?'

Pat looked at me as if I'd been deliberately, cuttingly rude; for a moment I thought she was going to snap angrily at me, and I turned away my eyes, prepared not to hear what she said; but then her fingers, which had stiffened in mine, relaxed. She gave a minute giggle, and said 'Oh, come off it, Bernard!'

We completed the next round of the dancing space without speaking again. I wished fervently that I had followed my instinct and left her alone. It was impossible to converse thus: to cut straight through to a direct expression of a feeling was, to me at that time, a destructive act, destroying as it did all room for manoeuvre, bringing immediately to a recognized head matters which should be approached obliquely, with eyes firmly fastened elsewhere. And yet in the dismay Pat's direct approach caused me there must have been buried a faint challenging thrill; as when, in making love, one's partner calls up, by an unexpected caress, responses which one had long ago disowned as being too shameful for indulgence. I wanted at once that the dance should end and not be repeated, and that the agony should continue, bear fruit of some kind, however humiliating.

And so, like a suitor pressing for the words he least wants to hear, I said 'Well, what did you mean, anyway?'

I suppose my tone told Pat that I genuinely wanted an answer, even if I already knew it, for she smiled quite warmly as she replied 'Oh, you just seemed to be avoiding me, rather, that's all.'

I steered Pat abruptly backwards into the nearest couple, Peredur and Gwyneth, for there was no reply to so obvious a truth. When the abuse and apologies were over, the record had come to an end. A few couples drifted apart, others stood with their hands hanging idly, smiling with very slight embarrassment at their feet, while others, less selfconscious, still clung together, sketching a few experimental steps as they waited for the music to begin again. As I had dropped my arm away from her quickly when the last record ended, Pat made as if to move back to her corner under the eaves, where she had been sitting with Peter and Helen when I asked her to dance. But I found myself, without thinking, reaching out to touch her elbow, inviting her to stay with me for the next dance. She accepted, smiling, but I saw her eyes move for an instant towards the gramophone, behind which, smiling brightly, sat Moira, alone. I hadn't yet danced with her that evening; nor, so far as I knew, had she been approached by anyone else, and I realised that this dance with Pat must for the moment at least be the last. Before it was over I wanted something to have occurred, I wanted – though I was so little conscious of this that I looked upon this dance with Pat as an indifferently enjoyable duty – to be challenged yet more directly and to be unable to escape some fundamental form of committal.

'You'd better dance with Moira next, or you'll be in trouble!' Pat said lightly.

'Yes,' I said.

'Where's your friend Raymond tonight?'

'Epsom? Oh, I dunno. He's not so keen on dancing.'

We were dancing a waltz, which I had only recently mastered, but I found that with Pat, sensitive to my every intention, the steps came with amazing ease. I was beginning to enjoy myself in the repeated rhythmic movements, the successful swishing turns, and had for the moment forgotten my partner's identity in the appreciation of this new-found pleasure.

'Bernard,' Pat then said casually, 'why do you never dance with Kathy?'

'What?' I said, preparing to execute a particularly daring reverse turn. 'Why do I what?'

'Never dance with Kathy? Now you've danced with me, I've seen you dance with every girl in the Club... except Kathy.'

I muffed the reverse turn so completely that we lost the rhythm, and had to stop on the corner, preparing to start again. And then the music ended once more, so that we dropped our arms, and were left looking at each other.

'Thank you,' I said. 'I enjoyed that.'

'Well, why don't you, Bernard? It's becoming rather obvious, you know. Don't you like her?'

'Oh, don't be silly, of course I do! It's just...'

'Just what?'

'Oh, you wouldn't understand!'

We were walking slowly down the room, side by side,

156

back to Pat's corner. If I would, I could not have explained to Pat why I had never danced with Kathy, for not only did I not myself understand, but until that moment the whole matter had been so deeply buried that I had never allowed the question to arise.

'Well, I think you ought,' said Pat, as we reached her cushion in the dark corner. 'The longer you don't the more difficult it will get, and that's silly. It makes it awkward for everyone.'

Pat settled herself neatly on her cushion, turning and turning about like a dog before squatting finally into her skirt; and I stood looking down at her, not seeing her, but seeing instead, for an illuminating moment, my own patterns of behaviour through another's eyes.

'Well, thank you for the dance, Bernard!' said Pat, looking up enquiringly as if to remind me that I still stood, blank-eyed, between herself and the rest of the room.

'Oh yes,' I said absently, 'thank you, Pat.'

I went off to dance with Moira, to bounce comfortably but unrhythmically upon her resilient bulging bosom and listen with half an ear to her scattered, disconnected comments upon the various significant changes in partnership which she had been busy observing throughout the evening. It seemed to me that whatever I did, or did not do, the pressing nonsensical emotions of others formed up insidiously to encircle me with a ring of inescapable traps. No matter how much I tried to avoid them, no matter with what care I abjured any action that could involve the emotions of others, the traps would still set themselves, and, when I was least expecting it, ensnare me in their webs of unplumbable feeling. To fall into the web, no action of mine was required. Not to kiss Kathy, not to dance with Pat, not to dance with Kathy, not to dance with Moira, was positive action. But to dance, to kiss, was also positive action; to exist at all, it seemed indeed, was positive action. Indifference failed as soon as it was achieved, rakehood failed as soon as it was believed in, detachment failed... but did detachment fail? Never having attained to it, I couldn't know. I thought of Epsom, wondering if he had found without seeking the fortress which I had laboured in vain to build.

Nine

One came into the Room, as it were, head first. The door was at the head of a steep flight of steps, and, having opened it outward, one continued on up another nine steps, emerging into the Room as if through a trapdoor. Thus one's head was level, at one moment of entering, with the floor. Girls standing near the stairhead would move away when they heard the door being opened, out of modesty.

No girls were standing near the stairhead on the day I went up to the Room determined to dance with Kathy, and the noise was such that no one heard my entry. I paused with my eyes at floor level, unobserved but observing. Possibly because it was the end of the term, everyone, as far as I could see, had turned up; even Epsom, who had been avoiding the Club lately, having sunk into one of his periodic 'thinking fits'. He was dancing, I saw at once, with Kathy: a performance watched with glee by the non-dancers, for she had not the physical strength to guide him, and his heavy-footed, bulldozing technique cleaved a way for them down the room only at the expense of everyone else on the floor. As I watched, Epsom attempted a reverse turn, twisted his legs spirally together, sat down heavily on his backside, and stayed there, resolutely refusing to move.

Dewi, who had found in dancing the perfect exercise for his rapidly mending legs, moved up instantly to take his place as Kathy's partner.

Dora was dancing rapturously with Peredur. Isabel and Moira were dancing together, shuffling automatically through the simple steps with their eyes darting everywhere in the room, looking for drama. Gregory was presiding over the gramophone, and beside him the Crow, his hair rumpled and his eyes wild, beat out the rhythm of the dance with two table forks on the bottom of an empty biscuit tin. Red, mournful eyed, screeched tunelessly through a tissued comb. The tune was 'The Umbrella Man'. Ann was leaning against the gable wall with her arm around the neck of, I was mildly interested to observe, Kenny; and together, tenor and uncertain soprano, they provided a not unpleasant vocal accompaniment:

> En-ny umber-ellas
> En-ny umber-ellas
> TO-mend
> TO-day!
> Ber-ing, your para-sols
> Di-dum di-dee, di-dum di-da...

The noise was deafening. The electric kettle, unnoticed, was quietly steaming the varnish off a handsome mahogany bedhead under the eaves. Some crockery had been smashed, and the broken pieces pushed roughly into a corner. Peter Hatchett had something grey and disgusting in a corked-up milk bottle, and was going from wallflower to wallflower exhibiting it, to a delighted chorus of horrified shrieks.

I emerged into the Room.

160

'Why, Jampot Smith!' exclaimed Epsom, from his squatting position on the floor at the Crow's feet, 'looking like
stout Cortez!'

'Hello, Epsom,' I said, pleased to be welcomed.

'Silent upon a peak in Darien!' said Epsom.

'What?'

'Get out of the bloody light, Jampot!' said the Crow. 'I
can't be seen with you in the way.'

I squatted on the floor beside Epsom. He was looking
more himself tonight, his eyes grotesquely protuberant, his
huge crooked teeth gleaming brilliantly in the artificial light.
Gone, or at least in abeyance, was that withdrawn, musing
look that had seemed to cut him off from me increasingly
during the past month. Sweat from his recent effort on the
floor still glimmered along the side of his nose and across
his retractable upper lip; and he had sucked, as he always
did when in a comical frame of mind, his under-lip up below
his upper incisors, giving his jaw a rounded, smooth, ape-
like appearance.

'Ber-ing, your fal-de-rals, your fol-de-rols, your musty wig,
I will mend them all, with what you call, a thingumijig!'
he sang hoarsely.

'Ker-rist!' shouted the Crow. 'A toad, Jones, you're a toad!'

'Voice like a suff'ring hangel, I've got!' Epsom asserted,
and continued to sing. Peredur had manoeuvred Dora into
a dark corner, and there they stayed, their arms about each
other, moving their feet slightly when a record was played,
but otherwise just standing, leeched firmly together,
looking into each other's eyes, for the rest of the evening.
Dora had taken off her glasses and applied more than the

normal ration of lipstick. It was good to see her happy for a change, for she was a sad girl.

'Kettle's boiling,' I told Epsom.

'Kells bilin!' Epsom shouted hoarsely at the room in general, just as the record on the gramophone ended. Dancing always stopped for tea, which it was normally Dora's duty to make, but which on this occasion, Dora being so obviously occupied, was made by Nancy. There was a rush for cushions, for there were never enough of them to go round. Epsom and I were joined by Isabel and Moira.

'I didn't think you were coming tonight, Bernard!' said Moira accusingly.

'I didn't say I wasn't, did I?'

'No... but you usually say you are, if you are, don't you?'

'Now then!' Epsom cut in. 'No fighting in front of Jones, if you please! He's in a very nervous condition tonight.'

Isabel, sure that any such condition could only have a sexual root, pressed to know why; and continued to press, long after Epsom had attempted to turn the conversation away from himself. The remark, made lightly enough, and mainly in order to save me embarrassment, had, I could see, sufficient element of truth in it for him not to want it probed.

'Come on over and fetch some tea, Epsom,' I said, straining at his arm in an attempt to lug him to his feet.

As we walked down the room together towards the tea-table, Epsom muttered 'Thanks, Jampot. The Merry Wives... oh, dear me! Oh, fudge, old truepenny!'

'A bit pressing, sometimes,' I agreed.

Epsom muttered again, so low that I could scarcely distinguish the meaningless words 'Give me my scallop shell!' he seemed to say.

A crowd pressed and swayed about the tea-table, behind which Nancy and Gregory were dispensing cups of tea and an assortment of cakes. Epsom and I drifted round the fringe of this crowd until we were hidden by it from the two girls at the other end of the room. Epsom, putting his chin down on his chest and leaning his shoulders against the sloping roof behind, wrinkled up his eyes at me as if that way he could examine me more closely.

'Well, Smith,' he said, 'how goes the war?'

'The war? What – ?'

'The war against women, I mean. Your war.'

Epsom, head bent and eyebrows raised, was looking soberly up at me as if awaiting some significant reply. Not knowing whether I was being mocked at or not, I could find no light answer. I said stiffly 'I wasn't aware that I had one, thanks all the same.'

'Oh, rats!' said Epsom kindly. He gazed blandly round the room. 'Who's the target for tonight? Not much choice, really, I suppose, everyone seems pretty occupied. How about Isabel, for a change? Don't mind me, I'm expendable.'

'Let's get some tea,' I said. I didn't want to enter into such banter tonight, it cut too near the bone.

Epsom, always quick to recognize that he had struck the wrong note, sucked his teeth apologetically as we edged in to collect tea and biscuits for ourselves and the girls. I found myself next to Pat Hughes, who smiled and said 'Hello, Bernard,' with the casual ease of an old friend.

'Who's that girl you spoke to?' asked Epsom, as we carried our cups across to Moira and Isabel.

'New member. I used to go out with her once, before I knew you. Not a bad kid, really.'

163

'Well, well, well!' said Epsom.

From my seat on the floor next to Moira I could see, across the room, what Epsom called my 'target for tonight'. Kathy wore a pale, olive-green jumper, high in the neck and long in the sleeves, and a pleated skirt of light fawn flannel; she had brown walking shoes on her feet, and around her left wrist that frail gold chain. She might have dressed deliberately to achieve anonymity, yet the effect, among the bright frills and flounces of the other girls, was the opposite. I wondered how she and they got on together. I knew that she was loyal to her friendship with Dora, but they could have little in common; with the others, Kathy was neither intimate nor withdrawn; never deliberately excluded from their giggling councils, but never, I would guess, sought out as a desirable conspirator. I had never seen her, as one often saw the other girls, circling the school playing grounds with her arm about another's waist, heads together, giggling wildly at some private joke. Kathy never giggled; she laughed.

Epsom and I went downstairs to the lavatory together. As I waited for him to finish, I spoke to him through the half-open door.

'I'm going to dance with Kathy tonight,' I said.

There was silence from the closet. I turned to the mirror above the washbasins and began to slick back my lank dark hair. I was glad to have committed myself thus, it made the whole proposition seem suddenly easier, less serious in intent.

I heard the closet flushing behind me and Epsom came out, holding out his hand for my comb.

'Not because of Moira?' he asked.

'What about Moira?'

'She seemed to me to be getting a bit serious. Well, not serious, really – settled.'

'Yes, there's that of course. But she's no trouble, really. It's just that... well, Pat said it was becoming obvious.'

'Pat who?'

'Pat Hughes.'

'The one you spoke to?'

'Yes.'

'What did she say?'

Said I never danced with Kathy and it was becoming obvious.'

'So it is. What else did she say?'

'Oh, nothing much. Something about it being awkward for other people...' I covered this with a laugh, for the conversation was making me uneasy.

'So you're going to?' Epsom said, handing me back my comb and staring fixedly at his own image in the glass. 'You've left it a bit late, haven't you?'

'I have, rather.'

Epsom began absentmindedly to wash his hands. He did it very slowly and thoroughly, like a doctor, taking so long about it that I found myself running water in the neighbouring basin and washing mine, too, just to have something to do.

'Well,' Epsom said, after a long silence, 'you're a mystery to me, Smith. But I'll tell you what I think, for what it's worth. You're playing with fire. The girl's dotty about you.'

'Oh no!' I said quickly. 'Oh no, I'm sure you're wrong! It's just that...'

'Just that what?'

'Well, we... I mean, we were a bit friendly once and it didn't come to anything, so it's all a bit awkward, that's all.'

'You were friendly with Ann once, and Dora, and Helen, but they didn't come to anything. Are they awkward too?'

'No, but it's different with Kathy somehow, she's so – '

'Exactly. So dotty about you. That's why I say you're playing with fire, Smith.'

We were both wiping our hands, using opposite ends of the same towel. Epsom looked directly at me, and, forgetting my pride, I appealed to him despairingly.

'Well, for God's sake, man! What should I do? If I don't dance with her, it'll get more and more impossible, and if I do...'

'If you do?'

'I dunno!'

I shook my head hopelessly, glad that he should see the full extent of my dilemma. Epsom folded the towel carefully, hung it over its rail, cocked one buttock over the lip of his washbasin and folded his hands in his lap, as if settling for half an hour's gossip.

'Well, I'll tell you. If you do dance with Kathy, you may fall for her. If you didn't know she was dotty about you you'd dance with her like a flash, probably even flirt quite openly with her. Wouldn't you, Smith?'

'Yes,' I said, looking at the floor and nodding heavily.

'So you do know she's dotty about you, don't you?

'Yes,' I said. I hadn't known it until that moment, although, knowing it now, it seemed incredible that I should not have done.

166

'Well, then,' said Epsom, 'the issue seems to me fairly simple. If you don't feel you're ever like to feel the same about her you must leave her strictly alone. Dance with her tonight, to break the ice, but not again for several weeks. She'll soon get the idea. On the other hand, if you are attracted to her, for God's sake find out now whether it's real or not, and don't leave it until everything's become impossibly complicated!'

'But what about Dewi?'

'Ah yes, Dewi. If Kathy's keen on you, and you're likely to be keen on her, Dewi hasn't got a chance anyway. It's better he should find out sooner than later. The whole thing hinges in fact, Smith, on how you feel about Kathy.'

There was a slight, uninsistent question in Epsom's voice on these last words, and he waited for me to reply. But I couldn't say, I didn't know.

'I don't know,' I said, with real misery. 'I hardly know her!'

'You've never given yourself a chance to know her, man!' Epsom said sharply. 'You shy like a frightened horse whenever she looks at you. Why? Why, Smith? What makes you so terrified of her?'

'I don't know!' I said again.

Epsom unhitched his leg from the hand basin, looked all round the washroom as if to satisfy himself that everything was in place, and said 'Well, dance with her, man, and find out!'

When we arrived back in the Room dancing had begun again, with practically everyone on the floor. Kathy, however, was sitting alone, for we had passed Dewi descending the stairs as we came up. I walked straight over to her and asked her for the dance.

I can't say why I did this. I had entered the Room almost as indecisively as I had left it. Epsom's command, indeed, still rang in my ears, but the compulsion that sent me round the edges of the Room towards her was deeper rooted than that: was connected in some way with the mysterious flush of power that had come to me when I realised – or at last admitted – that I was loved. It was something so far removed from the ordinary traffic of emotion that I use the word 'power' only for want of a better. It was a pulling together of the strings of my personality; it was like being given the thing which one most wants, and only then realizing that one had always wanted it.

Kathy said 'Hello, Bernard,' quite as if we danced habitually together once a week. As we danced she looked downwards over her right shoulder, never altering the poise of her neck and head, even when we turned or changed direction. I believe that we said nothing throughout the dance – what could we have said after all, that would not be banal or embarrassing? – and yet there was the sense of an endless conversation, speech passing not by our lips but through our arms and hands. What might have been a grotesque anticlimax, through our not speaking was not.

When the dance ended, and our arms dropped, became encumbrances once more, then I became aware of the Room again and its occupants. Very little notice was being taken of us, though doubtless tongues would wag in the girls' cloakroom at school, or in secret corners, later. Dora, whose intelligent Jewish eye I might have feared, was still engrossed in Peredur. Moira, catching my eye, smiled sweetly, used to my peregrinations among the other girls and attaching no significance, probably, to my dancing with Kathy. Isabel raised her eyebrows a little sharply perhaps, but this might simply be due to the fact that I hadn't yet, as I usually hurried to do, danced with her that evening. Pat I could not for the moment see.

This was the anticlimax: but one of relief rather than disappointment. It came immediately to seem ridiculous, that I should so long have feared to break the spell, and should have feared, too, the consequences of an act which appeared to have none.

Kathy said 'Thank you, Bernard!' smiling with her head on one side.

Dances were arranged in sets of three of a kind, and the one just ended had been the second of its set. As the music of the third began, and Kathy and I moved together once more, I saw, over my right shoulder, Dewi erupting gracelessly upwards into the Room. Then we turned at a corner, and, as the floor filled with swaying bodies again, I lost sight of him.

I was filled now with the desire to make Kathy talk, to hear her voice.

'Well, Kathy,' I said, banally, perhaps, but with real interest in my voice. 'How's life been treating you?'

Kathy flicked a surprised glance up at my face, and immediately turned her gaze back over her right shoulder.

'Oh, very well, thank you, Bernard,' she said meaninglessly.

'How's Wiggy?'

'Wig…? Oh!' Kathy looked me full in the face, an unhappy little frown setting a single crease absurdly between her eyebrows. 'Oh, don't you know?'

'Know what?' I said apprehensively.

'He's dead, Bernard,' Kathy said quietly. With horror, I saw a threatening brightness film the lower lids of her eyes.

The jogging rhythm of 'The Donkey Serenade' kept our feet moving in jerky zigzags around the perimeter of the floor… one, two, together; one, two, together… and it became important to me to keep our motion as smooth as possible, that no sudden jerk should spill the rim of moisture in Kathy's eyes, tears being not acknowledged tears until they fall.

'Oh dear, I am sorry!' I said. 'How… how… ?'

'He was dr…' Kathy swallowed, and said quickly 'I threw the ball into the sea for him and he swam out for it and got drowned!'

'Poor old Wiggy! Was it rough, then?'

'No. No, it wasn't rough, Bernard.' Kathy looked up at me as if appealing for an explanation. 'He just… he just sank!' she said.

'Well, it wasn't your fault, then, was it?'

'No,' said Kathy, without conviction, 'I suppose it wasn't, really.'

Kathy's eyes, bright with their unshed tears, appeared to ask me to destroy the past, make Wiggy alive, undrowned. 'So I sing, to my mule,' sang the vocalist from the black box at the end of the room. I thought that to keep Kathy talking might be the way to keep her tears at bay.

'Was anyone with you?' I asked.

Kathy whispered a name.

'Who?'

170

'Dewi.'

'Dewi?' Kathy had said the name so softly that even on the repetition I was not sure of having correctly caught it.

'Yes. He... went in. He had all his clothes on, Bernard. But he was dead. He was terribly wet.'

I was not sure whether she referred to the wetness of Dewi or of the dog, and for a moment I had an absurd vision of Dewi drowned, being brought to shore by the glistening, yapping, tail-wagging Scotch terrier. Then I saw Dewi, standing near the entrance, looking fixedly at me; his eyebrows were raised, not so much in surprise as blank horror, and he was working his lips, pursing them forwards and then sucking them back flat against his teeth, as if about to explode into uncontrollable invective. I returned his blank stare with one of cold, narrow hatred, hating him for having been present when Wiggy was drowned, for having plunged into the sea – too late, of course – with all his clothes on, for Kathy.

Kathy said 'We've got another Scottie now,'

'What's his name?

'Anthony Eden. But Daddy calls him Wiggy, too. Only... only he's not a bit like Wiggy, really!'

'I expect,' I said aimlessly, 'you'll get just as fond of him after a while.'

'Oh no!' Kathy exclaimed vehemently, looking straight at me with eyes open wide in astonishment. 'Oh no, Bernard. I couldn't possibly love two dogs, could I?'

'Oh, but surely, Kathy, I mean... !' I couldn't complete what I had intended to say, for the words, if not the sense, appeared too brutal.

'But don't you understand, Bernard!' Kathy pleaded

desperately, squeezing my left hand as if to emphasize her need to be understood. 'I loved Wiggy! Of course, I quite like Anthony Eden, but that isn't the same, is it?'

I didn't answer, being preoccupied for the moment with an injection of unreasoning fear into my own tangled emotions.

'You do see that, don't you, Bernard?' Kathy insisted.

The Donkey Serenade ended on a sustained braying note, and automatically I twisted Kathy round and round so that her pleated skirt flared out between my knees, and her brown hair swung round across her face and back. The forgotten, unshed tears slid then from the corners of her eyes, one out on to the bridge of her nose and one across her temple.

'I'm sorry for poor Anthony Eden,' I said.

Kathy's eyes widened again in surprise. 'Oh, Bernard,' she said, 'you are naughty! You do understand, you're just pretending not to. I told you, I do like Anthony Eden, he's really very nice, but he just isn't Wiggy!'

'That's why I'm sorry for him,' I said, 'After all, he's the one that's alive, surely it's more important to love the living than the dead?'

I felt that, quite accidentally, I had said something profound. I caught Dewi's eye again, scowling and motionless by the entrance, and felt myself obscurely blushing. Kathy, moving back towards her wooden stool at the far end of the Room, had not seen him. She laid a hand, unthinkingly, on my arm, as if in supplication; and, if she was unaware of it, I was uncomfortably convinced that she was the only person present who was.

'Bernard,' she said. 'Bernard, that's a terrible thing to

172

say! If you love... love something, you should love it whatever happens!'

The repetition of this word 'love' was making me uneasy – as indeed was the whole form of the conversation. If I could I would have escaped then; I dared not enter Kathy's world too abruptly, for I had long forgotten, if I had ever known, what paths I could safely walk there. But it would have been gratuitously rude to leave immediately, and so I sat down, tentatively, beside her on the long wooden stool. Down the length of the Room I could see, as in the opposite direction I had before seen Kathy where now I was sitting, Isabel and Moira, their bent heads almost touching, whispering urgently together. Many couples had left, and I saw, without much surprise, that Epsom was dancing with Pat. Dewi was nowhere to be seen.

I watched Epsom. He had locked his upper lip down over his teeth, obscuring them, the stretched flesh narrowing his nostrils and pulling down his lower eyelids, making his face look long, drawn, and immensely serious. He was clumping heavily, without any sense of rhythm at all, through a tango. Pat, following meekly, amusedly, was deftly avoiding the undisciplined gyrations of his feet, while apparently managing to listen intelligently to whatever he was saying. The faint pang of jealousy I felt might have been for either of them; and faded instantly, as, turning, I found, what I had forgotten, Kathy smiling inwardly beside me.

I was about to ask her to dance again when the Crow, one of whose nicer habits was to dance now and then with every girl in the Club, whether he liked them or not, slid suddenly to a stop in front of us and demanded, bowing to me with burlesqued old-worldliness, my permission to ask her for the dance. As he whirled her away, revelling in his own high-stepping, flamboyant style, I left the wooden stool and drifted undecidedly round the edge of the floor to where Moira and Isabel were squatting below the gramophone. Obviously I couldn't sit alone and inactive at one end of the Room while they were pretending not to mind being neglected at the other, but I winced at the idea of having to endure Moira's confident chatter when the only certainty my mind could hold was that her confidence must soon be killed. I would dance with Isabel.

But as she saw me approaching, Moira stood up and came forward to meet me, her arms rising to the dancing position, as she had come forward so often in comfortable good humour to welcome me back from one of those sorties among the other girls which she seemed to understand so well. There was nothing for me to do but grin an acceptable apology at Isabel and allow myself to be enveloped in Moira's amorphous softness. Perhaps she sensed a fall in my face as we interlocked for the dance, for the first thing she said was 'What's wrong, Bernard? Have I done something wrong?'

'Good heavens, no! Why?'

'Oh... nothing, really, I suppose. You look a bit peeved, that's all.'

'Well, I'm not.'

But my voice, as I heard it, sounded peeved; and, anxious as always to avoid giving pain, I added apologetically, untruthfully 'I'm not feeling up to much tonight, though. I expect that's it.'

Moira became immediately, radiantly solicitous.

'Oh, poor Bernard! Are you all right? Oughtn't you to go home? Have you got a headache? You ought to take an aspirin. Now who's got aspirins? Oh, I know, Kathy has; she's always got everything, you ask her for one, I know how horrid a headache can be, I'm sorry if I was nasty, if I'd known – '

'You weren't nasty, Moira!' I broke in, 'and honestly I'm quite all right. I will ask Kathy for an aspirin in a moment, but it's not bad, I was only apologizing for being peevish...'

Moira chattered on; but my eyes were following Kathy in her swooping progress round the room in the arms of the Crow. She laughed as she danced, and I knew that the laughter, though possibly excused by the Crow's never-ending flow of wisecracks, had no origin in humour at all. She knew I was watching her; sometimes would catch my eye, and then, acknowledging this contact with the slightest inclination of her head, she would seem to be sharing her laughter with me. I felt myself sliding, as one slides to sleep, towards a drowsy, uncaring acceptance of the warmth with which the sight of her filled me.

The dance, luckily, was the last of its set. I led Moira back to Isabel, arriving beside her just as Epsom and Pat, continuing the dance after the music had finished, shambled clumsily to a stop on her other side.

'Bernard's got a headache!' Moira announced immed-iately, triumphantly, as if she had been responsible for diagnosing a rare disease. 'I told him to ask Kathy for an aspirin.'

'How fascinating!' gushed Epsom ridiculously. 'You must

tell us all about your ghastly illness when you feel up to it, Jampot!'

'There's nothing funny,' said Moira reprovingly, 'about having a headache! I know!'

'Oh, but I wasn't laughing!' said Jones, as if horrified at the idea. 'I wouldn't laugh at Smith! Why, Smith is the classical example of a tragic figure! True tragedy means that for the hero death is the only possible solution to his dilemmas, and the hero is glad, at the end, to die. You'd adore to be dead, wouldn't you, Smith?'

'Has he ever been alive?' asked Isabel.

'Much more of you lot,' I said, 'and I shall die of boredom anyway. I'm going to get that aspirin!'

Moira said something about going home, as I left them, but I wasn't sure she was addressing me, so pretended that I hadn't heard.

The Crow, with unthinking kindness, was still standing beside Kathy near her stool, unwilling to leave her all alone but having, obviously, nothing to say to her outside the brittle convention of his humour. He grinned as I came up, waved a hand towards Kathy as if to say 'All yours!' and, thanking her pleasantly for the dance, left us once more together.

Even now, as I settled myself on the stool beside her, Kathy showed no surprise. It was as if the months, during which we had scarcely recognized each other's existence, had not been.

'Moira said you might have some aspirins, Kathy,' I said. 'I've got rather a headache.'

'Yes, I think I have,' Kathy said, reaching for her bag. 'Is it a bad headache?

'No. Very slight.'

'I didn't know boys had headaches, too.'

Kathy's handbag was a capacious affair of plain leather, very smart on the outside, but the inside crammed with such an assortment of curious equipment that a glimpse of it was like having peered momentarily through the half-open door of a market town junk shop. Kathy could produce, at any time, almost anything one might ask for; or, if not the article itself, at least an acceptable substitute; biscuits for dogs, lump sugar for horses, bandages, ointments, sal-volatile, ink, carbon paper, string, razor blades, fruit, sweets, scissors, adhesive tape, wire, nails, screws... not only was it difficult to stump her, but, once the bag was open, it was very difficult to prevent her from giving away as many of her stores as she could find willing recipients. On this occasion I asked only for one aspirin; but nothing would satisfy Kathy but that I should take the entire bottle. Shutting her bag with a decisive snap, she said 'Go on, Bernard, you've got them now and I'm not going to take them back. If it's a cold, you might need more of them later on. Anyway, there's several bottles at home. Mummy won't miss one of them.'

Eventually, after unsuccessfully attempting to force the little bottle back into her handbag – Kathy just laughed happily at me, and sat on the bag – I had to admit myself beaten and pocket the whole bottle, feeling an impostor. But the incident had obviously given Kathy great delight. There was something almost coquettish in the way she laughed, with her head down and on one side, looking up at me from the corners of her screwed-up eyes. When I looked at her then, the Room, everything about us, the town, the music, Moira, Epsom, Dewi, Pat... all fell away blankly on every side, leaving us, as it were, isolated together on a private peak of shared pleasure. It was unlike anything I had experienced with the other girls, and strangely had about it an element of intense loneliness. It was as if I had caught an emanation from Kathy's own mental world, and I became aware, in an unknowing way, that this sense of being alone was something that Kathy had with her always.

'Aren't you going to take one?' she asked, still smiling sideways as if to mock me.

'I can't take them without water,' I said. 'I'll have to go downstairs,'

'I must go soon.'

'Wait 'til I come back, Kathy. We'll have another dance before we go.'

Hearing that inadvertent 'we', both of us blushed together. 'Perhaps you ought to...' Kathy said soberly, obviously. 'Yes. But just wait, that's all.'

I had no idea, as I left the Room, what I intended to do when I returned. The vague hope that Moira might have left, Dewi failed to return, had little substance to it. The second part, I felt uneasily, might well subsist already; but in that case, unless by some miracle Moira should of her own volition leave with Isabel, Kathy would be left without an escort to take her home, which by our simple but rigid code of ethics was unthinkable. Yet I would not, I knew, have the effrontery to stand Moira down publicly, though whether regard for my own good name or for her pride, held me from that crude solution, I could not say.

I was glad of the aspirin excuse for escaping momentarily from the Room and its problems; and had an optimistic grain of faith in the ability of such problems, if left to ferment quietly alone, to find their own solutions without assistance from me.

Outside the washroom I met Epsom, coming out. I had not seen him leave the Room.

'Ah, Smith!' he said, with his hand cupped over his mouth, 'I was just coming up to fetch you.'

'What for?'

Epsom didn't answer; didn't even look at me. Instead he turned, opened the door of the washroom, and stood back to let me enter ahead of him.

Dewi was sitting in one of the hand basins, his legs, from the knees down, hanging over the rim, his bottom wedged between the taps, his chin cupped in his hands. He watched me come in without altering his position or expression; his eyes were quite blank, his lips pursed slightly as if in a soundless whistle.

As soon as I was properly in the room, before I had had time to register more than curiosity, he said expressionlessly 'I'll fight you, Smith.'

I heard the door close quietly behind me. I turned, expecting to see Epsom, but there was no one there. When I turned back, Dewi was pushing himself off the edge of the hand basin.

'What are you talking about?' I said. Involuntarily, I followed the words with a silly giggle, which echoed hatefully in my ears.

Dewi walked towards the door. As he passed me, he

looked sideways at me – but not quite at me – and said again in the same flat voice 'I'll fight you.'

Then he opened the door, put his head out, and shouted 'Epsom! Come on back!'

With his back turned to me, he held the door half-open until Epsom appeared, busily combing his hair.

'I didn't think you'd want me,' he said, looking at neither of us.

Dewi closed the door behind him. 'I'm going to fight him,' he said. He walked purposefully across to the hand basin, where, instead of taking off his coat, as I fearfully expected him to do at any moment, he settled back again into his old position between the taps. The brackets of the basin creaked slightly as it took his weight.

I wasn't afraid of Dewi. I knew that he was quick, determined, and full of endurance, for he had made it his business, to an obsessive degree, to gain control of, and to harden, the body which had once so badly betrayed him. But I had often fought with him in the gymnasium at school; playfully, it is true, but with determination to win on both sides; and had found no difficulty, with my longer reach and surer balance, in keeping his fleet, furious attacks at bay. Anyway, I was no physical coward, and had the odds been fairly heavily against me I would not have shrunk from a challenge for that reason.

But I was determined not to fight Dewi now. I knew exactly what he meant, all he implied, when he said 'I'll fight you.' I was not even very surprised to find him here in such a mood, for the sense of his presence and absence had been heavily with me ever since that first dance with

180

Kathy. I knew that, whatever Moira might do, Dewi would not allow me to escape scot free.

I appealed to Epsom. 'What's he raving about?' I said, raising shoulders and eyebrows as if in utter bewilderment.

'Do you really not know?' asked Epsom. I saw that I could expect no help towards evasion from him. 'He knows!' said Dewi.

'I can't see what good a fight's going to do!' I said indignantly, choosing now rather to admit by implication my understanding of Dewi's motives, than to suffer open examination of barely admissible emotions.

'I do!' said Dewi, showing for the first time a spark of animation, 'I'd slaughter you, that's what good it would do!'

'You wouldn't! You couldn't slaughter me, not in a month of Sundays! I'd slaughter you, more bloody likely. But what's the good of it, anyway? It doesn't solve anything!'

'Scared, Smith?' said Dewi tauntingly, hoping perhaps thus to goad me towards violence. Epsom heaved himself off the door of the closet opposite Dewi, puffing out his cheeks like a businessman inspecting dubious goods.

'Come off it, Dewi!' he said. 'Smith ain't scared of you and you know it. He's a tough nut and you'd be a fool to fight him, as far as all that goes. I think a fight's stupid, anyway. Like he says, it won't solve anything.'

'It'll solve his dirty whoring lust!' said Dewi quietly. I thought I must have heard incorrectly; but Epsom said loudly 'Stuff that, Dewi! I don't care which way you two solve this. You can fight if you're determined to, but I'm not going to listen to that sort of muck!'

'I'm not going to fight you, Dewi,' I said.

181

'You'll leave Kathy alone or you'll fight!' said Dewi. 'You can take your choice.'

This was the first mention of Kathy. I had been wondering, determined not to use her name first, if Dewi would endeavour to conduct the whole business without bringing her in at all. But now, seeing his blank, tight expression dissolve, his eyes catch fire, I saw that he didn't care what he said, how much he committed himself. He was prepared to strip his own and my emotions naked if necessary. Hurriedly I began to prepare myself for the ordeal, drawing in the tender tentacles of sensitivity, obscuring my mental vision with a smoke screen of indifference, determined to hear and understand as little as possible of whatever was coming.

'I'm not going to fight you,' I said again, with dull monotony.

'Then you're going to drop Kathy! You're not fit to be in the same room with her, Smith! You're not clean! You smell of lust!'

'Dewi!' exclaimed Epsom angrily. He took a pace forward, and at the same moment Dewi slid off the hand basin to the floor and faced him, flushed and tense, gripping with both hands the rim of the basin behind him. He squeezed the rim so hard that the flesh of his fingers went blotchy white, his nails white with a dark crimson half-moon of blood cutting across them.

'Well, he does!' he shouted, looking, not at me, but at Epsom. 'He's played the fool with every bloody girl in the Club, one after another, and now he wants to try his filthy hand with Kathy! He has, you can't deny it, Epsom, everyone knows it. God, man, it's a standing bloody joke! Smith the smasher! My God!'

'Shut up, Dewi!' said Epsom.

'I won't shut up, by damn! Look, why did you call him Jampot? It's your name, you gave it him! You know bloody well why! Because the bloody girls buzz round him like flies round a Jampot, that's why! You can't deny you gave him that name, can you?'

'Shut up, Dewi!'

'Answer my question, damn you! Do you deny – '

'No, I don't deny it!' Epsom cut in loudly, 'but you don't know the history of the name and you don't understand the joke. So just shut up for a minute, will you, while I – '

'I'm buggered if I'll shut up!' shouted Dewi, pushing himself backwards and forwards, swinging from and towards the washbasin behind him. 'The joke's as plain as my arse, just like I said, he's a bloody Jampot and the bloody girls – '

'Dewi! In the bowels of Christ, will you shut up! Just to dispose of this stupid Jampot business once and for all, and with apologies to you, Smith, I called him that simply because he's scared stiff of the women, and that, Dewi, is the joke. Now, for God's sake, calm down and use a bit of common sense, will you?'

Dewi stopped swinging, leaning forward in the outward position. 'Do you expect me to believe that?' he asked scornfully.

'Scared of women and spends his whole time chasing one after another! Scared of women! My aunt!'

Epsom sighed heavily. 'Dewi,' he said, 'you're pretending to be much more stupid than you really are. Certainly he chases them but he does that just because he is scared of them!'

Epsom turned to me, grinning ruefully, as one who has been compelled to spill the beans, 'I'm sorry, man,' he said, 'but it's true isn't it? We've got to make this maniac understand that, haven't we?'

'Yes,' I said ambiguously. I was busy retreating further and further into myself, and the less I had to do with the controversy the better. I was rapidly achieving the detached attitude of an interested spectator at a dog fight, with a faint but easily exchangeable interest in one of the dogs.

'If you asked any one of those girls, Dewi,' Epsom resumed, 'they'd all tell you the same thing. He doesn't get further than a peck in the dark, I promise you. And if they peck back, he scampers for dear life! You can't call that lust; you're just being bloody-minded! Why, man, I've gone further and fared worse and more often than old Smith, only I don't put advertisements in the papers about it the way Smith does. But you try calling me a lecher and you'll get the fight you're wanting! Now for God's sake let's get back to the old brass tacks again, shall we, and drop these fancy notions of yours!'

Epsom stood back towards the closet door again, leaving me closer to Dewi than he. Dewi, looking a bit put out, as if he'd forgotten the origin of the quarrel, put his head back and stared up at the damp-stained ceiling.

'All that's as may be,' he said uncertainly, 'but the fact remains, whether he pecks or pushes or stuffs, he's run through the whole Club like a dose of salts in the last few months. You ask anyone! Smith, they'd say, blimey, he gets about a bit. And all I'm saying is, he's got about quite enough without having to go mucking about with Kathy.

184

Kathy's my girl, and I'm not going to have any Smiths or Joneses or any damned man sticking their snouts in where they're not wanted, that's all.'

Epsom looked at me, as if waiting for me to make a move. I looked at Dewi, He had calmed down considerably now, his fingers on the basin's rim were no longer discoloured, and he was sniffing heavily as if he needed to blow his nose. Every time he sniffed, he jerked his head up, and the hair on the crown of his head rose like a flap and dropped again.

'What,' said Epsom quietly, 'if he is wanted?'

Dewi stopped sniffing, froze; his eyelids lowered, he looked first at Epsom, then at me, then back to Epsom again, as if scenting a trap.

'What's that?' he asked.

'What if he is wanted, Dewi? You said you wouldn't have Smith sticking his snout in where he isn't wanted. I quite agree, he mustn't do that. But how do you know he isn't wanted? Surely that's something only Kathy can decide, isn't it? And how can she decide it if you deprive her of any chance of ever finding out?'

'You're too clever by half, aren't you, Jones?' Dewi said indistinctly. He had resumed his sniffing again, but this time kept his head motionless. 'I can't see it's any business of yours anyway. All I asked you to do, as a favour, was go and fetch bloody Smith and bring him down here. And here you are trying to queer the issue with all your clever-clever talk. Why don't you leave us to settle it alone?'

'Oh, cheese, Dewi!' I said mildly, judicially, as if the point had only an academic interest for me. 'After all, you asked him to come back. He wasn't going to stay, was he?'

185

'I didn't ask him to poke his long nose – '

'Oh, drop it, Dewi!' said Jones wearily. 'Being nasty won't get you anywhere. Look, can't you see that all this is rather silly? Let's put it plainly! You like Kathy, and quite naturally want to keep her to yourself. If she likes you, that's surely easy enough, and Smith isn't doing you any damage by dancing with her occasionally – after all, it would look bloody odd if he never danced with her. On the other hand, if she isn't so keen on you as you are on her, you're being very unfair to her if you get up on your high horse every time another man speaks to her!'

'It isn't another man!' Dewi growled, shooting a venomous glance at me. 'It's Smith!'

'Exactly!' said Epsom. 'And why Smith? Not because he's been about with the other girls, Dewi, you know that as well as I do. But because you know he's always been keen on Kathy, and you're afraid she may still be keen on him. Isn't that it?'

It was appalling that the cat should be dragged so clear of the bag as this; but such was the intensity of the emotional torpor with which I had surrounded myself that only in the abstract was I at all dismayed; in the event, I merely looked with mild curiosity at Dewi to see how this all too plain view of the cat would be received.

Dewi was looking at his feet. There was a long silence, into which the sound of an old-fashioned waltz, faintly penetrating the room, injected, for me, a curious air of unreality. I would not have been surprised, then, if Dewi had looked up, grinned, and said 'Let's go on a wield!'

But he didn't in fact look up at all. He pushed slowly away from the wash basin, walked towards the door, and, as he opened it, said, without once looking back 'You're a rat, Jones.'

'Dewi!' exclaimed Jones suddenly, starting forward, 'Dewi, come back! What are you going to do?'

Dewi, already drifting up the stairs, called softly back 'I'm going to take Kathy home.'

Epsom looked back at me. 'Going to stop him?' he asked. I shook my head, too weary to speak, let alone act. I wanted, now, not Kathy, not Moira, not even Epsom; I wanted to be alone, quite alone, for a long, long time.

Epsom hovered in the doorway. 'Sorry about that, man. Had to be done, I'm afraid. Hasn't settled anything, but at least he knows where he stands. I think that if you really feel you must, you could go on with Kathy from there. He won't put up a fight again.'

'Thanks,' I said.

'Coming home with us?' Epsom asked diffidently. By 'us', he meant Isabel, Moira, and himself.

'No, thanks,' I said. I roused myself, and stretched my face into a grin. 'Thanks all the same. Tell them my bloody headache, got worse, will you? I'll slope off, now.'

'All right. Goo' night, man. See you.'

'See you. Goo' night.'

As Epsom closed the door behind him, I began washing my hands, humming the waltz tune which still filtered into the room. It seemed to have been going on for hours. As I washed my hands, I washed too, with every mental detergent I had ever discovered, all memory of the scene I had just witnessed from my mind. I sang, on the way home, and laughed sometimes, almost hysterical at the emptiness of my mind.

Ten

I don't believe that I spoke to a girl throughout that Easter holiday. Nor, for one reason or another, did I see much of Epsom. It was not that we had broken with each other; certainly there was never any question of our deliberately avoiding each other's company; it had simply ceased to be axiomatic that we should meet daily; parting in the evenings, we no longer said 'See you tomorrow,' with the certainty that whatever one was doing the other would do as well.

How Epsom occupied himself when he was not with me, I never discovered. For me, a visit to the Public Library became an almost daily occurrence, for I was reading voraciously at this time, as if my life depended upon an ever-increasing consumption of the printed word. Hounded out of the house by my exasperated mother, I would take my book with me up to the cliffs above the Haulfre Gardens, where, from a rocky eyrie, I could look down over the town, southward to the mountains or eastwards along the coast where the white line of surf carved on into the haze.

When Epsom and I came together again, at the beginning of the summer term, picking up our intimate friendship as if it had never been suspended, I found that he had changed. He was quieter, less self-confident, tentative in both thought and action. That quality, which had both impressed and irritated me, of seeming always to have known those human truths which I had to fight so hard to learn, had left him. Now it was his turn to long for guidance through the fog of his uncertainties. 'Sometimes I feel,' he said, 'as if I had two separate personalities, and I've absolutely no idea which is mine. They think differently, they act differently, they even,' he added with a snort of laughter, 'want different girls.'

I gave him Dr. Jekyll and Mr. Hyde to read, but he dismissed this as an over-simplification. 'Not the same problem, anyway,' he said. 'My two selves exist side by side, both at the same time.'

He had become interested in religion, and, out of friendship, I undertook to go to church with him on Sundays. These were enjoyable occasions; I liked the singing, and the virtuous, newly washed feeling of coming out of church into the quiet Sunday mornings. But though I continued, through summer into autumn, to attend church with Epsom, I soon knew that I was a stranger in this world of the spirit and likely to remain one. I had none of Epsom's capacity for belief, and what little I had was all needed for believing in my own existence.

It was a year curiously barren of incident, so far as we two were concerned. As the summer progressed we had drawn away from the activities of the Club, which had rapidly swollen beyond our control. Many of our original group were occupied with School Certificate examinations, and though Epsom and I were not considered fit to sit for it that year our interests, like theirs, became increasingly academic even out of school hours. We read poetry together – with a preference for full-blooded, declamatory stuff which would lend itself to being shouted aloud into the teeth of the wind beside the sea, with the waves breaking a dull counterpoint along the shore. We wrote a verse play together, a play with two characters, in which I wrote the words for the comic Scotsman, MacIver MacWheeble, and Epsom those for the mystical millionaire, J. J. Orifamme. It was a very bad play, but this was not anyway an art we were practising, it was an elaborate private game.

I had severed, after the incident at Easter, all communication between my consciousness and whatever compartment of my mind dealt with Kathy. She had become for me like some persistent ghost, ever-present at the back of my thoughts, unapproachable in any direct sense because of her ghostly status, but, through familiarity, a ghost with whom I was on superficially easy terms. I deliberately avoided thinking about her in any practical sense. Determined not to allow the old situation to grow again, I made a point of dancing once with her each evening, while Epsom and I were still attending the Club dances. If Dewi were there too, I would be uncomfortably conscious of his glowering presence, of his distrustful eyes following our progress round and round the floor; and when, at the end of the dance, I escorted her back to her seat beside him, he would look up at me with a sort of half-challenge in his eyes. But even if he were not there – and, as the term progressed, the pressure of school work kept him increasingly away – I never exceeded my ration of a single dance. Kathy appeared to accept this convention without question, coming to her feet always with a welcoming smile when I approached and thanking me demurely for the dance when it was over, as if it had meant no more to either of us than the similar single dances which we each had with other members of the Club. But she, like Dewi, must have wondered endlessly what my intentions could be, how the situation, obvious in its existence to all three of us but differently interpreted by each, was to be resolved. I, it appeared, was the only one in a position to take action, mine the responsibility for solving the tensionless triangle.

But in fact I had no intentions, could not face, even in my thoughts, the responsibility which, against all my wishes, had been placed in my hands. Had I brought myself to think about the situation, I would not have been willing to admit that any such responsibility existed. I had done nothing, said nothing; in all directions I was uncommitted; how then could I be responsible for a situation which was none of my making? I had, I would have said, acted honourably; had ceased, when the extent of Dewi's anguish became apparent, to give him further cause for it; had never wittingly betrayed to Kathy the fact that I loved her, for I had hidden this even from myself. Somehow, from the very beginning, Kathy had been unapproachable for me, and, love her as I might, there seemed no hope of change. Therefore I did not love her; and expended, instead, my shallower emotions on less vulnerable objects.

Epsom, for his part, wanted no love affair. Someone to kiss in dark corners late at night, someone to fondle on the sand dunes on hot summer evenings, someone on whom his eyes could rest with pleasure... these he wanted. But the emotion of love, which seems to be the crock of gold in search of which so much of our energy is expended, was not to his purpose.

Some unexplained quarrel had separated Isabel and Moira during the Easter holidays; perhaps Isabel could not stand whatever boy had supplanted me in Moira's emotions. And so there came about, as the summer term progressed, an oddly piquant situation: Epsom and I together keeping company with Isabel, competing earnestly for her favours but valuing them not at all. It was a game, with Epsom and I playing intently to win, Isabel attempting with honest concern to decide which of us she preferred but having, had she but known it, no volition in the matter; and none of us more deeply concerned than if we had been playing whist.

The game was made more easy to play, if less amusing, by the growing friendship between Isabel and Ann; which, though it could come to little while Ann was working for her School Certificate, burgeoned suddenly into an inseparable companionship as soon as the summer holidays began. Thus she became the recipient of whichever suitor Isabel had temporarily cast off; and, if she saw herself in this role, which I doubt, she was certainly content with it, allowing the wind of her passion to back or veer according to the vacillations of Isabel's uncertain cyclone. Ann was attractive enough herself to satisfy either my or Epsom's modest demands, and it was only by accident that Isabel took first place in our attentions. Perhaps Ann recognized this, and so was unperturbed by Isabel's ascendancy. Certainly they were a fine pair, dark and fair, tall and short, robust and petite, gay in their summer dresses, revelling in our harmless game of love. During those summer holidays we ceased entirely to visit the Room. We had little need of it, anyway, for an endless succession of hot, windless days made it more congenial that our headquarters should be the beach. We fell into the habit of meeting, in the mornings, among the tumbled rocks below the Little Orme, and in the afternoons in a particular hollow of the sand-dunes on West Shore. Often we would all bring our lunch, sandwiches, fruit, bottles of lemonade. We would assemble in the forenoon before the mouth of a cave under the rising cliff of the Little Orme and from there, throughout the sweltering noon hours, drift backwards and forwards between the warm, sticky sea and the hard, burning stones, our bodies browning or freckling or peeling, white lines of salt forming in the wrinkles of our flesh, feeling ourselves being pumped full of energy to bursting point by the sun, but kept always from expending it by the paralysing pressure of the continuing heatwave. After lunch someone would say 'Let's move to the dunes!' And, as if in the grip of some compulsive ritual, we would all gather our clothes and belongings together, collect our bicycles from the bus-shelter at the bottom of Penrhyn Hill, and cycle languidly, still in our bathing costumes, a mile across the isthmus to the Maes Du Bridge; leave our bicycles by the Club House and walk across the burnt turf of the golf course to our favourite sandy hollow near the concrete pillbox, and there settle ourselves on the pale shifting, baking sand for the rest of the day. As, towards evening, the air cooled sufficiently to allow

193

of some cautious movement, we would come down from the dunes on to the hard-ribbed flats below; and play cricket, beach tennis, or dodge-ball in the slanting golden rays of the declining sun. The heatwave seemed to have gone on so long that we could scarcely remember the taste and feel of rain, and the thought of snow was like a dream which one knows can never attain reality. And so, while through the gritty sands of Africa Rommel was pushed back, step by step, across the desert he had lately won, we, on our softer sand dunes, lay waiting for our unwanted youth to wear away.

It must have been some time in November of that year that Epsom and I, with the two girls, visited the Room for the last time. We had not been there for several weeks and knew that few of the old members of our group attended now. Even so, we were not prepared for what we found.

We could hear the noise from the bottom of the stairs: not the rhythmic shush-shush of ballroom dancing to which we were accustomed, but the wild, irregular stomping of 'jive'. When we opened the door it was like emerging into some titanic conflict: legs flailing in all directions, shrieks and yells of excitement, and above all the crazy barbarous beat of the music... it was another world to the one we had created. Crates of beer stood around the edges of the room, bottles and cups were everywhere, and the room was so full of smoke it was hard to distinguish faces across the width of the floor. Most of the faces were unknown to us, and we realised at once that the girls, without exception, came not from the school, but from the town.

Epsom and I hurriedly closed the door and ushered Isabel and downstairs again. Isabel was furious, she would have liked to have pitched in there and then and thrown the interlopers bodily down the stairs.

'What's the use?' said Epsom. 'It's their Club now, not ours. They don't know the history of it, they probably think they've got more right to be there than we have.'

'But they've no right at all!' cried Isabel angrily. 'It's our Club, not theirs.'

'Still, they think it's theirs,' I said, 'which comes to the same thing.'

'I think it's a rotten shame, all the same,' said Isabel. I realised suddenly that she was near to tears, and as we came out into the cold night I put my arm round her shoulders. She stood still, turning her face into my chest to hide the tears which she could no longer withhold. 'Oh, Bernard!' she cried. 'I know I'm silly but I can't help it, it was our Club, I don't mind what you say, we made it out of nothing, and now they've got it and messed it all up and... Oh, I think it's horrid!'

'I feel rather the same, you know,' said Epsom. He had one arm round Ann's waist and with the other hand now took Isabel's elbow, so that the four of us marched off, linked together, down the dark Promenade. 'And what do you think, little Ann?'

'I think we're just getting older, that's all,' said Ann solemnly. 'Nobody likes things they've got used to change, but everything's changing all the time. It's rather sad, really.'

'Getting older,' repeated Epsom. 'You know, I hadn't thought of that.'

We tackled the Crow about what we had seen up in the Room the next day. It was soon clear that we were not telling him anything he did not already know. He had not been able to bring himself to go to his father and confess that the Club had now got out of hand and had degenerated into a sort of illicit drinking and dancing saloon, but he was haunted by the fear that some oaf, unable to carry his beer, would commit an act of hooliganism in the hotel and bring the whole disastrous situation to light.

We urged him to approach his father before it was too late; but as it happened an event occurred a few days later which took the matter out of his hands. We heard the details at second-hand, for the authorities were very discreet and we knew nothing of the approaching storm until it was nearly over. Nevertheless it was a nine-day wonder in the school. Red was arrested, accused of larceny, and tried at the County Court, Caernarvon.

He had been away from school for several days, and we had imagined that he was sick, before this shattering news came to light. The announcement of his arrest came first in the local newspaper: simply a statement of the fact and the charge against him, without details. Remembering our own association with him on many a hocking expedition, we wondered fearfully if he had been caught at a similar activity, and, asking for previous offences to be taken into consideration, would incriminate us. But next day, after morning prayers, the headmaster gave us a short, pungent, and immensely chastening address on the subject. Whatever it was he said, he seemed to imply that he knew all about us and our exploits, had had his X-ray eye on us for some time, and hoped that we would take this as a warning of what would happen to us if we persisted in our criminal ways. The cutting little sentences must have sounded an even more personal note to the boys in the form below us, for they were even then at the height of their adventures in a field which we had abandoned the year before. But at the time it seemed that the Head was talking straight at us, looking straight at us, knowing every detail of our inglorious careers. We left the hall feeling as if we had been whipped.

Red's crime, with which he was immediately charged, was apparently the theft, from the Goods Yard at Colwyn Bay, of a number of iron girders. It was not stated what he wanted them for, nor how he managed by himself to move them, nor where he secreted them once stolen. But, in the course of evidence, it came out that he had committed a number of more serious thefts, of such diverse articles as a wheelbarrow, twenty-seven army blankets, a motorbicycle, the hairdryer from a ladies hairdressing saloon, and numerous other bizarre objects, the eventual resting places of which were never discovered.

Two of these objects were the record player and loudspeaker which Red had presented to the Club. This fact didn't emerge until the Crow, worried to death by the turn events had taken, told us privately that the police had visited his father, been taken up to the Room, and had confiscated the two black boxes. Miraculously, there were no beer bottles on view, otherwise the affair might have had more serious consequences for the Crow and his father than it did. As it was, the Crow was called for questioning, and had to tell the story of our search for a gramophone and Red's unexplained presentation. At one moment it was even thought that he would have to go into the witness box, but this was an unfounded rumour, for Red's trial was only for the theft of the iron girders; on which count he was found guilty, with one hundred and forty-two other offences taken into consideration; and remanded in custody for an examination by a psychiatrist.

This was the last we heard of the case. But at school it was discussed endlessly, to the point of boredom; by Epsom psychologically, by Peter speculatively, by Gregory legally, and by the Crow personally: for the Crow, a much chastened individual now, had had to bear the brunt of his father's condemnation when the signs, obvious when they were looked for, which the Room bore were correctly interpreted and the whole story of the Club's fall from innocent music room to near-brothel was extracted from him.

'The stupid thing is,' said Epsom, plainly worried about his own responsibility in the matter, 'I knew all the time!'

'Knew what?'

'Knew about Red. I knew he'd pinched that damned gramophone. But I couldn't prove it, so I just let it be. Didn't you even suspect?'

'I may have done,' I said vaguely, 'but I didn't know. I didn't really think about it.'

Epsom came back to this knowledge of his several times. I wanted to ask him what he'd thought about the hocking expeditions, but it didn't seem to be quite the sort of thing one asked. I could not see, and told Epsom so, that there was anything he could have done about Red. But he was not content. 'You don't know what you can do until you try. Look at Dewi. He didn't seem good for much when we first knew him, did he? I ought to have had a go at old Red, you know.'

Now that the Room was closed to us, the winter weather made us cast around for some other place where we could meet regularly in reasonable comfort. Soon it was established that we should foregather, on Saturday nights, in the dance hall attached to one of the town's cinemas. It was a poor substitute for the Room; we had to pay for admission, pay for refreshments, and the sense of intimacy which had been the Club's most valuable asset could never be recovered. It was better than nothing though, and as winter advanced we established for ourselves in this unfamiliar territory, a new and acceptable home.

Epsom and I had become very independent, and would never commit ourselves, as Isabel and Ann wanted us to, to attending; but whatever we set out to do on a Saturday evening, we usually found ourselves ending up in the dance hall, finding, as often as not, an entire corner of the hall or the adjacent buffet occupied by erstwhile members of the Music Club. Isabel, Ann, Dora, and Moira were invariably there, probably with the Crow and Peredur in attendance. Kathy, who had a trick of turning up in unexpected places, looking as if she had more right to be there than anyone, would often arrive alone, drifting up to the crowded tables and sitting down so unobtrusively that it was impossible to tell, from her demeanour, if she had just arrived or had been at the dance all evening. Dewi, who had decided to take the Higher Certificate in one year instead of the normal two, seldom came.

I now no longer observed my self-imposed limit of a single dance with Kathy. Perhaps because of that same lack of intimacy which in the abstract I deplored, I felt free here to dance with Kathy just as often as I liked. I was not even afraid, now, of what the others in the party might say or think; for a new freemasonry had developed between the sexes since the summer, the tensions of adolescent discovery had relaxed, and we moved among ourselves without that precise attention to the emotional significance of every act which had characterized and confined our meetings in the Room. Kathy herself seemed now an easier person to be with, no longer threatening me at every turn with the intimacies which I at once desired and feared. Indeed, so noticeable was the change in her demeanour towards me that, perversely, I felt cheated, disappointed, as if some offer, which I did not wish to accept but of which it pleased me to have knowledge, had been withdrawn.

Pat, too, put in a regular appearance on Saturday nights, so that I began to see more of her, that winter and spring, than ever before. Pat's movements and attachments had always been something of a mystery to me. In the summer she would join us on the beach quite often, but it was never possible to know what she did with herself when she was not with us, nor pin her down to any particular attachment. Her friend Freda had, like my 'friend' Gregory, grown away at a tangent from her; if any one girl could be said to be more in her company than another, it was, when I came to examine it, Kathy; if any one young man, Epsom. But neither of these dispositions impinged on my consciousness that winter. Pat seemed always to be a free-lance; and if Epsom should chance to walk home from the dance hall with her, that was because Isabel had had to leave early; and if she should chance to arrive with Kathy, then in all probability they had met at the door.

The rivalry between Epsom and myself for Isabel had petered out gradually through the autumn, more from our desire for the privacy of our own company than from any swivel of our interest towards another girl. At the dance hall we kept the fiction up in a desultory fashion, because it was amusing, and because it seemed to be expected of us. But though, if Epsom claimed Isabel too often for the dances, or by some stratagem abducted her from the hall at the end of the evening, I would make the correct gestures of morose disgust for the benefit of whoever happened to be present, we were no longer able, as once we had been, to carry the pretence into our private life, so that the whole game had now lost much of its once piquant flavour. I think that the girls, too, were beginning to tire of it; Ann, certainly from the New Year onwards, showed more interest in John Stockwell, the Dreamy Scientist who had joined our group through Peter's agency, than in either Epsom or me.

Thus I found myself, on Saturday nights, when Ann and John Stockwell, Isabel and Kenny, Epsom and Pat, Peredur and Dora, were away on the dance-floor or in the buffet together, left often alone with Kathy, whether I liked it or not.

I did like it. I discovered that it was possible, as with Pat, to sit at Kathy's side at the deserted tables, watching the circling, swaying couples on the floor, without feeling impelled to keep up the endless chatter and repartee which Isabel, for instance, would have demanded. The mutual pleasure of these long silences was for me heightened by all that was being left unsaid, that might have been said. Yet sometimes, feeling the silence stretched between us like a sheet of white paper ready to receive a message, I would long to break it with some startling, shattering intimacy, to smash down the shield of impersonal friendliness which I had forced Kathy to build for her protection.

I had ceased to worry what the others thought. It occurred to me, sometimes, that, seeing Kathy and me so often alone together on those Saturday evenings, the other girls must have formed an estimate of the relationship between us which could have little in common with the truth. More often, I wondered what Kathy thought, how she balanced in her mind her continuing friendship with Dewi and her weekly companionship with me.

It was a curious relationship that we built up out of the long silences and the careful platitudes of those evenings. We sat together as might a divorced couple, thrown together at a party, having so much potentially between them that the field of safe communication was narrowed almost to nothing. Comment about the affairs of others was impossible, for it suggested parallels; speculation about the future was as perilous as reminiscence about the past; and anything that involved a knowledge of the other acquired during a previous period of intimacy had to be strictly abjured. To mention Wiggy I or Wiggy II would be to acknowledge the past.

And yet somehow the delicate structure of a new amity came slowly into being, pieced together out of the minutiae of bare existence – the tone of my voice as I offered Kathy a second cup of coffee in the buffet, the sense, when I arrived at the dance hall later than usual, that she had been watching the door, the expected mockery at a familiar foible, the faces of strangers on the floor gradually emerging into individuality; these things, mutually cherished as common property, were the materials of the hypostasis that was forming between us. We arrived at the hall alone, or in company with other friends; and it would have been unthinkable, it never occurred to me as a possibility, to have walked home with Kathy, or even to the tram stop, when the evening was over. The conventions which we had accepted were rigid; they drew the magic circle within which we were safe. Outside, was chaos.

But hanging over all of us was a threat which we had long ignored, and the time came when we awoke, one by one, to the fact that the distance between ourselves and the School Certificate examination was to be measured now in weeks instead of months. In March, when Moira failed to appear at the dance hall one night because, it was said, she had started swotting, it was just funny; in May, when Peredur proffered the same excuse, it was understandable; but by June we had all been gripped by the same fever, and for the time being the meetings at the dance hall came to an end.

For five weeks every activity but work was suspended. We ceased attending A.T.C. parades, ceased almost to know the girls. We had three years' work to cram into five weeks.

'Five weeks!' said Epsom. 'Nothing to it! What we want is a system! The whole set-up's loony, anyway. Look at Gregory: mind like a washtub, and he gets five Credits! If he'd used his nut he'd have got five Distinctions. I'll lay you ten to one you get three yourself!'

So we laid a bet, of a hundred cigarettes against ten, on the possibility of my getting three distinctions.

'It's a shame to take your money!' I said. But the bet had crystallized the issue for me, and I became determined to lose it. Five weeks, I thought: well, perhaps it's just faintly possible.

We made our swotting into a sort of fierce, fast game. 'Facts,' said Epsom, 'the buggers want facts. Never mind understanding what it's all about. We'll bloody give 'em facts!'

We took each subject as if it were a sponge, squeezing it until we'd expressed every last factual droplet, and throwing away the dry, irrelevant shell of meaning. The system was based on the method used at the school for teaching History: each subject had a separate, pocket-sized notebook in which, in minute handwriting, the bare facts were arranged as headings, sections, subsections, and sub-sub-sections, so that the whole of the Industrial Revolution could be compressed on to one page, the whole of Welsh History on to two. In three weeks we had applied this system to History, Geography, Art History, and French, carrying in our pockets notebooks containing synopses of the whole field of each subject, ready to be stamped on to the memory through the remaining weeks. Chemistry, Physics, and Mathematics, however, would yield only in a limited sense to this kind of condensation, and in these we had to employ as well the common principle of rejection and selection: rejecting all those areas of knowledge which had been the basis for a question more than once during the past five years, and concentrating on those areas which had turned up only once or not at all. Thus, in five weeks of concentrated effort, Epsom and I equipped ourselves for the world.

The weeks seemed, at the time, to pass like days; in retrospect so crammed with unaccustomed mental activity were they, like years. The examination was on us and past us almost, it seemed before we had properly come to consciousness about it. It was as if one had suddenly, without warning, had to enter a boxing ring for a fight of such intensity that all sense of time and the world outside were lost; and then, after staying there, fighting like an automaton, for an indeterminate period, suddenly to find the bell ringing, and be free to stagger forth, punch-drunk, still fighting, dodging, feinting into a slowly stabilizing world. For days, weeks after the examination was over, I found myself, walking along a street or lying in bed at night, going over and over the lists of facts and figures, many of which I had not had to use, and most of which, during the succeeding weeks, dropped out of my mind, having, since they were divorced from meaning, found no context there in which to spread holding roots.

The last examination took place on a Friday. As we left the school that evening, the Crow accosted us.

'Don't forget tomorrow night!' he said mysteriously.

'How can I forget it?' Epsom asked innocently. 'It hasn't happened yet, so there isn't anything to forget!'

'Don't be dim, man bach! I mean the dance! We're all going. Celebration. Coffee, women, and song! Don't forget!'

The Crow treated Epsom and me now with a sort of embarrassed deference, as if at a wrong word we might royally turn on him and banish him to the outer darkness. I'm not quite sure why this should have come about; but it is true that, almost without our being aware of it, Epsom and I had somehow attained to a position of respected insularity in the school. We were, I suppose, rather more self-contained than most, took no part in sports in any competitive sense, did not attend such activities as the Debating Club or House Meetings; had created for ourselves, in fact, a world outside the school, a world containing, as its very centre, ourselves, and needing little more to be complete. Our manner was perhaps a little aloof, but more through self-sufficiency than superiority.

Girls, of course, being creatures anyway of another world, were affected less by this exclusiveness than the other men. Nevertheless I was surprised when, on Saturday morning, Epsom announced that he had arranged to take Pat to the dance that evening. Since we had abandoned the game with Isabel, we had always arrived at the hall and left afterwards together. This new departure, though on all precedent unobjectionable, seemed to me heavy with significance, to such an extent that I even contemplated not going. Dewi, I thought, would be sure to be there. But I had nothing else to do; and it was, after all, an occasion. If I didn't go, something exciting was bound to happen.

I never liked arriving at the hall alone. One had to pass through, either on one's way to the cloakroom or to the dance-floor, the crowd of unattached girls who always gathered hopefully in the raised carpeted entrance passage between; and one was followed resentfully by all those eyes, critical eyes, hopeful eyes, indifferent eyes, as if by failing to stop and ask one of them for a dance one had slighted them all. Then there was the long walk, an agony if it happened to coincide with an interval, when the floor was empty, right down the side of the hall, watched by the safely seated hundreds on either side. Our tables, which, being some way back from the edge of the floor, were seldom in demand by others, and to which, by long use, we had established a certain right of tenure which was recognized by the habitués, were in a corner commanding a view of the entire room. Only the orchestra was out of sight, a fact which we didn't mind but which helped to keep the corner clear of intruders. As I approached (I had taken the usual precaution of the diffident in being late) I saw that this was indeed an occasion which it would have been maddening to miss, for almost the whole of the old Music Club had assembled in our corner; an amnesty, it seemed, had been declared by everyone for their enemies; factions and sub-factions and schisms had all been suspended, and I saw for the first time the full extent of the Club which had grown so arbitrarily out of my fifteenth birthday party. I had never realised how many of them there were; without counting, and with several more to come, one could safely put the figure at over thirty. Seven tables were in use. The usual three, all that had ever been required on a Saturday night before, had been pushed together, and round these sat, in valedictory triumph, my own group, the backbone, the unbroken heart of the Club; Isabel and Ann, Gregory and Helen, Peter and Moira, Epsom and Nancy and Pat.

But it was ironical, I thought, that the Club should never have assembled *en masse* until it was to all intents and purposes dead, dispossessed, on the brink of final dispersal. For, with the term over, and with no headquarters, it could not now hope to survive the summer. There would be meetings, no doubt, on the beach or in the town, possibly in this hall. But in any complete sense this was bound to be the last real meeting of the Club as such. It had died unhealthily months before; this was a brief resurrection, ghostly with self-consciousness.

In a fortnight, the Crow would be leaving for the Air Force and a week later Kenny would follow him. Peredur was a volunteer for the Navy, due to leave in early September; also in September Isabel would leave to start a Domestic Science course at Sheffield; Dora was to start work in July at an hotel in Caernarvon. And in November, Epsom, too, would leave. The pieces of our world were breaking away one by one. And though I looked forward still, no less eagerly than always to the future, to glory, to freedom, I would at that moment, seeing the parts of my private universe gathered together for the first and last time, have stopped the clock and gone back to savour the best of the days which I had so incontinently wished to fly.

Three chairs stood empty, between Epsom and Helen, at the tables occupied by my own group. I sat down next to Epsom, waving to others at our and neighbouring tables. Almost at the same moment the announcer mumbled something incoherently into the microphone and the music for the next dance began. As I sat, others started to rise, so that I was spared, by the confusion of all this sudden movement, the awkward first few moments of a new arrival in an already established group.

'Quite a turn-out, eh?' said Epsom, shooting his teeth out of the side of his mouth in a lop-sided grin. 'Where one or two are gathered together in the name of Sex… we ought to hold a service to Venus, and spatter each other with the bile of a pregnant bat!'

'Who are the other two chairs for?' I asked casually.

'Kathy and Dewi. Only Dewi can't come, Peter says. He's got another exam on Monday.'

'Bad luck,' I said.

'Bad luck on Dewi, yes. But Pat says Kathy's coming.' Pat was sitting on the other side of Epsom, smiling benignly at me. I leant across Epsom and asked her to dance.

'Traitorous crew!' growled Epsom as we stood up to leave him.

Epsom rarely danced now; he preferred to sit hunched in a corner of the hall (or, preferably, the buffet, for he had an insatiable thirst for coffee) watching the comings and goings of the crowd and inventing fantastic, and usually scabrous, biographies for any stranger whose face excited his interest. Pat, on the other hand, loved dancing. We danced well together, reacting in the same way to the rhythmic demands of the music, seldom speaking, enjoying the smooth working of our bodies, the automatic responses of our muscles. But Pat this evening was, for a change, inclined to talk.

'Well, how did you like it, Bernard?' she asked; meaning, of course, the examination.

'Ghastly,' I said. 'Failed the lot, I should think.'

'I bet you didn't!'

'I bet I did!'

'I bet I failed Latin. It was a stinker!'

'Do you? I bet I failed Physics, too!'

'Do you?'

One by one we examined each subject in turn, explaining to each other exactly why and how we confidently expected to have failed them all. I had already been through this ceremony with Epsom, the Crow, and Isabel, and had by now almost succeeded in convincing myself, and resigning myself to the fact, that I had indeed done as badly as I pretended. It was a necessary insurance policy.

'Are you staying on, if you get matric?' I asked; assuming, despite her denials, that Pat would have done moderately well in the examinations.

'No fear! I'm going to be a nurse.'

'A what?'

'A nurse.'

'You're not!'

'I am!'

'You're cuckoo! You work like a slave and get no pay. My mother was a nurse in the last war, so I know.'

'Still,' said Pat, smiling cheerfully, 'that's what I'm going to do. I'm starting at Bangor, at the C. and A. in December.'

'You're crazy!' I said. 'How old are you, Pat?'

'Seventeen in December.'

'Why, you're just a baby!'

'It's you who's the baby!' Pat retorted.

In fact Pat's age, sixteen and a half, was about normal for taking the School Certificate from the Fifth Form. We were, as it happened, a particularly backward crowd, possibly because the majority of us had been uprooted from schools in the south, often missing one or two terms in the process and inevitably wasting a year in the attempt to readjust ourselves to a new curriculum. The Crow, who hadn't this excuse, must just have been unusually stupid. When we arrived back at the tables we discovered that Kathy had slipped quietly into the empty chair beside Epsom. I took the chair next to her, leaving Pat the one on Epsom's other side.

'Hello, stranger!' I said. I had not seen Kathy, except in the distance, for six weeks.

'Hello, Bernard. How did you like the exams?'

'Failed the lot, I should think. How about you?'

'I didn't think they were too bad, really. I answered quite a lot of the questions. I think I shall pass – but only just.'

There was a moment of silence at our table; heads turned to see – or to confirm – who could be tempting fate in so blatant a manner. Kathy, blithely unconscious of having said anything unusual, produced from her bag copies of the examination papers, and began to question us about what forms of answer we had given. It was quickly apparent that she had not distinguished herself.

But I was only half-attending. Something in Epsom's manner, his flippancy, the way he was sunk into his chair, with his chin withdrawn and an expression of benevolent inanity on his face, told me that he was preoccupied with something other than examinations. Coming back to my chair later, after a dance with Kathy, I found him deep in a serious, private conversation with Pat. As Kathy and I arrived, he turned and grinned, and I sensed that our arrival had brought the conversation to an end. Pat, now, looking up to acknowledge our presence, wore a troubled look on her round, usually contented face. I felt that irritable disturbance that comes when one detects an unshared secret between mutual friends.

We moved then, on Epsom's suggestion, to the buffet, where we found a large group of Club members already established at the two largest tables in the middle of the room. There was no space for us with them, so we joined Peter and Moira at a smaller table in the corner near the coffee urn, from which position Epsom was able to replenish his cup without leaving his seat.

After a couple of coffees apiece, the three girls excused themselves. Much as I liked him, I wished that Peter too would leave us for a moment. But even if he had done so, I doubt if I would have brought myself to challenge Epsom, for he was in his most unapproachable mood: silent, for the most part, or, if not, sardonically obscure. He loved speaking in quotations, and would often introduce a phrase from a poem into his normal speech so that, if one didn't immediately recognize it, one was often baffled by an apparently irrelevant remark. The more he wished to be left alone, the more obscure his remarks became.

When the girls returned, I asked Pat to dance again, feeling vaguely that, if Epsom would not confide in me, I would at least prevent him from doing so with Pat.

After we had been round the floor twice, Pat said 'Epsom's older than you, isn't he?'

'Yes. Three months.'

'When are you joining up, then?'

'Next February. They won't have me any earlier.'

'Did you volunteer?'

'Yes.'

'Did Epsom?'

'Yes.'

'So he's due to go in November?'

'Yes. Why? What are you getting at?'

'Me? Getting at? Why, nothing, Bernard!' said Pat with

wide-eyed innocence. 'I just wanted to know when he was due to leave, that's all.'

'I don't believe you,' I said. But Pat wouldn't rise to this, nor to any of the other accusations and probes with which I tried her. I was convinced that her questions were in some way related to her conversation with Epsom, though I could not imagine how. I was still no wiser when we returned to the table in the buffet. Peter and Moira had left, but Kathy was still sitting, apparently quite contentedly, with Epsom.

'More coffee?' Epsom asked, as we joined them.

Pat and Kathy shook their heads, and Epsom ordered two cups. I drank mine as fast as possible, and then suggested that we should all move back to the dance hall. An uneasy silence had fallen between the four of us.

'Not me,' said Epsom. 'Still thirsty. But you two go, if you want to.'

Kathy rose instantly, and I had to follow. I didn't want to leave Epsom and Pat alone together, but there seemed nothing I could do about it. Kathy and I picked our way through the crowds to the tables in the corner of the hall. The Club gathering had thinned out slightly now, broken up into smaller groups, so that Kathy and I had a table to ourselves. As we arranged ourselves at it, I happened to glance across the table at my companion. She was looking at me; and I realised with a shock, as if I had not seen her face before that evening, that my companion was Kathy.

I was so startled that I got up immediately, excused myself, and went off to dance with Ann. I needed time to digest the situation which, apparently without volition on my or Kathy's part, had suddenly revealed itself to me. There was no escaping the fact that Kathy and I were behaving just as if an established, accepted relationship existed between us; and there was no doubt that it was intensely agreeable to both of us. But this had come about, as it were, behind my back. The tenuous hypostasis which had grown accidentally out of our mutual reserve, had suddenly manifested itself as a *fait accompli* relationship too definite to be denied. But what of Dewi? What of my own doubts and fears? As I danced with Ann, forcing my mind to grasp the intangible which I had just perceived, I realised that, whatever I might think about the Dewi-Kathy situation, or about Kathy herself (and I was incapable still of deciding what I did think), it was obviously impossible that this thing that had come to a shallow maturity between us should be allowed to remain confined solely to a corner table in a dance hall which change might prevent us from visiting together again.

When, after delivering Ann to John Stockwell, I returned to our table, Kathy had already risen to accept an invitation from Peter. She smiled sideways away from me as she left, as if to conceal something from me. I watched her move out slowly on to the crowded floor, her eyes on her own feet and the hand which Peter held poised, curved, like a bird. Her pale-yellow skirt flared suddenly outwards in a turn, and then they were both gone, swallowed by the revolving crowd.

On the table was Kathy's bulging leather handbag, an enormous affair with a catch which would never fasten. Looking at it sitting there, so much a part of Kathy's personality, and thinking how well I knew the overflowing bric-a-brac inside it, it seemed to me to be a symbol of our intimacy. I could not remember how many times I had teased Kathy about it, nor how often she had produced from it, as if she had suffered foreknowledge, the very article that the moment demanded: camomile lotion for sunburn, petrol for stains, salt at picnics, needle and thread for embarrassing tears... she hoarded things like a jackdaw, indiscriminately. I remember how, after hearing Ann complain that she couldn't find any milk chocolate in the town, Kathy arrived on the beach next day with a staggering selection, perhaps half a dozen different brands, which she forced upon everyone present, laughing, insisting that she never touched the stuff herself. One of her peculiarities, at a time when cigarettes were for the first time in short supply, was to carry in her bag a slim box of Benares brass containing an array of every imaginable kind of cigarette, Virginian, Turkish, Russian, French, Egyptian, American, which she must have been collecting for years. She did not herself smoke, but she delighted in offering this box to anyone who showed the slightest signs of wanting a cigarette. Giving, for Kathy, was a luxury, almost a sin.

When she returned from her dance I asked her, more because I had been thinking about them than because I really wanted one, for a cigarette. She laughed when I asked her: with pleasure, I suppose; and gave me the sidelong look, a mixture of complicity and shyness, with which I had become so familiar. I laughed with her. It is a wonderful relief, to laugh for no reason at all when one's emotions are so hopelessly tangled and buried that one scarcely dares to frame a coherent sentence. The orchestra was playing 'Thanks for the Memory', very slowly, languorously, and our laughter was muted to the mood of the song. I noticed that a lock of

Kathy's hair, the forelock or quiff, was fairer than the rest.

'Kathy, do you bleach your hair?' I heard myself say. Her hand flew to her crown.

'It's the sun!' she said. 'Honestly! I can't help it!' Her face glowed, scarcely a blush, more an acknowledgement that I had been looking at her. I was appalled, for a moment, by what I had said, for it was a remark too personal to pass between convenient acquaintances. Then, as the words settled, and as Kathy, leaning over her handbag with her eyes still pleading for belief in mine, parted her lips and closed them again, allowing something to escape from her, I was content that whatever had to come, should come.

'It's funny the sun didn't bleach the rest of your hair, while it was at it,' I said.

'Oh, Bernard! You are a beast. Don't you believe me? You must!'

'If you say so,' I said, pretending meekness.

'Oh, but you must, you must really believe! Say you really believe, Bernard!'

'I'll have to think about it. What about that cigarette? Perhaps that'll help me to think.'

Kathy started to rummage again. 'You can't really think,' she assured herself, 'that I'd dye my hair. You just can't, that's all.' There seemed to be some difficulty in finding, among all the junk in her bag, the little brass box; and she had to empty some of the contents on to the table. Among the apples, pen-knives, bandages, pens, and ointments which the bag disgorged, was a very pretty little cigarette case, of the narrow kind which holds five cigarettes only in each leaf. Each side was of black lacquer, with a Japanese design set into the

lacquer with mother-of-pearl. While Kathy rummaged still in
the recesses of her bag, I picked up this little box and turned
it over idly, admiring the beautifully executed design, the
perfect surface, the way the mother-of-pearl, with its constantly changing colours, seemed to be a natural view in the
lacquer, like the vein in marble.

'Why don't you use this for your cigarettes,' I asked,
'instead of that nasty brass box?'

Kathy looked up; and, seeing what was in my hands,
became immediately, agonizingly distressed.

'Oh, Bernard, please give that back to me! Please!' she
cried. 'I'm not going to pinch it,' I said. 'I'm only looking.'

'I know, but give it back now. Please, Bernard!' It was as
silly of me to have taunted her with it as it was for her to
arouse my curiosity by her pleadings. I knew, without knowing why, that I ought to hand the little lacquered case back
to her without question, but I didn't. In such circumstances
as these a curious compulsion seems to seize one, paralysing
the will and forcing one on to acts which in retrospect can
only be condemned. I held the case up with my thumbs on
the latch, looking mockingly at Kathy, as if to say 'Why,
Kathy, surely you haven't anything to hide from me?'

Kathy leaned forward and tried to take the case from me,
knocking to the floor several of the objects still scattered
about the table-top. I held the box away from her, uneasy
now, but still thinking that some joke could be made out of
her distress.

'Give it to me, Bernard!' cried Kathy commandingly.
'Give it to me. Oh, don't be so silly, you must give it to me!'

But I didn't. With Kathy stretching desperately across the

table between us, I swivelled on my chair, and, holding the case out of Kathy's reach, opened it. It was empty. But scratched with loving care on the pale blue surface of the left leaf was the message: *To Kathy, with all my love for ever, Dewi.*

I closed it with a snap, turned it over once in my hand as if completely mystified, and threw it carelessly on the table among the rest of Kathy's precious belongings.

'Why,' I said, 'there's nothing in it! Can't see what all the fuss is about!'

But Kathy wasn't deceived. She knew I had seen the message.

So quietly that I scarcely heard the words she said 'You shouldn't have opened it, Bernard. You shouldn't have!'

She started sweeping all her treasures back into her bag, picking up the things from the floor, keeping her head lowered and the bag clutched firmly against her chest, as if I might wish to snatch it away.

'Kathy, what's wrong?' I protested. 'It's a very nice little box! I can't see why you should make such a fuss just because I opened a completely empty cigarette case!'

'You shouldn't have opened it!' she said again. Then, clutching her bag, she rose from her chair and pushed past me. 'Excuse me!' she said politely, as she squeezed past. I reached out in an attempt to grasp her wrist, but she twisted away.

'Kathy, where are you going? Come back!' I called. But she was already far away, circling round the edge of the dance floor towards the cloakrooms at the other end of the hall, running. I realised that she had already, when she left me, started to cry.

For several minutes I sat on alone at the table, staring out unseeingly into the gyrating crowd, completely stunned by what had happened. Not puzzled, for I understood approximately how Kathy must be feeling; nor yet angry with myself, for I was still too close to my action to condemn it; my mind, in a sort of self-protective reaction, had simply immobilized itself, so that for a short period I thought and felt nothing at all.

Then, still without formulating an intention, I moved slowly round the edge of the dance floor towards the cloak-rooms. I had no real idea how long had elapsed since Kathy had left me, it might have been two minutes or ten. As I reached the steps leading down into the lobby, on either side of which were the cloakroom doors, I met Ann coming up.

'Hello!' she said. 'What on earth have you been doing to Kathy?'

'Where is she?'

'She's gone home. Pat went with her. She said I was to tell Epsom.'

'Who did? Kathy?'

'No, Pat. I think he's in your cloakroom.'

Ann looked at me curiously, as if on the lookout for some quality which she had hitherto missed.

'What happened, Bernard? Why was Kathy crying?'

'Was she crying?'

'You know she was!'

'I didn't know. Honestly I didn't!'

Ann gave a little toss to her head, to show her disbelief. 'I don't think you're very nice to Kathy,' she said. And

219

added, as she walked round me towards the hall 'Tell Epsom, will you?'

I found Epsom in the men's cloakroom, washing his hands.

'Ann said to tell you that Pat's gone home,' I said, joining him at the hand-basin and searching for my comb.

'What!' he exclaimed. 'Gone home! Cheeky wench! Is she ill or something?'

'She's gone home with Kathy.'

'Why?'

'She was crying.'

'Who? Pat?'

'No. Kathy.'

Epsom suddenly started to execute a little dance of rage in front of me, flicking his wet hands in my face and spluttering incoherently.

'What is it, Smith? What's up? Pat! Kathy! Crying! Ann! Gone home! What the blazes is it all about, you great stuffed MacWheeble, you! Tell me, man, can't you?'

'You needn't lose your wig, old man,' I said calmly. 'It's quite simple. Kathy was crying in the girls cloakroom, so Pat went home with her and asked Ann to tell you and Ann asked me, that's all.'

'Why was Kathy crying? Come on, Smith, give! Give!'

'I don't know.'

'My aunt!'

'I don't!'

'You're a bloody menace, that's what you are! Does Ann know?'

'I don't think so.'

220

'Did you ask her?'

'No. I mean, yes.'

'Well, did you?'

'No. She asked me.'

'And you wouldn't tell her?'

'I don't know,' I shouted violently, heaving the wet hand towel in Epsom's face. 'Now stop being a bloody lawyer, will you?'

'Well, you needn't get in a tizzy about it,' Epsom said, and added, as I made for the door 'And where do you think you're off to now?'

'Home,' I said, and slammed the door.

Epsom joined me in the lobby, carrying his raincoat. 'I'm coming with you,' he announced. I didn't want him, but couldn't very well say so; and, once we had emerged into the cold sanity of the sea-drizzle that was drifting in from the North shore, I was glad that he had forced himself on me.

Despite the drizzle, we decided to walk back along the Promenade. When we reached it, I suggested that we should go right down to the sea's edge, and walk along the shingle in sight of the faint guiding line of the surf. Down here, on a black night, with the few glimmers of light from the blacked-out town hidden by the steep bank of the beach, and the tireless sea knocking and sucking at the loose shingle beside us, one had a sharper sense of isolation than on the highest mountain or the bleakest moor. The unconfined sea, unseen, evoked itself to ear and nose so over-poweringly that one's own consciousness seemed no more than a minute, ephemeral point on the unthinkable plain of infinity; in which the crunch of one's own shoes, the movement of one's own mind were swallowed completely. There was a nihilist pleasure to be had thus; it was as near as one could get, alive, to a suspension of one's own existence.

When we emerged once more, half a mile further on, on to the Promenade, Epsom said unexpectedly 'Well, Smith, tell me all about it.'

'About what?' I said. Epsom, undeceived, simply waited for an answer without replying.

I was genuinely surprised at his question, for never before, in such a matter, had Epsom sought to probe without invitation; and in this case I had clearly indicated that I wasn't prepared to enter a discussion. Even now I made an attempt to evade the issue.

'I don't know why Pat went with her,' I said. 'After all, her tram passes the door of the hall, it isn't as if she had a long walk in the dark.'

'Don't be daft,' said Epsom patiently. 'What happened between you and Kathy.'

'Oh, nothing, really. Nothing to cry about.'

'Nothing at all?'

'Oh, well, there was some silly business about a cigarette box, that's all. I don't know what she – '

'Tell me about the cigarette box,' said Epsom.

And I found myself telling him; reluctantly at first, with disclaimers, sighs, verbal shrugs; but with a growing sense of relief. I started, at one point, trying to invent excuses for having withheld, and opened, the little case, but soon realised I didn't have to. Epsom didn't question the action, apparently understanding the sort of compulsion under which I had been acting.

'It's a pity,' Epsom said when I had finished, 'she knew you'd seen the inscription.'

'Yes. I only had it open for a sec, but you know how it is, you don't have to read a short sentence like that, if you just catch sight of it.'

'I know.'

We walked on in silence, nearly as far as the Little Orme, before turning back again towards the town.

I was glad, now, that I had shared my part in the incident with Epsom, for not only did this sharing lessen the sense of guilt which had begun to creep up on me in the cloakroom, it also put us on a new and exciting footing, so pleasurable as almost to justify the unpleasant incident which had brought it about. I had completely forgotten, in my own turmoil, the mystery of Epsom's earlier private gloom.

'It's a pity about Dewi,' said Epsom at last.

'Yes.'

'He's certainly nuts about poor Kathy.'

'Yes.'

'And Kathy's certainly nuts about you.'

'I suppose she must be.'

We were talking judicially, as if about persons known to us only at second-hand.

'The question is, of course,' said Epsom, asking his question of the black wet night about us, 'are you nuts about her?'

'I know,' I said.

'Or likely to be in the foreseeable future?'

'Quite!'

After another silence, during which we reached the

point, outside the North Western Hotel, where our ways parted, Epsom said 'If I were you, I know what I'd do.'

'What's that?'

'Become a monk. It seems to me to be the only possible solution for you, Smith.'

He sounded quite enthusiastic. 'After all, man, secular love is only a pale, temporary substitute for spiritual love. The love of God, man!' he cried, slapping my shoulders. 'That's what you're cut out for! The church represents all mankind, love the church, and you love mankind! That's the answer for you, Smith. I can't imagine why I never saw it before! It comes to me like a vision, man, Father MacWheeble Smith, S.J., the Thomist of Gogarth Abbey!'

Epsom was joking, of course; short of dropping the subject helplessly, he could do nothing else, for there was no sort of advice he could give me that would not be ridiculous or offensive. But I was alarmed all the same by the joke, for I had detected, buried under all the absurdity, a particle of earnestness. I didn't know what a Thomist was, nor what S.J. meant, but I did understand that when Epsom had said 'Become a monk' rather than, for instance, 'Shoot yourself', he was hinting, possibly without even realizing it, that I was unable to love.

To be unable to love is, for any man, the greatest tragedy that can possibly afflict him. The bare idea, half-formed, so unrealised that I could not have expressed even a faint ghost of it, was enough to make me shiver involuntarily, as I walked home down the Conway Road through the silent, penetrating drizzle, as if I had been touched by a ringer colder than death. And in reaction I began suddenly to affirm to myself what I had never before affirmed: I do love Kathy, I told myself, I do love her! And, thinking of her thus, calling up a picture of her (poised, laughing, ready for flight), I saw her freshly in the catalytic light with which acknowledged love suffuses its subject, and realised that indeed it was true; I did love her. I loved her.

I love Kathy, I said to myself, first listening to the sound of the three words, and then erecting them deliberately in print before my mind's eye, drawing every last drop of meaning from each of the separate words. And then, as I neared home, I took the meaning of the three words together into my mind, and found myself laughing out loud, as if an explosion had occurred inside me, filling me with expanding, choking fumes which only through laughter or sobs could be allowed to escape. I no longer thought of Kathy and Dewi and myself as an insoluble triangle. I thought vaguely: I shall have to do something about Kathy... But it didn't matter what. Something would turn up. I started running, still laughing, with my head up and the drizzle coming down on to my face, and arrived home breathless, surprising with my laughter the unsteady figure of my father, fumbling for the keyhole on the wrong side of the front door.

Eleven

As it turned out, I was not to see Kathy again for several weeks. Even if I had known this, I would not have minded. I needed time to get used to the idea of loving her, and I still had no idea what, if anything, I was 'going to do' about it. Just as my mind was capable of at once disbelieving in the existence of God and being apprehensive of His wrath at my lack of faith, so I could hug to myself the knowledge of my love, cherishing the most vivid visions of declaration, response, consummation, while at the same time being perfectly aware that Dewi's single-minded constancy was something I would not dare combat. I had no sense of contradiction, of conflict; the two parts of my mind acted independently, were mutually exclusive. I believed that 'love will find a way'; and I believed that Dewi's tenancy was unchallengeable.

The summer holidays began dourly, with ten days of almost continuous rain. In such moods Llandudno is not an hospitable town. The two Ormes, behind their veils of descending water, were unattractive lumps of uniform, surly grey. Between them the town sprawled wetly, uninhabited except in the shopping centres, where housewives skipped impatiently from doorway to doorway and trams splashed

226

noisily along their parallel canals. A few unlucky holiday-makers glared patiently from the porches and windows of their boarding houses. On the deserted Promenade eccentric old gentlemen strode briskly through the puddles, their faces lifted rapturously to the rain. And every morning, without fail, at eleven o'clock, Ann, Pat, and Isabel, Gregory, Epsom, and I gathered at the same table in the big downstairs room at Sumner's for morning coffee.

We all seemed to be living in a state of suspension, as if the release from our unaccustomed burst of work had left us limp, divorced by those few weeks of intense activity from our normal pursuits and without the energy to pick them up again. Ann and Gregory, who had matriculated the year before, lacked this excuse, but even so seemed to share our lassitude.

Epsom, in particular, appeared to have sunk away from the world. As soon as the term had ended we had started reading the works of Galsworthy together, but, though we had made half-hearted attempts to invest the Forsyte family with our own personal fourth dimension, we had completely failed to bring these bumbling Victorians to life. Often Pat and Epsom and I would sit on in Sumner's, long after the others had left, and, while Epsom silently sipped his way through six cups of coffee, all three of us would remain sunk in private, and, on my part, almost blank-minded reverie.

But out of these three-handed coffee sessions there arose, as there had arisen between Kathy and me at the dance hall, a kind of pleasurable companionship which came increasingly to be acknowledged by each of us. I first became aware of it, as something outside the accidents of friendship, when, wanting to suggest to Epsom that we should visit the cinema that evening, I found myself impatiently awaiting the departure of all the others at the table... except Pat. I realised then that I wanted, or, not wanted, but expected, Pat to accompany us. And when, after the others had gone, I finally made the suggestion, enquiring equally of Pat as of Epsom, it was accepted by both without a moment's selfconsciousness. In our world, where precedent had the weight of law, it was a matter of significance to make a new departure in personal relationships, and this significance was I think apparent to all of us. Our visit to the cinema that night had something ceremonial about it; a mute acknowledgement that a new pleasure had entered our lives.

We took, thereafter, to arriving at Sumner's at half past eleven, instead of eleven, so as to have less time with the others, more on our own. And when, finally, the rains came to an end and a period of fine weather began, the three of us went out on our bicycles in the afternoons, or sometimes for the whole day, to explore the little local lanes and villages, Pydew, Glan Wydden, Bodysgallen, Llangwstenin, and the Pabo Hills which for some reason we seemed never to have had time to investigate before. We began visiting obscure churches and chapels, and ruins, and examining with interest nameless landmarks which had hitherto been nothing but unremarkable features of a familiar world.

For me, at least, this was a peaceful time, full of quiet riches. Though Epsom was, in a sense, more distant from me than before, concentrating as if by a deliberate policy on the impersonal outside world, obsessed more and more with the past – preferably the ecclesiastical past – this did not now bother me as once it would have done. I had now my own secret, a private emotional life of which he – and everyone else – knew nothing. I carried it with me like a talisman which I could touch and fondle at moments of distress.

I saw Kathy, for the first time since the dance, on a wet day some three or four weeks after the end of term. I was on my way to Sumner's, already later than usual. Kathy's bicycle was leaning against a tree outside the Library; I had just recognized it, and stopped to gaze, when its owner appeared at the top of the Library steps. She came down on to the pavement before she saw me.

Because it did not pleasantly fit the love story which I was busy constructing around Kathy's person, I had dismissed the incident of the lacquered cigarette case from my mind. It was an intrusion too deep in its complexities for simple solution; and since I could entertain no vision of our coming together but that of instantaneous rapprochement, it had been necessary to erase the memory altogether. Now, seeing Kathy face to face like this, the difficulty of reconciling fiction with reality was too great for me; my mind went completely blank.

Possibly Kathy turned and went up the steps into the Library again immediately she saw me; it seems most likely. The impression I retained, though, was that we stood there, staring inactively at each other, for about ten minutes before she moved. When she had gone, I crossed the road, walking on towards Sumner's, hurrying for fear of missing my friends. I was not at all depressed by the meeting; rather, I was elated. I was content that I should have seen her, so beautiful there on the Library steps, the miraculous object of my love. I felt that the meeting had had a profound significance; and that she had turned back through a sudden access of shyness on seeing in my face the love which, I felt, to her must now be so obvious.

When I reached Sumner's, Epsom and Pat were there alone. I ordered myself a coffee, and another cup for Epsom.

'That's your seventh!' said Pat accusingly.

'It isn't, it's my fifth!' Epsom retorted. 'You can't count.'

'Yes I can. And you've already had six. Ann said you'd had two before I arrived, and I've seen you drink four, so there! You'll poison yourself!'

'Nonsense! Very nourishin' stuff, coffee. Full of barbitocalotherms and things. Anyway, it's too late now. Here it comes.'

This was ritual. Pat always insisted that Epsom would make himself ill if he drank so much coffee, and had ruled that six cups in one morning was the absolute limit. Epsom played this game, of trying to outwit her vigilance, every morning. He took a simple, touching delight in succeeding.

'I've just seen Kathy,' I announced suddenly, for no particular reason. Epsom looked at me with curiosity, Pat with interest.

'Oh, is she coming? Did she say anything about the place? Does she like it?' Pat asked. It seemed to me that she was asking some other, unaskable, question.

'Like what? What place?'

'Didn't she tell you?'

'Tell me what? No, I didn't have a chance to speak to her. But what... ?'

230

I realised suddenly the irrelevance of announcing that I'd just seen Kathy, if I hadn't spoken to her; plainly, that was the cause of Epsom's frown. He was looking into his coffee cup, listening intently.

Pat said 'But don't you know about the... she's learning shorthand and typing at the Secretarial College at Colwyn Bay. That's why she hasn't been around lately. Surely you – '

'I didn't know. Nobody tells me anything. And I haven't seen her since – '

I remembered suddenly about the lacquered cigarette box; and that it had been Pat who had seen her home, in tears. I blushed, not so much with present embarrassment, as at the realization that throughout the past fortnight, in my company, Pat must have been conscious at the back of her mind of the incident which I had wilfully expunged from mine.

Epsom said, surprisingly 'I told Pat about that. I was sure you wouldn't mind.'

'It wasn't your fault,' said Pat.

'Well, in a way...' I said. I was glad Pat knew; otherwise she might have thought, as Ann thought, that I had treated Kathy with deliberate cruelty. Ann had lost no opportunity, for the first few days after the dance, of letting me know that she thought I ought to be ashamed of myself.

'Did Kathy say anything?' I asked. I saw – I thought I saw – Pat's eyes meet Epsom's for a moment. She appeared to be thinking back, trying to remember.

At last she said 'Not about the box.'

'About what, then?'

Again I thought Pat sought some help from Epsom.

'Nothing... nothing to do with – ' Pat began.

'She said,' Epsom said slowly, still examining the dregs of his cup, 'she said she didn't want to see you again.'

I laughed, and they both looked sharply at me, as if I were being sick. I don't know why I should have laughed, but I suppose if one wants to cry, and can't, one laughs instead. But there was more to my laugh than that.

'Did she say why?' I said, hearing the oddness of my own voice.

'No,' said Pat.

'Yes,' said Epsom, 'she said... what did she say, Pat?'

'Well, she did say you just think she's funny. I don't know what...'

Yes, I believed that, I could hear Kathy saying that: not aggrieved, rather as if she knew she was funny but couldn't help it and wasn't really: he just thinks I'm funny!

'What should I do?' I said; I was asking myself, really, thinking aloud. I couldn't yet properly appreciate what I'd just heard, it assorted so ill with the romantic picture of our falling wordlessly into each other's arms which I had so carefully cherished during the past weeks.

'Do you want to do anything?' asked Epsom pointedly. Pat was watching me with her lips parted, as if wanting to speak for me, will words from my mouth. I thought of Dewi, fiercely proprietorial. I thought of Kathy.

'Yes,' I said hoarsely; then I swallowed, and said, 'Yes!' again in a more normal voice. 'I don't think she's funny.'

What I wanted to say was: I love her. But how could I, how could I face Epsom and Pat across a coffee table in Sumner's, and say 'I love her'? The words were not in our vocabulary.

232

But I think I was well enough understood. Pat said 'That's what I told her. Of course, I didn't know about the cigarette case, then.'

Pat, I noticed, was blushing; I suppose at the naked affirmation of the inscription; one ought not to know about such things.

'It may be difficult for her to face you, now,' Epsom said. 'Anyway, I'm not sure – '

'What?'

'Nothing.'

Suddenly I discovered that the waitress, without my noticing it, had placed fresh cups of coffee in front of Epsom and myself. I hadn't seen them ordered.

'Eight!' said Pat. 'You'll die!'

'Six!' said Epsom complacently.

I didn't see either Epsom or Pat for a few days after this. I had to go to Crewe to attend a Naval Selection Board, for I had applied earlier to be accepted under the 'Y' scheme as a potential officer, and had, at Easter, attended a curious series of 'Intelligence Tests' at Caernarvon. I was terrified of the interview, but I think managed to answer the questions coherently, if not intelligently. They seemed surprised that I had only just sat the School Certificate examinations, and asked me to send them the results as soon as they were out. 'You'll be hearing from us,' they said, ominously, as I left. Then I went into the next room and took all my clothes off in front of a very ill-tempered doctor, but that was quite a relief after the interview.

I had cycled to Crewe in one day, having sold my railway warrant at two-thirds its value to my Father, who wanted, for some reason, to go to Wolverhampton on the same day. But I took my time about returning. My bicycle was hung about with the oddments of camping equipment. I had a tent and blanket-roll in the saddle-bag and money enough for several days, so I enjoyed a leisurely, solitary ride down through Shropshire to Builth Wells in Brecknock, across to the coast and northwards within sight of the sea for forty miles to Harlech; and from Harlech round the flanks of Snowdon to the Conway Valley and home. I didn't wish that anyone was with me; I was enjoying, for the first time, a sense of absolute freedom, of being my own master, choosing my own roads, stopping when I wanted, speeding when I wanted, choosing my own resting place at night. Once, having risen late, I cycled on far into the night, past midnight, pleasantly scared by bats and owls but feeling a deep, almost mystic companionship for the night animals, the hares and rabbits and stoats that my masked headlight disturbed, and the trees closing overhead, and the hidden streams in their black gullies, and the stars that appeared and were lost and appeared again, and all the silent breathing countryside on either side. This was a sort of reality I could understand.

When I turned up at Sumner's again, after my absence, I found a whole crowd from the school there, more than ever before: Peredur, Isabel, Dora, Pat, Epsom, Gregory, Peter, and many more, several of them having nothing to do with us and our circle. I went across to join Epsom, Pat, and Peter, who were sitting at our usual table, taking a chair with me as I went.

'The man himself,' said Epsom, 'MacWheeble Smith. You owe me ten cigarettes, MacWheeble.'

234

'Nonsense!' I said at once. Epsom, if he wanted to borrow five shillings, always used the formula 'You owe me five shillings, Smith!'

'Oh well!' said Epsom, shrugging. 'If you'd really rather I gave you a hundred, I'll drop a note to the examiners....'

Then the penny dropped. 'The results, my God, the results! Where are they? Did I pass?'

'The lady,' said Epsom, 'has got the list.'

Pat handed me a slip of paper, an extract, I supposed, from the complete list which must have been posted up in the school that morning.

'SMITH, Bernard Evan,' I read, 'Mathematics C., Art C., English Lit. D., English Lang. D., History C., French C., Phys. P., Chem. P., Geography D.'

'I'll buy you a hundred!' I said.

'Buy me a coffee, boy, that's more to the point.'

'Four!' said Pat.

The relief was exquisite, yet I knew now that I had not been seriously worried about the result. I also knew that if I had had to take it again, that week, I would have failed.

Epsom had done even better, with four Distinctions – the same as mine, and History – and the rest Credits. My own failure – for a Pass meant ludicrously low marks – in Chemistry and Physics was only to be expected. I noted that at some other tables there was rather less jubilation than at ours. Pat's result was exactly the same as mine, though the Passes, Credits, and Distinctions were differently disposed. Peter grinned at us all benevolently. I thought of Kathy, and searched again through the list. She had passed – but only just.

235

After the first shock I found that I was more excited than dismayed by Kathy's remark about not wanting to see me again. Though it meant readjusting my mental ideas of the eventual reconciliation, I now found it possible to assimilate the incident at the dance hall, and began to plan a series of improbable situations in which I would use the incident as an introduction, a lead-in, to the declaration of love which I had now so often rehearsed.

But I was in no hurry to take action; indeed, when I daydreamed, I imagined no action I could take; the situation was resolved, as it were, from outside: Dewi would be killed mountaineering, and at his funeral Kathy would read on my face the naked signs of devotion which through the years I had so selflessly concealed; or she would come to me, unable to bear it longer, and throw herself on my mercy as the only man in the world who could make her happy.

And so I let the summer drift by in dreams, in which time and place were mixed, and Kathy was present on some distant battlefield to witness my heroic (and useless, of course, for he would be dead when I brought him in) rescue of Dewi from under the very muzzles of enemy guns. Epsom, Pat, and I remained together, seeing little of the rest of the gang, immersed in ourselves and our discoveries. Pat revealed an interest in, and knowledge of, architecture which surprised us both, for we had imagined that the subject was limited entirely to churches and ruins. So our bicycle rides began to extend themselves to take in places which, if I had known about them at all, I would never have imagined could hold any interest for me. Epsom had discovered Donne and Hopkins, out of which ill-assorted pair he produced a hybrid poetry of his own, mystical, rich, and obscure. I found, solitary and unwanted in a secondhand bookshop, a ragged copy of Spender's Poems and, keeping it hidden from Epsom, produced a number of Spender-like verses which plainly had him puzzled until he discovered the source of my inspiration.

'You'll never make a poet,' he said once. 'You're ashamed of using your nut. You wouldn't write at all if you hadn't got a masochistic impulse to confess. You ought to become a Catholic!'

He was right about the impulse to confess; but becoming a Catholic was the last thing my temperament leaned towards. I could not have been further from a religious frame of mind than I was that summer. Yet, so great was my inertia, so ingrained my ability to think one thing and do the other, that I continued, through habit, friendship, laziness, and perhaps to a small degree because I could not escape the feeling of virtue which it gave me, to attend regularly with Epsom the services at Trinity Church on Sunday mornings. Indeed, my impulse to break away was less strong now than it had been at Christmas. My faith, if it had ever existed, had died completely; but I had so deliberately fostered the divorce between the words I heard and said, and their meaning, that I was now capable of attending church, a complete unbeliever, without any sense of hypocrisy. I knew that when Epsom left me in November, I would cease to attend. Meanwhile there was the singing, and Epsom's company, and the pleasure, the sense of occasion, in being clean and tidily dressed, and the fresh, settled feeling of joining the subdued, respectable crowd at the church gates, almost as if I had a right to be there.

But Epsom came to me one day with a bombshell which made me wish I had revealed my deceitfulness long before. We were alone in Sumner's that morning, Pat having gone to Bangor in connection with the nursing vacancy that awaited her there at the end of the year. I had been conscious, from the rapidity with which he was getting through his cups of coffee, that Epsom had something on his mind. Even so, I was caught unawares, in the middle of an heroic daydream, when he finally broke the silence.

He said 'Listen, Smith, I've been thinking. Do you have any particular conception of Good and Evil?'

'What do you mean?'

'Well, how do you think of them? Do you imagine a sort of army of Evil, with the Devil as General, and an army of Good with God as General? Or do you think of them as attributes distributed among men and women rather like fair hair and dark hair... no, I mean like being muscular or being feeble, because although you inherit one or the other, will power can overcome one or weakness undermine the other? Or do you think of them as being like magnetism, something which exists around us without having any form, but which can nevertheless pull us in opposite directions? Or... well, how do you think of them?'

'I don't think I've ever thought about it,' I said. 'But I suppose the magnetism is the proper way....'

'What do you mean, proper? Orthodox?'

'I suppose so.'

'No. Oh no, that's not orthodox. I think the first one, the armies, is the orthodox one. But I don't think about them like that at all. Look: you think of life for a minute as a river, with a big mill pool, and a mill standing on its banks. Now, we're all standing around the pool, and our job is to keep the mill race running, stop the banks from falling in, keep the weeds out of the pool, so that the mill can keep on grinding away. That's the Good, you see. If we do nothing, or push stones into the mill race, or plant weeds in the pool, that's Evil. Now Good feeds off the flour which the mill produces, and Evil feeds off the slime on the pool when it gets stagnant. So the great thing is to keep the water running. You can think of the river above the pool as the future, and below the mill as the past. And since the past affects the future, you want the water to keep on running, because if it doesn't there won't be enough water in the sea to be evaporated and come back as clouds and fall as rain to keep the river full and the mill running. And if the mill isn't running there won't be enough flour ground to feed us with Good so that we can go on working to keep the water flowing. Do you see what I mean? Let's have some more delicious coffee.'

'Yes,' I said. I didn't entirely understand; but I remembered a very involved poem of Epsom's in which the same image occurred, and which I now began to appreciate for the first time.

'Like Nellie Deane?' I asked; that had been the title of the poem.

'Good man! Yes. Does it make sense?'

'I think so.'

'Good. Now then, do you agree that if my picture of Good and Evil makes sense – and it's only a personal picture, just the way I look at things – then you can say that Good feeds on Good and Evil on Evil?'

'I'd say that anyway, without the river business.'

'Well, yes. I just wanted to make myself clear. So if I clout you over the ear 'ole, you're going to be much more likely to clout someone else if you get the chance than you would otherwise?'

'No, not necessarily. I might forgive you.'

'Ah, but only if you'd had plenty of that nice flour to eat! And remember, though you might be well fed at the time, and forgive me, my action in clouting you has bunged up the mill race and diminished the supply of grain. And the next time someone trod on your corns you might be hungry, and clout them on the ear 'ole yourself. And that would bung up the mill race still more, so there'd be even less flour ground... and there's still this element going around with a cauliflower ear just waiting for someone to tread on *his* corns. See what I mean? It all adds up.'

'So what?'

'Exactly. So what? So if someone commits an evil act, and you commit another evil act in order to get your own back, though you may stop him from committing another evil act, you have, by committing one yourself, made it more likely that someone else in the future will commit one. You've diminished the store of Good in the world.'

'Two blacks don't make a white, in fact.'

'No, more than that. Two blacks make another black, and three blacks make five, and five blacks make eight. Compound interest.'

'What about if you do nothing?'

'If you do nothing, you get the law of Diminishing Returns. That's all right, but it only works if a lot of people

240

do nothing and a lot of people work for Good. It's much better to repay an evil act with a good one. Do you agree?'

I was beginning to wonder where all this unusual speculation was to lead us. I was certain by now that Epsom was pushing me towards a conclusion I would find unacceptable, and I was seeking frantically for flaws in his argument. But unfortunately our minds worked on such different levels that, while the discussion was still centred around his river analogy, I was at a disadvantage: for although I understood it, I could not visualize it in terms of human life as I knew it. So far, I had concluded that I was being forced to accept some article of Christian dogma and was determined to resist.

'Do you mean to say,' I said, 'that if we had a great bully at school, who was always going around beating up the smaller boys, and you knew you could stop him by giving him a good thrashing, you wouldn't?'

'That's right. I certainly wouldn't.'

'But that's... You can't say that, man! There he is, committing evil acts all over the place, and you'd let him go on instead of stopping him! You'd be committing a good act, if you stopped him.'

'No, no, that's just the point, it wouldn't be a good act. It's never a good act, to thrash somebody. Never! It leaves a mark, it increases the store of evil. Certainly I'd try to stop him, I'd talk to him, do things for him, follow him about, make a bloody nuisance of myself. I'd stop him, in the end. And he'd remember it. He'd be a power for Good, after that.'

'What if he turned on you and said he'd push your face in if you didn't leave him alone?'

Epsom spread out his hands on the table, stretching his blunt, spatulate fingers as if considering the strength in them that he did not want to use.

'I'd let him push,' he said. He was silent for a moment; then, grabbing his cup, he drained the dregs of coffee in it, put it down quickly, crookedly, in its saucer, and began to speak very fast, urgently.

'Listen, man, you can't go on hitting someone who doesn't hit back. Let him hit. Then go back for more. Let him hit again. And go back for more again. He couldn't keep it up. Say he killed me. There'd be someone else to pick up where I left off. The man isn't born who could keep that up. I doubt if he'd ever get around to hitting me a second time. And remember, all this isn't happening in a vacuum. There's other people watching. It has an effect on them, as well as on him. You can't resist goodness, naked goodness. It's overpowering, when you really see it and recognize it. It's like love, it fills you. Of course, it is love. And evil can't resist love. Can you think of anyone, in the whole of history, who was entirely evil?'

'Hitler?' I said at once; history wasn't my strong point.

'Good heavens, no! Very evil, but not entirely evil. Wrong-headed. But what about the roads he built, the social reforms he introduced? Of course, he went about everything the wrong way, because he didn't know Good from Evil. But even the worst things, the concentration camps and killings and all that, he did because he thought the end would be good. Barmy, of course, but not entirely evil. If you're entirely evil you do evil for Evil's sake, not for a mistaken idea of Good. No, there's no such thing. But there's been plenty of entirely good people, from Christ downwards.'

'That's not the Christian view. What about original sin?'

'I'm talking about acts, man, acts. I know we can't help having the possibility of evil in us, as long as we're born into a world which contains evil, but if a man never commits an act of evil, then we can say he's entirely good. But on the other hand, it's impossible never to commit an act of good. Impossible. If a man like Hitler never did anything good in his whole adult life, there'd still be the time he gave half his banana to his kid sister when he was six years old. Somewhere in his life, if only we knew, we'd find someone that he had loved for a moment. No, man, you've got to admit, the Good's got an edge on the Evil. The problem is to increase that edge, bit by bit, until the Evil goes under once and for all.'

'But look here, Epsom!' I protested. 'What about if something evil beats something good, because the good won't fight it? You've then got a victory of evil, which will lead to more evil and so on....'

'That,' said Epsom, sighing slightly as if at last coming down to brass tacks, 'is the point. Now, look: take the case of two very small nations, one of them very very evil, and one good. You would say that the good one ought to fight the evil one, would you?'

'If they were attacked, yes. Perhaps even if they weren't, if the evil seemed bad enough.'

'My God, how low can you get, Smith? You've reached expediency now. It's not money, it's expediency that's the root of all evil. Listen, say the evil nation attacked the good one, and the good one refused to fight. Just sat there and let the evil one walk in. The whole world's watching, remember, and is influenced by the sight of so much goodness. Of course, a lot of idiots say the good nation ought to have resisted, but they can't help admiring a chap who has principles, and sticks to them. Then what happens? The evil nation goes on and attacks the next good nation. Say this nation, inspired by the martyrdom of the other, also martyrs itself? The rest of the world is now deeply moved by all this, and what's happening in the conquered countries? The army of the original evil country is scattered throughout the lands of the other two. The soldiers, who went there intent on rape and murder, find themselves being invited into people's homes and fed and given affection. They begin to wonder what all the fuss was about. Some of them marry girls from the conquered country and have children. They discover that a nation is only made up of human beings who want a patch of land to lie down on, a good meal, a laugh, a drink, and someone they love to take to bed. Maybe the leaders of this once terribly evil country manage to round up enough of their soldiers to make an assault on the next peaceful nation. But if this third nation takes off its hat politely when the tanks and armoured cars come pouring across the frontier, and says 'Welcome, come and have a drink'... well, I mean, that's the end of that. Evil can't stand up to that sort of treatment! And think of the effect on the rest of the world of watching a practical demonstration of the defeat of evil by good, like that! And stupid people,' Epsom concluded sadly, 'only understand experimental proof.'

I was aware of having been emotionally swayed by Epsom's peroration. But I wasn't convinced. The implications of his argument were so foreign to me that I felt sure there must be a serious flaw in his argument. Only I couldn't see it.

'But that's just an ideal picture, it's a dream!' I protested. 'That isn't the way things happen! There's no such thing as a good nation which would lie down like that under an evil one! If the Jerries came over here now, would you invite them into your house, or let one of them marry your sister, if you had one?'

'No, I don't suppose I would. But I ought to. If I was strong enough, and courageous enough, I would. Of course, I'm surrounded by evil. I can't help being influenced. If our hypothetical bully pushed my face in, I might intend to take it, and forgive him, and try again, but in fact it's much more likely that I'd lose my temper and bash him back. But that's no argument for intending to fight him in the first place! Perhaps I wouldn't invite the Jerries into my house, but I ought to! To do that sort of thing needs a kind of courage stronger than any a soldier will ever need. And if I did find the courage, perhaps it would help other people to do the same. It's only another drop of water in the pool, but it all helps. We've just got to try. Not just in the big things, like going to war, but in the small Jones, like the cup of coffee you're going to buy me and the fag I'm going to give you. It all adds up.'

I was baffled. I couldn't see where he was wrong, but he had to be wrong. Was his whole conception of Good and Evil wrong? It must be, but there was no way I could see of demolishing it. And I had nothing to put in its place.

When the new coffees were being placed in front of us, a thought struck me.

'What about the Resistance Group, then?' I asked. 'What about all that stuff up at the bothy?'

Epsom rested his teeth on the rim of his coffee cup, grinning at me through the steam. Then he closed his eyes, took a sip, and put the cup down.

'I burnt the lot,' he said calmly. 'Of course, we left the food and blankets and things. But we burnt all the arms, and chucked the ammunition in the stream. Pat and I went up while you were at Crewe. She thinks I'm off my head!'

'My God, you must be! Damn, man, what about my old man's revolver?'

'Burnt.'

'Iyssi Christ! And the two-twos?'

'Burnt. Burnt the whole lot. We had a smashing bonfire, and then bashed 'em about with a hammer and piled rocks on top of them. You ought to have seen Peter's fire bombs going up – splendid, they were. We left the padlock unlocked, by the way, so someone's going to have fun when they find the other stores.'

'You're crazy!' I said. I was so astonished I couldn't even protest against the loss of my father's revolver. I really did think he was crazy, then. After all, it's one thing to natter about good and evil over a cup of coffee, but quite another to go around burning and hammering into scrap-iron a perfectly good collection of weapons. Also, I couldn't help remembering the labour of carrying all that wretched stuff up from the Room, and the way Epsom had flogged us on until it was done. 'Absolutely off your bloody rocker!'

'But I thought you agreed with me!' said Epsom, with false innocence. 'You didn't disprove my argument, did you? The other thing's just a logical conclusion, that's all.'

'No, I didn't disprove it,' I said, beginning to get slightly angry. 'But I'm sure you're wrong. Damn it, man, you're behaving like a bloody pacifist!'

'Yes,' said Epsom.

He dropped that affirmation off-handedly into the space between us, as if it were of no importance. But I knew, as soon as I saw his lips framing the word, that it was the point at which he had been aiming from the beginning. I remembered then the signs which I had noted before, the withdrawal, the pensive silences; and remembered too a number of other little incidents which had not seemed significant at the time, like his attempt at arbitration between Dewi and myself, but which now fell into place. 'I think a fight's stupid,' he had said, 'it doesn't solve anything.'

But then, I had agreed with him. Now, in trying to apply a principle to the field of world politics, which I could only consider valid in the limited parochial sense, I felt he had overreached himself. There must be a flaw in his argument somewhere; if I couldn't see it, and I was aware of my limitations in dialectics, I was sure that older, better-equipped men would be able to.

Epsom said 'I'm going to see the Sprocket this afternoon,' (the Sprocket was our Maths master, Mr. Brock, and Commanding Officer of the school A.T.C.) 'to resign from the A.T.C. Would you come?'

'I suppose so,' I said doubtfully. I still felt that if only I could find the hinge I'd be able to lift the lid off his argument, and, as I saw it, release him.

'Look here,' I said, 'do you mean to say you're going to resist call-up? Refuse to serve?'

'Yes. I shall have to register, of course, and there'll be a tribunal. I shall have to write to the Navy people. It's rather a pity you talked me into volunteering, it'll weaken my case a bit. But I don't mind if I don't win it. I still shan't serve.'

'But damn it, man, how can you sit there, a boy of seventeen, and calmly announce that the whole British nation is wrong except you? Do you want the Nazis to win?'

'Don't be stupid!' Epsom exclaimed, with a flash of anger. 'If there's a fight between Good and Evil going on I want the Good side to win. But I still think it's evil to fight at all. My little gesture won't affect the war one way or another, I'm perfectly aware of that. But it's a drop in the mill pool, it all adds up, and one day there'll be so many of us that in the distant future the politicians won't be able to have war, because there'll be no one willing to fight it. Then they'll be chucked out and we'll have the first Pacifist Government. It'll spread. It can't help spreading. Evil has had a good run for its money, but its days are numbered. Even you, Smith,' Epsom said, fixing his bulbous eyes humorously on mine, 'even you, after this conversation, will never fight a war with an entirely easy mind.'

I found myself beginning to splutter. The whole thing seemed so crazy, yet so firmly rooted in the inflexible logic of nonsense, that I didn't really know what to say, what attitude to take.

'But, God Almighty, man, think of all the clever people, the lawyers and bishops and writers and philosophers, who support this war! They can't all be wrong, and you, a boy of seventeen, be right!'

248

'Christ,' said Epsom apologetically, 'was right when he was ten.'

'I suppose you think you're the Second Coming?' I said.

Immediately I wished the unthought words unsaid. It was a terrible thing to say. I saw a flush came up slowly across his face, and was glad that his eyes were closed to the shame in mine. But he didn't say anything. He just sat there, with his palms closed about his cold coffee cup, his eyelids lowered, shining purple, his lips sucked tightly against his teeth, letting the silence lengthen; and I had a spiteful thought 'Practising,' I thought to myself, 'at being Good.'

At last, awkwardly, hurriedly, I said 'I'm sorry. I shouldn't have said that. I didn't think. You've got me all confused, that's all.'

Epsom opened his eyes, and gradually his face, which had been tight, cracked, his upper lip flew up, his eyebrows rode up his forehead, and he was grinning.

'I have, haven't I?' he said, 'By damn, I have got you confused!'

Suddenly he put back his head and shouted with laughter, drawing the frowns of the nice waitress and the nasty housewives at the other tables. The laugh stopped as suddenly as it began, and he was serious again.

'You're not a Christian any more, are you?' he asked.

'No.'

'I've known for a long time. What is it? Anything particular? Christ? God? Holy Trinity?'

'All of 'em,' I said, with beautiful relief, amazed to find how easy it was. 'I don't believe a word of it!'

'Why did you keep on coming to church, then?'

'Oh, I dunno. Lots of things. I like the singing. I didn't want to... oh, I dunno. It was fun, in a way.'

Epsom looked at me wryly. 'I've often wondered about you, Smith,' he said. 'What is it you've got that's so precious you can never quite bring yourself to give it away?'

'What on earth do you mean?'

'If you don't know that, chum,' he said, 'you don't know nutting. Well, come on, let's go and have some lunch and then tackle the Sprocket.'

Epsom barked suddenly with laughter again.

'Poor old Sprocket,' he said. 'All alone out there in the Infinite, dressed in a reach-me-down Quantum Theory! I bet he's cold!'

By mutual agreement, we did not mention the subject of pacifism while we were having lunch (at my house) or walking to the Sprocket's house at West Shore afterwards. I wanted to see Pat, alone, before I involved myself in argument with Epsom again. I felt sure that if she and I, similarly convinced, could talk it over together, we would find the flaw which must exist in his argument. As we walked down the long straight road from the gasworks to Maes Du I felt slightly uplifted by my mission, as I saw it, of saving Epsom from himself; and at the same time was able to admire in myself the loyalty that made me stick by him, even though I disagreed with him, in his hour of trial.

While Epsom was in the Sprocket's house – one of those semi-detached villas that always seem to be in imminent danger of being swallowed by the drifting sands from the dunes – I sat alone in a shabby little cafe near the tram terminus, reading the commonplace book which Epsom had lent me.

It was a very fat book, pocket-sized, bound in black leather, and I had been with him when he bought it for two shillings in the Mostyn Street antique shop. The pages were of plain glossy paper, browning towards the edges. Already, Epsom's notes, quotations, comments, ideas for poems, filled nearly a third of it.

As I turned the pages, I was aware of a curious, disturbing impression, growing stronger the more closely I examined the book: it seemed to me to be the casual accumulations of a mind which I did not know; a book compiled by a stranger.

There were, of course, things which I recognized: the first sketch for the plot of our verse play, odd gobbets of poetry which we had discovered together, or to which he had introduced to me, detailed analyses of ideas which he had first tried out, conversationally, in my presence. But there were pages upon pages which reflected a conscious-ness, a direction of interest, which did not at once connect with the Epsom I thought I knew.

Most of his quotations were unacknowledged; and though I felt fairly certain of recognizing his verse when I saw it, much of the prose which I was able to pin on him simply from internal evidence, might well, I felt, have been a quotation from some eighteenth-century essayist:

It is this mass of unclean world that we have superimposed on the clean world that we cannot bear.

Under the feet of the living is this great pyramid of the dead, not still, but writhing restlessly, making our stance unsteady.

When one has put forth all one's strength to raise what seems like an enormous weight, it is annoying to find that the dumb bell is made of cardboard and could have been lifted between two fingers.

There is always a way to heaven, even from the gates of hell.

It might as well be assumed, as indeed it generally is assumed by implication, that a murder committed with a poisoned arrow is different from a murder committed with a Mauser.

I am not strong enough to bear such tokens of your love.

It should read: 'Let us honour if we can
The committed man
Though we emulate none
But the indifferent one.'

It is possible to see, in the reproductive habits of the slug, a microcosm of mankind. For indeed we are but hermaphrodites of the spirit uncertain of the nature of virtue, and when our good and our evil copulate together neither can be said to have seduced the other for they have become one.

Lincoln said 'The world will little note nor long remember what we say here, but it can never forget what they did here.' But in fact the Address is far better known than the events of Gettysburg!

Out of such pages as these I found it almost impossible to sort quotation from direct comment. Often I was unable to see any significance in the short sentences which he had noted down, yet it was obvious that for him they must have had some special importance. Then, too, there were quotations which seemed to reveal an acquaintance with whole areas of knowledge or literature whose existence I had not even suspected. I wondered constantly, where did he read this, when? When was he thinking like this? And tried to extract from the past some picture of Epsom that would fit the page in front of me. But I could not. And I realised then that the reason I could not lay in my own self-absorption, my habit of always seeing Epsom – and, indeed, everyone else – as an extension of myself. I believed only in what little reality I was prepared to lend to other people, never suspecting that behind the two-dimensional facades which I accepted as the whole person might live and grow deeper, more complicated human beings than myself.

In Epsom's case, of course, the facade had been lent, by intimacy, a certain apparent depth. But all the more so because of this, I had never imagined that there was still hidden this other person, this privately thinking, feeling stranger that the commonplace book revealed. Reading it now, I was moved by sadness, that somewhere, at some point in our friendship, I should have failed in sympathy to such an extent that Epsom had had to let this other self grow in solitude.

When he came into the café to rejoin me, I could see that he was angry. He came in quickly, forgetting to slouch, and ordered two cups of tea in a brusque, impatient voice as if certain that, when it came, it would be of an inferior quality.

'I'm furious!' he said as he sat down. 'I ought not to be, but I can't help it. He's a guilt-raddled old atheist. Do you know what he said to me?'

'If he had his way he'd have you shot?' I asked facetiously.

'No, I wouldn't have minded that. No, he said, "Jones",
he said, (Epsom imitated the tinny squeak of the Sprocket's
voice), "Jones, I can't help feeling you're being very selfish.
Think of the reputation of the School!" he said. "Think of
the shame we shall all feel at having produced a Conchie!"
Do you know what I said?'

'No?'

'I said, "Bugger the School, Mister Brock," and walked
out. I know I shouldn't have, but I couldn't help it. My
God! Think of the reputation of the School!'

'You didn't really say that, did you?' I asked.

'Yes, I did. I'm sorry about it now, I suppose I shall have
to write and apologize, the poor man can't help being a
fool. He said he was a Logical Positivist, whatever that is.
He thinks God is the square root of minus one, Ovid was
Christ, and Einstein's the Second Coming! I told him that
when we had World Government all mathematicians would
be put to work on collective farms because Maths drives
people mad and is therefore antisocial. Now he thinks I'm
a bloody Bolshie.'

'You didn't say that?'

'I did. I was getting angry by then. Come on, let's go,
this tea tastes like a squeezed flannel.'

I had never known Epsom as he was that afternoon.
Something – perhaps his conversation with the Sprocket –
seemed to have released a spring in him, so that all the
pent-up energy his mind had been storing was now
restlessly searching for an object on which to unleash itself.
He walked quickly, with his head up, talking, talking,
talking, changing the subject constantly, scarcely listening

to my replies. He talked about religion, about mediaeval poetry, about the nature of love, about Welsh history, about the Club, about Peter's theory of Creation, in which Science and the Bible were superbly reconciled. He talked as he had never talked to me before, and I began, for the first time in our relationship, to feel that something more than the ever-present barrier between one consciousness and another separated us; began, indeed, to see the quality of my mind as coarse, immature, amorphous.

Pat came in to Sumner's the next morning, but I was not able to see her alone until the following day, when Epsom had an interview with the Headmaster at about the time we usually met for coffee. But by this time I felt I had the answer; had found, if not a flaw in the argument, at least a compromise that might save him from the worst horrors of his position.

I did not tell Pat this. I told her that I had an idea that I wanted to put to him, but wouldn't say what it was. I had intended to, expecting to elicit her support. But, when Gregory and Helen, who had overstayed their welcome so far as I was concerned, at last left us, and I was able to reveal to Pat that I now knew what she had known ever since that night at the dance hall, she told me, with the faintly smiling gentleness that I had come to value in her, that she was 'on his side'.

For some reason the phrase irritated me.

'I'm on his side, if it comes to that,' I said, 'whatever he does. I'd be on his side if he committed a murder. I just think he's wrong, that's all.'

'I think he's right,' said Pat simply.

'And everyone else in the country is wrong?'

'Not everyone. There's three thousand Conscientious Objectors in prison now – or if they aren't still there, they have been. In 1916 there were twenty-two thousand of them, and nearly seven thousand were arrested. I looked it up. And there's masses of people who think the way Epsom does but haven't the courage of their convictions. The more Conchies there are, the more there'll be.'

'Mainly religious cranks!' I said.

'Sometimes,' Pat said, 'you do say stupid things, Bernard!'

'I'm sorry,' I said huffily, 'I can't help saying what I think.'

'You think Epsom's a religious crank?'

'I didn't say that! No, of course I don't! But – '

'Or me?'

'I don't know what your religion is. I don't think you're a crank.'

'I haven't got one. But there you are, you know me quite well, but you didn't even know what my religion was. And yet you'll dismiss thousands of people you've never even met or heard of as 'religious cranks'! That doesn't make sense!'

I said 'I'm not making much sense this morning, I'm afraid.'

Although said in a grumpy voice, this was an apology, and Pat took it as such, smiling with squeezed-up eyes over her coffee cup. She always settled herself in a chair like an animal, shoulders hunched, head sunk, knees drawn up; and held her cup in both hands just below her chin; a compact, comfortable person, enjoying the sense of being herself.

At last Epsom arrived, beaming, thirsting for coffee. There was a cold cup already on the table, bought by Gregory for Helen who hadn't wanted it. Epsom drank this while the waitress was getting a fresh one. He raised it to me in a mock salute before taking the first gulp.

'Until the Conversion of the Jews!' he said.

'How was the Beak?' I asked.

'The Beak's a lovely man!' Epsom said, as he finished the cold coffee in a second prolonged gulp. 'I love him dearly. I always thought you had it in you, Jones! he said. Not that I agree with you, he said, in fact, he said, I think you're up the bloody pole, he said, or words to that effect. But what I've always held, he said, is that a man who's willing to back his conscience can't go far wrong even if he's a fool. And I don't for a moment think you're a fool, Jones, he said. So I said, I don't think you're one, either, sir! in my best prefect voice. So then his mouth started twitching and he tried to look at the end of his nose and he said: I fear that you are unique among my pupils in that, Jones! And that was that. Oh dear me, yes! I love the man passionately!'

'The Sprocket won't go much on that,' I said.

'We will pray for the Sprocket,' said Epsom, ' – later.'

'Listen,' I said, employing Epsom's own formula, 'I've been thinking. You know when we had this discussion the day before yesterday, and I said: What about if you do nothing?'

'Yes, and I said you get the law of Diminishing Returns

but that it's much better to repay evil with good. Right?'

'Yes. Well, look here, aren't you just proposing to do nothing, and isn't that pretty useless?'

Epsom shifted in his chair, and before he could speak Pat said 'But he isn't doing nothing! He's taking a positive action!'

'Yes, there's that,' Epsom said, 'but it's very complicated. I don't agree that I'm doing nothing, because I think an actual physical refusal to fight is, morally speaking, doing something. But what you meant is that I'm not doing anything in the reverse direction, is that it?'

'Well, yes. I mean, I know you can't do anything to bring about a peace, but – '

'Something like fire-fighting or ambulance man, is that it?'

'Yes.'

'Well, the thing is, you see, they won't let me. I'd willingly fight fires or be on a bomb disposal mob or drive an ambulance, but I've still got to have this tribunal first, because of conscription.'

'Do you want a tribunal?'

'Not particularly. I'm not the type for martyrdom, really. I know I can't stop the war, and I'm too young to influence people in any way. That's the part of it that bothers me. But I can't fight. I won't.'

When Epsom said that, I couldn't help thinking what a magnificent soldier or sailor he would have made, with his chunky body, his firm mind, and his will power, all of which I now saw going to waste.

'Hasn't it ever occurred to you,' I said, 'that you could be an S.B.A.?'

'What on earth's that?'

'Sick Berth Attendant. In the Navy. They don't fight. They don't have time to. They're always busy putting people together again. Of course,' I added off-handedly, 'it's rather dangerous, stuck down in the bowels of the ship like that, I wouldn't like it.'

'I don't like blood,' said Epsom.

'You'd have to get over it. I know it's not a nice trade but it's useful, it's practical, it really is doing something! Of course, you might not be able to stand it, I suppose, all the blood and the smells, and that.'

'You can stand anything if you have to!' Epsom growled.

I had deliberately laid on the unpleasant side with a generous trowel, knowing that a challenge to will power was meat and drink to Epsom. And he was thinking about it. He hadn't yet come back with the obvious refutation. I thought I had a chance.

Pat said 'But he'd be in the Navy, wouldn't he? How do you know they wouldn't make him fight?'

'I could always refuse!' said Epsom. The thought obviously delighted him.

'I just know,' I said,

'Yes, but how?' Pat said. 'You don't know – '

'My Uncle Euan,' I said crushingly, inventing fast, 'was an S.B.A. in the first war. He said he never came out of the Sick Bay when they were in action. And when his ship was sunk at Jutland he was one of the last to leave, he nearly got trapped below trying to get all the wounded out. He said he didn't know one end of a gun from another. He said he thought he'd never get the smell of blood out of his nostrils....'

'Let's have less about the blood,' Epsom suggested.

He still hadn't opposed me.

Pat said 'And of course, as you say, if they did try to make you fight, you could always refuse, couldn't you?'

'They wouldn't,' I said firmly. 'You don't train a man to make motor-cars and then use him for breaking them up. Any fool can wield a hammer.'

'A snappy image, Smith!' said Epsom.

'Listen,' I said, suddenly inspired. 'What do your parents think about this?'

Epsom pulled at his upper lip, looking sideways at me. 'I haven't told them yet,' he said. 'They're not going to like it one little bit. My old man was in Italy in the last war. He thinks war is the Great Game. He's an overgrown Boy Scout.'

'Don't you think it will cause them a lot of pain?'

'Undoubtedly.'

'Isn't it evil to cause pain?'

'Undoubtedly. It's very difficult to avoid evil in this world, Smith. I might almost say bloody difficult.'

'But oughtn't you to do everything in your power to avoid giving pain to people that love you?'

'Undoubtedly.' Epsom's voice was becoming heavy, I noticed.

Pat said suddenly 'I think Bernard's right. I think you ought to do that, if it's possible.'

'If it can be done, yes.'

I saw, incredulously, that I had won. I could scarcely believe it, I didn't dare say a word. I had never for a moment really believed that it would be possible for me, with my less subtle mind, to steer Epsom away from a course he had

260

decided upon. I could see, too, that Epsom was himself surprised. He was looking at me speculatively now, as if I had unexpectedly laid an egg and might at any moment do it again. But I knew that I had shot my bolt. I had nothing left to say. I could only sit tight and pray that the idea which Epsom had so guardedly admitted to his mind would take root and blossom into action.

I shall, I suppose, never know in what proportions Epsom's own natural desire not to divorce himself from his fellows, and his fear of causing pain to his parents, were balanced in the decision which, at my prompting, he had taken. Even at the time I wondered if he were aware, as I had been from the beginning, of the flimsiness of the compromise. But he showed no signs of having second – or third – thoughts about the matter, and the day after our conversation in Sumner's applied, through the recruiting centre at Caernarvon, to be accepted as a volunteer S.B.A.

I was uneasy in my victory. For one thing, I had far more knowledge, being nautically minded, than Epsom of the internal workings of the Navy, and was perfectly well aware that, although his first application would probably be accepted, once he was in the service the authorities might easily decide that they had enough S.B.A.s or that Epsom was psychologically unfitted to be one. He was surprisingly ill-informed about military matters, and, though he might know more than I about the 'situation' in the Middle East, was almost completely ignorant of ranks, ratings, means of selection, training, and promotion, which to me were the ever-present tenets of a faith. Also, I was disturbed by the very slight shift which had now occurred in Epsom's attitude towards myself. He seemed to be treating me with caution; on several occasions I caught him with a look in his eyes which he had never turned on me before; a puzzled, almost suspicious look; a look which I had surprised on Pat's face many times during the summer, but which in her case I had always attributed to some speculation concerning Kathy.

I had thought that the interviews with the Sprocket and the Beak might have made it more difficult for Epsom to change his mind; but should have remembered that the one danger of which he had never been afraid was loss of face. His resignation from the A.T.C. would anyway be allowed to stand. And a few days before the new term was due to begin, he had a further interview with the Beak, explaining the position, and arranging that, for the seven weeks before he left, he could be a sort of honorary member of the Sixth Form, with the use of the Library, and a corner in which to study First Aid and elementary medicine.

He settled to his new studies, when term began, with an intensity that seemed to me almost neurotic. He would talk of nothing but fractures, ligatures, haemorrhages, streptococci, gangrene, as if by concentrating thus on the frailties of the human body, he could ward off the dangers inherent in those of the human mind. Pat, of course, herself marking time in the Sixth Form to no particular purpose, encouraged him in this, and together they spent their days poring endlessly over the big, gruesomely illustrated books which Pat had been lent by the hospital at Bangor. I found myself, during those seven weeks, spending more time alone than I had since before Epsom arrived at the school two and a half years before. I tried to emulate them. I borrowed the

Admiralty Manual of Seamanship and the Manual of Navigation from the County Library, and set myself to learn the habits of ropes and pulleys and lights and winds and tides and anchors and all the other exciting mysteries which are there set forth so obscurely, like the rites of a complex sect whose meaning can only be glimpsed after the neophyte has passed blindly through all the stages of the Order towards the final uplifting Light. But I was not capable of Epsom's concentration, and the days sat dully on my desk, mocking my inability to sidestep them into the future.

I wrote poems to Kathy. On several occasions I wrote long, morbid letters to her, describing her beauty and what it did to me, and exculpating myself for my own course of inaction. Poetically, I mourned the years of happiness which we might have had together, and attempted to explain the powers which had held me from her, which I did not myself understand.

None of those letters was ever posted.

I saw Kathy only twice during this period. Once she was with Dewi, leaving the Odeon on a Saturday night after the first house, just as Epsom, Pat, and I were entering for the second. We all smiled and waved. Dewi said something to Kathy, who shook her head; and then he grinned, straight at me, while Kathy looked away, and I was able to guess what it was he had asked her.

The second time she was alone. We came face to face on the Promenade one Sunday morning in October. It was blowing half a gale from the north, and I had decided to walk down to Graig-y-don along the front, and back home across the fields. The breakers were sending their heaviest armour up the beach steps and over the edge, to explode in bouncing white spray high into the air. Even by the edge of the flower-beds, on the landward side of the Promenade, I was lashed by the driven spray, denser than any rain, and soon drenched to the skin. But it was raining, anyway, and I wanted to immerse myself in the noise of the roaring, thumping water, and think of myself out there in that white fury, clinging grimly to the corner of a destroyer's bridge, my salt-caked eyes searching the erupting water for a glimpse of the enemy.

And then I came across Kathy, sitting alone on a bench by the flower beds, with her hands buried, almost her whole self buried, in an old oilskin of her father's, her head up and her hair blown back, facing the sea. She did not see me approaching, and I was almost on top of her before I recognized her. Her face was streaming with water, the bare crown of her head sleek and dark, but the wind kept the bulk of her hair moving loosely above her shoulders. Her eyes were screwed up against the driven salt spray, and she was smiling.

She continued to smile when she saw me, but the smile tightened, losing whatever of happiness it had held. When I spoke a greeting, the words were blown back into my throat, and I had to shout again to make myself heard. Kathy didn't shout. She said something, but I couldn't hear, and she immediately turned her face to the sea again.

On an impulse, I sat down beside her.

'Isn't this lovely!' I shouted.

Kathy nodded, not looking at me.

'I haven't seen you for ages!' I shouted again.

She looked at me quickly and away again, her lips forming the word 'No'.

It was obviously impossible for us to carry on any sort of conversation, and I dimly apprehended that Kathy had anyway no wish to speak. I leaned back against the hard wooden rail behind the bench, feeling awkward and stupid. Having sat down beside her like this, I could not immediately get to my feet again and walk on: but so much now stood between us... the cigarette box, her remark about not wanting to see me again, and how much else?... that we could not possibly be at ease again in one another's company until something had happened to change the whole tenor of our relationship. I wished, now, that I had not sat down.

Kathy stood up, turning to say something to me; but she could not have wished to be heard, for she did not raise her voice. As she turned her hair was blown sideways across her face, isolating, for an instant, her eyes and forehead: and isolating too for me the moment from other moments so that the image I had of her then, leaning against the wind in her huge flapping black oilskin, with her hair cutting softly across her face and her head tilted against the wind, joined with those other images, registered in moments of heightened visual perception, to form the complex picture which I carried with me always of her physical beauty.

I, too, came to my feet, and moved off beside her down the Promenade. She was to seaward of me, her face turned to the spray, and I had an impulse to take her arm, then, and turn her towards me and without explanation or apology kiss her wet, glowing face. The impulse exploded in me strongly, catching me unawares, for I had never with

Kathy, as I had with other girls, been pricked towards a desire for kisses. This impulse was different, stronger, had nothing to do with the irritations of the flesh. It was an emotion, and it seemed to originate in my stomach and rise to my throat like an involuntary cry, which, held back, twists agonizingly inside one.

I moved away from her, sideways, putting yards between us. My hands in my raincoat pockets were clenched hard. I saw that we were nearly opposite the Washington Hotel, and Kathy had already started to swerve away from the sea towards the gap in the flower beds that would allow us to escape from the Promenade.

As we crossed the road into Clarence Street, I saw that our ways lay together for less than a hundred yards. The noise of the waves receded rapidly behind us, and once in the lee of the Washington the wind abruptly dropped, so that for a moment we were both off balance and swayed lightly against each other, our elbows touching.

Now, in this dangerous calm we had entered, Kathy kept her head lowered, watching the pavement in front of her feet. She was walking quickly, and yet with a sense of reluctance, as if torn between duty and desire. I wanted to say something, anything, that might lie down as the first stepping stone across the river between us.

'Do you like the Secretarial College?' I asked.

'It was all right,' said Kathy. 'I've got a job now, though.'

'A job? Really? Where?'

'In the Ministry of Food. Colwyn Bay. It's not bad.'

Her mouth was buried in the collar of the oilskin, and she made no attempt to make her words distinct. We were approaching the corner of the Broadway, where Kathy would turn off, and we were speaking like strangers. I made a last effort.

'It's good about Dewi getting his Bursary, isn't it?' I said.

Kathy did turn to look at me then, just for an instant, but I couldn't read her face. She didn't answer me. All she said was 'Oh, Bernard!' in a voice which mingled agony, reproach, and despair. Then she started running, with the desperate, swinging urgency which I had noticed before I even knew her name. I called out a goodbye to her, but if she answered I failed to hear. She didn't look back. It was a long time before I realised that I ought not to have mentioned Dewi.

Dewi had become for me, since his brilliant entry into the Sixth Form, increasingly unreal. My attitude towards him was compounded of respect and fear, the respect for something, a cast of mind, which I did not, could not, understand; the fear for his emotions, the obsessiveness of his loves and hates. I had never known him do or say an unkind thing, except in heat, when they could be forgiven. But even if I had not, that night in the washroom below the Music Club, seen and been shocked by the gritty tension of his emotions, I believe that I would have sensed them beneath the level doggedness of his surface.

He was, I suppose, one of the most brilliant scholars the school had had for a long time. Despite the fact that he had missed two vital years of the curriculum, had been, on his arrival in 3D, a year older than Epsom, and yet still behind us, in a single year he had passed us, in the next had passed those already ahead of us and now, with the Higher Certificate behind him and a Bursary in his pocket, was already advancing in his chosen subject towards fields normally reached only at the University. Mathematics was his subject, but it was a mathematics bearing only a very distant relationship to that which we had learnt for the School Certificate. He attempted to describe one day, to Epsom and me after we had joined him in the Sixth Form, the pleasures, the 'beauty' as he put it, of calculus and solid geometry. After a particularly highly coloured eulogy on the imaginative purity of the Theory of Numbers, Epsom said 'But that's poetry you're describing, not maths!'

'It's the only sort of poetry that makes sense to me!' Dewi growled.

I did not understand him, found it difficult to take him seriously. Yet at the same time he made me uneasy. I said once to Epsom that I thought Dewi would be quite ruthless in getting whatever he wanted.

'Oh no!' Epsom protested. 'Not ruthless! It's just that he knows what he wants and he doesn't care if everyone else knows too. But he wouldn't hurt a fly if he could avoid it. To tell you the truth, I'm rather sorry for him. You can't have a happy life with a will like that.'

I thought, but didn't say, that Epsom might have been speaking of himself, but I could see that there was a difference. Dewi's will was a force inside himself, scarcely will at all, rather a refusal to come to terms with life; while with Epsom it was something which he imposed from outside on his own weaknesses; Dewi's will was a horse in full gallop, Epsom's was a guiding rein.

A rather non-committal reply had come from the Navy to Epsom's request for acceptance as an S.B.A.: a reply to the effect that the request had been received and its contents noted. But by that time Epsom was already immersed in his nursing studies and had thought himself into the part of an S.B.A. so thoroughly that it was inconceivable to him that he should be anything else. And as November closed greyly about us and the time approached for him to leave, he slipped into using phrases like 'When I'm in the Navy', or 'When I'm a sailor', as if the urgency of his convictions had faded during the past two months. Then, one day, only about a week before he left, Pat said to me 'Epsom's not really happy about this S.B.A. business, you know.'

'He hasn't said anything to me,' I said.

'I know. But he has to me. I think he thinks you'd just pooh-pooh his doubts if he told you about them.'

'What doubts, anyway?'

'Well, as he says, it's all very well for you to say he won't have to fight, but you don't really know, do you? And once he's in the Navy he's in it, isn't he? I mean, if he refused to fight then, it's much more serious than if he just went to a tribunal. And it doesn't really mean as much.'

'I'm sure it'll be all right,' I said.

'I hope so,' said Pat, looking distrustfully at me.

But I wasn't sure it would be all right. And I was unhappily aware that Epsom was further from me now, during these final days together, than he had ever been, that Pat was more his confidant than I. It wasn't that they conspired together, or attempted in any way to shut me out, but simply that I had the impression constantly of discussions which had occurred in my absence and which were never resumed in my presence. I was unhappy, and slightly ashamed, for I sensed dimly that in some obscure way it was my fault, that I had failed Epsom, not at any particular point, but over the years, in little things, which had one by one accumulated so that now, with this big thing, he could no longer trust my understanding. I wanted to go to him and put my point of view afresh, stressing the pain he would cause by being a Conscientious Objector, and the good he would be able to do as an S.B.A.. But he never seemed to give me an opening, and when the day of his departure arrived the matter had still not arisen between us again.

It was, for me, a dismal, unsatisfactory parting. He had undertaken to insist on saying goodbye to his parents at home, so that Pat and I could see him off from the station. The train left at 8.15 and there was an icy wind blowing through the station as the three of us stood there, huddled in overcoats, waiting impatiently for the train to leave. For me it was an agony of reticence, for I seethed with the unsaid and the unsayable. I could not tell him now, again, that I was convinced he was doing the right thing. And there was no time to try to express the importance which he had had, and still had, in my life; a thing which, anyway, if there had been time, I could not have brought myself to say.

'Send your address as soon as you've got one,' I said. 'We'll write then.'

'The Cells, R.N.B., Portsmouth, should find me,' said Epsom.

Pat said 'It's going to be dull without you.'

Epsom said 'Look after the youngster, won't you, Pat? Keep him out of mischief.'

I said 'I shall be a rest cure for Pat after you.'

A whistle blew somewhere in the station, and we all

turned hopefully towards the guard of Epsom's train. He was chatting nonchalantly with an elderly, wizened little porter, his green flag furled under his left arm. We turned back to grin self-consciously at each other.

Epsom said 'Look here, it's perishin' cold, you two had better go. There's no point in waiting.'

Pat said 'I want to wait.'

'So do I,' I said.

Epsom pulled viciously at his upper lip, stretching it outwards and then downwards over his teeth. Then he grinned, and the lip shot up and the teeth popped out, and for a moment he looked not one day older than the boy I had met on the sands the day the mad woman walked down the breakwater.

'Listen, Smith,' he said, grinning. 'If you get a commission, don't you ever expect me to call you "sir".'

'You'll be clapped in chains if you don't!' I said.

'Midshipman MacWheeble, the Scourge of the Seas!'

'Oh damn!' said Pat, violently.

'What's the matter?' Epsom asked.

'I wish you weren't going, that's all!' she said angrily. She looked at me challengingly, and I felt that her anger was directed at me. There was an uncomfortable little pause, and I wondered what Epsom would say, what possible thing he could say.

'Thank you, Pat,' he said.

'I wish I was coming with you,' I said.

'So do I, boy!'

Then a whistle shrilled again, nearer this time, and the guard started to unfurl his little green flag.

'That's me,' said Epsom. He came and shook hands with me, clasping my right hand in both of his.

'Thanks for coming,' he said. 'See you.'

'See you,' I said.

Then he put his arms round Pat and kissed her, not passionately, not emotionally, but in a nicer, more moving way than I had ever known about. I turned away, searching for cigarettes. When I turned back Epsom was already in the train, leaning from the window, and the train was moving. We waved until the curve of the coaches as they left the station hid at last the black shape of his head and moving arm.

As we left the station, Pat took my arm. She had often taken it before, but only when Epsom had been on her other side. Now she gripped it tightly with her fingers, and walked fast.

'Let's have some coffee,' I said.

'All right. At Sumner's.'

'We could go in the Avondale, it's not so far.'

'I want to go to Sumner's!' Pat said angrily.

'Oh, all right!' I said in a surprised voice: Pat was so rarely anything but calm. Now she shook my arm, half in anger, half in apology.

'Damn it, Bernard!' she said. 'Can't you see I'm crying?'

We were passing the Avondale then, and I could see that she was. So we walked on to Sumner's.

Twelve

'My stupid mother!' said Pat, about three weeks later. We were in Sumner's again, drinking coffee. The term had not yet ended, and we still attended school in a desultory fashion, for something to do; but we had dropped into the habit now of leaving at about eleven-thirty and walking along to Sumner's for coffee and biscuits.

'What's stupid about her?' I asked.

'She's suddenly decided that I ought to have a sort of farewell party before I leave for the Hospital. If she'd thought about it earlier, it could have been a farewell party for Epsom, too.'

'Never mind. Perhaps he wouldn't have been too keen, under the circumstances.'

'Nobody but us knows the circumstances. I think he'd have been tickled pink.'

'Shall you still have the party?'

'We might as well, don't you think?'

'Thank you for the 'we',' I said.

Pat smiled. Quietly, we enjoyed each other's company. Now that Epsom had gone, Pat revealed more of herself to me than she had ever done while he was with us, and I think I too gave more of myself away.

'Let me have another look at the letter,' I said.

Pat had that morning had a letter from Epsom, the first. Previously we had both had postcards. Mine had said: Just to give you my address. S.B.A. business all fixed up. Should be O.K. . Too much square bashing. Will write. Epsom. Pat's had said: All according to plan. Neat little black suit. Wish you were here. Love, Epsom.

Pat handed me the letter. It was on cheap absorbent paper, black-ruled, and headed 'Mess X12, Block B., R.N.B., Portsmouth.'

My Dear Pat,

This letter is for MacWheeble, too. I don't have much time for letters at present, nor very much to say. I'll write separately later.

This place looks and smells rather like a multiple edition of the school, with a few huts scattered about the playing-fields, a rifle-range on the tennis courts and playing grounds [parade grounds] about a quarter of a mile square. Everyone is either in a tearing hurry, and hasn't time to tell you anything, or has nothing to do and knows nothing. I'm one of the latter. I have nothing to do, but can't do anything I want to, like write or read, because I'm always supposed to be doing something. But I never know what.

I was already registered as an S.B.A. . I had an interview with a doctor-officer who asked me if I knew what a fibula was. He seemed rather surprised when I did. Then he asked me what a haemorrhage was, and began to get quite angry when I answered correctly. After a few more questions, all of which were easy, he was getting really furious. Then he let me go, having apparently exhausted his stock of questions. I think he learnt medicine out of the same book as we did.

So then I was allowed to go and draw a uniform, what they call 'fore-and-aft rig' which is just a very badly cut little black suit, with a short coat and trousers that bag at the seat. It looks black to me, but I'm told it's blue.

Food is plentiful but lousy, and the NAAFI coffee is undrinkable. We do a lot of square bashing, and to my dismay some rifle-shooting. But I'm prepared to blink an eye at this as long as it stops when I'm fully trained. I've found an 'oppo'. His name is Henry. He's very short, has a huge head, huge shoulders, and tiny little feet, like a W. S. Gilbert Bishop. He's a quarryman from Bethesda, and has just come out of cells – after a fight in which he broke his opponent's arm. Somehow, MacWheeble, I can't see you settling comfortably in among this lot. The ironic truth is, I suppose, that I'm much more suited to service life than you are.

Pat, I'll write again. This is being written after Lights Out by the light of a forbidden candle, with the paper on my knees. The night is hideous with snores, not the least stentorian of which issue from the mouth of friend Henry on my left. Keep MacWheeble away from the women and I hope Operation Cupid blooms.

Love,

Epsom

'What's Operation Cupid?' I asked; I had read the letter before, alone, and had forgotten about this.

'Oh, it's just a silly joke we had,' Pat said. I saw that she was blushing, and didn't press the matter. I had often wondered just how deep the relationship between Pat and Epsom had become, and took this to be a sign that it had been rather more serious than I had suspected. On the surface they had been no more than close friends. Certainly their attitude towards each other had been proprietorial, their manner in my presence often touched lightly by innocent uxoriousness; but these were traits which Epsom

275

and I ourselves on occasion would display, for the benefit of others, when we were most in sympathy and proud of it. Yet they had spent much time alone together; and for over six months neither had entered into liaisons with others. It seemed improbable to me that there should be no more between them than was apparent from the even surface which they presented to the world, even if one wrote off Pat's tears at Epsom's departure as no more than a feminine expression of what I was myself feeling.

'Who shall we invite to the party?' Pat asked. 'There aren't many left, are there?'

'Not many worth asking. Peter and Moira, of course.'

'Yes. And Ann. That means having John Stockwell. I hardly know him. What's he like?'

'A bit dim. Dreamy Scientist. But he'll do.'

'Isabel will probably be home for the holidays. Who does she go with, now?'

'Well, she was all over Peredur until he joined up. I expect she's got someone new in Sheffield by now. You can't not ask her, though. Of course, there's always Gregory.'

'Yes, there'll always be a Gregory. That means Helen, poor thing. I'm sure she'd much rather be invited without him, only we're a bit short of manpower. We'll have to think.'

I was thinking of Kathy, whom neither of us had mentioned. I knew that Dewi was going to Glencoe for the snow climbing over Christmas, so I said 'What about Dewi? When were you thinking of having it?'

'Mother wants it on New Year's Eve. Dewi won't be back, will he?'

'No, I don't think so.'

'Well, we'll have to think of someone else for Kathy, then,' Pat said, keeping her face perfectly straight; from it, I could not guess whether she meant what she said, having assumed that my interest in Kathy, whom I never now mentioned, was dead, or was after all mocking me. Both seemed equally unlikely.

Just before Christmas I had a letter from Epsom. Pat also said that she had 'heard from him' but had not offered to show me the letter, so I assumed that it was too personal for my eyes, and took this as evidence that there was more than friendship between them. My letter said:

Dear MacWheeble,
This is your Christmas letter and has to be short and snappy, as we, that is myself and a louche character called Cohen, are leaving today for a place called Dunfermline, near Edinburgh, where we are to be taught How to Treat Siphyllis Without Catching It.

Pat tells me you and she are having a party on New Year's Eve. I wish I could come, if only for the pleasure of watching you agonizing over whether you would be endangering your freedom by offering the Spam sandwiches to Miss X for the second time. Take it from me, boy, freedom is relative. The worst cage you can ever get into is yourself. Time is the dangerous element in illusions of freedom. It's nice to be free, and again it's nice to be still free and later on but rather wanly it may still be nice to be free. Not only of persons, but of opinions, convictions, commitments, responsibilities. But the time comes when you add one freedom to another all along the line and look at the result and find that it is infinite nothing. Who the hell wants to be infinite nothing?

While we're in the Home Truths Department, let Auntie Agatha whisper another little secret in your maidenly ear. A person who is too proud ever to give away anything of him/herself is like a plant that grows up tall and strong and flowers and has fruit and is so proud of these fruits that it can't bear to drop them on the dirty ground where anyone can pick them up or tread on them. But the seeds of its own survival are in those fruit and if it doesn't drop them it will wither away without regeneration. That's not an analogy to be pursued too far, but you can see what Auntie means.

And now since it's pissing down with rain we will sing We'll roll the old chariot along once more and you can all bugger off 'ome.

Write to the same address until I send you a new one.

Happy Christmas and Committed New Year.

Your childhood sweetheart,

Oracle Jones

It was an odd letter for Epsom to write to me, and I read it several times. I was sorry he didn't tell me more about himself and his surroundings, for I was hungry for inside information on the Navy, although he did add a mysterious footnote which said: Henry has permission to grow. If Henry was so young as to be still growing, I couldn't see that they could do anything about it, permission or no permission.

I could not interpret the enigmatic 'Committed New Year', although I did connect it with the earlier paragraph about freedom; nor could I see how any of this could be applied to myself, and decided that Epsom had only used the letter to me as an excuse for lecturing himself. Perhaps, I thought, he found it difficult in his new surroundings to keep his anti-military convictions alive, and needed to bolster them up by expressing their importance on paper. I felt rather flattered that he had chosen me, rather than Pat, as the recipient of such musings, for it seemed to indicate his acceptance of the existence between us of the kind of mental contact which I had always sought from him, and which, except in unsatisfactory patches, we had failed to achieve.

I showed this letter to Pat, after hesitating for some days on account of the rude words in it. Eventually I decided that either she didn't know them, or, if she did, then they could scarcely shock her. It was Christmas Eve, and we were in Sumner's again.

Pat read the letter with her lips twitching, and grinned as she handed it back.

'He's coming out into the open, isn't he?' she said.

'Yes,' I said, taking her to mean that he was expressing in writing aspects of his convictions too complicated to be expressed conversationally. I thought Pat looked a little puzzled by my simple affirmation, so I added 'I expect he finds it a bit tough, trying to hold on to his beliefs in an atmosphere like that. It probably helps him quite a bit to have someone to write to about them.'

Pat, looking more puzzled than ever, asked to see the letter again. This time she read it – or the first page and a half – with a frown of concentration. Then she put it down on the table, shaking her head indulgently; indulgent of myself, or of Epsom, I did not know.

'You're a funny boy, Bernard,' she said affectionately.

I didn't know, or much care, what she meant. I knew that we both had thoughts which we withheld from the other; our friendship was based on the right to do so. Often I found Pat difficult to understand, as she, I think, did me, but these differences were no bar to our affection. Thinking back, I know that I valued my companionship with her more highly than any of the flirtations I had indulged in over the past two years, and though we had never so much as briefly kissed goodnight, I was warmly aware that such tokens, as tokens, were superfluous, and we did not desire them for other purposes. I liked it that Pat had grown so much more attractive during the past year and was proud of the difficult rewarding relationship we had established.

It looked at one moment as if Pat's party was fated to be disastrously ill-balanced, for, try as we would, we could not find more than four acceptable males, while of the six obvious females none could be dropped without giving offence. The guest list sorted itself out, eventually, as guest lists do, by the defection of Isabel, and the unexpected arrival of Bill, Pat's brother, who had hitherto been no more than a name to me. His name, the fact that he was a year older than I and had been an Engineer Apprentice in the Navy since the age of fifteen, and Pat's assertion once, after I had behaved rather raffishly at the Music Club, that I had been 'as bad as Bill', had given me a picture of a stalwart, cheerful extrovert, world-weary and fearless. The reality, when I came across it in Pat's large but over-furnished villa at Llanrhos on the afternoon of the party (I was 'helping', my mother having undertaken to provide a share of the food), proved so wanly unassertive that I thought there must be some mistake; this must be another brother, also, for some reason, known as Bill. He was quiet, slight, and smelled of oil.

On the surface it was a tame party, unambitious, vale-dictory, as we had intended. It had a dying fall about it, as if everything we said ended in a sigh, everyone we looked at was a lost opportunity. I could not in any detail remember anything that we did, said, or ate, because Kathy was there. But I remember the feel of the party, the way none of the males could interest themselves in Pat, because she was about to leave the town, and none of the females work up that enlivening spirit of rivalry which had inflated so many of our parties into landmarks, because the alternatives to their existing arrangements were so unexciting. Moira stuck to Peter, Ann to John Stockwell, Helen to – or if not stuck to, remained becalmed near – Gregory. Pat and Bill fussed uncertainly, like caricatures of a host and hostess, on the fringes of the party, looking distrustfully at each other as at unwelcome gate-crashers. Yet it was a pleasant party. A quiet concord of muted regret bound us together. Each unexciting little game passed with a faint murmur of acknowledgement as the last of its kind, as something which had not been well loved but which through association had come to earn a small corner in the affections. It was not a party about which, in after years, we might say 'Do you remember when... ?' But at it we consolidated the memories of those other parties, elevating them into epics, discarding the irrelevant and concentrating on the hilarious, performing a service of remembrance to keep at bay the past's mortality.

But for me there was only, really, Kathy. I watched Kathy, talked to Kathy, thought of Kathy, sat by Kathy. She wore a dress which I had not seen before, of pale gold damask, which (she said) had been a Japanese kimono of her mother's but which now (I thought) looked as if it had existed always, had watched humanity for centuries, before finally selecting Kathy as the one woman fit to wear it. I knew, immediately she came into the room (last, as usual), that something had occurred, or that she had made a decision, affecting myself. She smiled at me across the room, shyly, tilting her head; and moved like a swan towards me. I saw Pat watching her, and achieving somehow both a small smile and a small frown at the same time. I saw Gregory, his hands cupped in front of him as if to receive a gift of rice, hee-hawing with laughter at something he had just said to Moira, bewildered but politely smiling. I heard, on my left, Peter explaining to Bill that something called nuclear fission, invented by somebody called Rubberfoot or Rudderboard, would have replaced all existing forms of power within ten years, and that he (Bill) was wasting his time learning about anything else and that he (Peter) wouldn't be surprised if within the same period the same force made future wars impossible. I saw John Stockwell surreptitiously stroke the inside of Ann's left arm (he was sitting on the arm of her chair) and I saw that Helen, who was talking to Ann, was oblivious of the fact that Ann was not listening. I sipped my sweet cider and kept my eyes off Kathy, but every nerve of my body told me where she was, how she looked, and what she would say when she reached me.

'Hello, Bernard!' she said quietly, without emphasis, just as I had made up my mind to hear it.

'Hello, Kathy,' I said. We stood beside each other as if we were holding hands secretly in a crowd; and indeed her elbow brushed mine once, and later I made it do so again, and then again, until the scarcely felt contact had assumed the stature of a conversation.

I didn't know what had happened; I didn't care. I felt strong in myself, capable of keeping afloat in the deepest waters. Dewi, in Glencoe, hacking monotonously at steep ice, was abroad, away, might never return. Kathy was here, no longer kept from me by complex webs of reticence and fear, conversing freely with her bare elbow, her hair (I knew, without daring to look) alive with light.

Then we had a game, one of those pointless little paper-and-pencil games which we inflicted masochistically upon ourselves in order, perhaps, the better to experience the pleasure of doing nothing when it stopped. There were two teams, but I was never clear who was in which nor who won. I found myself at one moment doing something with Bill, and wondered who he was. Then we had another glass of cider, and Kathy told me she could type at however many words per minute it was she could type at. She also told me about an elderly lady in her office called Miss Mace, who was a spiritualist and had told Kathy that she (Kathy) was a natural medium.

'Medium what?' I asked, and Kathy coasted away on a soft roll of laughter that carried us into the next game, the ubiquitous 'drawing game'. And then it was time for supper.

It was a 'buffet supper'; it always was at our parties, a bad system because one ate only the things one particularly liked and ate too much of them so that one ceased to like them. I had a passion for cheese straws, and could consume platefuls at a sitting. I always had indigestion afterwards, but since I am incapable of learning from experience I went on eating them at party after party until I loathed the sight of them, as I still do.

The corner chairs were all taken, so I took Kathy across to the grand piano, wedged her in behind it so that she couldn't get out, loaded the lid with plates of dainties, and tried to make her eat.

She would not, of course. She nibbled at a cheese straw, ate a Spam sandwich the size of a postage stamp, and then said she had had quite enough. Kathy seemed not to have the normal human appetites for drink, food, and drugs.

I was myself, I suppose, slightly drunk: not with cider, but with Kathy. I kept turning to look at her as if I had invented her, and wanted to confirm that what I had made was good. It was. She was lovely. I couldn't think what all the other males in the room were about, gesturing, talking, laughing, eating, with their backs to her or their eyes not on her. And then I caught Bill looking at her, not at her face, but at her waist, and I wondered whether to go across and kill him.

'I had a letter from Epsom,' Kathy said.

'Great Scott!' I exclaimed. 'When? What did he say?'

'Last week. I'll tell you about it later. Not now.'

'You are honoured! He hardly ever writes letters. I've only had a couple myself.'

'I know,' said Kathy. She smiled mysteriously at me. I could not imagine what might have prompted Epsom to write to Kathy, whom he had never known well. All sorts of fantastic explanations, connected with his pacifism, with myself, with Pat and his private life, flashed through my mind, but none of them seemed plausible. I toyed briefly with the idea that Epsom, remembering our last conversation about Kathy, at Sumner's in the summer, had decided to

284

write to her and tell her... tell her what? Tell her something about me that would change her attitude towards me, thaw the icy wall of reserve which she had erected against me. But what? What could he tell her? I did not believe he would do it, and I could think of nothing he could say if he did.

'May I see you home?' I asked.

'The party isn't over yet,' said Kathy, smiling sideways.

'May I, when it is?'

'Yes, please.'

I found I was grinning inanely, and to stop the grin filled my mouth with cheese straws.

'If you eat any more cheese straws,' Kathy said, 'you'll be so ill...!'

The party, after supper, seemed to drag on interminably. Pat and I had agreed that there should be no 'Murders'; we had not the heart for the game, for it was a game designed to open up possibilities, and we were busy bidding farewell equally to taken and lost chances of the past. And without the Crow, Kenny, Red, Isabel, Epsom, Nancy, Dora, how could we play 'Murders' without feeling our arteries harden, the wind move round to the east?

But the long hours shrivelled away at last and died. And then we all awoke to the valedictory nature of the party, and became suddenly interested in one another. It was discovered – I discovered myself, having forgotten the fact – that I would not be returning to school in the New Year, would be leaving for the Navy at the beginning of February, in five weeks. Gregory made a sudden and embarrassing all-out attack on my affections, attempting to establish for himself an important position there as Oldest Member. Repulsing him,

I found Ann achieving as near a leer as her innocent, triangular face could encompass as she reminded me with poorly veiled hints of our past brief intimacies. Even Helen did not wish me to forget, as I had indeed forgotten, the half a dozen evenings on which, in dark doorways near bus stops, we had lingered hopefully over a kiss. It seemed to me now irrelevant, all this. And when, at midnight, the wireless was switched on, and the bells sounded, and we all pranced round, interlocked, singing Auld Lang Syne, I felt, below the shallow emotionalism of the moment, a sort of irritable hilarity at the spectacle we were providing for the laughing gods; felt how tawdry was our little burst of bonhomie, how soon to fade the mutual charity with which we were flushed.

We gave ourselves time, after this embarrassing demonstration, to taste the odd sound of nineteen-forty-four, confess our unkeepable Resolutions, and promise the letters, contacts, arrangements which in a week would be forgotten. And then at long last we were all in the hall, struggling into coats, winding scarves. There was some poorly timed kissing under the left-over mistletoe. Suddenly Bill sprang to life, and started darting out at the girls, as they passed under the mistletoe, to assault them with kisses. I edged Kathy past hurriedly, fixing him with a proprietorial glare, and we achieved the door in safety.

Pat arrived at the door with us.

'I'm leaving tomorrow,' she said. 'Had you forgotten?'

'No,' I said, although I had.

'I don't expect I'll see you again.'

'I suppose not. Well – '

'Well... Have a good time. Don't get yourself killed.'

'Don't be silly. It's been a good party, Pat. I'll write.'

'Has it? Will you?'

Pat suddenly seemed to me to be what it would have been fantastic a week ago, the day before, that morning, to have conceived her as: pathetic.

'Well, Bernard....'

'Well, Pat....'

Pat then put her hands on my shoulders and her face up to kiss; and – unexpectedly at such a moment, with Kathy standing beside me – I experienced a sudden and quite unique tenderness; we kissed with that rare and cherishable kiss which I had seen and envied between Pat and Epsom on the station that morning... passing from one to another something durable and deeply needed for which I knew no name.

Out in that cold river of darkness, the Conway Road, Kathy and I walked in silence for many minutes. We had a long walk before us, over a mile, and could take our time. Kathy's hand was linked through my arm. Without thinking I took my hand from my pocket, moved her hand into mine, and squeezed it gently. She skipped a pace, like a little girl; and then returned the pressure; and then laughed.

'Bernard,' she said.

She was always saying my name, without any particular expression: like saying 'damp' or 'windy' or 'warm', stating a fact.

'You like Pat a lot, don't you?' she said.

'Yes, I'm very fond of her,' I said.

'I know she's always been very fond of you.'

'It's funny, about Pat,' I said. 'And Epsom.'

'Yes,' said Kathy, 'I know.'

'What did Epsom's letter say? You said you'd tell me.'

Kathy squeezed my hand, as if to reassure me. 'Wait till we get home!' she said. 'There's a light in the porch, you can read it there.'

It was strange, with nothing said to alter the facts of our last meetings, to be walking hand in hand with Kathy, as if it had been thus between us for months past. I was hilarious with the strangeness of it, the warmth, the ridiculous pulsation of my own emotions, I wanted to laugh, or cry, or sing. But in fact I walked sedately enough at her side, content for the moment as she seemed to be with the silence. Carmen Silva Road is a long road and Kathy lived at the very end of it. It is lined with trees. Clouds zipped across the stars like an endless chain of curtains, invisibly connected. There were a lot of cats, and they all made noises like a whole crêche of babies being strangled. Once we passed a drunk, clinging to a tree. He shouted some obscenity at us, and I replied 'Happy New Year!'

'What's muckin' 'appy abaht the muckin' thing?' he shouted back. When he swung round the tree again, I could see that he was in naval uniform. A thin white scarf flapped loosely to his waist on either side.

'Poor man!' said Kathy as we hurried on.

I knew Kathy's house well from the outside. I had cycled past it often in the last six months, watching the windows, hoping to learn something about Kathy or meet her. All I learned was that her family was richer than mine, that they had a car, that someone in the family was a good flower gardener, and that she had a young sister (I supposed a sister) of about ten years old. Kathy had never mentioned

her. She was very blonde and very pert and had an expensive pedal car which she could drive very fast. The house
was large and looked fairly new. It had a big bay window
each side of the front door, a large porch like a conservatory,
and a pan-tiled roof, Georgian style, short, steep, and
broken by two nicely proportioned dormer windows. It was
a nice house.

There was, as Kathy had said, a light in the porch. There
were also blackout curtains which had to be pulled across
the glass of the door and the side-panels before we could
switch the light on. When it was switched on, I saw that
there were benches on each side of the porch. We both sat
down on the side where there was no potted palm. Kathy
rummaged in her bag.

'Here,' she said.

Epsom's letter was very short, and had been written
from Dunfermline on paper that looked like lavatory paper
but wasn't.

Dear Kathy (it said),
As you see, I'm serving the upstarts from Hammer in the land
of our Rightful Ruler. A droll place, this, full of drunken sailors
from Rosythe and very elderly Wrens from Cheltenham. I know
you'll be surprised to have a letter from me, but the reason is that
I have discovered among my papers (that sounds very grand, I
really mean, between the pages of my common place book) a
letter addressed to you, obviously from Bernard. I could I suppose
have sent it to him, but thought it would be a good excuse to write
to you, and, who knows, you might write back, which is a thing
he never does. I've never needed letters before, but I do now,
though I seldom seem to have time to write them myself.

Here I'm learning all about how to treat boils and pains in the tummy and ingrowing eyebrows and suchlike, which will make me a useful husband to some lucky girl. Candidates please queue behind the white line. The only trouble is we haven't any patients, so have to practise on ourselves. And you know me, Hyperchondiac Jones. As soon as I have to start imagining I've got a pain in the tummy, I actually get one. Too much aptitude for faith, that's me.

Well, look after yourself. Give my love to everyone, but only a short ration to Bernard, who doesn't write.

Ever yours,

Epsom

P.S. Can't find the letter now.

P.P.S. Found it.

'Have you finished?' said Kathy.

'Eh? Oh. Yes, thanks,' I said. I had almost, for a moment, forgotten that she was with me, I was so used to thinking about her in her absence.

'I must turn off the light, then,' she said, and did so. Returning to my side, she tripped, and I put out an arm to save her from falling. My arm went round her waist. She turned round inside it and sat down, so I left it there. It seemed quite natural. I was beyond caring for the delicacies of significant gesture, now.

I remembered that letter, one I had not been able to find when I burned the others. It was not one of the most maudlin, but it was bad enough. It committed me utterly. I had said everything in it that it is possible to say to a girl one loves, and a lot of things it would under ordinary circumstances be impossible to say. I had tried to explain

290

why I had always held back from her, apologized for looking at the cigarette box, confessed to having seen the inscription, and pleaded that it wasn't her fault and anyway people always say embarrassing things in inscriptions. There was nothing really terrible about the letter except that it had not been written to Kathy; it had been written to myself. Now that Kathy had read it, the world, I felt, must change. The unthinkable had happened. It was like a husband announcing to his wife and family that he had a previous wife still living. The whole method of thinking about life must suffer a metamorphosis.

But after the first horror, came beautiful relief.

'You see?' said Kathy simply, saying thus all that needed to be said about her behaviour that evening.

'Yes,' I said. 'But I hadn't meant to post it. It was such a ghastly letter!'

'But you wrote it, didn't you? And it's a lovely letter. It's the most wonderful letter I've ever had. I cried and cried and cried when I read it!'

'Good heavens! I'm sorry!' I exclaimed, appalled at the thought.

'Oh no, you mustn't be sorry!' Kathy laughed, and I felt her turning towards me. 'You don't understand! It was lovely. I was only crying for joy, and because... well, it's been such a long time, I mean....'

She was crying at the wasted years, I thought, knowing the strangled feeling of having got something one had yearned for too late.

'Bernard,' Kathy said.

I said 'It's true, Kathy, I mean, what I said in the letter.'

Kathy said 'I know. Say it.'

'Say... ?'

'You know. Say what you said in the letter. Please!'

I almost didn't, almost couldn't. I knew what she wanted, but it was so much... it was something I had never in my life said, except to myself. But again it was impossible not to, the thing had to be said, however hard it was, however much my whole nature revolted against the saying of it.

'I love you, Kathy,' I said.

'Thank you,' she said, 'and I love you. But I won't make you say it again if you don't want to.'

Then I did love her, when she said that, perhaps for the first time that evening, properly.

'Darling Kathy!' I said. 'I love you!'

It was quite easy, really, I found. It would come out as if I meant it, with practise. And I did mean it.

'How long have we got?'

'Five weeks. February the sixth, I have to go.'

'Five weeks. Oh, Bernard, lots of time. I'll give up my job. I can always get another.'

'Do you think you ought?'

'Of course I shall, don't be silly!' Kathy laughed, and I knew not only that she would give up her job but that she would, if I asked, follow me from station to station through-out my naval career, seeing me when she could, living by herself in boarding houses, working in strange towns... it was a terrifying thought.

I tightened my arm about her waist as the thought hit me; and Kathy, putting one hand behind my neck, the other on the lapel of my coat, said 'Now let's kiss.'

Chastely, we kissed.

'Well,' said Kathy. 'I like that. Now you must go.'

I kissed her again.

Later, as I stood, shivering in the cold wind, waiting for the chinks of light which I had seen appear at her bedroom window to go out, thinking of her, up there, in bed – wondering what sort of nightdress she wore, in what sort of room she slept – I felt the world suddenly to be a weightier, more difficult place than I had known, fraught with peril, threatening. But knew also that until I had felt this the world had been a pale place indeed, myself a dim figure in it.

A flake of snow blew against my cheek, a cold touch, but gentle. Eventually the chinks disappeared. The snow increased rapidly. Tomorrow the earth would lie quiet under a freshly laundered white sheet; one would be reluctant to step out across it and spoil with one's footprints so pristine a prospect.

Thirteen

From my bedroom window I could see, across the fields behind the Links Hotel, the sprawled roofs of Craig-y-don, with behind them, like a crouching elephant, the grey hump of the Little Orme. By counting blocks, and running over in my mind the street topography of the huddle of houses, I could determine which roofs, which chimneys, belonged to Carmen Silva Road. Almost I could imagine that there, certainly, that one, that chimney, belonged to Maelgwyn, Kathy's house; could imagine that beneath that roof Kathy was waking, dressing, eating breakfast, reading again the letter I had never meant her to read but which now I would not have her not have read.

When I looked out on the morning of the first day of January nineteen-forty-four it was still snowing. The snow came gently, falling, so still was the air, erratically like scraps of paper, borne up by the warmth over chimneys, sucked down into the cold valleys between houses, drifting idly a few feet above the ground as if uncertain where to alight. The flakes were large, grey against the sky and the fallen snow. But now the fall had almost ceased, the flakes were few, not enough to obscure, across half a mile, the chimneys of Kathy's house.

We met in the front room of the Avondale at eleven o'clock. Kathy was already there when I arrived, sitting in the window seat, her chin in her hands. I saw her when I was halfway across the road. She waved, and turned to beckon the waitress. At the door I paused, conscious of a tremulousness in my breathing which I could not control.

Kathy was huddled into a big green tweed overcoat and had, on the table beside her, a fur muff, something I had not seen in use before.

'Hello, Bernard' she said, as shyly as ever, looking at the table.

'Hello, Kathy.'

When the coffee arrived, Kathy took from her handbag a tiny bottle, about three inches high, and poured half its contents into my cup.

'Hey! what's that?' I asked, thinking of medicines.

'Brandy,' said Kathy complacently. 'Keep you warm.'

'Good lord!' I tried the coffee, and found it delicious, a new experience. It tickled my throat with vapour from the brandy, almost making me sneeze.

'Aren't you having any?' I asked.

'I don't like it,' Kathy said.

We looked at each other, smiling. I noticed that there was a red, slightly inflamed patch on her left cheek, high up on the bone.

'What's wrong with your cheek?' I asked.

Kathy put her hand up to her face, turning her head sideways, so that I couldn't see. 'Oh, don't,' she said. 'It looks horrible. It's just a kind of blood poisoning, I often get it. You mustn't look!'

'It doesn't look horrible. It's hardly noticeable. I just thought you'd bruised yourself.'

'I look diseased!'

'You look like... like... you look good enough to eat,' I said.

Kathy put her right hand inside the fur muff and extended the muff towards me across the table. I put my left hand in the other end and there, in the warm soft centre of the muff, our fingers met and interlocked.

When we had finished our coffee we walked through the town, our arms linked, our hands, inside the muff, entwined. Softly, as if to remind us that there was more still to come, a few flakes of snow continued to drift down between the shops. I was acutely conscious that, with our arms linked publicly thus, we might meet someone we knew, friends, masters from the school, my mother, Kathy's mother; almost, I wanted to. I would have been embarrassed, but I wanted the thing to occur, public acknowledgement to be made. But we met no one. We seemed to be alone in the town (for the people we did not know, serving in shops, buying, driving motor cars, were merely part of the town), left over from some enveloping cataclysm, the last man and woman in the world.

We walked along Gloddaeth Street towards West Shore looking at the 'stills' in front of the Odeon and Palladium, debating whether to go to the pictures that night or to the dance hall, and deciding on the dance hall. We talked only of trivialities, but no matter what we said our conversation was private, intimate, full of significance. We wandered. There was nothing for us to do, but we were content to do nothing. The snow at West Shore had drifted, as the soft sand drifts, into beautiful whorls and ridges and valleys, blown by the gentle morning breeze that comes in from the sea. There was a place where, by some eccentricity of the moving air, the snow had drifted up in opposing directions, forming two cornices which each, at their highest, ended in an overhanging point. These points were almost, but not quite, touching; had almost, but not quite, formed a bridge. The distance between them was perhaps a quarter of an inch. There was an exquisite, painful tension about this perfect poise, this sublime incompleteness.

'It's like,' said Kathy, 'when a violin goes higher and higher, then can't go any higher, and then does. It makes you ache all over.'

'It's like looking at you,' I said. It was, it was just like looking at Kathy.

'Oh, Bernard!' said Kathy, hiding her face.

'It makes me ache all over, looking at you,' I said.

'Bernard.'

'What?'

'Bernard, I almost can't bear it; I'm so happy!'

'What, Kathy? What can't you bear? Why?'

'You'll have to kiss me.'

So there, by the sea, standing in snow, we put our cold faces together and kissed for the third time. There were small boys throwing snowballs twenty yards from us, and a youth of fourteen or fifteen, wearing a lumber jacket and a school cap, slouched past, whistling, while we kissed. An ugly boy, he was, with a satirical look in his eyes.

'That's better!' said Kathy, after the kiss.

Kathy made me telephone my mother, to say that I

would not be back for lunch. She had already told her own parents that she was going out for the day. I had to confess that I had very little money, about three shillings.

'I've got some,' said Kathy. 'Lots of it. After all, I've been earning three pounds ten a week for four months, and it doesn't cost anything to live at home. We could – well, we could do anything we want, really.'

But there was nothing we wanted to do. We lunched in a little café in Deganwy, not by choice but because our walking had carried us there. Afterwards we walked on to Conway and across the golf course to the Morfa, where, among the reeds and warrens of the saltings the winter sea-birds, Stints, Dunlins, Knots, Godwits, Whimbrels, Turnstones, Plovers, and Oystercatchers, stalked on frail legs over the snow, whistling mournfully. And here, for the first time, we heard that most disturbing of all bird calls, the deep, resonant 'Boom' of a male Bittern; and though we could not see him out there in the marsh, could imagine the sharp bill pointed at the sky, the long neck stretched upwards, the heavy brown body quivering with its own effort in the snow. It was a sound such as might have come from the last member of an extinct species, calling to its forbears across the centuries; a noise to associate with fog and ice and the lonely wastes of the Outer Isles. Kathy and I, our arms about each other, listened to it with a thrill of fear, and then turned our backs on the marsh and walked quickly away through the cold dusk, to the warm tea-shops of Conway, the tall stone walls, the solid accumulations of defence which men through the centuries had piled up against the cry of the Bitterns, the salt marsh, and the lonely mists of the sea.

We had tea in Conway, a large tea – High Tea – celebrating in many ways our return from the wilderness. We were becoming easier in one another's company now, and I realised, facing Kathy across the crowded table, that I had that morning in one sense been dreading this first day together, envisaging the agonies of post-mortems, explanations, recapitulations. But as the day advanced I saw that Kathy wanted no more than I such time-wasting irrelevances to mar the short time we had together. She was like a little girl who will cry for an hour, two hours, for the sweet she has been denied, behaving as if for her mother she could feel nothing but consuming resentment; but, the sweet obtained at last, the cries die on the instant, tears vanish, smiles crease wet cheeks, and all is love, the hours of crying forgotten.

It was dark, quite dark, when we queued in the Square for the Llandudno bus, our hands, parted by the tea table, now locked together again. I seemed to have held Kathy's hand for years, across half the world. I knew all about it, how long the thumb was, how clearly articulated the nails, how, without moving the thumb, Kathy could tense or relax the muscle in the ball of the thumb, making it hard or soft, a barely perceptible caress.

In the dark square, dim figures in front of us and behind, the street lamps masked to thin slits of light, I could hardly see Kathy, yet, holding her hand, I felt myself to be holding all of her. It was as if, by holding her hand throughout the day, I had drawn down into it the essence of herself, could now feel there, there, where the tips of my fingers fitted precisely into the soft hollows between her knuckles, the real tangible part of the person I loved, of Kathy. It seemed to me that no future pleasure could ever surpass or even equal this which, holding Kathy's hand in the dark Square with the flakes of snow tapping at our cheeks, noses, eyelids like moths, I was now experiencing. The day had been one of quiet, sustained, mounting elation, as impossible to describe as to repeat. The world was all ours, for us; the snow fell for us, drifted into exquisite forms for us, enamelled the hills and fields for us; curious people walked abroad for us, beautiful and ugly; boats rode on water for us, Bitterns boomed for us, teacakes smelled uniquely delicious for us, queues formed their mysterious entities for us, buses created their private enclosed civilizations for us. And later, a dance was arranged for us, a band played for us, the table we did not want to sit at was occupied for us, and when we came out into the hard clear night the stars were all there for us, every one perfectly positioned, keeping their precise stations for us in the faultless sky.

We walked down to Craig-y-don on the Promenade, with the sea rustling gently among the tide-wrack along the shingle. I had learnt nothing more about Kathy – that is, about her family, her way of life, her interests – than I had always known. But I had learned that day something about herself, about the way she lived in the world, which I had never suspected: that for her the important part of life was not then or when but now, here, this instant; that for her the past was not an accumulation of forces building up towards the future but a series of instantaneous nows which happened to have culminated in this all-important, happy or unhappy now; the past could no more be regretted than the future feared, for neither were important. If she was unhappy now, her life was a tragedy; if happy, she was a child of Good Fortune.

After a whole day spent with Kathy it was impossible not to know this; and, knowing it, it seemed to me remarkable that the habit or cast of mind had led to neither stupidity nor shallowness. There must be in her, I thought, some other hidden sense of the cohering stream of time, for there was an innocent, accepting wisdom in her that made my own hesitations about life seem superficial, immature.

She said, in the porch of her house, as we kissed good night 'I'm so happy, Bernard!'

'It's been a wonderful day. I can't think how we're ever going to beat it,' I said.

'How do you mean, beat it?'

'I mean, have one as good, or better.'

'Oh, Bernard, you do say funny things! Why, there's thousands of things we can do; we can be happy for ever and ever and ever, now!'

I couldn't say that our ever and ever was limited to five weeks, none of which contained more than seven days of twenty-four short hours apiece, so I kissed her again instead. But I was thinking as I kissed her that 'for ever and ever and ever' had no meaning for her beyond 'tomorrow'. And I knew already, young as I was, how soon tomorrow becomes yesterday when one desperately wants it to be today.

Love has a baffling logic of its own. One falls in love with a person about whom one knows nothing, and only then, after the first impulse has been obeyed, does one start slowly to discover those qualities which, in later years, seem to be the essence of one's love. Thus with Kathy I came first to realise how little I knew of her, and then to uncover the treasures which in retrospect I would have said made me love her. Yet I loved her first. It is an old riddle.

Kathy would often say 'I have a theory...' and follow with some utterly unexpected contradiction of what is generally accepted as the truth. Sometimes they were simply whimsical yet expressed something one had oneself often felt, as, 'I have a theory that mountains are higher in winter than in summer!' or 'I have a theory that clocks go faster by day than by night' or 'I have a theory that rocks have nerves....' But occasionally her theories were more substantial. One day she said to me 'I have a theory that spring starts in December'; and, challenged, took me off on a long bicycle ride to show me daffodils in small bud at Gloddaethisaf, crocuses at Bodafon, snowdrops in the woods on Bodafon Hill, japonica in waxy bloom over the doorway of a ruined cottage near Llangwstenin, flowers of wych-elm, the spotted catkins of poplar. I was not convinced. December, I said, had been unusually mild, these flowers deceived; they would regret it now that the snow had come.

'If it wasn't for the snow,' Kathy retorted, 'I could show you hundreds of little flowers, and you'd have to agree with me!'

'There isn't really,' she asserted as we rode home, 'any such season as winter. There's simply late autumn and early spring.'

Like all Kathy's pronouncements, this had a mad relationship to the truth. And after a week of her company

I began to see that other of her confident statements, such as 'We can be happy for ever and ever and ever, now!' were not so out of touch with reality as I had imagined. For Kathy, 'for ever and ever' meant simply 'until it is ended'. It might end in death tomorrow, or by the machinations of outside powers the next day, or by my leaving her on February the sixth; whichever it was, whatever happened, while we were together we were together for ever and ever.

'I always think I'm going to die tomorrow,' said Kathy. She did. She behaved as if whatever she were doing, seeing, eating, having, was for the last time. Perhaps it was this that gave all her actions that urgency which, seeing her as an unknown girl run across fields over thirty months before, I had sensed in her. Every cup of coffee she drank, kiss I gave her, laugh we shared, was the best ever. When, unthinking, I spoke sharply to her once, she looked at me as if I had cut off her hand, and I saw that for her the momentary displeasure I felt was as much for ever and ever, now, this instant, as had been the love it had displaced and which would succeed it. Reality for Kathy was as we were now. She might (I felt she felt) die the next instant with my sharpness in her ears as the essential quality of life. I determined never to speak sharply to her again.

The snow consolidated itself; put down a new layer on two successive nights, thawed slightly on the third day and then froze hard. Kathy shared my love of abnormal conditions. We delighted in the brittle sheaths of ice encasing spears of reeds, in the line of frozen froth across the little beach at Pigeon's Cove, the bubbles and mounds and bridges of ice which the stream at Dwygyfylchi had

303

erected. As, day by day, the temperature dropped, the roads became icy, we abandoned our bicycles and used what buses were still running to escape from the town.

It had now become necessary, for our peace of mind, to keep away from the town as much as possible, for Dewi, we knew, must have returned from Scotland. We had never mentioned him; indeed, had never even obliquely referred to the past, except to talk of people with whom neither of us had been intimately connected. The only exception to this rule was Epsom, who had for Kathy the fascination of a foreigner from a romantic country. She loved me to talk about him, repeat his sayings, imitate his gestures and his voice; and, like a child, liked best to hear those stories which she already knew. 'Tell me,' she would say, 'about how Epsom got to know Isabel...' or, 'Tell me about how you met him and the mad woman and the fight you had...' or, 'Tell me about the Resistance Group...'

One day, after we had been speaking of Pat, and I had told, humorously, the story of my first meeting with her, I suddenly started to tell her about Epsom's pacifism. I hadn't intended to, because it was a subject which still made me feel uneasy. I was led into it in an effort to demonstrate an aspect of Pat's character about which we disagreed; and then I was in the middle of it all and experiencing a certain sense of relief in the telling.

Kathy listened gravely, nodding her head. I tried to put Epsom's arguments across fairly, but felt that I was doing less than justice to him. I kept stopping and saying 'Do you see? Is that clear? I can't quite...' And Kathy would nod impatiently, and say 'Yes, of course, go on, go on!' When I had finished, explaining too my part in his decision to become an S.B.A., and Pat's agreement, Kathy said 'Well, I must say, I do think that's silly!'

'What's silly?' I asked.

'Being a whatsit, joining the Navy after all. I mean, it's the protest that matters, isn't it? He ought to have refused to have anything to do with the war.'

'You mean, you think he's right, then?'

'Of course he's right, you silly!' Kathy exclaimed, laughing, as if it was ludicrous to think in any other way.

'But you don't mind me joining the Navy, do you?'

'Of course not, but you're not Epsom,' she said. 'It would be ridiculous for you to be a Conchie!' Kathy laughed again, presumably at the picture of me as a Conchie.

'Well, good heavens!' I exclaimed, exasperated. 'What on earth do you think, then? We can't both be right!'

'Oh, but you can, you are!' Kathy asserted confidently. 'It's right to be the thing you are, that's all. It's when you act against yourself that you start nasty things happening. It's a question of balance.'

'Balance?'

'Yes. I've got a theory that the world is a balance. It's all right as long as people go on being what they are, but as soon as they try to be things that they aren't it upsets the balance and you get all sorts of nasty things like war and unemployment.'

'I don't believe you really think that,' I said indulgently.

Kathy was quite indignant. 'Oh yes I do,' she said. 'It's my philosophy, you see.'

I couldn't argue with her, any more than I could argue

305

with Epsom. It was as if, talking of such abstract matters, words meant different things for each of us, communication became so imprecise as to be dangerous.

But Kathy kept coming back to the subject, urging me to write to Epsom and find out how things were working out. I agreed. I wanted to write, but for some reason I did not. My days were full of Kathy, my nights full of the thought of her. There would be plenty of time, I felt, for writing to Epsom once this brief idyll was over.

One day Kathy announced that she had herself written to Epsom. 'I sent him your love,' she said.

'What did you tell him?'

'Oh, everything. I thanked him for sending the letter and told him how marvellous everything is now and how happy we are, thanks to him. And I said you'd told me about his views about the war and I thought he was quite right but shouldn't have let himself be persuaded to join up, and all that....'

'But you don't think he's right about the war!' I said. 'You shouldn't have said that, Kathy!'

'If I was him,' said Kathy obscurely, 'I'd think he was right!'

'You shouldn't have said that!' I said again, shaking my head, I was troubled by the thought of her letter, wished that it had not been written. Yet I could not blame Kathy. She was (I thought, thinking in her own manner) only doing what in such circumstances she would do. It was my fault for having told her about Epsom's views in the first place; as perhaps I should never... but no, it was inconceivable that I should have been wrong.

It was inevitable that one or both of us should meet Dewi eventually. I had hoped – I supposed that Kathy had hoped – that we could live out our five weeks without his ever knowing; or, since he could hardly help but learn the truth from others, without meeting him. He knew that I was due to leave in February, and could console himself with the thought. When we eventually met him, the circumstances were worse than any I had imagined. We had taken the bus over the Sychnant Pass to Dwygyfylchi, walked up beside the frozen stream and along the Jubilee Path on the lower slopes of Foel Lus to the Green Gorge, where, Kathy had a theory, the wild ponies would be grateful for a ration of lump sugar. Kathy was right. The ponies, made fearless by the snowy conditions of their chosen beat, were so grateful that a troop of them followed us right down towards Penmaenmawr, sniffing at our pockets and jostling each other to get near us, until I feared that we would both be trampled to death. Kathy, not the least bit scared, was delighted with her shaggy, hungry friends, and only sorry that we could not take them all down into the town and let them loose in a greengrocer's shop.

'Poor things,' she said, 'if Epsom were here I bet he'd organize someone to take some hay up to them!'

I thought that she was probably right; but knew that such things were not within my scope. There had been no hint of reproach in Kathy's voice; one of the advantages of her 'philosophy' was that she never expected one to do something which it was not in one's nature to do, simply because she knew that someone else would have done it.

It had been a wonderful walk, on snow crusted so hard

that even on the deepest drifts one's feet indented the surface only just enough to give one purchase, never so much as to impede movement. The air was brilliant, fed with light from above and below. Wherever bracken or reeds came through the snow, or trees were embraced by ivy, the colours seemed to glow and pulse, the white of the snow whiter, the green or the brown greener or browner, than one would have thought possible. Kathy and I, hand in hand, came down into Penmaenmawr like travellers returned to the ordinary world after having trafficked for strange webs with Eastern merchants. We felt ourselves almost to be lean mountain ponies sent down as spies into the cities of the plain to plunder, wreak havoc, drum laughing through the town on hooves of ice and fire. Since breakfast we had subsisted all day on nothing but laughter and love and snow melted in our warm palms and now were joyously hungry. We knew a cafe down on the front near the station where the bread was homemade and real butter was served in generous rations with it. We came into it as if we owned it, laughing, our arms about each other's waists. It appeared to be empty, and we stood in the middle of the room, stripping off scarves, coats, gloves, and calling through the open door of the kitchen to let the waitress know we were there. And then behind us we heard the noise of the door opening, and, turning, saw Dewi, a small figure in climbing boots and an anorak, with an ice-axe hanging by a thong from his wrist, going out. At the table in the curtained window embrasure, where we had ourselves many times sat, was a full, steaming cup of tea and a plate with a half-eaten Bath bun on it.

Through the glass door we watched Dewi hurry away, without looking back, grasping his ice-axe like a weapon of offence. The bell above the door swung, creaking but not ringing. Except for that creaking, it was very quiet in the cafe.

'It was Dewi,' I said.

'Yes,' said Kathy.

We sat down at an inner table near the kitchen door. The thin, amiable waitress appeared, greeting us as old friends.

'What's happened to the other gentleman?' she asked. 'Left his tea he has!'

'He's gone.' I said, superfluously.

'Didn't pay for his tea, neither. Nor his Bath bun! There! That's a fine thing!'

'He was in a hurry,' said Kathy, surprising me.

'Might have left his shilling, hurry or no hurry. But there, that's what happens when you trust people! Now then, what would you like? Nice homemade bread and butter and a pot? Cakes?'

She peered inquisitively at Kathy, who was drawing with her thumb-nail on the chequered tablecloth. 'Cheer up, bach,' she said, 'a cup of tea's what you need!'

Kathy and I, waiting for our tea, said nothing. I tried desperately to think of some consoling, philosophic phrase, but nothing came. The waitress brought tea, chattered again, went again. Kathy continued to incise deep lines across the tablecloth with her nails. I poured the tea, helped myself to one of the greyish irregular shaped pieces of bread, and started to butter it.

Kathy, looking at the tablecloth, said suddenly 'I can't

help it. It isn't my fault. I never said anything. It was always him. He was always there, it would have been silly if I'd just refused and refused and refused to go out with him. I did refuse, sometimes. But I didn't want to hurt him. He was always insisting on things. He insisted on taking me to the pictures when I didn't want to go, and on giving me that silly cigarette case... I tried to refuse, honestly I did, but... well, it didn't seem then that you would ever... I've always loved you, Bernard, you see. It's his own fault.'

'I suppose it is, really,' I said.

'Oh, it is!' said Kathy with sudden passion. 'It is, it is!'

'Once.' I said slowly, 'at the Music Club, when I danced with you – '

'The first time?

'Yes, the first time. We danced, and then I borrowed an aspirin.'

'I remember.'

'Dewi was in the washroom when I went down. He wanted to fight me. Epsom... Epsom wouldn't let him.'

'You weren't afraid of him?'

'Of course not. Not of fighting. But I didn't know. I wasn't sure – '

'What? You didn't... Bernard, you didn't think I loved him?'

'I didn't know. I didn't know what to do.'

'Oh, Bernard, I wish you had fought him! There you are, you see, it is his fault. What right had he...? I'd never said anything....'

'No,' I agreed. 'It's his own fault.'

But it wasn't. I knew it wasn't. I knew that it had

nothing to do with him, really, nothing to do with the incident in the washroom. I didn't know how, where, what, but I felt, I knew, that the root of Dewi's present distress was buried in my own inadequacy. The world, as I had always known, laid traps to ensnare one, traps that can only be evaded by courage and honesty. Somewhere, perhaps at one moment, perhaps at hundreds, these had not been with me. I didn't know where. I couldn't, at that moment, see the history of my relationship with Kathy in any completeness. I didn't even think, with the cogitative surface of my mind, any of these things; but I apprehended them, and when I said 'No, it's his own fault,' said it dully, without conviction.

As we left the cafe, I excused myself and went back inside for a moment, as if I had left something behind. When I came out again, Kathy asked what I had gone back for.

'To pay for Dewi's tea, I said. 'It was our fault, after all that.'

'Well, you see,' said Kathy, taking my hand, 'that's why I love you!'

The meeting with Dewi had spoiled our day; but, by releasing us from the restraints which had kept us before from ever discussing or even mentioning our mutual past, made it possible, in the two weeks that remained, for us to become closer than ever.

On the day after our walk to Penmaenmawr, the thaw set in. For three days the town was covered by a thin, warm drizzle. The snow retreated slowly, leaving its bones in spoiled drifts under walls or at the edges of escarpments. I was sorry to see it go, for I loved the silent, special world it created; found in its beauty some element of purity, of profitless untouchability, that appealed to a streak of austerity in my nature. Man could, I felt, do nothing with snow: it could not be sold, would bear no harvest, feed no one, provide shelter for no one; it would never be territory for which men might go to war, or murder, or steal. Its beauty could not be taken away to museums or framed and hung on walls, its marvellous purity remained only so long as one refrained from laying covetous hands on it. One could do nothing with snow but look at it; my mind's eye will never tire of conjuring over and over the lovely sweeps and funnels and curving edges of snow that my physical eyes have rested their gaze against.

I told Kathy of my regret, as we walked one day through the warm mist of rain near the lighthouse on the Great Orme.

'Rain's lovely, too!' she said, lifting her face to it, licking the water off her lips. While the snow was there, nothing, for Kathy, could be as wonderful as snow; but now it was raining, and rain was lovely.

'You're lovely!' I said. 'I love my love with a – '

'With a what?'

'A Kay.'

'Kay for Kathy?'

'No. Kay for Kiss!'

There was something in what she said, about rain. I loved to kiss her when her face streamed with water, when rivulets of rain ran down between our noses as our lips met. Sometimes, in rain, we sat with our cheeks together, the skin of our faces adhering with the viscosity of the thin film of water between. There was always something in what Kathy said: she would make it so. If the east wind cut into one's bones, and the pain of cold feet had become almost unbearable, Kathy would say, shivering 'What's nice about being cold is getting warm again!' When she said it, I might think it a ridiculous thing to say; but later, sitting in some warm cafe with our hands clasped about cups of hot coffee and our feet, with shoes kicked off, extended to the fire, I saw that she was right: this particular pleasure, which was exquisitely satisfying, would have been impossible had we not first become painfully cold.

Kathy met me one day in the Avondale, looking unusually troubled. As I sat down she pushed a piece of paper across the table to me.

'It's a letter from Epsom,' she said.

The letter was addressed from Dunfermline again. It said:

Dear Kathy.

I never expected it. I really didn't! But you'd think your trouble well taken if you could have seen my pleasure on receiving your letter. It was a very nice letter. Thank you.

I'm glad about you and Bernard, really glad. I have wished often that I could say something to you to let you know how he felt about you, and have tried often enough, goodness knows, to persuade him... well, anyway, that's all past now. I will confess to you – don't tell him! – that I don't properly understand Bernard, he's an odd fish. Happily though I have come to realise that one often understands least those one loves best; otherwise how could we ever love properly?

As to the second part of your letter, I may say that the situation has now become so tricky that I'm afraid I completely agree with you; I have made a mistake and will no doubt have to pay for it. For myself, I don't particularly mind. I have learned quickly how to be self-contained. In two months I have I think matured more than in the previous two years. Prison holds few horrors for me. But I regret the pointlessness of being condemned (as I suppose it will pan out) for disobeying an order, instead of having refused to have any part in the war. One more Conscientious Objector is a drop in the ocean towards persuading people to examine their consciences. But one more awkward sailor is just one more defaulter.

I can't, as things are, see how it is to be avoided. Up here I have attended half a dozen lectures on elementary first aid, which I already know, and spent the rest of the time marching up and down with a score of other lunatics with a weapon of death on my shoulder; or have been made to learn the intestinal details of Bren guns, Lewis guns, Oerlikon guns, dropping to sleep at night murmuring, not 'The presence of bile in the deeper layers is due to obstruction of the common bile duct,' but 'The rear-seer-spring-retainer-keeper is held in place by the pressure of the keeper on the lower lip of the retainer which takes up against the upper machine surface of the breech....' Quite apart from the fact that that way madness lies, it seems to me a sinister hint of the future, that a male nurse should be taught more about the insides of lethal weapons than about the insides of their victims. I haven't made up my mind finally, but I'm trembling on the verge of action. If this sort of nonsense goes on for another week, the parting of the ways must come. Bernard may be able to go to church without believing in God; I can't.

So tell Bernard to write while his letter can still reach me. And, Kathy, dear, kind Kathy, if you want my undying gratitude, write to me again yourself.

Love from

Epsom

'You must write, Bernard,' Kathy said. 'I've already written again... before I came out this morning.'

'Of course I will. What did you say?'

'Oh. I just said that of course he was right, he couldn't possibly go on like that, and perhaps he could get his case into the papers and do some good that way. That sort of thing.'

'But, Kathy!' I protested, 'How can you write things like that! You don't believe the war's wrong, do you?'

'Of course I do, Bernard! Everyone does, surely!'

'But, Kathy,' I said, trying to be patient, 'you said yourself that Hitler was wicked and had to be stopped!'

'Well, so he is, and so he must. But that doesn't make war right. Don't you see, Bernard, it's quite right for you to fight the Germans, but not for Epsom. Epsom mustn't ever fight, except fight against war.'

'Do you mean you think pacifism's right, then?'

'Oh no, not for everyone! After all, someone's got to fight Hitler. But someone's got to be a pacifist. And then one day we'll all be pacifists. Germans and Americans and Japanese and everyone, and then there won't be any more wars. It's a question of narrowing the balance.'

'Kathy, you're impossible!' I said, laughing because I could find no terms on which to meet her. Kathy laughed too, delighting in her image.

'I've got a theory, you see,' she said, 'that at the moment we keep the balance with arms which are opposed to each other. People like you are good at keeping the two arms in balance, but people like Epsom are good at making the two arms get closer and closer together until finally they meet over the point of balance.' And then Kathy concluded happily, 'there won't be any more wars! It's as simple as that.'

'I wish it was!' I said. But looking at Kathy there across the table, laughing at me with screwed-up eyes, her head tilted delightedly at her own cleverness, I almost believed her: believed that she would make it so.

That night, with difficulty, I did write to Epsom; a long, hesitant, shambling letter, a mixture of my delight in Kathy and my sorrow at his anomalous position. I told him that Kathy and I disagreed, without rancour, as to what he should do, and exhorted him to stick it out to the last moment, not to call his hand unless he was ordered to take actual offensive action. I assured him, without conviction, that he would not be.

I also wrote a short letter to Pat. At the top of this one I wrote the date: January 30th, 1944, and realised with a shock that in seven days I would have to leave. It was ironical that now the day to which I had so long looked forward was nearly upon me, I no longer wanted to go.

The next morning there was a note for me from the School Secretary: The Headmaster would be grateful if you could call to see him at 11 a.m. on 31st Jan. . I had arranged to meet Kathy at eleven at the Avondale, but fortunately she was, as I had counted on her being, early, and having asked her to wait where she was, I hurried round to the school, arriving only a few minutes after eleven.

I had never had much to do with the Head. As Chemistry Master for the upper forms he had brushed briefly against me; and on one occasion, for I forget what offence, Epsom and I had had to present ourselves in his study for what was known at the school as a 'whipping': that is, a whipping from his tongue. But he was a kind, humorous man; I think he must have had a vocation for teaching, for he could keep perfect order without either inspiring fear or forfeiting respect. After our 'whipping' he had asked Epsom to stay behind when I left. 'Jones,' he said, 'you might murmur in Smith's ear that it is disconcerting to admonish a boy severely and be met by a bland grin. Smith always gives me the impression that he's laughing at me, it's enough to try the temper of a saint!' Epsom reported this to me, and, so approachable was the Beak, I went straight back to his study and apologized, explaining that my grin was only nervousness and I hadn't known I was grinning. The Beak said 'Good. Well, I should try to control that grin if I were you, Smith. It's so bad that I had to send you out of the room and say what I wanted to say through Jones. I felt you'd only grin even wider if I said it to you then!'

Heads, I thought, were only human after all. This was practically my only passage-of-arms with him; and that a mild one. Nevertheless, I felt the usual flutterings which any schoolboy, or only-just-ex-schoolboy, must feel in the circumstances, as I tapped that morning at his door.

He was a tall, thin man, with a larger head than his body needed, and sat very straight in his chair. I had imagined that, knowing I was about to leave for the Navy, he had sent for me to make a formal farewell. But, after the greetings and enquiries, pleasantly man-to-man, had put me at my ease, he said 'You're a friend of Dewi Hughes, aren't you, Smith?'

'Well,' I said, 'sort of, sir. I didn't know him very well. He didn't have many friends in the school.'

The Beak looked at me sharply, and I realised that I had been speaking of Dewi in the past tense.

'That's what I thought,' he said. 'But he was associated with you and Jones at one time, wasn't he? And Owen and Thomas?'

For a moment I couldn't think who Owen and Thomas were; then I remembered: Kenny and Peredur.

'That was before he went up to the Sixth, sir. I haven't seen much of him since then.'

'Hm. I see. I rather hoped...' the Beak covered his mouth with a clean, hairy hand, frowning. 'The fact is, Smith' he said, 'Hughes has done something I can't understand... I thought perhaps you knew him better than you seem to. You might have been able to explain – '

'I could try, sir,' I said helpfully, wondering what on earth could be coming.

'You know, I suppose,' the Beak said, hunching himself over his desk and staring at his blotting-paper, 'that he succeeded in winning a County Bursary, and had been accepted by Manchester University? He was to start there in April.'

'Yes. I know that, sir.'

'And so far as you know he's always wanted to get to the University?'

'Ever since I've known him, yes, sir.'

'He's worked hard for it, hasn't he, Smith? And he was still working hard right up to the end of last term. And now this happens!'

'What, sir?' I asked. I had already guessed, vaguely; and wondered tremulously whether I was being interviewed now simply, as he said, as Dewi's only remaining friend, or... for some other reason.

'Two Mondays ago, I had this letter....' The Beak flipped with a long nail an open letter at one side of his desk. 'He says that for 'personal reasons' he has decided to forfeit his Bursary and intends to... to join the Army! It's,' – the Beak spread his hands, distended his eyes – 'it's incredible to me, Smith! The most brilliant scholar we've had for years, keen, intelligent and ambitious, with a wonderful future... and he wants to join the Army! Have you any conception of what can have come over him?'

'I... I'm afraid I haven't, sir. I'm sorry,' I said. I could hear my voice, thin and squeaky, and was amazed at having been able to get the words out. The Beak didn't seem to notice. He shrugged slightly, his expression almost despairing. I was touched to see how much he cared. He obviously, to my relief, knew nothing that could connect me with those 'personal reasons' with which Dewi had excused his sudden apostasy.

'I was afraid you wouldn't know. It was just a chance – personal reasons – you might have.... Ah, but I'm wasting your valuable time, Smith, you must be very busy just now. I shall have to go and see his parents of course. Possibly it is too late already. But I wouldn't feel easy in my mind if I didn't... hadn't...'

I saw that the Beak was talking to himself, 'Oh dear,' he ended, almost plaintively, 'this is very distressing for me, Smith, very distressing!'

I could see that it was; that for him to lose the most brilliant of his litter to the Army, where he would almost

319

certainly go stale, possibly get himself killed, was a loss actually touching his emotions.

I took the opportunity of this visit to say goodbye. The Beak, I saw at once, had quite forgotten my own imminent departure. He looked suddenly very old and worn.

'Oh dear,' he said, 'are you going too, so soon? How old are you, Smith? Seventeen and a half? Well, I suppose they know what they're doing. It's all very sad – '

He was talking to himself again; for a moment was not the alert, intelligent headmaster I thought I had known, but another man, feeling his middle-age, wondering if in the end all his labours were futile; allowing himself a pause in which to sag with the thoughts he normally dared not have. Then he brightened a little.

'And how is your friend Jones getting along? Have you heard?'

'He seems to be managing, sir,' I said. 'It can't be easy,' – I wasn't going to involve myself in a discussion of Epsom if I could help it. I wanted to get away quickly, to think about Dewi.

'No, no it can't be easy. I hope he does – er – manage, as you put it, but fear that he won't. Not Jones.'

The Beak looked up at me (I had stood to take my leave) and the firm, humorous expression I was accustomed to was back on his face.

'I always liked Jones,' he said. 'He doesn't believe in what he has just done, like the rest of us; he does what he believes in. And he doesn't... truckle?'

The Beak managed to make the word truckle sound richly humorous.

After we had said again our farewells, and I was standing once more in the draughty, dusty hall, I noticed a small boy, in wide slacks and a green blazer, hovering inconspicuously near the notice board. The Beak, in his doorway, noticed him too.

'Oh, Jones,' I heard him say, 'you wish to see me, don't you? I hear that you've been experimenting in an interesting way with the school plumbing....'

Hearing the name, Jones, I looked back, half-expecting to see Epsom entering the dreaded door. But it was only, after all, a grubby little boy of fourteen or fifteen, absurd in baggy trousers and out-grown blazer.

Kathy was waiting for me in the Avondale, I had to rejoin her straightaway. I wished that I had time to think, before meeting her, about Dewi. But what was there to think? I knew it all without thinking. I decided not to tell Kathy, though, for the moment. She would be bound to hear, from someone, but by then I would have had time...

'I'm sorry I've been so long,' I said, sliding into the window seat beside her. Beneath the table she found my hand, taking it in both of hers.

'I've been quite happy,' she said, 'thinking about you. What did he say?'

'Oh, just to wish me luck, and all that. Wanted to know if I'd heard from Epsom.'

'Did you tell him?'

'No. I said I thought he was managing. I didn't want him to – '

'No, of course not,' Kathy agreed. 'But what are you so gloomy about?'

'Am I? I'm sorry, I didn't mean to be.'

I smiled at her, squeezing her hand. 'There! Better?'

'What did he say?' said Kathy.

'What do you mean? I told you what he said!'

'What else did he say?' Kathy insisted. When I shook my head, as if not understanding, she laughed, and said 'Oh, Bernard, you're such a silly boy! You know you can't fib to me! Now then, what was it?'

'It's Dewi. He's joined the Army.'

'Joined the Army! Dewi? Oh no, Bernard!'

'He has. Or he's just going to. He'd written to the Beak. He said it was for 'personal reasons'. The Beak thought I might know.'

'He doesn't know anything? About us, I mean?'

'No. I said I didn't know him very well. The Beak was quite upset about it.'

'Oh, but it's so silly?' Kathy exclaimed. 'It's all wrong! He didn't have to do that!'

I said angrily 'It's just the sort of damn' silly thing he would do! I always said he was ruthless!'

'That's not ruthless,' said Kathy. 'It's just silly!'

I realised after I had said it that it was not ruthlessness that had made Dewi react in this violent way, but... what? An inflated sense of destiny, I might have said. If I had known about such things, a too dramatic sense of himself as the centre of the world. But he was being ruthless only with himself. As he had driven himself to become a mountaineer, to make himself into a scholar, so he had driven himself now to abandon one thing that he desperately wanted because he could not have another.

322

I said, out of my thoughts 'It's my fault, really....'

'It isn't!' Kathy exclaimed passionately. 'It isn't your fault, Bernard! You can't help it if he's such a... such a mutt! I won't have you say it's your fault. And it isn't mine, either! I didn't ask him to... to – '

'It's so complicated,' I said vaguely. 'It all goes back such a long way.'

I didn't know what I meant when I said that; but I sensed perhaps that the roots of tragedy (I thought of Dewi's life, already, as a tragedy) lie not only in what we have done but also in what we have not done, not only in what the victim (I thought of Dewi, too, as a victim) is, but in what other people are not. One cannot say: I will stand aside from these problems because I do not wish to be responsible for hurting someone; because by standing aside one is taking action which must affect others, and for which, whether one likes it or not, one must eventually hold oneself responsible. No matter how big the world, how small the individual, he cannot expunge himself from its affairs without being responsible for what takes his place there.

Kathy said 'You don't know whether he's actually joined or not yet, do you?'

'No. The Beak didn't either.'

'We ought to do something, it's such a waste. I wish Epsom was here! Neither of us can... I mean, it would only make it worse if I tried to see him.'

'Or me.'

'Can't you think of anyone, Bernard?'

I couldn't. It was extraordinary, I had never realised it before, but Dewi had succeeded in spending nearly three years at the school without making a single close friend. He had, of course, been associated with the rest of us in the Music Club and the Resistance Group, and at that time any one of us would have said of him 'Oh yes, he's a friend of mine.' But he was not. He was One Of Us, but not a friend. I knew, when I came to think about it, practically nothing about him, not even where he lived, beyond the fact that it was up under the Orme, in Church Walks perhaps. I knew that when he went climbing he did so with a group of other climbers whom he had met at the Youth Hostels and Club Huts in the mountain valleys; but now, realizing his essential friendlessness, I suspected that these climbing companions were not friends, had no existence for him except as calculable forces on the other end of a climbing rope. I thought of the people now left in the Sixth Form: Gregory, whom Dewi despised; Peter, who admired Dewi's mind but found him unapproachable as a person; John Stockwell, a quiet, sensual biologist who once described Dewi as 'A naked Life Force... they put in the will power but forgot to add the human being...'; none of them were any use, none could, even if they would, approach him on any acceptable terms. The only person who knew him at all well was Kathy, and she was debarred from approaching him by being at the very centre of his crisis. Only Epsom, had he still been with us, could have carried out such a commission. But I doubted if even he could have influenced Dewi away from the mad, wasteful course he had chosen.

Kathy and I did not discuss Dewi any further that day; but all day, and the next, he was with us, a reproachful ghost, staring down any glint of delight we might show in each other's company, lurking everywhere about the town in which we had known him. We tried to avoid him; would not visit the dance hall because of the table at which I had discovered the inscription in the cigarette box, nor the Odeon because we both remembered the occasion on which Kathy had said to Dewi (I guessed), on seeing Epsom, Pat, and me in the second house queue 'No, come on, I don't want to see him... !' We avoided Sumner's, took care not to pass the hotel in whose attic the Music Club had lived and died, found subjects which had before amused us closed by their associations. And how many these subjects were! – music, mountains, the Club, the School, parties, dancing... even Epsom, it seemed, could not now be mentioned without, by some complicated web of relations, throwing the image we wished to forget across the screen of our thoughts.

We kept, as much as possible, away from the town. But the weather, continuing wet, made it impossible for us to spend all our time in the open, and we were beginning to tire of the little cafes, snack bars, milk bars which we had made our homes. My mother, too, was beginning to tire of the endless succession of wet clothes, the constant demand for dry ones. What Kathy's parents thought, or said, I don't know. She never mentioned them, and I doubt if they knew that I existed. Kathy was a very competent liar, but I can't imagine how she explained her daily absences from home. Perhaps she just forgot to mention that she had given up her job at Colwyn Bay.

Knowing that we were bound, one day, to meet my mother in the town, I had early decided to forestall her curiosity by telling her a little about Kathy. We were very distant, these days. She may have wished, I thought I detected signs of her wishing, that in these last weeks or days of my life at home some brief sympathy could be established between us. But she must have known it was too late, had for years been too late; it was too late as soon as she decided, or perhaps was forced, to look for love outside of her family. I suspect... I shall never know... that her own affairs were at this time coming to an acute head.

I told my mother simply that, since I would not be seeing Kathy again for several months, I was spending as much of my time as possible in her company. It seemed unnecessary to enlarge on this, to give the when, where, and how much of our relationship. We treated each other with the tactful consideration of complete strangers; there was nothing else we could do.

Rebuking me mildly for my endless wet clothes, Mother said 'Why don't you bring Kathy here in the afternoons? You can make yourself tea, I'm never back until after six, you know that.'

I said I would. Sometimes, I knew too, Mother did not return until the late evening, eleven o'clock, midnight, or after. She would tell me in the morning if this was to be so, so that I could make my own arrangements about an evening meal. It was on one of these days, the third day after my interview with the Headmaster, that I brought Kathy to my home for the first time.

'What a pity,' Kathy said, 'we didn't do this before!' We were sitting each in an armchair, either side of the fire in the sitting-room, a little selfconscious about being alone together in a house for the first time. It was, ironically, the first of the spell of fine days which ended my life in Llandudno. We had lunched in Bangor after a bus ride to Betws-y-Coed and through the Nant-Ffrancon Pass to the coast, arriving back at my house soon after four in the afternoon. Between us, on a wicker stool, was the tea tray. The fire, which Mother had banked up before leaving the house after lunch, was still flickering cheerfully when we came in out of the grey February dusk.

'Do you realise,' I said, 'what the date is?'

'Yes, Bernard.'

'The second of February. We only have four more days. Three, really. You can't count the day.'

'I'm coming with you, part of the way,' Kathy said. 'It'll be fun in the train.'

Kathy had an aunt in Rugby, and had contrived to arrange a visit to her to coincide with my own journey to Skegness.

'Still, it's only three days,' I insisted. 'It's silly to pretend it'll never come to an end.'

'It won't, really,' said Kathy confidently. 'Not ever. Bernard....'

'What?'

'Nothing. Well, something, but not now.'

She had become very quiet ever since we entered the house, her remarks disconnected, her smile abstracted. I had deliberately brought up and played upon the diminishing sands of our hourglass, thinking that it was perhaps this which troubled her. But she was not exactly troubled... there was a serene, subdued excitement about her which troubled me more than it did her.

She kept looking at the room, so different (I imagined) from her own home; a rather austere, clinical room with its carefully arranged bookcase, the tables clear of ornament, the mantelpiece supporting only an ormolu clock and a pair of silver snake candlesticks, the family's sole heirloom.

'When we're married,' Kathy said, 'I'd like to have a room like this. It's clean, airy, there's room to do things!'

'Not very cheerful,' I said. 'I like a room that's full of things, sort of left about.'

'Oh no, Bernard!' Kathy exclaimed. 'Our house is like that and it's horrid! You're always moving something to make room for something else!'

I had not proposed to Kathy, the thought would not have entered my head; nor had she to me. But when Kathy first said – it must have been on our second or third day together – 'When we're married...' I didn't even register the phrase. Later, during one of those moments of self-consciousness that occasionally touched me in Kathy's company, moments when, as it were, I broke the surface for an instant, took a quick look round, swallowing involuntarily a gulp of 'reality' before sinking back into the vivid 'unreality' of Kathy's world, the words 'married', 'marriage', 'wife', did flicker startlingly across my memory like the recollection of a troubling dream. There was no question, here, of intention. It was natural and right for Kathy to speak of our being married almost as of a fait accompli; but had someone from 'outside', my mother, perhaps, asked me 'Do you intend to marry Kathy?' it would have taken me several seconds to grasp what they were talking about. 'Well... yes, of course!' I would have said; but in the voice of one who says also

'You obviously don't understand the situation, or you wouldn't have asked.'

It was not that I did not regard Kathy, now, as the living and vital core of my life; or that a cautious corner of my mind warned me that it would be as well, being so young and not knowing what adventures the future might have to offer me, to retain a moral freedom. I had no reservations about Kathy now; had allowed myself to be borne away by the river which I had been afraid might drown me, and found it bearing me up, carrying me to countries of which no rumour had ever reached me. What Kathy visualized when she said 'When we're married...' I cannot guess; but I, repeating the words with no less sincere confidence, saw only a prolongation of the state we were in now....

How could I conceive of a future? No more than any soldiering youth did I imagine myself physically mortal, but I was very conscious that in going to war I was in a sense parting company with the only self I knew, I would not, of course, be killed; but if I thought of a Bernard Smith as existing in that inconceivable limbo 'after the war', it was of a stranger. How could I underwrite the emotions, desires, place in the world of someone I had yet to meet?

Kathy said now, looking into the fire 'I feel as if we were married already, don't you?'

'Yes,' I said.

'I mean, us just sitting quietly here by the fire, and the tea-tray and that – '

'If we were really married we'd probably be quarrelling about whose turn it was to do the washing up!'

Kathy, her head cocked sideways, looked curiously at me.

'You do say funny things, sometimes, Bernard!' she said. She didn't mean amusing things, I knew; and I knew that my facetious remark had been out of key with her mood. But I couldn't tell her that I did not, in fact, feel as if we were married, I felt only as if I were sitting privately in a warm room with the girl I loved, sensing between us the growth of some tension which I could not understand.

To help my understanding, to bring, as it were, the situation up to a pitch of 'reality', I told myself now (picturing to myself this room complete, the fire, I in my chair, Kathy in hers, bound together in the small world of firelight) that we had only three days, three days... there was surely something, in such a circumstance, that one should say or do? What did it mean, this picture which I formed in my mind, what significance would it immediately hold forth to someone more in touch with 'reality' than I? Kathy, I felt... I felt it in the shy, downward-looking smile with which she met my frown, in the gesture with which she impatiently refused my offer of more tea... Kathy was surely waiting for some sign from me, some... as, I suddenly remembered, with a little flush of shame, she had in this house sought a sign from me two and a half years before. Then, I had known what sign, what gesture, would have been an unequivocal declaration. But now, I only saw that her fingers, clasped in her lap, were restless, her eyes, when I raised mine to them, bright.

'I've always wanted to live in Spain,' she said. She said it as if she were not particularly interested, but felt she ought to say something.

'It would be lovely,' I said, as if she had said 'on the moon'.

'We could have one of those square stone houses with tiny windows and no glass, and you live on the balcony among the flowers. Wouldn't you like that, Bernard?'

'What would I be?' I asked, smiling indulgently. 'A bull-fighter?'

Kathy looked disappointed, almost she pouted. 'I haven't decided yet,' she said, 'what you're going to be.'

'If I get a commission, I shall probably stay on in the Navy,' I said vaguely. I hadn't thought of it until that moment, but it seemed quite a good idea. Ridiculous, of course, like any other vision of the future, but not indefensible.

Kathy widened her eyes in horror. 'Oh no!' she exclaimed, 'you can't possibly do that!'

'Why not?' I asked, laughing.

'What! And leave me to look after the children all by myself while you're away?'

I burst out laughing, but Kathy didn't laugh, she was quite serious; so after a moment I stopped laughing, and became confused.

'Don't laugh at me!' Kathy said, wide-eyed. 'I mean it. I want five children, three boys and two girls, and they'll all look like you. But you'll have to have a job that lets you stay at home most of the time!'

'Kathy,' I said (I couldn't think of anything else to say), 'I love you!'

'Yes, well!' she said reprovingly, as if to say also 'But that isn't enough!' But what else could I say? I had a sudden uncomfortable feeling that she wanted – it seemed fantastic, but all girls are fantastic, particularly Kathy – wanted us actually to be engaged, with a ring and plans

331

and... no, it was too absurd. I wasn't unwilling... I loved Kathy, didn't I?... but... but...

But it didn't fit, it wasn't part of our reality. Our reality, this reality, was not one of spoken pacts, affirmations, arrangements, mutual exchanges of personal knowledge; these were things I had coped with often in the past, giving and taking solemn promises with the ease of one who knows well their ephemeral nature. Kathy and I used more dangerous change, the unspoken assumption, the intimate secret revealed by a smile, the tone of voice in which a name was spoken. As I had known from the first moment I spoke to her, a girl on her bicycle laughing in the middle of the Conway Road, Kathy was all secrets, or none. She gave herself away, once I had allowed her to start giving, with every sentence she spoke, smile she smiled, glance she tried to hide; and could accept only the same terms from me.

'Bernard,' she said.

'What?'

'Oh... just, Bernard.'

In all our years together, in all the five weeks into which we had packed years of happiness, I had never felt as I felt now; heavy with the weight of what we had created, the ghostly third person to whom we had given life, of whom we would have loosely spoken as 'our love'. I felt as a man must feel who, standing waist deep at the edge of a river which he must swim, carries in his hands a bar of gold; he cannot swim carrying the gold, but he must cross the river; there is no one to whom he can hand the gold for safe-keeping, and anyway it is possible that the river may drown him or by its force prevent him from returning to his point of departure; is he then to throw the bar of gold back up the bank on to dry land, or carve his name on it (which is to defile it), and bury it neatly in the mud at the river's edge in the faint hope that he might one day return to dig it up?

The room was now quite dark save for the inconstant movement of yellow light from the fire, the glow of red about our feet.

Shadows, on the far wall, grew tall, wavered, and subsided. Among the moving curtains of light and dark in which she quietly sat, Kathy kept still the two minute specks, the twin inverted images of the fire, that lived in her eyes. Growing in me, coming up to my throat to choke me, was an apprehension of futility. I remembered, and put quickly from me, the silent inevitable death of Porphyria; and into my mind came two lines of Marvell which I thought I had forgotten:

> Let us roll all our strength, and all
> Our sweetness, up into one ball,

I would have liked, then, to have rolled our strength, our sweetness, our five weeks, our ghostly third person, up into one Ball, and... cast it from me, be done with it; to have said to Life 'Thank you; exquisite; but enough!'

I did not want three more days with Kathy. I loved her. I would have repudiated as ridiculous any suggestion that I didn't love her. But one cannot continue to drown indefinitely; it is said to be a blissful death but a point must come when the bliss ceases and death begins. I had been drowning for five weeks; I wanted now to cross over into death.

Kathy said 'How long will it be before you get your first leave, Bernard?'

'I'm not sure,' I said. 'But probably about six months. You don't get much leave when you're under training.'

'Let's sit on the sofa,' Kathy said, 'then you can kiss me.'

I had difficulty in making my limbs move; I seemed to have become detached from them, and only by a painful effort of will was able to enter my body again.

The sofa was of the collapsible type; I let down one end and lowered the back a few notches, so that Kathy could put her feet up in comfort. Then I sat down, sideways, on the edge, facing her. Kathy smiled confidently up at me, one hand on my right elbow.

But there was something wrong with the situation. Previously we had kissed only in porches, bus shelters, on public seats or beds of heather, bracken, damp grass. It had always been too cold for us to make love for long. Nor did I care to kiss Kathy too much at any one time, though the desire to kiss her had often arisen passionately in me, like a great bubble of warm air, when we were simply walking hand in hand by the sea or sitting beside one another in a tram or omnibus. But the cold and the damp had always been, for me, the welcome prophylactics of desire. After I had kissed Kathy too much the edges of my emotions became blurred, the sharp sweetness gone from the aura we carried with us.

Now, as I bent to kiss her, her face a pool of sweetness

cupped in a cushion of hair, I was afraid. I was aware that I had made a fatal mistake in bringing Kathy back thus to an empty house on a winter evening, in the fag end of our days. It was madness. This physical privacy was not our element; or, since Kathy appeared to feel no restraint, not mine. Out in the world, in cafes, on the streets, walking on hillsides, we had had privacy enough; by the very fact of being together, we had been safely enclosed. I had been able, on those terms, to give myself to Kathy with the abandon she desired. But here, on a soft sofa in warmth, in firelight, I was overcome by a sort of emotional claustro-phobia. Yet how could I, my lips pricking from contact with hers, plausibly suggest a walk, the dance hall, the cinema?

Touching Kathy was like touching flower petals, rose petals; my fingers moved on her flesh with delicate caution, lest some bloom be lost, ineradicable scar be made. I was afraid, always, having touched her, to look at her, so sure was I of having marred by my meddling her beauty. And yet I could not stay myself. She lay, always, silent, wide-eyed, breathing shallowly, and would say, after I had kissed her or lain a hand tentatively for a moment within her blouse 'Thank you, Bernard.'

For me, kissing was merely kissing, a farthing in the hand of the begging flesh. For Kathy, it was something more, her emotions were deeply, specifically involved. Except when, suddenly conscious of my love, I wished to express it and chastely kissed her (anywhere, immediately, in the pouring rain or a deserted street) my emotions, when I began to kiss her, seemed always to suspend themselves, let the flesh take charge. Kathy became no less beautiful, my delight in kissing her was still bound up remotely with love. But it was a beautiful girl that I loved, that I kissed, not Kathy. Kathy was... the air about her, her laughter, her shyness, her urgency, the world she created by moving through the world; these, I could not kiss.

But Kathy, kissing me, was kissing what she loved, all of it, Bernard. Where I was, a specific object, there her love lay, and could be expressed by kisses.

I understood too well, and feared now, in this darkened private room, the depths in Kathy's kiss. And if I should, say (as I did), allow my left hand to find the velvet softness of her right breast, that beautiful unemphatic mound, it was for her a gift not, as it was for me, of wondering sensual delight, but of absolute love. Her breast, she felt, was a better, a worthier, part of herself for having been touched by me. Not to have touched her, then, to have succumbed to my apprehensions, would have been a base meanness.

And so I touched her, kissed her. She seemed, I thought, after a kiss, to vibrate like a touched fiddle-string. Her breath, when she allowed it slowly to come out, shuddered down a scree of notes; or, like a mountain stream, fell suddenly from the confining gorge above to the open boulders below.

'Bernard,' she said, 'kiss me for a long time.'

I took her face between my hands to kiss her, covering her closed eyes with my thumbs, the tips of my fingers plunged into the roots of her hair. I kept my lips on hers: soft; hard; parted slightly; closed... for I know not how long. But I was not in the kiss. My body was in it, but not my mind. While the nerves of my body twanged onwards up the intolerable scale, my cold mind, centred behind my open eyes, looked blankly towards the future. My eyes examined with impersonal interest the minute, almost invisible hairs which started from Kathy's forehead below the actual hair-line, and which caught now some goldenness from the fire, giving her skin a double surface. It was beautiful, but it meant nothing, had nothing to do with whatever it was I loved.

When I pushed myself up from kissing her, Kathy opened her eyes to look at me. She was trembling.

'Thank you, Bernard,' she said.

Still looking at her face, I moved my left hand down to touch her breast again... and touched it. I saw then that, while I had been kissing her, she had with her free hand opened the front of her black cardigan, and of her grey woollen dress, and slipped down the shoulder straps of her vest, leaving her breasts exposed. I had felt her moving, but had thought only that she was settling herself more comfortably.

I let my hand lay where it had fallen across her breast, the nipple pressing up between thumb and forefinger. I had to look at her hair, and then beyond her hair to the cushion behind it, to the floor carpet, the skirting board, the wall below the window. I could not look either at her face or at what lay exposed below it.

Kathy put up her right hand and laid the palm flat against my cheek.

'Bernard,' she said.

My eyes had to be forced back to hers. She was smiling, still trembling. Absently, I moved my hand across her soft flesh, and felt my body stirring again.

'Beautiful Kathy,' I said.

But I wanted now to stop, get up, leave the room; and to come back, switching on the light, to find Kathy sitting quietly in the deep armchair beside the fire, her dress buttoned, this incident expunged.

'Don't frown, Bernard,' Kathy said softly, 'you mustn't frown. Listen, Bernard: I love you!'

'And I love you, Kathy,' I said, swallowing whatever obstruction had risen in my throat. It was intolerable, the pain of looking down at her thus: her eyes wide and dark, her hand trembling against my cheek, her bosom exposed to the unsteady tongues of light that licked around us.

Kathy said, 'Bernard: do you... know how?'

'Know how?' I echoed stupidly, blinking, knowing.

'To make love. We must make love now, Bernard, mustn't we? I mean, we must! Oh, Bernard, listen: I love you, don't you understand?'

Kathy's anguished, urgent voice... and yet also her accepting, contented voice... twisted in me, hollowing out the area below my ribs. My flesh had gone cold: I was appalled.

'But, Kathy – ' I started to protest.

'No, Bernard, you don't understand!' Kathy said quickly. 'I want you to make love to me. Don't you see. I want you to! Oh, Bernard, you know how, don't you, surely you know how?'

'Yes. but... Oh, Kathy, please. I can't! How can I? We're... you're... it isn't right, Kathy!'

'It is, it is right!' Kathy exclaimed. 'Don't you love me?'

'Of course I love you, Kathy! But – '

'Well, then! And I love you. Don't you understand? I love you! Oh, don't be so silly, Bernard, don't you see, this is... this is what... I want to belong to you, Bernard, because I love you, I want to be... Oh, Bernard, please!'

Kathy put up her other hand, her right hand, to my face, and started to draw my head down towards her bosom. She was trembling so violently that her palms made an audible tapping noise against the flesh of my cheeks. But I could stand it no longer. I was being choked by a flux of emotions which only violent movement could, I felt, prevent from killing me. I took her wrists in my hands, pulled them apart, and stood up. Then... the gesture was quite unconscious... I reached down and pulled the edges of her dress together in an attempt to cover her breasts.

'Stop. Kathy!' I commanded. 'You must stop! I can't! I won't! You must try to understand, it wouldn't be right, it would spoil everything... !'

'Oh, Ber...' Kathy couldn't complete my name, it was blocked halfway by a sob. Violently she threw herself over on to her face, her body heaving with convulsive, silent sobs.

'Kathy, I'm sorry...' I started; but knew she couldn't hear me. I walked across to the window; noticed that the black-out curtains were not drawn, drew them, and walked back again to the sofa. Kathy, her body twisted at the waist, had buried her face in the cushion behind her. Her hands pressed the cushion to her face. I saw how lovely the whole sweep of her body was, how rich her hair; and had I dared I would then have knelt and buried my face in that hair. But how could I? Kathy was a stranger, someone I had never known.

A noise came from Kathy, a terrible, rasping noise, as she drew in her breath. It was not a sob, it was worse than a sob, it was the abandoned choking of utter despair. There flashed into my mind the image of myself, fifteen years old, opening an unseen door in the dark and hearing, from the room within, the anguished sobs of a grief-stricken girl. I remembered how I had sworn to myself that never, never, would I allow myself to give cause for such grief. But this was worse than grief. Kathy was crying as if she wished to choke herself to death, would be glad to die. I knew. I felt what she felt, knew what shame, remorse, loss, racked her mind. Had I known how I might have joined my tears to hers.

I walked away from the sofa, across to the windows; parted the curtains and looked out into the darkness. My only conscious thoughts were: why does one always, at moments of crisis, look out of windows? and: when will it end, when will it end?

I walked back. Kathy was silent now. Her shoulders shook still, the hair across her frail neck quivered, but no sound came. I thought dispassionately how beautiful her hair was, and my hand itched to stroke it. I walked away, and back; looked down at her, remote, untouchable, two feet away from my useless, clumsy hands. I walked away, and back.

Kathy turned her head on the pillow, to face, not me, but the back of the sofa. She said clearly 'I want you to go away. Upstairs.'

'Kathy...'

'No, Bernard, please. You must do... that. I'll never ask _ '

She turned her head back to the pillow, starting to tremble again. I knelt on the floor beside her, resting my fingers on the elbow.

'Kathy, please!' I pleaded. 'You must try to – '

'No, Bernard! Can't you just... just do one thing I ask? Please, please leave me alone!'

I went. I went to my old refuge, the lavatory at the top of the house, and sat there with my hands over my ears, trying to block the sound of her voice asking me to leave her. But I couldn't block it. Like the Bittern's boom, her voice had had more lonely grief in it than the heart can stand. Like the grit in the soft belly of the oyster, it would always be there. I would have to learn to live with it. But though I weave the most elaborate cocoons of unreality about it, no comfortable pearl will ever grow.

When I at last came downstairs again, having heard the careful closing of the front door, I found the room as it had been when we arrived there, two hours before: the sofa re-erected, the cushions plumped up, the tea tray removed. Only the hollow cave of the coals, their life spent, was different. It was as if Kathy had never entered the room. I began to wonder if she ever had.

Fourteen

Gregory, his information system as efficient as ever, turned up at the railway station four days later to say goodbye. How he had discovered the date and time of my departure, I don't know. I had only seen him once since Pat's party, and then had exchanged no more than the briefest greetings. Nor did I understand what had brought him early from his bed into the grey drizzle of this bleak winter morning. Nothing, absolutely nothing, had ever passed between us that could be construed as the muted flame of friendship. But always, no matter how I ignored him, forgot his existence, snubbed him, he had persisted in regarding me as his friend. Lugubrious, ubiquitous Gregory! I wished him well, but well away from me.

And now we stood together, dim and embarrassed, beneath the sooty girders of the grey station, waiting for our release. I wished he were not there. I had nothing to say to him. Alone, I would have made myself comfortable in my chosen compartment, and read again, for the last time, the letter from Epsom which had arrived the day before. I wanted to read it while I was still in Llandudno. The impulse was obscure, but strong.

I felt nothing but relief in my departure. Gregory was

superfluous, and his attempts at jocular, last-minute reminiscence painful. I had contrived, so far, to keep my going emotionless, meaningless. My mother had not betrayed me. If she had been surprised to find me suddenly anxious for her company during my last three days at home, she had not shown it; had busied herself sensibly with preparations for my departure, buying or making the various personal impedimenta, a 'housewife', a sponge bag, shoe-cleaning material, which it had never occurred to me that I would need. My father had avoided me until the last possible moment; then, on the night before I left, had come shyly, almost apologetically, to my room, to lay two five-pound notes on my dressing-table.

'You might find a use for these,' he said.

We looked at each other in mutual embarrassment, both of us realizing, I suppose, that we knew no more about each other than might two reserved travellers at the end of a long journey, thrown together by chance and each determined to reveal as little of himself to the other as possible. He looked, to me, to be a very, very old man. He was fifty-six.

'Well, you'll be off before I'm up in the morning,' he said. 'We'd better say goodbye now.'

'Yes,' I said.

'Well... goodbye!'

We shook hands. He muttered something about looking after myself. I said I would. Then, turning away, he patted my shoulder, and left hurriedly.

Mother was even less demonstrative. She referred constantly to 'Your first leave'; as if I would be back home again in a few weeks. She was up long before me in the morning, had my breakfast ready to take out of the frying pan when I came downstairs, and kept herself busy in the kitchen while I ate it. At the door, when I was ready to leave (I had taken my luggage to the station the day before), she allowed herself to say 'Well, have a good time. You might write to me occasionally.'

'Of course I shall,' I said.

'Good boy. Well, off you go, now.'

She kissed me on the cheek in the casual, offhand way she had always kissed me; squeezed my elbow; and let me go. As I walked up the Conway Road towards the town I ran over in my mind, deliberately, the nautical 'Rule of the Road' which I had learned from the Manual of Navigation. At the station, I felt only irritation when I saw Gregory hovering near the platform gates. If I could have evaded him, I would.

Most irritating of all was his smugness in being the only member of my farewell party.

'I thought there'd be lots of people,' he kept saying. 'I was sure Pat would come. She's home, you know, for the weekend.'

'Oh, is she? I didn't know.'

'Yes, I saw her yesterday, in Sumner's. She was with Kathy. I'm surprised Kathy didn't come!'

'Perhaps she didn't want to,' I said. I could not think of Kathy at all, but I was hurt that Pat, who had promised on a postcard that she would try to get to Llandudno to see me off, had been in the town, and avoided me.

'Oh no, I expect she just didn't wake up early enough!' Gregory assured me. 'I found it a bit difficult myself.'

led into the corner of the compartment and unfolded
m's letter, 'thank you!'
som's letter was from Dunfermline.

ar Bernard, he wrote (a strange form of address, coming
him, I thought):
is may well be the last letter you have from me for some
I've at last stopped shilly shallying, and have informed my
onal Officer that I can no longer continue to take part in
drill, target practice, etc. That I wish to serve as a Sick Berth
dant or not at all, etc. I ought to have done this long ago,
ept hoping that all that nonsense would cease after the first
veeks. Far from ceasing, it had increased. The straw which
broke this camel's back was bayonet practice. There were
f sandbags, dressed up as Jerries, hanging from a suspended
and we were expected to charge at them with bayonets. 'In,
out!' the instructor kept shouting. 'Cut the bastards wide
' and similar obscenities. When my turn came I refused to
Was put on a charge, and then submitted my case to the
He thinks I'm mad, of course. I explained that the only mad
I did was to join the Navy at all, and that I did that as the
of having been incorrectly informed about the duties of an
. (Peace, oh Smith! You didn't know any more than I did.)
w I'm in the Guard Room, waiting to be charged with, in the
nstance, refusing to obey the order of a senior officer. Where
from there, I don't know.
e D.O. said, like a solemn cow 'You realise, Jones, that if
ersist with these views of yours you can only end up in
?' I said that I did. 'You can get two years, you know!' he
I said that middle-age held no horrors for me, and he
ht I was taking the Micky out of him and brought the
iew to an end.

I tried to make myself thank him, but could not bring
myself to say anything that might delay his going. He
seemed not to notice the omission, however, continued to
grin just as inanely, so pleased with himself that I could
have hit him.

'I wonder if you'll bump up against old Epsom?' he
speculated, 'That would be a laugh, wouldn't it? I mean, if
you went along to the Sick Bay to have your piles looked
at, and found old Epsom holding court there! Gosh, you
would have a laugh!'

'I don't think it's very likely,' I said.

'Oh, you never know! Funny things happen in the Services,
you know. And there's old Peredur, he's in the Navy, isn't he?
You might bump into him. And Dewi... oh no, he's going in
the Army, isn't he? Now that was a funny thing!'

'Killingly funny,' I agreed.

'You'd never think Dewi'd do a thing like that, would
you? Well, there you are, you never know. He was always
a bit of a dark horse. I was always surprised...'

'Well, what?'

'Oh, nothing really.'

I was grimly delighted to see Gregory at last embarrassed.
It had penetrated even his thick skull that he could not
speculate about why Dewi and Kathy had parted company
without annoying me. Had he not been made, for him,
sensitive by my imminent departure, I believe that curiosity
would have won, he would have risked my disfavour in the
hope of learning some scandalous secret. He contented himself now with looking knowledgeable, a grotesquely
unsuitable expression for his bland, pudgy face.

'I expect you gave him an inferiority complex,' I said. 'He was always annoyed that your memory was so much better than his.'

This was completely untrue, only a fool could have believed it. Even Gregory had to make a show of disclaiming any such superiority; but the idea evidently delighted him, a dreamy expression came into his brown, soft eyes. I took this opportunity to climb up into my compartment, and continued the conversation through the open window.

'Well!' Gregory said, 'the School won't seem the same now you've gone.'

'It won't be the same, if I'm not there, will it? It'll be that much different, for better or worse.'

'Oh, you know what I mean. I mean, you hardly notice a person until he isn't there any more.'

'I'm sorry you didn't notice me,' I said gravely.

'Oh, you know what I mean!' Gregory said again.

It was a ludicrous conversation, and I was deliberately keeping it on that level. As long as I could find Gregory funny, it wasn't necessary to be openly rude to him; though anyone else would long ago have left in disgust. In order to be rude to Gregory, one actually had to call him by unpleasant names; and even then you had to be careful... if you went too far he would just laugh, thinking you were being funny. His expression now, solemnly anxious, was an attempt to impress upon me that this was no time for being funny. This was an occasion, and he wanted to make the most of it. I listened impatiently for the guard's whistle, watching the clock.

'It's funny,' Gregory said, lifting his moon-like face anxiously towards me, 'the way things have turned out! I mean, you and me being friends right then me being the only one to see leaving!'

'Killingly funny!' I said, looking wi from awe into his insensitive bovine I felt, he would start talking about Lo incredulity almost amounting to del forming on his face; his face, belov stirred slowly by an eccentric stick.

'It's like,' he said shyly, 'one of the you know right from the beginning come together again at the end.'

I could hardly believe my ears. laughter. 'Oh magnificent Gregory!' that I have denied myself the delight so long!' I was, then, truly grateful to had made in coming to see me off. Ho this town than on a note of ironic la the whistle blowing at last, saw the green flag. And I was able, leaning o hand, to say sincerely 'Thanks for co made an enormous difference. I was I arrived here, but I feel much better some time!'

A smile of pure bliss suffused G struggled hard to say something. All I you, Bernard, thank you!'

Then the train, moving at last, bo a joyfully waving figure on the curvi to my sight. 'Thank you, Gregory,' I n

The Guard Room Petty Officer is a friend of mine, and will be posting this letter (strictly illegal) for me. After this I don't suppose I'll be given a chance to write. I thought you'd want to know how things turned out. I feel a bit guilty towards you, letting you down like this. But honestly, man, I did try to be reasonable. As in all things, though, one's acts are shaped by emotion as much as by logic. It was that sadistic sod shouting 'In, twist, out!' that really finished me. Logically, it's no worse than Bren gun practice. But a gun, like a bomb, is an impersonal weapon, well-fitted for the practice of casuistry. The more we reduce killing to a scientific problem, the easier it is for those who hate killing to kill. I wonder how our smart, civilized bomber pilots would get on with a bayonet in their hands and a series of human bellies to rip open? Wouldn't their stomachs turn? Wouldn't yours? But the bigger the bomb the better.

I've written to Pat, and a short note to Kathy, who very sweetly wrote to me, as I expect you know. She is the nicest, kindest girl, that one, and I hope you realise how lucky you are to be loved by her. Treat her with care. Love is a beautiful house to live in, but oh! so vulnerable! But I'm sure you will. You never wittingly hurt anyone in your life.

This letter should reach you before you leave for what my respected Pop would call 'The Great Adventure'. I know that I will never make you think as I do about war, and, believe me, I don't blame you. 'Bernard,' as Kathy profoundly asserted in her last letter to me, 'is Bernard.' But I believe that in your nice warm heart you would agree...

I read no more. I had read it through twice before, and during this final reading the suspicion which had at first found a difficult foothold in my mind had matured into a certainty. Holding the letter in my hand I stood up and opened the compartment window. The train had carried me

349

away from the town which I had not favoured with a single backward glance, and was curving now away from Llandudno Junction Station, giving me a last glimpse of the Conway Valley, Glan Conway, and the hills behind. For a moment I indulged dangerously in memories; then, remembering my purpose in standing there, I screwed Epsom's letter up into a tight ball and flung it with absurd violence through the open window. The wind of our progress snatched the light ball of paper hungrily; and I closed the window, crossed the compartment, and settled to watch, on the other side, for the curving line of surf that would soon be coming into view.

Perhaps in my nice warm heart I did agree with the comforting, steadying moral certainties propounded in the last four pages of Epsom's letter; perhaps not. Perhaps I would know one day, and when I knew would know also why I agreed, or disagreed. And if I agreed, it would not, I was now sure, be for Epsom's reasons.

For, 'Bernard' as Kathy had said, 'is Bernard'; and if nothing else was clear to me it was at least clear now that Bernard was not Epsom, nor was Epsom simply a projection of Bernard. I remembered something else that Kathy had said, one day when I had been masochistically extolling Epsom's virtues and denigrating my own. She had laughed openly into my face, shaking my arm reprovingly. 'You're an old silly!' she had said. 'You think Epsom's so jolly wonderful, and you never realise how wonderful you are yourself! You say Epsom believes in Good and Evil and you don't believe in anything, but you do! You believe in Truth and Falsehood, and that's much harder to believe in and a lot more valuable in the end.'

350

'And what do you believe in, Kathy?' I asked.

'I believe in you,' said Kathy.

I did not think I was wonderful and I was not at all sure that I knew the difference between Truth and Falsehood; but I did, now, believe in myself. I did, at last, know that I existed as a separate personality, not just an amalgam of contending forces brought into play by others... by Epsom, by Dewi, by Kathy... by Gregory... I knew that I had a way to go that was my way, not anyone else's way; and that the rules that I was so haphazardly, and with such difficulty, unearthing, though they were my rules were just as good rules as anyone else's; and made sense for me, as Epsom's rules, Kathy's rules had not.

Past Colwyn Bay the railway line runs beside the sea. In the monotonous light of early morning the shore looked bleak, the water uninviting. It was very calm. The ripples came in slowly, to spread themselves with unhurried grace across the sands, and withdrew, leaving behind the faint patterns of their foam. The train, swaying as it gathered speed, clattered metallically onwards, and I peered sight-lessly out of the compartment window, grinning insanely, finding it difficult not to burst out into wild, aimless laughter. I was still filled with the excitement of heaving Epsom's letter out into the wind. It was a wonderful thing to have done. A wonderful thing to have done.

Foreword by Merfyn Jones

Professor Merfyn Jones is vice-chancellor of Bangor University. His numerous publications include *The North Wales Quarrymen 1874 to 1922* (1982) and the book of his television history *Cymru 2000: A History of Wales in the Twentieth Century* (1999).

L I B R A R Y of W A L E S

The Library of Wales is a Welsh Assembly Government project designed to ensure that all of the rich and extensive literature of Wales which has been written in English will now be made available to readers in and beyond Wales. Sustaining this wider literary heritage is understood by the Welsh Assembly Government to be a key component in creating and disseminating an ongoing sense of modern Welsh culture and history for the future Wales which is now emerging from contemporary society. Through these texts, until now unavailable or out-of-print or merely forgotten, the Library of Wales will bring back into play the voices and actions of the human experience that has made us, in all our complexity, a Welsh people.

The Library of Wales will include prose as well as poetry, essays as well as fiction, anthologies as well as memoirs, drama as well as journalism. It will complement the names and texts that are already in the public domain and seek to include the best of Welsh writing in English, as well as to showcase what has been unjustly neglected. No boundaries will limit the ambition of the Library of Wales to open up the borders that have denied some of our best writers a presence in a future Wales. The Library of Wales has been created with that Wales in mind: a young country not afraid to remember what it might yet become.

Dai Smith
Raymond Williams Chair in the Cultural History of Wales, Swansea University

LIBRARY OF WALES
FUNDED BY

Llywodraeth Cynulliad Cymru
Welsh Assembly Government

**CYNGOR LLYFRAU CYMRU
WELSH BOOKS COUNCIL**

LIBRARY OF WALES

So Long, Hector Bebb	£6.99	
Ron Berry	978-1902638805	
Border Country	£8.99	
Raymond Williams	978-1902638812	
Cwmardy & We Live	£9.99	
Lewis Jones	978-1902638836	
Country Dance	£6.99	
Margiad Evans	978-1902638843	
Ash on a Young Man's Sleeve	£7.99	
Dannie Abse	978-1905762255	
The Dark Philosophers	£7.99	
Gwyn Thomas	978-1902638829	
A Man's Estate	£7.99	
Emyr Humphreys	978-1902638867	
In the Green Tree	£7.99	
Alun Lewis	978-1902638874	
Rhapsody	£7.99	
Dorothy Edwards	978-1905762460	
The Withered Root	£7.99	
Rhys Davies	978-1905762477	
Sport	£9.99	
Edited by Gareth Williams	978-1902638898	
Poetry 1900–2000	£12.99	
Edited by Meic Stephens	978-1902638881	
I Sent a Letter to My Love	£7.99	
Bernice Rubens	978-1905762521	
Jampot Smith	£7.99	
Jeremy Brooks	978-1905762507	
The Voices of the Children	£7.99	
George Ewart Evans	978-1905762514	
Congratulate the Devil	£7.99	
Howell Davies	978-1905762514	